Mesmerized

"Wow! What a sexy and fun read. Dane has a way of making the futures seem so real and believable with characters that just pop off the page. Love it!"
—*Fresh Fiction*

"From the first chapter, *Mesmerized* grabs you by the throat and leads you through an exciting twist of sensuous romantic and science fiction adventure . . . A well-told blend of hot sensual romance and science fiction."
—*Night Owl Reviews*

"No one combines space opera and erotica quite like Dane. If you thought the only thing missing from Joss Whedon's *Firefly* series was a little explicit sex, you have to check out *Mesmerized*."
—*RT Book Reviews*, 4½ stars

Insatiable

"The story line is fast-paced and loaded with action as the irresistible force meets the unmovable object when two enemies from different life stations fall into heated love . . . This is quite a sizzler."
—*Genre Go Round Reviews*

"Dane has created a fully realized, intricate world with thoughtful, sympathetic characters, which makes it easy to lose oneself in the romance . . . The cliffhanger ending will leave readers panting for the next installment."
—*RT Book Reviews*

continued . . .

"Filled with heat and erotic passion . . . *Relentless* is a do-not-miss."
—*Joyfully Reviewed*

"This terrific science fiction erotic romance is fast-paced and filled with action in and out of the bedroom."　　—*Midwest Book Review*

"Fiery, erotic and rich with plot, this book is definitely a keeper on my shelf."　　　　　　　　　　　　　—*Night Owl Reviews*

Undercover

"Delicious eroticism . . . a toe-curling erotic romance sure to keep you reading late into the night."　　　　　　　　　—Anya Bast

"Sexy, pulse-pounding adventure . . . that'll leave you weak in the knees."　　　—Jaci Burton, national bestselling author of *Taking a Shot*

"Exciting, emotional and arousing . . . a ride well worth taking."
—Sasha White, author of *One Weekend*

"A roller coaster of emotion, intrigue and sensual delights."
—Vivi Anna, author of *The Vampire's Kiss*

Berkley titles by Lauren Dane

CAPTIVATED

HEART OF DARKNESS

NEVER ENOUGH

THREE TO TANGO
(with Emma Holly, Megan Hart, and Bethany Kane)

MESMERIZED

INSIDE OUT

INSATIABLE

COMING UNDONE

LAID BARE

RELENTLESS

UNDERCOVER

Captivated

lauren dane

heat | new york

THE BERKLEY PUBLISHING GROUP
Published by the Penguin Group
Penguin Group (USA) Inc.
375 Hudson Street, New York, New York 10014, USA
Penguin Group (Canada), 90 Eglinton Avenue East, Suite 700, Toronto, Ontario M4P 2Y3, Canada
(a division of Pearson Penguin Canada Inc.) • Penguin Books Ltd., 80 Strand, London WC2R 0RL,
England • Penguin Group Ireland, 25 St. Stephen's Green, Dublin 2, Ireland (a division of Penguin
Books Ltd.) • Penguin Group (Australia), 250 Camberwell Road, Camberwell, Victoria 3124, Australia
(a division of Pearson Australia Group Pty. Ltd.) • Penguin Books India Pvt. Ltd., 11 Community
Centre, Panchsheel Park, New Delhi—110 017, India • Penguin Group (NZ), 67 Apollo Drive,
Rosedale, Auckland 0632, New Zealand (a division of Pearson New Zealand Ltd.) • Penguin Books
(South Africa) (Pty.) Ltd., 24 Sturdee Avenue, Rosebank, Johannesburg 2196, South Africa

Penguin Books Ltd., Registered Offices: 80 Strand, London WC2R 0RL, England

This book is an original publication of The Berkley Publishing Group.

PRINTING HISTORY
Heat trade paperback edition / May 2012

Library of Congress Cataloging-in-Publication Data

Dane, Lauren.
Captivated / Lauren Dane. — Heat trade paperback ed.
    p.   cm.
ISBN 978-0-425-24736-5
1. Imaginary wars and battles—Fiction   I. Title.
    PS3604.A5C37   2012
    813'.6—dc23   2011040585

PRINTED IN THE UNITED STATES OF AMERICA

10 9 8 7 6 5 4 3 2 1

*This one goes out to all the fans of
the Federation Chronicles.
Thank you all so very much for supporting these books
and allowing me to continue to write futuristics.*

Acknowledgments

First and foremost, my thanks always go to my husband, who is my biggest cheerleader even though I hardly ever kill people off the way he suggests I should.

To Laura Bradford, my agent and my friend, for all the hard work you do for me every day.

I really can't overemphasize how important it is to an author to have a great fit with her editors, and in Leis Pederson I am so very fortunate. Thank you, Leis, for being shiny and awesome.

And a big giant thank-you to Fatin, Mary and Renee, who kindly beta read this (and many other of my books) and gave me so much wonderful input.

Chapter 1

She rocked because it brushed her hair over her skin. It was the only way sometimes that she remembered she was still there. The sound of her feet shuffling across the floor, the way the blanket felt when she pulled it around herself tight, the songs she sang in her head—she knew she was real.

They wanted her to forget. Wanted her to forget she existed before they brought her here. They wanted to break her and tear her from reality, but she would not let them win. Because if they won, it meant she'd cease to believe she was real.

She was real.

She was real.

She was real.

"My name is Hannah Black. My parents are Shelby and Bertram Black. My name day is in midsummer as the grain is above my head."

She spoke to herself to hear the noise. Her voice was rusty, and she wondered if she even sounded remotely human anymore. She repeated the words her mother taught her in the time before she started at school. Several times every day, because it helped her remember the person she was. *Before*. When she got up every day and went to work. When people spoke to her, touched her, when she laughed with friends at large dinner parties. It was real and they would never take it from her.

A banging noise. She didn't bother to look. They liked to taunt her sometimes. She didn't know if they realized the isolation was less when they made sound, but she never responded in any case. There were some lab workers who tried to help when they could. And others who liked to harm when they could.

Some of the latter liked to underline how much power they had over her. Just in case it was a physical lesson she slunk from her cot and headed to her corner, taking her blanket with her. Once, in the very beginning when they still interacted with her, they tried to take it and she took something from the guard instead. She smiled to herself. She kept her blanket and he had a prosthetic eye.

Of course then they'd gassed her room so she was unconscious when they came in. But they never tried to take her blanket again. And from then on they'd used the gas before anyone entered. Fear made a well-learned lesson. Her father used to tell her that so she whispered it to herself over and over as she rocked.

The door slammed open and she looked cautiously through the veil of her hair. It had been a long time—months—since she'd seen another person. Klaxons rang in the background and when she truly saw him, she knew he wasn't one of them. She backed up, trying to make herself smaller.

"My name is Vincenz Cuomo and I'm here to help you. I'm a Federation military officer, and we're about to blow this place up. Do you want to live?"

It took a moment to focus on the words. It had been a very long time since anyone had actually spoken *to* her. She was afraid to speak. Afraid they'd hurt her. She licked her lips and gripped the bed to stand on legs fear had rendered a trembling mass.

She nodded her head and took a step toward him. Willing herself to believe it was real. Willing herself to believe this wasn't a trick and she was getting out of this chamber of horrors. But her legs didn't support her very well and she had to hold on to the bed to keep standing.

Klaxons. Something was happening. Panic began to eat her insides. What if he got impatient and left?

But he didn't leave. He took a step to her and caught her against his body. She gasped and began to shake all over at the glory of the contact.

"I have to pick you up. Is that all right?" His words were firm, but gentle. He wanted to make her better. She understood this in her belly. Though she wasn't sure if she could trust it anymore, she knew this might be her only chance to get out.

So she managed another nod, ignoring the nausea. He gently swung her up into his arms, and she put her head on his chest as he rushed out, his heartbeat against her ear steady and strong. She swam into the rhythm of that sound, held on.

There were orders being shouted over his comm, but he remained absolutely resolute as he brought them away from the labs, taking the inner stairwell. Up and up. She jiggled and held on. Nothing mattered but getting out of there. Then staying free.

Outside. Light. She moved her face away from the shelter of his chest and looked around. Her eyes hurt but it didn't matter.

He spoke to others about her, but didn't put her down.

He called her a victim. She *felt* like a wild animal. She clutched the pieces of herself tightly. A group of people came out onto the roof—soldiers. A woman with them looked to Hannah and started. Hannah wondered briefly just what she must have looked like.

The pretty man with the long, dark hair had been giving orders and then he made a sound that wrenched her heart. She knew the sound. Made it herself. There was yelling as Hannah saw the scene play out as if it were on a vid screen.

There was weapons fire and the man shoved the woman who'd been staring at Hannah down to the pavement. In the cockpit of the bird that had landed, the one she was hoping to escape in, a dead man slumped against the seat, blood a bloom of crimson across his chest.

She didn't scream. Screaming would call attention to herself. So she clung tight to her savior as they crawled toward the woman looking toward the bird, screaming. Vincenz tried to put Hannah down, but she clutched at him tighter, not knowing if she could face being alone, even though she saw the screaming, weeping woman with the braids needed his help.

He crooned to the weeping woman and dragged her to a nearby doorway. Hannah had to concentrate very hard not to tear at his uniform to keep hold of him. There was no way she'd go back in the building. She'd jump off the helipad and end her life before she'd go inside again.

Her muscles tensed and Vincenz made eye contact. "I'm not going to leave you. Do you understand me?" She swallowed hard and believed.

He held the other woman, Piper, she heard him call her, but didn't let go of Hannah. Spent shells rained down, the sunlight glittered from them with deadly beauty. Plas-rockets were being shot off time and again and the air stank. The humming lived in her belly. The helo hummed, the plas weapons hummed, there was shouting and shooting and that hummed too. All around them weapons fire hit the ground. Pieces of it tore into her leg but she didn't cry out.

And then it was over. The other man came to gather Piper and they headed toward the helo. The man who'd been killed had been covered with a drape. The woman sat, staring. No longer screaming. It smelled like blood and burning things as the soldiers spoke in clipped tones. Panicked reports came over an in-dash comm system. The Parron Governance Portal was telling everyone to get out and do it now.

If she died, at least it would be as a free woman.

But if she lived, she'd spend every moment from then on working to destroy the people who did this to her. They'd stolen her life from her for how long she wasn't exactly sure. Made her into little more than a scared animal, always reacting.

There would be a reckoning. How she'd manage it, when, she didn't know. But the knowledge of it, sure and deadly, lived in her belly, keeping her going.

Then there was a shaky landing and she was carried—again by Vincenz—into yet another ship. It all seemed to go very fast. She could scent the panic, knew people were worried they wouldn't make it out. But she turned it all off and looked only at his face as he gave and took orders. He wasn't panicked so she could hold on.

He had her.

Their bird took off. There was more chaos, noise from what sounded like a series of explosions, shouting over the comms to get out, get out, get out, and they were through the portal.

Once things had smoothed as the transport had fully engaged and they were safely in the portal, Vincenz carried her deeper into the ship, waving away anyone who tried to take her. She held him fiercely;

though her eyes were screwed tight and her muscles trembled, she wanted to survive and he would help her with that.

He managed to sit down while still carrying her. "Have you traveled via portal before?" He spoke to her softly but firmly, and she slowly opened her eyes.

She nodded.

"Can you speak?"

She paused, as if she didn't know. "Yes." Her voice was full of snags and burrs.

"I'm going to strap in so I need to touch you."

Her fingers tightened in his shirt and then he saw her force herself to relax enough to let go. *What had they done to her?*

"You can stay in my lap. We're just going to hit some disturbances in the energy flow. They've collapsed the portal on Parron so we need to move far more quickly." He strapped them both in as he explained.

She nodded.

"What's your name?" He'd seen it on the log back at the lab, but he didn't want to lose her and she seemed so very far away in her mind right then. Fear lived in her gaze as she scanned the room.

"My name is Hannah Black." She paused as if she wanted to say more, but then didn't.

"Hannah, my name is Vincenz. I said it back there, but it was sort of hectic. You're safe now. No one is going to hurt you."

She looked doubtful but didn't say much. Her color had risen to something close to normal, which he was encouraged by. Andrei held Piper and they shared a look. Piper had broken down utterly after seeing what happened to her brother and Andrei had given her a sedative. He rocked with her, slowly, rubbing a hand up and down her back.

His friend had found something entirely wonderful in Piper Roundtree. Vincenz hoped it would help Piper get through the grief.

"Would you like something to eat?" She was thin. He could feel her bones, so very close to her skin. Fragile, and yet he sensed she was a very strong woman despite that. Maybe *because* of that.

She nodded and after they were able to get some distance from the collapsed portal, the ride smoothed out. "We have a small bathing suite here. If you'd like to clean up a little."

Wonder flashed over her face and then she bit her bottom lip. Worry and fear were back on her face.

"What is it, Hannah?"

"Would you . . . stay?"

His chest tightened at the entreaty in her voice.

"Of course." He unstrapped and stood, placing her carefully on her feet. She took his hand and he had no desire to take it back. Leading her through the ship toward the sleeping berths, he took in the way she ate up every detail. And that's when he noticed her limp.

"What's wrong with your leg?" He paused to kneel and examine it closely. Shrapnel had torn through the skin. "I'm sorry I didn't see this earlier. We need to clean it up. Sit while I get the triage kit."

She held very still, her gaze taking in every move he made as he cleaned out the wounds. "I'm going to hold off on the numbing gel until after you bathe."

She swallowed hard and shook her head. "I'm fine."

He didn't want to argue with her so he stood, taking her weight as they finished the walk. "Here we are." He pointed toward the bathing suite. "I can't vouch for the heat in the water, but there's soap and it's big enough to get clean. I'll see if I can't find you some clothes."

She looked to the door and then back to him. Over and over. And then she slid to the floor, her shoulders shaking as she wept.

He went to his knees and hugged her, not knowing what else to do. "What is it?"

"I'm . . . I'm sorry."

"How long did they have you in there?"

She reached up and touched her scalp. "Eleven."

"Weeks?"

She shook her head. She paused, clearly thinking, and he wondered how hard it was for her just to simply speak to another person after her ordeal. "Months, I think."

Nearly an entire standard year? What would that do to a person?

He took a deep breath even as he sent his most fervent prayer that his father simply drop dead and end this misery for everyone. "Alone? All that time?"

She nodded and he closed his eyes a moment, needing to find patience when he just wanted to hurt someone.

"You're safe now. Is that what's got you so upset?"

She shook her head.

Fine tremors worked through her. He watched her hug that wretched blanket around her body and calculated the odds of getting it away from her long enough to at least launder.

Perhaps it was the fear of being alone again? "I'll come in with you. Would that help? I'll close my eyes. And I won't leave the room."

Her eyes were greenish brown. Pretty. Filled with gratitude as she looked up at him. "Yes."

He helped her to stand and one-handed, he grabbed a drying cloth and some clean clothes before leading her into the room.

Not knowing how close to stand or what she needed, he hoped she'd indicate it if he wasn't doing it right. He showed her how to turn the water on and turned his back when she began to undress. Not soon enough to miss the scars on the backs of her legs. He fisted his hands again but kept quiet. She didn't need his anger on top of everything else she needed to process.

She stepped in and he caught sight of her in the nearby looking glass. Her head was bowed as the water rushed over her. Fascinated, he watched her touch the soap and make a lather. The frosted glass on the shower door hid most of her body, the parts not normally on display anyway, but she slowly and surely soaped herself from head to toe in an orderly fashion, paying attention to the shrapnel wounds in her calf without even a flinch.

*H*er hair was longer than he'd thought. He noticed it when she got out of the enclosure and wrapped herself in the drying cloth. Back still turned, he spoke. "Clothes are there. They're probably too big, but there's a belt too. We'll be in Mirage shortly so we'll get you something more appropriate there."

"Thank you."

He slowly turned, waiting for her to stop him if she hadn't gotten dressed all the way yet. Clean she was even more alluring. More wounded too. Her eyes had smudges beneath.

"How long has it been since you've eaten?"

She took his arm as they left, leaning into his body. "Don't know. I keep track. *Kept* track, back in the . . . place."

He clicked his teeth together, anger rushing through him. "I can't promise you anything truly good until we get to Mirage. But we've got protein bars. Looks like you might need some."

Her laugh was the barest whisper. "Probably." She hesitated when he guided her to the table in the small break room.

"What? You don't know me, but I do want to help."

She pursed her lips, concentrating. "What will happen now?"

He swallowed as he put a glass of watered-down juice in front of her. He didn't want her to get sick, even as he wanted her to eat.

"We'll stop in Mirage. Federation personnel will want to meet with you. Doctors probably as well to give you a checkup. They'll handle a debriefing as well. They can do it rather quickly via brain scan."

She paled so much it alarmed him. Shaking her head nearly violently, she snarled, *"No doctors."*

"Not like those back there. I promise. You'll be under when they do the scans."

She shook so hard she couldn't hold the glass without spilling.

He knelt before her, putting his palms on her knees. "I'm not going to let anyone hurt you. You have my word."

He had no right making that promise, but he had, and he would keep it no matter what.

Hannah Black had become his in a very real way. He didn't understand the whys of it beyond the fact that it had been he who'd saved her back on Parron. But he knew it was more. She needed his protection. And he'd give it to her.

Chapter 2

Weary to his bones, Julian rolled from the bed it seemed like he'd only just fallen into. People had come in. Vincenz's voice was clear.

But his normally calm, metered tone had sharpened. *Odd.*

Pulling on pants, Julian moved toward the talking, pausing to button and zip at the doorway. Across the large space, Vincenz stood, holding an apparently unconscious woman as he argued with two soldiers, one a med-tech. The woman's hands were bandaged and her clothes, obviously borrowed, swallowed her body.

"*I said no.* I promised her I'd stay with her. She's going to be right here." Vincenz forced his way past two Federation soldiers and into a room just off the main comm and command center of the house.

"She needs to be debriefed. We can take her to a med center where she'll get real help. We need to know what she knows." The soldier spread his hands, totally reasonable.

But the look on Vincenz's face was *not.* He was so fierce, Julian stepped forward to intercede. To offer his force to make whatever Vincenz wanted happen.

"What's going on?"

Vincenz put her down carefully and turned back to Julian. "This is Hannah. They kept her in a lab for nearly a standard year in almost total isolation. She's . . . she's fragile. And deathly afraid of doctors right now. I'm sure you can understand that." Vincenz turned his attention back to the med-tech.

"We can keep her under at least while we check her over. Operative Cuomo, she's clearly malnourished and emotionally unstable. You're not equipped to handle that."

Vincenz got in the med-tech's physical space and used it to push him back. "I *told* you not to approach! It's your own fault and now she's injured and her emotional state worse. You can examine her *here*. Now. I'm not leaving the room either."

"Are you saying I'd hurt her?" The soldier's features broadcast just what he thought of that accusation.

Vincenz batted it away just as angrily. "No. I'm saying I'm not going to let you make it worse. I made a promise to her and I don't break my promises. I'm staying because she wants it that way, not because I think you'd molest her in some way."

With a glare, the soldier took up his medical bag and got to work. Vincenz moved to the doorway, watching, his side touching Julian's.

"Hey." Julian wanted to kiss Vincenz just then. But they were on duty. But after . . . when the soldiers left, then he'd get that kiss and more.

Vincenz gave him a smile and Julian forgot some of his troubles. "I'm glad you're here. When did you get back?"

"Daybreak." And then he'd sat in the shower, hoping he could wash it all away. The water had gone cold and he still couldn't get the stench out of his nostrils. "What happened?" He tipped his chin toward the woman on the bed.

"Andrei and Piper are on their way to the Center. Kenner . . . her brother Kenner is dead. He was killed on the roof of the lab where I found Hannah."

Both men looked toward the woman on the bed and the soldier who'd slid her shirt open, carefully using his diagnostics on her. "A year?"

Vincenz nodded. "When I found her she was in a corner, rocking. Not quite filthy, but it was clear she had to make due with wet cloths. Though, that she took the care to try to stay clean speaks to how strong she is. She wouldn't let go of me, but even in the middle of a firefight she held it together. She's a survivor."

Julian looked at the curve of her cheeks. Pretty. Too thin, but with some time to recuperate, she'd be better. He hoped. Then again, he wasn't sure there was such a thing as recuperation anymore.

"What happened to her hands?"

Vincenz huffed a sigh. "I told them to back off, but they persisted. They wanted to interview her right there at the portal station. Gods. She was holding on to me and then sort of wrapped her hands up in the straps of my pack. They pulled at her. She screamed." His voice broke. "She screamed and screamed and screamed as they pulled at her. I kept telling them to stop. Finally they used a sedative and before she went under she looked at me like I'd done it to her. Her hands were bloody from where she'd tried to hang on." He scrubbed his hands over his face and Julian heard the ache in his voice.

They watched as the soldier did his diagnostics and turned back to them.

"She's underweight considerably. Dehydrated." He held up an IV bag. "She'll be out for several more hours so I'm going to at least get her hooked up to a drip. It'll help."

Vincenz paused, but after a few moments he nodded. "Just be sure not to strap her down."

"If she moves, she could tear the IV out. It's not to hold her, but to keep her from doing that."

"I know. But this woman was tortured for a long time. She was kept prisoner. You will not strap her down, not even her arm. I won't have her waking up and thinking she's back on Parron. She's had enough trauma for the day."

The soldier nodded and set the bag up and got it going, taping over the needle in the back of her hand. "She's got some scarring here and there. Consistent with beatings. I took some blood samples and I'll run them at HQ to run some tests. I need to get some internal film. She could have any number of health issues we can't see."

"When she's ready I'll bring her in. But you'll leave her for now."

"We have programs to help victims, Operative Cuomo. We're not the monsters who did this to her."

"I understand that, soldier. But this woman was used and abused. Today she deserves some fucking peace from that. You will *not* haul her off to a hospital and strap her down while you take diagnostics. Not unless there's an urgent problem, which we now know there isn't as you've given her a checkup."

Julian held a hand up to stay the soldier from speaking again. "It's not optimal, we understand. But you're not taking her anywhere. If you need verification from Comandante Ellis, I can get that for you."

The soldier paled and Julian wanted to pat the boy's shoulder and assure him that many people had the same reaction when Wilhelm Ellis's name came up. But it made the point, and after the soldier left some tonics and instructions on what she could eat for the time being, he was gone, leaving the place quiet as they moved back to watching her sleep.

"Thanks for the backup."

Julian put his head on Vincenz's shoulder. "I'm sorry you had to see it. Sorry she had to go through it."

"She needs us to protect her. You know how this'll work. They'll want to study her and take her in for debriefing. I don't know if she can stand it just now."

Julian looked at her again, his heart aching for a woman he didn't know. Aching because through Vincenz, he'd also taken on protective feelings for her. "We'll do everything we can to keep her safe. She can stay here with us if she doesn't want to go to the hospital or back to the Center."

"We'll take it a step at a time. Today's been . . . well, I'm sure for you too." He turned and Julian's arms slid around Vincenz's shoulders and Vincenz's around Julian's waist.

"Not my favorite thing, no. But we got the info we needed."

Vincenz looked into Julian's face and, Julian knew, saw everything. "I'm sorry."

Julian had to close his eyes a moment. "You can make it better."

Vincenz's expression changed and he got that little smile. That smile drove Julian to distraction. So fucking sexy.

"Give me five minutes to finish up."

"You've got three."

"Oh, it's that way? A challenge, hmm? All right, you're on."

Julian needed him. He watched Vincenz move, loving the ease of his muscles as he did. His hair had been standing on end, most likely because when Vincenz worked or thought things over he tended to pull at it.

Vincenz looked up, as if he heard the whispers in Julian's head. Their gazes locked and that was all there was to it. In three steps Julian had his fingers in that hair, tugging to angle Vincenz's head back so he could get at the long line of his throat.

Vincenz sighed roughly, and his hands slid under the hem of Julian's shirt and over the bare flesh beneath.

More. Julian needed more. He pushed Vincenz back until he hit the wall nearby. The sound he gave in response was threaded with need, shooting straight to Julian's cock.

"Gods, you're so hard," Vincenz murmured as he slid a hand into the front of Julian's pants and found his cock. Julian arched into that fist and then his teeth raked over Vincenz's throat. Tasted salt and skin.

"I've been hard just thinking about you. All day long as I headed back here all I could think about was this." These quiet, stolen moments when he didn't have to think about the war, or the things he'd had to do back on Ceres to get the much-needed answers. When he didn't have to think about all those they'd lost. In this place, with his hands and mouth all over Vincenz, there was nothing but that pleasure and comfort.

"I'm here now. You're here now." Vincenz unzipped Julian's pants to get at his cock better. He licked his lips as he looked down between them and Julian had to seek patience to not come just from that.

Vincenz pushed at Julian a little. "Turn around. Let's switch places."

Julian had no idea what he was about until Vincenz dropped to his knees as Julian leaned back against the wall.

"Yes."

A smug smile marked Vincenz's lips as he pulled Julian's cock free. And then he licked across the head and amusement was the last thing on Julian's mind.

"That's the way. Deeper. Suck my cock, Vincenz. Suck me so I can blow down your throat."

Vincenz shivered but Julian was helpless to do anything but

watch, fascinated, as Vincenz slowly took Julian's cock into his mouth, swirling his tongue around the head over and over.

There was affection as well as titillation when his fingers slid through all that golden hair. Soft, long enough to tug to get more of what Vincenz offered.

"You can take your cock out. Fuck your fist while you suck me. But don't come. Not yet."

Vincenz rolled his eyes up to meet Julian's. They had this delicious sort of push and pull, a struggle of two dominant men who expressed that dominance in totally different ways. It made for incredibly hot sex.

Julian didn't miss the sound of the teeth of Vincenz's zipper. *Click-click-click-click* as he took it down. The schuss of clothes and then the moan around Julian's cock as he got his own out.

And yet he didn't lose focus on sucking Julian's cock. "Such a brilliant multitasker." Julian didn't quite close his eyes, but he let the lids droop as he leaned back and simply took in the carnal beauty of Vincenz there on his knees, Julian's cock in his mouth, his balls in Vincenz's palm.

Julian waited, tense, knowing Vincenz had more planned. The man was brilliant at sucking cock. He pressed the pads of his fingers against that sweet spot just behind Julian's balls.

He widened his stance as Vincenz slid his fingertips over Julian's asshole. Caressed. Stroked. All the while keeping Julian's cock wet and hot as he took it so deep Julian grunted each time.

"Oh, baby, you're so good at this," Julian murmured.

Vincenz smiled and hummed his pleasure around Julian's cock.

"Are you hard?"

Vincenz moaned again and Julian leaned around to watch Vincenz fist his cock a few times in a rhythm with his mouth on Julian.

There was something so scorching hot about the way Vincenz had sex. So unabashed. In a man who was normally buttoned up tight and ultra calm, that wildness and burning intensity when it came to fucking felled Julian.

The hand on Julian's balls disappeared and then came back, slick from Vincenz's mouth. And this time those stroking, caressing fingers pressed in and sent the breath gusting from Julian's lips in response.

"Yes, yes, yes," he whispered.

Deeper those fingers quested until they found his sweet spot, stroking in time with the sucking. His vision seemed to gray at the edges it felt so good. He only barely resisted fucking Vincenz's face. Only barely.

But Vincenz took his cock so deep it tapped the back of his throat. So deep, and so in time with his fingers in Julian's ass it was a quick-silver, teeth-numbing rush into climax as the waves of it hit him over and over until he was weak with it.

Vincenz pulled away, gazing up at Julian, that smile on his lips.

"Don't you make yourself come, Vincenz. That's my job now." He jerked his head toward their room, which was just across from where Hannah lay sleeping. They'd be close enough to hear if she woke.

Tearing clothes off as they went, Julian grabbed the lube before he shoved Vincenz back on the bed. He straddled Vincenz's thighs, pouring the lube, which heated to his touch, over his own cock as well as Vincenz's.

"Is this what you want?" He held his cock along with Vincenz's, brushing them together as he fucked them with his hand.

Vincenz stuttered a breath.

"Hands on the headboard. Don't let go. This is mine."

That a man like Vincenz would submit to him was part of the al-lure. It wasn't always this quiet or this easy. Sometimes it got darker, rougher, with teeth and that was good too. Julian had only been with a man once before, so it wasn't as if he was an expert on all the hows. But he had a cock and he knew what felt good. And Vincenz had taught him a great deal about how to pleasure a partner with a cock as well.

He undulated his hips, mimicking the thrust of a good, hard fuck. Slippery cock to slippery cock. Before long, he was fully hard again and shivering as his balls brushed against Vincenz's.

Sweat glistened on Vincenz's chest as the pulse at his throat hammered, visible to Julian's gaze.

"Yes, baby. Give it to me."

Vincenz met his eyes. "Take it."

So he did. Tightening his grip and the speed of the thrusts. Hard breathing, the arch of backs. Gasps. And then the warm, silky rush of seed as Vincenz came hard. Julian followed, surprised he could so soon after the last time.

After they got their breath back, Julian tossed Vincenz a nearby cloth. "I'll watch her while you shower."

"Thank you. I'm glad you're back."

He was glad as all seven hells to *be* back.

Chapter 3

Fear jolted her awake. She stayed still as she swam to full consciousness. Old habits that had kept her alive. She remembered the day before. The lab. Vincenz. The portal station where they'd pulled at her, drugged her.

Anger washed through her as she slowly opened her eyes. Where was this place? A hospital? No.

She sat up, fighting the nausea. The needle in her hand attached to the drip brought consternation. Were they still drugging her? She pulled it out, biting back the whimper her body wanted to give up.

"You're awake." Vincenz came in slowly, carefully. He tipped his chin toward the IV. "You should have left it in. You're dehydrated. I just gave you a new bag about two hours ago."

Remaining silent, she watched him through wary eyes.

"There's no need to be afraid. This is my home and a headquarters of sorts for my . . . group. It's well defended. No one can get to you here."

She studied him. He was beautiful. The kind of man people would look at because how could they not? But he'd helped them drug her. She squeezed her hands into fists a few times, wincing.

He was there, at her side in a breath. "Shh. Don't do that. The doctor cleaned them up again when we brought you in last night. You got some abrasions from the straps of my pack. I'm sorry. I . . . say something, Hannah."

He looked so worried she forgot her anger for a moment. And then remembered it. "Never." She paused to clear her throat and to grasp the words she needed. "Never again."

He blinked. "You're never speaking again?"

She shook her head, frustrated that her words were fine in her head, but she couldn't manage to always put them into coherent sentences. "*They* drugged me."

He sat on the very edge of her bed. "I didn't. I know you didn't see everything and you were scared, but I didn't drug you. And they didn't do it the way the Imperialists did either. You were panicked; they were concerned you'd hurt yourself."

"*I* make choices now." It was important he understand that. She was no one's test subject anymore.

He took her hand gently. "Of course. Are you hungry? Julian—he lives here with me—is making breakfast. He's a great cook. You're underweight. The doctor was worried."

First she needed to clean up a little. "Bathroom?"

He blushed and she found herself charmed. And then wondering how long it had been since she'd been charmed by anything or anyone. He stood, holding an arm out and allowed her to get out of bed on her own steam. Still, she took his arm gratefully.

Because she needed it on shaky legs and because she needed to be touching someone. Needed to be touched. When he touched her, the confusion quieted and she felt a little less like tearing her skin off.

He took it slow. "You're welcome to keep the room you have or move to another. We have several empty ones right now. There's a bathing suite right here and one attached to our room too."

Our? He paused at the door and she made herself go in and close the door behind her and go do her business like a real person.

He spoke to her through the door, which helped. "There's a clean toothbrush there. Clothes that will probably fit you better too. Give me a moment and I'll go get them."

She looked at herself in the mirror for the first time in a very, very long time. Alone again she could hear the rushing of her blood and the beat of her heart. Panic began to rise as she forced herself to wash her face and brush her teeth. A nearby brush enabled her to take care of her hair, braiding it back away from her face.

"My name is Hannah Black. My parents are Shelby and Bertram Black. My name day is midsummer with the grain high above my head." She said it over and over until the ritual of it calmed and soothed. She jumped when he tapped on the door again.

She opened it, and he looked into her face and smiled as he handed over a bundle of clothes. "I like your hair like that. Here. These will fit you better. You and Piper should be roughly the same size. I'll wait right here for you to change."

Everything was so . . . much. Too bright. Too loud though there was no one else in the room. Her muscles trembled but not so much from fatigue as fear.

"Need to . . . I need to sit down."

"I'm sorry. Of course. I didn't even think of that."

He moved closer and bent, she knew, to pick her up. Though she'd have liked that very much, she needed to do it on her own. Or as much as she could manage anyway.

"Can walk." It was hard to remember to say things aloud.

"Yes, you can." He put an arm around her waist and she leaned into him as they made their way across to her room. Her room with windows. And a mirror and dresser. That's when the other one—Julian, she remembered from something Vincenz had mentioned earlier—came out and saw them.

He moved to them confidently, fitting against her other side. "Are you well?" Something about that calm confidence settled the jittery things inside her, pushed the panic back.

"She's just a little shaky." Vincenz looked at Julian and Hannah knew who the other person in the "our" comment was. These two had something deep and electric.

"Sit here." Julian turned them neatly and sat next to her. "I'm Julian." He took her hand, her hand that had been so injured yesterday, and kissed it in a gentlemanly fashion. "What do you need from us right now?"

That was the question, wasn't it? She swallowed and searched for all her words. She put her hands in her hair, letting it down so it brushed against her cheeks again. But she didn't rock and that was a victory. "I can get dressed."

He looked at her carefully and then over to Vincenz. "It's not shameful to ask for help. If you need it, we'll give it to you."

She jutted her chin out. "I can dress."

He grinned and his face transformed. She smiled in response, even without planning to. "I bet you can, Hannah. Vin and I will be right here. We'll turn our backs, but we'll be right here in case you need anything."

But if he liked men, it didn't matter if he looked at her. She wasn't sure if she should be relieved or disappointed.

It took her a while and she had to stop several times to catch her breath, but she managed to get changed and felt much better.

"Ready."

They turned as a unit and both of them studied her carefully.

"Let's break our fast." Julian simply scooped her up and carried her out. She didn't immediately snuggle into his body like she had Vincenz, but he made her feel safe, regardless. Safe here in this house.

Her stomach growled when they got into the large kitchen.

"Good! I like it when my guests are hungry." He put her down and Vincenz pulled a chair back for her.

"Take it easy, she hasn't been eating regularly," Vincenz warned as Julian began to make her a plate.

"Good call." He turned and put a plate of bread, fruits, cheese, nuts and a slice of . . .

She leaned close and breathed in the scent. "Spice cake?"

"I've got it on good authority that any time of day is the best time for cake. Where are you from, Hannah?"

Julian put a heaping plate of fried meat and eggs in front of Vincenz and then himself.

She sipped the juice and when it stayed without revolt, she moved to nibble at a piece of the toasted bread. "Sanctu."

"Me too." Julian smiled. "Though I'd wager we aren't from the same parts."

There was pain in his face and she wondered over the whys. Vincenz put a hand over his, just a brief touch.

She ate and felt better with each bite. It would be slow going, she knew, to get her health back, but she would. No one would strip her of that. She'd be whole again. She snorted a laugh and both men looked at her askance. Whole physically, not mentally. She wasn't sure that would ever happen.

"Share that joke?" Vincenz filled her glass.

"Silly thought," she reassured.

She liked that they left her alone without physically leaving her. There was so much to process, just being able to sit and try to unpack it all in her head was nearly too much.

What would happen to her now?

Could she go back to Sanctu?

Would she work again?

Her parents, yes, she needed to contact her parents.

"My family."

Vincenz looked at her. "Would you like me to get a message to them?"

She nodded. "My parents are Shelby and Bertram Black." She said it clearly.

"On Sanctu?"

"Seah." The name of the city.

"I'll get it done." He slid a palm over her head and she breathed it in like air. He stood and moved to the comm center nearby and began to work. For her. The first seeds of trust had been planted when he'd broken her free from the labs. And he'd been working to help her since. She could hold on and let him help.

Everything made noise, she realized as they began to bustle around her. She wanted to go back to her room, but didn't want to be alone. She pulled her shirt around herself tighter.

"Hannah?" Julian paused and sat at the table with her again, brushing her hair back with his fingers.

She swallowed hard. "I-I . . ."

There was some noise and talking out in the entry. Vincenz looked up from his comm station and stayed them both.

"I'll deal with it."

He left the room and she wasn't sure of anything all the sudden. She began to tremble and despaired. Would it always be this way?

"Hey, it's all right." Julian had been wearing a long-sleeved shirt over a T-shirt of sorts, and he took it off, placing it over her shoulders. She pulled it tight around her body and then he put an arm around her, holding her to his side. His warmth enveloped her, his scent as well. Soothed better than the blanket or the shirt.

"Vin and I won't let anything happen to you."

The roar of chaos in her head ebbed at his touch and she wanted so badly to rub against him like a cat.

Vincenz came in. Alone. "There's a doctor here. In the other room."

Julian stroked a hand up and down her arm.

"He'd like to give you an exam. It's totally up to you. This doctor is one who's treated me before. Three times actually. He's gentle and he knows you've been through a lot. But your blood tests showed some problems he'd like to help you correct. We know you've been through a lot. They want to be sure you're all right."

She swallowed hard and pulled Julian's shirt around her even tighter. Her heart beat so hard it boomed through her ears.

"Would it be better if we stayed with you? At least just outside your room?" Julian asked her quietly.

Vincenz kept his tone calm as Julian brushed his lips over her temple. "Your iron is very low. Your white blood count is off. He wants to get you back on track. You were in a bad situation for a significant amount of time. He wants to help you."

She grew up around doctors and scientists. Was both herself. But they'd done something to her. Instilled a fear that went very deep. She had to clamp her lips closed to keep from showing her teeth like an animal.

They'd need to talk to her. The Federated Governance people. She knew this. Understood it. Wished it weren't necessary but knew it was. She had to find her courage again.

"No drugs?" She was surprised she could get the words out without screaming.

Vincenz moved to her to kneel at her knees. "No, baby. I promise."

"Surviving this and making yourself even stronger is the best revenge." Julian brushed his lips against her temple and she took a deep breath.

And nodded.

Vincenz wondered why he felt pride at seeing her nod and then as Julian helped her up. She leaned into him as if she wanted to crawl into his body and then took a deep breath, standing taller.

Being touched helped her, he'd noticed. It made sense. For generations it had been accepted that humans needed to be touched to thrive. She hadn't been for a very long time.

He smiled and went to her, taking up her other side. "Consider us your bodyguards."

He'd explained to the doctor that in no way shape or form were there to be any drugs used unless fully disclosed and discussed with Hannah. The doctor had told Vincenz that he'd worked with trauma patients quite extensively, which made him feel better.

And Andrei had commed earlier that day asking about Hannah. If she knew anything they could benefit from, they had to debrief her. Had to not only be sure her health was improving, but also hear her story.

He wouldn't let them take her to some lab that, as far as Hannah would feel, was the same as the one she'd been held captive in. She was barely holding herself together as it was. But they were at war. He knew this. She might have intelligence they needed and so he'd have to help her get it to them in the most effective, but least intrusive way.

The way the doctor waited until they'd gotten her seated on her bed before he spoke only made Vincenz feel better.

She was like a scared animal and it broke his heart to see it. And what he'd learned about her parents would only make it worse, which is why he decided to hold off telling her for a while.

"Hannah, I'm Hal Pesch. I understand you're a doctor too?"

She swallowed around the wad of fear in her throat and nodded.

"I've seen your records, you should know that up front. One of my friends went to the same academy you did. Several years before you arrived. A respected medical and research facility."

Her father had gone there as well. It had been the proudest day of her life when she'd learned she'd been accepted there for her medical training.

"I need to touch you. I'll try to explain it all as I go so you understand, but you'll know what I'm doing anyway." He smiled at her and it wasn't full of lies like the doctors at the lab.

He poked and prodded. Took notes. Each new thing he did, he explained carefully, though as he'd pointed out, she already knew. It helped that he treated her like a colleague instead of a test subject.

And yet the scent of the antibacterial gel he wore on his hands reminded her of the labs. The clicking and beeping of the diagnostic tool he used made gooseflesh rise. Her heart rate was elevated, a fact that astonished no one.

Dr. Pesch put the diagnostic away and turned back to her. "I'd like to speak with you," the doctor said to Hannah quietly, "about what you might have endured. It will help me with a general diagnostic. And I'd like to see your skin. You've got some blood levels I'm worried about. Do you have any wounds that didn't close well?" He paused, waiting for her to process. But she couldn't. "They can wait outside with the door closed. I can get a female doctor in if you'd rather. It's difficult to know how to treat you unless we get a full exam and hear what you have to say."

She knew her eyes nearly bugged from her head as she scrambled backward, white noise a roar in her ears as spots pricked her vision. They started out this way. Nice. Friendly. *Just let us examine you for the project.*

The memories swirled around, sucking her under. Pulling her apart.

Julian thundered something at the doctor and it was the only thing that enabled her to pull herself back from the pit of memories. She didn't want anyone hurt.

"No!" She held a hand out, still breathing hard. Still choking back bile. "Don't hurt him."

Vincenz was already there, pulling Julian away, speaking to him quietly and calmly.

She shook her head and slumped to the bed, curling into a ball. "Sorry."

The doctor snorted a laugh. "It's all right. He wanted to protect you. We can do this another day. My purpose is not to make things worse for you."

She took a deep breath. "I should go." Avoiding looking toward the doorway, she tried to be brave. They saved her. She would not bring harm to them. "To hospital."

"You'll do no such thing." Vincenz was at her side in moments.

She didn't want to fall apart and yet, it was happening. Pieces of her fell through her fingers like sand. The darkness lurked in her head. She dipped her head and rocked slightly as she huffed the air, trying to calm down.

She knew she was about to pass out, knew the signs and yet she couldn't seem to stop.

Julian watched her fall away, lose her grip, and he moved the doctor aside and lay on the bed, pulling her to him. "On the other side, Vin. She needs touch."

Vincenz followed, snuggling up to her on the other side as they held her between them. Her heaving breaths and stuttered sobs slowed.

Between them she seemed so small and fragile, this woman who was beyond strong. Julian buried his face in her hair. "Stay with us, Hannah. Here with Vincenz and me. You can let go for now, but we're here to catch you."

Her whimper and full body shiver brought his gaze to Vincenz's. She clutched at his shirt, burrowing into him and they held her tighter. The doctor nodded, encouraging them.

They held her like that for some time until she finally went lax and her breathing smoothed, going deep and slow.

"Don't go too far." Vincenz looked back through the doorway to watch her sleep. "I don't want her to wake up alone."

"I'm sorry I was so angry. Before." Julian looked to the doctor, who'd been standing there the whole time. "Should we use something to help her stay sleeping?"

"Her body is working overtime to heal. She'll be out awhile. In fact, expect her to sleep a lot the first days she's back. Maybe even a month. Her internal sense of time will be out of synch. Given her reaction to my even suggesting a more comprehensive exam, I feel using any sedatives on her without her knowledge and consent would only hinder any trust we've created."

Julian nodded. "That makes sense. I just hate seeing her suffer this way. I want to help her."

"I know that. She knows that or she wouldn't have been able to get past her fear to defend and protect you the way she did." Dr. Pesch looked at his notes. "I'd like some of your time if you have it to spare."

"We need to check in. May as well be now." Vincenz indicated the worktable in the middle of the room. They'd debriefed in part the evening before after . . . Julian looked over to Vincenz and hid a smile . . . after they'd exhausted themselves.

"I've read the testing journals Vincenz brought back from Parron and did some investigation myself." The doctor took a seat at the nearby worktable where Vincenz and Julian joined him. They'd meet with him while they waited for everyone to get connected back on Ravena.

"Hannah Black was at the top of her class. A brilliant doctor and scientist studying disease out on the Edge. Her mother is . . . was from the Imperium. The daughter of a trader. It's how Ms. Black got involved with them to begin with. The program they took her from was a cross border initiative created to deliver health care and study fast-moving viruses among the frontier 'Verses. They killed four at the labs she had established. Several have disappeared and we fear . . . well, it's obvious what we fear."

Vincenz heaved a sigh. "Not thrilled to have to tell her what's happened to her parents. I want to make her smile, not shed more tears." Julian nodded, feeling the same.

"We'll tell her together."

"That will be good, I think. She seems to trust you two. Just make it brief and straightforward. She's going to need a lot of uncomfortable truth, but it has to be given to her. She deserves that." Dr. Pesch consulted his notes again. "They very rarely spoke to her or touched her over her time there. Except." He paused. "There's a note. They tried to take a blanket from her. She tore the man's eye out to keep it. They had to gas the room to get him out. They did it just to see how she'd react. They never wanted the blanket in the first place. After that though, it appears they doubled the amount of sedative in her food and water to keep her more subservient."

Julian growled, the rage eating at his belly. "I hope he wears those scars forever for his sins. I'd rip his other eye out if I ever met him."

Vincenz paled and Julian knew it was guilt. Guilt over something he had nothing to do with, but felt nonetheless. Because he was the man his father only wished he could have been.

Pesch continued. "She was beaten at random. Starved. They caught her keeping track of time in her room and made her stop with . . . severe punishments."

Julian scratched the beard on his chin. "Why would they kidnap her just to torture her? She's a useful target."

"Something we don't know yet. It's why it's so important we debrief her."

"Hal, you've seen her. She's in absolutely no shape to be taken to Ravena to be questioned by soldiers in a military compound. Much less hooked up to a brain scan." Vincenz leaned forward, intense. Julian rarely saw him this way. But he understood it. For whatever reason, Hannah was important to them. Important to protect. She had no one but them and that would be enough.

"I agree. She's stronger than you're giving her credit for. I think if we can manage to do it here, we should. I wouldn't voice support for any plan that removed her. Not unless she was getting in the way here. Are you two all right with her presence?"

Both men nodded. "Yes, yes, of course. We can keep her safe. We have the room and the access to medical care for her." And Julian would feel better knowing she was there where they could keep an eye on her.

"I'm going to return tomorrow. Give her a chance to rest and recover from today. I'll make my official recommendation that she stay here with you. If and when you have to go out on missions, it may be complicated. I just wanted to get that out there. But if she grows to feel secure here, she may be fine when you're both gone."

He stood and shook hands with them.

"Thank you. For coming out here." Vincenz was a little pale but he'd regained most of his composure.

"Of course. There's something about your Ms. Black."

Yes.

*T*hey connected with Ravena and waited for all the parties to get hooked in. Vincenz looked in her direction from time to time. Her door was open so he could see the rise and fall of her body. She tended to sleep bundled up in all her bedding. Tenderness skittered through him at the thought.

Ellis spoke without any preamble. "Vincenz, we're going to need you to appear at a corps meeting in four standard hours. Holo in. Julian, Ash Walker is on his way to you. I want you to brief him on the results of the interrogations on Ceres."

Julian took notes to keep from thinking too closely about Ceres.

"Andrei will stay here for the time being to coordinate next steps so be prepared for daily briefings." Daniel Haws, Wil Ellis's right-hand man, nodded in Andrei's direction. "How are we coming on the data you brought back from Parron, Vincenz?"

"I worked up a program that will spike every time certain parameters in the data are breached. I'll start with the anomalies."

Julian was proud of how intelligent and resourceful Vincenz was. If there wasn't a program to do what they needed, he simply created one. Brilliant.

On the screens, Ellis nodded, satisfied for the moment at least.

"We've raised security levels. Travel will be restricted for the time being."

"I saw the footage." Julian had watched the tapes of the Federated Universes' response to what Fardelle had done. He'd known then that the Federation would have to restrict travel and raise security presence on the streets. To ease the citizens' fears and to underline that they would be prepared if the Imperium got far enough through the portals to end up in a position to do them any further harm.

"Rank and file will leave you alone. You've all got the clearance. They don't need to know anything about what you're doing there."

As if he was freshly minted or something.

His annoyance must have shown on his face because Daniel snorted. "Oh, get that look off your face. I know you understand. But let's move along."

Chapter 4

"Why did they not just kill her? She's a high-value target, isn't she?" Daniel paced.

Vincenz watched as his friend worked through the problem. A problem he and Julian had discussed with Dr. Pesch just a few days earlier. Back then Ravena had agreed to table the issue, but it had to be discussed and Vincenz knew it couldn't be avoided any longer.

"They had her for almost a year. Why did they take her to start with?"

"All we know is that she was taken from the program she was granted to work with. Several others were also taken that day."

They'd been discussing Hannah for the last several minutes and it made him defensive. He knew they'd have to question her about her time in that cell, but she was fragile. Just barely making it through each hour; the idea of pushing her recovery back even further to debrief her was untenable. But he knew it had to be done.

"What does she say about it?" Ellis asked.

"She still can't keep her time straight. She has a difficult time speaking and keeping track of her thoughts. When she's alone she talks to herself. For hours. She retreats to a corner and wraps one of Julian's shirts around herself. This happens less the longer she's with us, but she's not ready to be debriefed." Vincenz wanted to make that totally clear. "She's barely holding on. To push her to relive her time there, right now, could be detrimental to her overall health."

Ellis nodded, a shadow crossing his features. "It is not my intention to harm the woman, Operative Cuomo."

"But the fact is, we need the information. She's been with you a week already." Daniel tapped his pen against the table. "They took her for a *reason*. They kept her alive for a *reason* and if they just wanted to torture someone to experiment on them, why not do it in their own territory where it's safer? They chose her for a *reason*, and there's no getting around the fact that the why of it could very well be integral to what we're doing."

"Dr. Hal Pesch would like to address our group. He's the person who's been working with Hannah. He's got level four clearance and I ran him again earlier today." Vincenz shifted, hoping they'd let Hal speak. He'd be a powerful advocate for Hannah, and she needed all the help she could get.

"Yes, yes." Daniel looked over the data on his comm to verify this information. "Patch him in."

In short order, Pesch's face was on a screen at the conference table in Ravena. Pesch was an unassuming person. He wasn't too anything. Just the right height, average weight. His voice was calm and measured. Vincenz liked the man a great deal, especially after he'd observed just how patient and kind he'd been with Hannah.

"Dr. Pesch, I'm Daniel Haws. Tell me, when can we expect to debrief Ms. Black? We helped her escape and certainly have no plans to do her any further injury. But we need to know what she knows."

"Hannah Black is suffering not uncommon results of having been held without any other human contact for months on end. She's exemplary on many levels. Many others in her place would not have survived. Not without having lost their minds. She needs time to get better. Time to process. Time to figure out her own internal clock, which is damaged. She's sleeping a lot, which is also common. Her kidneys are damaged, but that can be fixed."

"How much time? If you'll forgive my impatience, there's a war on. I need what's in her head."

Pesch paused for long moments. "There's an experimental treatment."

Vincenz knew he was shaking his head vehemently. No fucking way was anyone going to experiment on Hannah ever again.

"Tell me about it." Daniel looked to the hologram that was Vincenz, sitting in a room across the Universe while his body was back in Mirage. "Get over it, Vincenz. Everyone has to make sacrifices. Including Hannah."

The words he held back were bitter. But it was his job to shut his mouth just then and so he did. But there was simply no way at all he'd let them use any treatments on her without her complete and total acceptance. Period. She was in Mirage, halfway across the Known Universes. In his house where she would continue to be safe.

"I don't know if I agree with that, Operative Haws. This young woman has been held captive, abused, tortured, beaten and starved already. That's not enough for you?" Dr. Pesch cocked his head and Vincenz wanted to hug him. "If this is to be what she experienced in that lab under the hands of the Imperium and you'd wish me to replicate that, I'm going to have to refuse. That woman has done her part and more. If you'd like to hear about this treatment and if she decides of her own free will to undertake it, I'm happy to do so. If she refuses, well, I took an oath when I became a medical doctor. I will not participate in any experiments or treatment that is given against the will of, or that would be a detriment to, any of my patients."

Daniel sighed and scrubbed his hands over his face. "Tell me about the treatment, Doctor. I have no plans to experiment on this young woman for my pleasure. But people are dying every single day and it's my job to stop it."

"What Ms. Black has suffered has physical consequences. Obviously. She has some impaired kidney function as I mentioned. I've already begun treatment for that and I expect in a month or two she'll be recovered. Dehydration, which again, has been treated. Other problems like poorly healed wounds." He shrugged. "She'll have scars for the rest of her life though she won't be physically impaired by them.

"But she's also suffering from mental and emotional damage. Studies on long-term isolation are one of the many reasons we don't use solitary confinement in our corrections systems except in the very worst cases. To be blunt, her brain has suffered some damage and that's not as easy to treat. Not quickly."

Vincenz wanted to look over toward her room to assure himself she was all right, but the holo meant he couldn't. He trusted Julian and the doctor would do that if she awakened.

"She's . . . for lack of a better word, she's broken. Neural pathways are disrupted. She's angry. Resentful. Fearful. Worried she'll be sent off to a Federation facility and away from this small place of solace she's found. This is the sort of thing I'd treat with a combination of chemical adjustment and talk therapy. Over a long time. The brain is amazing. We discover new data all the time, even after all our history. So over weeks, months and years, she'll be all right again, though I doubt she'll ever be totally free of the shadows of what she's experienced."

Ellis made the scariest, angriest sound Vincenz had ever heard from the man. Who was already pretty scary. "I promise you, Vincenz, we will help this woman. It is not my aim nor the aim of the Federated Universes to perpetrate more harm. We will make those who did this to her, and to tens of thousands of others they've harmed and killed, pay. But we don't have months and years."

"This therapy works specifically on brain tissue and brain chemistry. The treatment is given daily in multiple segments. With Hannah, I'd suggest three times a day. Each will work to speed the healing of the damage to her neural pathways. It won't cure her. But it should ratchet back the worst of her symptoms. Her time issues should smooth out. Speech centers of the brain will also be affected and if it works correctly, while not totally healed, it should enable her to be debriefed. Give me three sessions a day for this next week and I think we can move her forward several months. Enough that she can do daily tasks without panic attacks and sleep regularly."

"You said it was experimental. Why?" Daniel asked.

"It's not fully accredited and approved by the Federation Medical Consortium. It hasn't been tested long-term. In some very rare cases it has caused irreparable brain damage. In all fairness, that was in the very beginning. And I hasten to add I've administered this treatment four times now and have never had any negative results. I'm one of the doctors who pioneered this treatment and I believe in it. Not for all cases, certainly. But this is not a usual scenario."

Vincenz had been in meetings all day. She'd done her very best to stay in the background and not make any noise or distractions for him. Though the doctor had brought a calendar in and she could see it had only been ten days since she'd arrived, she missed Vincenz if she didn't see him.

He had taken to working at the table just outside her room. It had soothed her fear of being left alone while letting her also be away from all the noise and chaos of the main parts of the house.

Sometimes it had felt as if she were wading back into a real life. Dipping her toe in and letting herself get used to it again.

Julian was out training people or doing something similar. He didn't say a whole lot but always made an effort for her. He was intense and hard, but smiled at her. His smile lit his eyes and softened the sadness lining his face. She liked him and wondered just what put the pain in his features. It felt safe when he was around.

"I thought I'd bring this in here." Vincenz poked his head into the room after knocking. He gave her a look as he carried a soft, comfortable-looking chair over and placed it in front of the window.

She'd been in the corner. She knew it was bad. Knew it was silly and made her look crazy, but it seemed to be something she did automatically.

He held a hand out. "No need to hide in the corner, beautiful Hannah. I brought you a chair so you could sit in the sunlight. Dr. Pesch says it's good for you."

She took his hand and allowed him to help her to her feet. "I'm sorry."

Vincenz shook his head and tucked her hair behind her ear. "Don't apologize. I don't want you to feel bad. I just want you to feel safe enough not to huddle in the corner. No one can hurt you in this house. You know that, right?"

What she knew and what she felt weren't always in accord.

"Now I'm the one who's sorry." He gathered her to his body and hugged her. Just the way she needed and hadn't even known it. She burrowed into his chest, breathing him in.

"Would you like to break for some food?" He held her back and looked into her face, taking careful notes. She was tired of careful notes. "Julian is free and we thought we could all eat together and talk a little. Dr. Pesch is also here."

She didn't hate the kind-eyed doctor. But she didn't like being poked and prodded either. She had no need of doctors just then. She'd spent all her time and energy just not going crazy. Had used up all her skills and knowledge to do so and she was . . . tired.

"I know you're wary of him. He's a good man. There's no way Julian and I would trust him with you otherwise."

She shook her head and made the extra effort to shepherd her words into the right order. "Not that. Let's eat." She didn't want to talk about it.

"First tell me if you're all right with where I've placed your chair." He winked and she smiled at his cheek.

He'd put it just exactly where she wanted it. It was in her favorite spot. Just outside that window was a small garden, enclosed by the high walls surrounding the compound where the house was. She'd begun to yearn for that garden. Sometimes she'd lay on her bed and look out at it, imagining herself out there, her hands in the dirt.

As for the chair? *Her* chair? Not as secure as having your back to the wall, but all things considered, it might be a place to perch. The afternoon in the sunshine seemed a very nice thing indeed. "Yes." She swallowed. "Thank you."

"Come on then, let's get you eating."

In the dining area, Julian had put out a colorful spread for the late afternoon meal. He saw her and lost the look of concentration he'd been wearing. Instead he grinned and moved to her, bringing her into a tight hug. She hummed, happy, hugging him back.

"It's our lovely Hannah." He kissed her forehead and pulled her chair out. "Sit."

Dr. Pesch sat across from her. She nodded her hello.

Once they'd all gotten seated and plates had been filled, she realized it wasn't just that Dr. Pesch happened to be there but that he had something to say. It agitated her that they hadn't just told her up front.

And she said so. Licking her lips and grasping her words tightly. "I am not feeble. If you have something to say . . ." She looked down and the brush of hair against her cheeks helped. "You should tell me that."

Julian took her hand, entangling his fingers with hers. "So fierce. We're not trying to be sneaky. It was time to eat and we wanted to talk with you about something. No harm in doing both at once."

"Tell me." After squeezing Julian's hand she managed to swallow past her fear and anger to take a few bites. It seemed like all she'd done since she'd arrived in Mirage was to eat and sleep.

"We're at war. I know you have heard part of what's going on." Vincenz helped himself to another spoonful of roasted vegetables, putting more on her plate too.

She had known something was wrong. Clearly soldiers didn't just show up in a lab with helicopters on the roof, start a firefight and blow the place up on leaving. But she hadn't known it was war.

"And you need something from me." Fear ate at her. But for them, she'd get through.

"Yes."

Dr. Pesch broke in. "You'll heal. Over time the emotional upheaval you're drowning in will ease. You'll remember how to react to non-emergency situations in appropriate ways."

"Will the anger ever stop?"

Vincenz's mouth hardened.

Dr. Pesch sighed, sorrow threaded through the noise. "It's healthy to be angry, Hannah. What they did to you was outrageous. If you weren't angry, I'd be worried. But it will lessen, yes. Over time."

Her thoughts were so scattered, it took an immense amount of will to force herself to stay cogent.

"Time you don't have."

He nodded. "There's a new treatment for people who've been through harrowing ordeals like the one you experienced. You understand of course that the physical damage is one thing, but the emotional and mental toll is harder to address. It takes time and counseling. This treatment speeds some of that process."

"Invasive?" Her hands shook so she put them in her lap and made fists.

"It would be three times daily. You'll be unconscious when treated."

"D-drugged?" Her heart beat so fast she was sure her skin throbbed in time.

"Sedated. So your brain waves are where we need them for the treatment to work. There's a small cap fitted to your head. Tiny electrical nodes that would be attached to monitor your physical situation."

"They had you for almost a year, Hannah." Julian moved his chair closer and took one of her fists, slowly unfurling her fingers to kiss her palm. He . . . disarmed her. So gruff all the time and yet when he turned his focus on her all that dropped away. He touched her like she was precious and that helped her listen. "They didn't kill you. If you were a prisoner, they'd have made to trade you or they'd have killed you. We need to know why they kept you alive."

Didn't they think she'd wondered that too? Had wondered if her life had come at some expense she didn't understand? "I don't know anything!" The rage boiled up and through her system. They'd kept her and hurt her over and over for no reason she could understand. "I studied viruses. I wasn't political at the foundation. Do you think I'd betray my Universe?"

The words shot from her mouth like bullets.

Julian's worried look faded a little. "I think that's the most you've said since Vincenz brought you home." He winked and she laughed. Just a gritty huff of sound, but it felt so very *good* to do.

"Even better, a laugh. No, we don't think you betrayed us. If you had, they'd have let you go, not kept you penned. But we need to question you about what they did to you and why they might have done it. And you are not in any shape to answer those questions much less dwell too deeply on what happened in that cell."

"We need to know what you know. You may not even know what it is. We have methods to help people go through these sorts of events. I'm trained to help you find what you may not know. But there is simply no way Julian and I would agree to such a debrief right now. Even if you could withstand it."

"And you couldn't." Dr. Pesch interrupted. "The kind of trauma you've endured is quite simply, more than most people could have survived with their sanity intact."

"Who says it is?" She rubbed her free hand over her face, leaving her hair there for long moments. Julian kept her other hand in his.

"You're the sanest person I know." Julian brushed a kiss over her cheek and she laughed again.

"You must not know a lot of people."

Vincenz tutted and waved that away.

Dr. Pesch spoke again. "This *will* help you. It won't cure you. But it'll get you to a place where you don't pass out from fear every time you see my instruments. I'd be the one to do the treatments, though Julian and Vincenz have both volunteered to learn how to administer the treatments as well."

Could she do it if they were with her?

"Tell her why it's experimental." Vincenz had wariness in his voice, and a little anger. She was glad he asked and more than a little curious as to why he responded that way.

The doctor told her about the newness of the process and the lack of long-term studies. He told her it might result in irreversible damage to brain tissue.

"I want to emphasize the rare part. The longer we do this, the better we get at it. I'm good at what I do, Hannah. Let me help you. Let me help you help us all."

She understood. Better than they thought she did. "I don't need a . . . guarantee. I know how this works." Her brain. Well, her brain had always been her strongest asset. If she damaged it . . .

"There is a chance that the treatment won't help at all. Though I've never had that result with a patient. In the end it'll take longer to heal with more aggressive medication to normalize." He shrugged. "I wouldn't be recommending this if I thought that would be the case. This is extreme. Much as your situation was extreme. But all my patients and those treated elsewhere have had forward momentum. Even if it was very small. You're a doctor; you know how this all works. I can't cure you with this treatment. But I can help you find a way to process what happened. And I can help you get to a place where you can help your fellow Federated Universes citizens by being debriefed."

"What do you think?" she asked Julian.

He grimaced and it made her feel better that he wasn't so superhuman he could hide his emotions in every situation. "I think it bothers me that you'd be manipulated into an experimental brain treatment by using patriotism. I don't like what happened to you."

"Do you think I should do it?"

"I think you should do it only if you want to. I believe Dr. Pesch is a good doctor, good at what he does, and I think if you plan to go ahead, he's the guy to go ahead with."

She narrowed her eyes, frustrated. Turning to Vincenz, she caught him watching her and Julian. "What do you think? And don't say only if I want to."

Vincenz laughed and he and Julian shared some private, intimate thing, and yet she felt part of it, not apart. "I don't like the experimental thing. You're a brilliant woman with a history of doing things that have helped others. I hate the idea that you stand a chance to lose that ability in the future."

She pushed from her chair and moved to the sink, looking out the window.

"You don't have to make the decision right now."

She turned slowly. "I appreciate that, Vincenz, but we know that's not true. This is rush-rush and my brain is broken. Too broken to be pok—" She wrestled back a sob and hated that weakness. "I'll do it. Let's get started so we can be done."

Her hands shook and all she wanted to do was be well enough to be alone so she could cry in peace.

"I know you're scared." Julian stood and moved to her. He slid his palms from her shoulders down her arms, holding her hips. "And I can't tell you not to be. I'd be scared too. But you're not broken. And you're brave. So very brave."

He hugged her, and she knew she got the front of his shirt wet from all the tears, but she couldn't help it. Momentarily, Vincenz was there, hugging her from the side. "We'll be with you. Every step of the way."

Chapter 5

"*I*'m going to take this slowly." Dr. Pesch sat next to her bed. Vincenz had opened the window coverings wide to let the sunlight stream into the room, but it was his presence that held back the darkness. He sat on her other side, squeezing her hand.

Dr. Pesch had already given her the sedative and she felt the cottony numbness fill her from the outer edges to her center. The fear wasn't so hard to manage. She needed to be grateful it wasn't the same heart-pounding terror she'd wrestled with only a few hours before.

But it wasn't enough. As much as she wanted otherwise, what had happened to her still lived inside. The memories fresh enough that she flinched and made an animal sound when Pesch held up the cap. Vincenz kissed her wrist, and Julian rubbed his hands up and down her legs where he'd settled at the foot of the bed.

Pesch fastened the nodes to her chest and set the monitoring machine. The steady hums and clicks brought a sheen of cold, sticky sweat.

"I need to put the cap on. I want you to take a deep breath and blow it out. Do it three times." Pesch's manner was calm and competent. But the tears still came until she closed her eyes rather than look at anyone.

The cap fit snug and the contact points shocked a tiny bit when they established contact with her brain waves. It was the oddest thing she'd ever submitted to willingly. The burn in the drip on her hand told her they'd administered the second dose of sedation. Pesch spoke to her, but it was Julian's continual slide of his palms against her legs and Vincenz's hand in hers that kept her eyes closed and let the oblivion of unconsciousness set in . . .

She surfaced two hours later, sitting straight up, nausea and cold sweat an assault. Fear clawed at her, making it hard to see as she screamed, pulling at the cap.

"Shh. Hannah, it's Vincenz. Honey, I'm here. Calm down. Let me help you get the cap off."

She slapped at his hands, the memories still so fresh she could taste the stench of the disinfectant they'd used back in the lab. The cold of the walls pressed against her.

Vincenz held her, gently but firmly, as he undid all the nodes in the cap and finally pulled it free.

Not a moment too soon as she rushed out of bed, tripping and falling right onto her knees as she made her way into the bathroom where she threw up the scant contents of her stomach and spent another however many minutes dry heaving.

A cool cloth against the back of her neck then drew her from the nightmare of the dream, brought her there to the place where Vincenz and Julian had let her nest and make a home.

"You're here with us, Hannah. With me and Julian. We contacted Dr. Pesch. He's on his way over. You surfaced quickly, he said."

She nodded, the nausea returning at the movement. "You don't need to stay." She leaned against the tile, letting the shock of the cold help push the sickness back. She used the cloth to clean up.

"Of course I don't."

But he didn't go.

Instead when she was ready he helped her to stand and walked with her back to bed, pulling the blankets back and helping her slide inside. The shakes came then and without a word, he got in with her and held her tight.

Dr. Pesch came in and checked her vitals. "As I explained, the first times will be the most difficult. Everything you've repressed since you've been away from the lab is really just there right beneath the surface. It'll be the first thing you'll have to confront. I'm sorry you were so ill when you came out."

He was gentle and kind, making adjustments for the next round of treatment that she'd insisted she was ready for, but she was relieved when he was gone.

"You can let go, baby." Vincenz kissed her temple. "Let yourself fall apart a little while if that's what you need. I'm here to hold all the pieces until you're ready."

At every turn, when things got to be so much she wasn't sure if she could hold herself together, one of them had been there to help her do it. Not to do it for her. But to help her do it, letting her get better on her own terms. She closed her eyes and pressed into him as much as she possibly could. The feel of his arms around her was more than comforting, it seemed integral. And so she let him be.

He'd been on his way back to the house when the sun had glinted off the wind chimes, catching his attention. Julian paused as he listened to the deep hum as the breeze sounded through the tubes, the louder resonant bong as they slid together.

She'd like that.

Julian had handed over the credits and was carrying the package to the house before he realized he'd done it.

She'd been there with them for four weeks. He and Vincenz had watched her try to regain herself. At first she couldn't leave her room alone, and then Vin had drawn her outside to the small garden the windows in her room and the dining area overlooked.

In between her treatments, she'd made that little garden her home. Vin had brought chairs out. Had made sure she had hats and other protection from the sun. And she'd sit out there with her face tipped toward the light, at peace.

Which is where he found her when he got home.

She twisted in her seat to greet him.

"I brought you something." He handed her the package and sat alongside her on the chaise as she opened it.

No ripping of paper from her. She always made a slow, steady study of the packaging on the various little gifts he brought home. And when she finished, she would fold the paper into whimsical shapes of all sorts.

He knew the following day there would be a bird or a horse sitting on his workstation. He'd come to look forward to whatever she'd gift him with.

"They're chimes for the wind." He stood, taking the chimes up. "Where would you like me to hang them?"

She paused as the breeze kicked up and the chimes sounded. "I can feel that sound in my belly." She nodded. "There perhaps?" She pointed at the corner of the overhang at the back doors.

It was quick work and not too very long before the sounds filled the air.

"Thank you. I like it when I can hear things inside." She said it solemnly and he knew it was a compliment.

In the time since she'd arrived, it had become his and Vin's goal to make her happy. To help her through the rough spots. They'd opened up the family the two of them had created and she'd fit there as if she was always part of it.

It helped Julian to know that not every part of his life was dark. He found refuge in Vincenz and now with Hannah.

Vincenz looked up from his comm as Julian entered the room. Hannah lay on her bed, the treatment cap on her head, nodes attached here and there; the steady click and hum of the machines monitoring her were quiet enough for him to hear her breathe.

He stood and went out into the main room, hugging Julian.

"Hey you." Julian smiled and dipped his head for a kiss. Soft at first, then the scratch of his beard against Vincenz's face as he deepened and his tongue found its way into Vincenz's mouth.

Vincenz slid his fingers into Julian's hair, which had grown out from his usual shorter cut. It was long enough to tug to pull Julian closer. Close enough to thrust his hips, stroking his cock against Julian's. Vincenz swallowed Julian's tortured groan, suckling his tongue as Julian broke the kiss.

"I take it you missed me too." He'd been out all morning with Ash Walker, another of the leaders of one of Ellis's special teams. They'd coordinated some of their efforts and mapped a few new ideas. They'd spent a great deal of time going over the films of Julian's interrogations back on Ceres and more recently those he'd done with some high-placed prisoners of war. They'd gained a great deal of intel and between the two of them, they'd been able to put some of their plans into motion.

It took him away from home more than he wanted, but it was his job and more and more lately it had felt as if they'd been making real headway.

"How's our girl?" He tipped his head toward Hannah. Ever since the first treatment he'd hated the way she looked while under. Hated the way she'd held on to Vincenz's hand as tears had slipped past her closed eyes the first several days. Hated the hard tremble in her legs and really had despised the way she'd shrank away from the cap with that sound, that hurt animal sound. It lay in his belly every time they started a new session, making him resent having to be gone.

And then the doctor had found the marks she'd scratched into her scalp. She'd explained in her medication-slurred voice that it had been her way of keeping track of time after they'd removed the tally marks she'd made on her wall multiple times. They hadn't seen the ones at her hairline. Brilliant woman, their Hannah. But the story of it, that she'd *had* to mutilate herself to hold on to her sanity, burned in his gut.

"Who knows? Her vitals are fine. She's lost that tremble she had in the early days. I hope this helps because I can't stand the thought of her confronting all this and it not working."

"Was it any better the second and third round?" She did her first treatment each day in the early morning and he'd been there that day before he'd gone to meet Ash. She had to follow with another just after the midday lunch and then another after the evening meal.

"She's not crying anymore. It seems better for her now." Vincenz paused, his Adam's apple sliding up and down. "Still, it's hard when she comes out of it. I had to do a vid comm with Andrei and when I'd come back she was in her corner again. Nearly tripped over her blankets to get to me when I walked in. She held on tight, trembling from head to toe, apologizing." He ran his hands through his hair. "I'd like to kill a few people after that."

"At least three times." Fucking Imperialist pieces of shit. Julian wanted to hunt them all down to make them pay for Marame. For Vincenz and Carina, the children Fardelle had driven away and continued to threaten. For Hannah, who in only a little longer than a month standard had become his too. "Oh, baby. I wish I could make it better for you. For our pretty Hannah. For this fucking 'Verse."

Vincenz brushed a kiss over his jaw before moving behind him to knead his shoulders and down his back. Julian let his anger out and put it all away. Here with Vincenz there was no need for it. Vincenz's hands kept all that away.

Vincenz encircled him from behind, pressing his body to Julian's back. "You do make it better. It's what you do. It's who you are."

He smiled, leaning back to kiss Vincenz. "Are you flattering me so you can . . . have my virtue?"

"In my mouth." Vincenz moved around to face him, leaving Julian a little breathless.

"You want my virtue in your mouth?" He ducked his head down to lick up the side of Vincenz's neck.

"No. I want your cock in my mouth. Maybe I'll let you put your virtue elsewhere."

Julian laughed as he backed Vincenz up to a nearby wall, pressing himself against his body.

And then all joking had passed. Replaced by the fire of need. Need to be touched and understood.

Julian had considered a long, slow seduction that evening, but Vincenz clearly had other ideas. His hand was down the front of Julian's trousers until he finally stopped, grasping Julian's cock and pumping a few times.

Julian arched, fucking himself into Vincenz's fist until the way became slicker as pre-come beaded at the slit of his cock and Vincenz gathered it with this thumb. The pleasure of each swipe of the pad of

Vincenz's thumb through that slippery, sensitive spot brought shards of bright pleasure and a tortured *yes*.

He wanted in. Vin's mouth, his ass, his fist, whatever. Julian wanted to be in him, to be surrounded by Vincenz, craved that.

"Turn around. Pants down. Shorts down. Hands on the table."

Julian swallowed, obeying. By the time he got his pants off, Vincenz had returned, placing a bottle of lube in Julian's line of vision. Julian's dominance was in his physicality. Vincenz . . . well, Vincenz liked to dominate in a different way. He used his mind, used Julian's needs, even those he couldn't say aloud.

To be known like that was ridiculously sexy. And reassuring.

Vincenz kissed the back of Julian's neck as he dragged his square, blunt nails down Julian's belly and thighs, ignoring his cock.

Urgency consumed Julian. "Hurry." He said it knowing Vincenz wasn't in any hurry. Knowing Vincenz would give Julian exactly what he needed, when *he* decided it was time.

Vincenz picked the lube up and shortly after that, the cool, slick of it slid over his hole and he may have groaned. It was hard to think with all the blood in his body currently in his cock.

"Do you know how hard it is not to just slick my cock up and thrust hard and deep into your ass?" Vincenz murmured this as he reached around Julian's body to grasp his cock with one hand and held his own cock with the other. Brushing slowly, slowly over his hole.

He wanted to thrust back, swallow Vincenz's cock, to feel the burn and stretch all around the invasion. Patience wasn't his strong suit, but he knew Vincenz would reward it.

"Why are you not doing it then?" Julian rolled his hips, fucking slowly, tortuously into Vincenz's slick fist.

"Because you want me too so badly. You want me to rush. But I want it slow. Because you feel so good."

In time with the strokes around his cock, Vincenz used his fingertips and then fingers to stretch Julian, readying him. Never with another man had Julian given this. Had Julian *received* this. But with Vincenz there was nothing to do but give him all, and to take all Vincenz had given equally.

The burn gave way to the right kind of heat, especially when Vincenz found his sweet spot and stroked it while jerking him off.

"I think you're ready."

Julian groaned . . . so close . . .

"You'll get there. I promise. But for now, widen your stance so I can fuck you like you've been squirming back on my fingers, begging me for."

Past blushing, Julian stretched to get a better grip on the table's edge as he stepped wider and put his cheek against the cool of the wood.

She panicked as she began to surface to consciousness, her brain quicker to respond than her body in long moments of paralysis. Then remembered and swallowed a scream.

The treatment. Yes.

The sedatives had left a dull film on her brain, leaving her thoughts sluggish. But the longer she forced herself to breathe slowly and keep calm, the clearer things became.

Things had slowly improved the longer she'd undergone the treatment. After the first week or so she didn't panic as much when she came to. Her heroes, Julian and Vincenz, had what seemed to be a bottomless well of patience with her. They seemed to greet whatever mood she had with an ease that had allowed her to accept those quirks along with any bumps in the road to recovery.

It had been an unexpected but very needed gift. They let *her* get through things. If it was too much, they gave her support, but they seemed to understand how important it was to her that she do this on her own when she could. Everyone else wanted to do *for* her. They wanted her to do it for herself but were there if she stumbled.

Which is why she trusted them more than she would have in any other circumstance. They'd been nothing but her champions and had listened to what she needed, not just what others thought she did.

And because of them and that understanding, this time her eyes fluttered open and adjusted to the lower light of evening. No tears. The trembling in her hands and legs was gone too.

As she lay there, getting her bearings, she let herself find comfort in her room. Lights were on in the rest of the house and she could see the outline of her chair at the window. The chair Vincenz had brought her. With the wrap Julian had left on the seat for her to discover when she sought the space out to read or just daydream.

When she turned just a little she heard them.

The soft sounds of hushed speaking. Mumbling?

Her eyes fully adjusted as she set to remove the cap. And her hands stilled as she realized just what it was she was hearing.

A tremble went through her, but it wasn't from fear. No, it was something she hadn't felt in over a year.

Julian was bent over the worktable in the main room. The light gleamed off his bare legs and ass. Strong, powerful thighs. Tawny skin. He was so very big and braw. Vincenz stood behind him, one arm around Julian's waist, his hand clearly on Julian's cock.

A flush heated her neck and face.

She'd never, in her life, seen anything so beautiful. Breath quieted, she watched, unable to tear her gaze from Vincenz's ass as he thrust forward. Until Julian groaned, ragged.

Afraid to move or even breathe loudly and break the spell, she watched, her gaze snagged on this powerfully sexy and intimate moment between her two saviors. Vincenz groaned.

"All the way in. You're so fucking tight."

Julian's response was a strangled laugh. "Move. You're going to kill me if you don't move."

"Wouldn't want that." Vincenz leaned down and kissed Julian's neck and the tenderness of the moment tore at her. Strong, brusque Julian went soft when he was with them in private. And this . . . well this was beyond her wildest imaginings. Though she had imaginings in her life, she was pretty sure she couldn't have made up something as hot as what she watched just then as Vincenz began to move, fucking Julian.

She swallowed hard as Vincenz braced his hands on Julian's shoulders.

"Fuck your fist."

She blinked several times and held absolutely still, not wanting to interrupt and not wanting the moment to end.

Julian moved his hand and she wished so much that she could see just exactly what he was doing then. Wondered what he looked like stroking his cock.

This was wrong. It was wrong to spy on them. She knew it. But she couldn't look away or close her eyes even though she knew it's what manners dictated.

Vincenz continued to murmur to Julian. "So, so good. I never imagined it could be this good."

Julian's movements sped and she imagined what he would feel like in her hand. She opened her fist, flexing her fingers. The wave of this newly surfaced sexual desire washed through her. Quieting the chaos. It was as if her body and her brain realized there were other things to feel. Remembered things like pleasure and joy. She did close her eyes then, against tears of relief that she hadn't completely died inside and been left with only the capacity to survive at the basest of levels.

In the background she heard a snarl and opened her eyes to watch the last moments of this beauty between Julian and Vincenz. Heard Julian's moan. "Gods, yes, yes, right there." He hissed and then Vincenz's posture straightened as he cursed.

"Can't last. Gonna blow."

And then he pushed in a few more times and with a long moan, stilled for several moments before pulling his shirt off and cleaning Julian up. They stood, face-to-face, smiling. They had something, and instead of envy, she was grateful to see it. Grateful to know such connection existed still in the world after she'd been in the dark for so long.

They moved into the washroom, still talking quietly, only now about work, she could tell.

When they came out, she gave them a few more minutes before she began to stir loudly enough they heard and came in.

"You're awake." Julian bent to kiss her. The same way he had for the time she'd been there. A brief, comforting touch to reassure her. But this time on the mouth. A whisper of a touch. And she gulped, licking across her lips and tasting him.

His gaze snared with hers and she realized she'd probably burst into tears if he apologized. *Please, not pity.*

"There you are," Julian murmured as if there'd been no pause and made it better. He removed the last few electrodes carefully.

Vincenz fluffed the pillow at her back and helped her to sit up. "I bet you'd like to eat." He kissed her temple and she scented clean sweat and Julian.

"I'm not very hungry." Her head didn't feel right. It didn't feel bad. She wasn't in pain. But it felt as if someone had riffled through it, like a drawer of clothing. Pesch had warned her, but it left her off balance and out of control.

Which wasn't so very uncommon anyway.

"You should eat. You didn't touch your meal earlier. But if you don't want to, at least have a cup of tea."

"I know you have work to do. I know where the kitchen is if I need to eat."

"If you don't eat what I cook, I have less opportunity to cook. It really is about me." Julian winked and kissed her knuckles. Sex apparently made him jovial. Watching other people have sex made *her* sort of antsy and sweaty.

"Would you like me to run you a bath? You can do that first and then eat?" Vincenz used to brush the hair back from her face, but he seemed to realize she needed that veil to block out the world. So now he drew a fingertip down her jawline.

There was so much other stuff all the sudden. Like a ship, she mentally and emotionally listed to the side. Some of the anger had gone, but the other emotions, long repressed and absent from her life in the time she was held at the lab, had returned.

"Hey." Vincenz simply pulled her into his embrace. "Would you like to talk about it?"

"No." She tried to shake her head, but he held her so tight she couldn't move. And that's when a rush of pleasure brought a gasp from her lips. So much sensation to be held so tight. So much dark sweetness that she could struggle in his hold and it wasn't fear. It felt so *good* to be totally surrounded. The sheer amount of sensation was ramped up a thousandfold. Gooseflesh broke out.

She was wrong to feel this way. Wasn't she?

"Are you all right? Did I hurt you?" He pulled away, examining her flaming face.

"No. No." She licked her lips and he looked, just a little too long. Was it too long? Did she imagine? Yes. It was the treatment stirring stuff up, had to be.

Hannah shook her head again, this time firmly. "You didn't hurt me." She could still see the way they looked together. He wasn't interested and she was not a good bet anyway.

She needed to learn how to live again. On her own.

"I'll run my own bath."

Julian looked to Vincenz and it annoyed her enough to get out of bed.

"Do you want company?" Julian looked at her carefully.

That was a good question and one she didn't know if she could answer. She did, of course, like it when they were around, but she wouldn't be there forever.

"I can do things on my own." She stomped to the door and turned, sorry. "I apologize. You've both been so good to me. I'm out of sorts right now."

Julian snorted. "You're entitled, you know."

"I'm not an animal. I'm capable of acting like a human being. Eventually I'll have to go about my life. When my parents are contacted I'll go to them. You can't possibly keep me here much longer. I know you have jobs to do." Watching them together showed her they had a life. They'd let her share in it, never made her feel excluded. But the fact was, she wasn't a soldier and they were at war.

And she felt fragile, brittle in places. To go depending on these men when that wasn't how things worked would be stupid.

"Are you unhappy here?" Vincenz asked, simply following her into the bathing suite and opening the taps to fill the tub.

"I'm all sorts of things," she mumbled, standing motionless in the doorway.

"This is your home as long as you wish it to be." Vincenz walked back past and retrieved a drying cloth.

She sighed and pulled her clothes off, not thinking about it until she stood naked and his eyes skated down her body. Then she blushed. Again. "I'm sorry. I say I'm not an animal and then flash you."

His smile settled her jangled nerves a little. "I've seen a lot of animals." He shrugged. "None of them look like you." He put his hands on her shoulders and kissed her lightly. "Get in and soak. We'll be just outside getting a meal together and working. Come when you want to."

She stepped into the tub and sighed at the warmth. This was something else she couldn't seem to get enough of. Baths and showers had been totally absent while she'd been in the lab. Her entire body submerged in nearly scalding hot water was a delicious treat. Julian joked she was going to grow a tail where her legs used to be and turn into a sea nymph. She found some peace in the large bathing tub. Weightless, she could close her eyes as the water supported her, surrounding her. Like a warm, full-body hug.

She knew they'd ask her how she felt. How she thought the treatment was going. Or worse, that they *wanted* to ask but thought she was too fragile to say. But really she just didn't know. She hadn't felt normal in so long she wasn't sure she'd even know it again. But the anger that sat in her belly like acid seemed to have lessened enough for her to take a deep breath.

She did, filling her lungs and then falling beneath the waterline to listen to the world that way. Her heartbeat thundered in her ears until she came back up. Alive still. The thing they hadn't stolen from her.

Her anger had lessened and now she was sort of titillated by what she'd seen. The difference in how these two things felt was enough to give her pause. The memories of her life before had begun to flit around her brain and she hoped they'd settle in so she could figure out whatever it was they did to her and why.

No matter how much she'd wanted to stay in the tub and ignore the other two, the scent on the air as Julian began to cook set her system to rebel against her dumb ideas. Her stomach growled enough to make her sigh and go about the business of getting clean.

Chapter 6

*I*t had been over two months since she'd come to live in Mirage with Julian and Vincenz. Six weeks of the treatment. Pesch had eased it back to twice a day from three times.

She'd expected the transition to be easier and found herself frustrated that it in fact had not been.

"My head is a jumble." She narrowed her gaze at him when she'd come out of treatment to find him at their kitchen table.

"You'll adjust in a day or two. Your system was used to three times a day and you've just given it less. I told you it would be difficult at first but then easier." He sipped his kava and she felt the irrational need to smack it out of his hands.

Julian came in through the front door. He'd been gone four days on some mission somewhere. Vincenz had been gone for two of those four days and she'd been there with Pesch, who had left her alone when she'd wanted it. She hadn't needed a babysitter, but she'd appreciated not being alone in the middle of the night when she woke up from a bad dream.

"I'm home and I have a present for you, beautiful Hannah." He handed her a bright blue package and she sat at the table to unwrap it. First the silky ribbon it was tied with, which she set to the side carefully.

He watched patiently, never urging her to just rip it open as many would have.

"It has two sides." Delighted, she discovered the bright blue outside had a sunset orange inside. "Like fruit."

"When you cut into it," Julian said to Dr. Pesch, who nodded, understanding Hannah's comment.

Inside the little box lay nestled a pair of earrings. Red glass with threads of silver all shot through it.

"I thought they would catch the light."

She smiled at him. "Thank you." She put them on and tried not to hurry from the room so she could look at them in the mirror in her bedchamber.

They did catch the light beautifully when she wore her hair away from her face. He thought he was so sneaky, that man. She laughed to herself. He liked her hair back and so he enticed her to do it. It was so adorable she pretended she didn't know what he was up to.

She could do that. In their home with one of them there. She caught some back from each side of her face and clipped it back with the combs he'd brought her only a week or two before.

He grinned when she returned. "They look beautiful on you."

She sat back at the table trying not to get caught inhaling him. The sun had left an imprint on his skin, he smelled warm and strong. "Thank you again."

"Dr. Pesch says Vincenz has been gone this week as well? I'm sorry to have left you without one of us."

"I'm fine. You have a job to do." She was so pleased to see him she had to give herself a stern mental talking-to not to rub herself against him. "I went to two treatments a day."

He squeezed her hand and pushed a slice of cake in her direction. "Cake!"

Julian laughed then and kissed her quickly. "I'm glad you're pleased."

"Pleased is a mild word for what I feel." She leaned forward and then turned to him a little. "Having my hair back is a good thing so I won't get frosting in it."

He received those words like the gift they were and enjoyed himself watching her breathe in the chocolate in her cake. A weakness for sweets, had their Hannah. It pleased him unbelievably to bring her pleasure. To tempt her, spoil.

She picked up the fork as she examined the cake until she'd decided just exactly where she wanted to cut into it. The perfect ratio of cake to frosting as she raised it to her lips, took a breath and slid the fork into her mouth as she made a sound that shot straight to his cock.

He paused as she savored the taste of it, guilty for a moment as he thought of Vincenz. Captivated by the way she enjoyed the fuck out of that cake. Gods above and below, he should not be thinking this way about her.

"This is the best thing ever created. Thank you for bringing it to me. I'll even share with you and Dr. Pesch even though he said going to two days would be easier and it has been a challenge instead."

She arched a brow and charmed Hal Pesch when Julian knew he'd meant to be stern with her. Several weeks ago Julian had noticed her do it to Vincenz. He'd figured it was a fluke, but it had bloomed into this Hannah.

She was getting better, he realized as he watched her. He noted the strain around her eyes but also the genuine joy in her body language. She liked Pesch when she'd been steadfastly wary of him in the beginning.

She'd gotten some color from working in the garden. The thinness she'd come to them with had disappeared as she'd gained weight and muscle from the workout he'd created for her.

This Hannah was the full, three-dimensional-in-vibrant-hues version of the near ghost she'd been. It looked good on her.

"I'm going home to have dinner with my wife." Hal stood up. "I'll see you tomorrow."

"That's all right, Hal. I'm here so I can do it."

"Are you sure?"

"What's her new schedule again?"

Hannah watched, astonished by the way they had a complete conversation about her without consulting her a single time. She knew they didn't do it to hurt her feelings, but she wasn't invisible.

Vincenz came home and it was like the sun had come out again. He swept in and dropped a silk-wrapped bundle. "Tea from . . . well, from my travels."

They were very good to her. Spoiled her with these little treats of theirs. "Thank you, Vincenz." She stood. "I'm going to make some; would anyone like a cup with me?"

But Vincenz had been drawn into the conversation Julian and Dr. Pesch had been having and unbelievably also seemed to have all sorts of opinions about her but no need to ask her.

"I'm not a piece of furniture."

The three of them looked to where she'd just slammed the kettle onto the grill.

"What?" Vincenz asked.

"I appreciate what each and every one of you do for me. I can't tell you, Dr. Pesch, how truly thankful I am for the treatment. Even when it jumbles my head, I'm still better than I was yesterday, and the day before. Julian, to you and Vincenz, who alter your schedule to be there when I am in treatment. But I am not invisible."

Vincenz took a step closer but she held a hand out. "Of course you aren't. Why would you say that?"

"You just talked about me for several minutes. Consulting each other on scheduling, on frequency of treatment and the eventual tapering down to once a day. You discussed how I reacted to these changes. How I was improving in this and that way. Talked about my sleep patterns and how well I'm eating. Not once did any of you include me in the conversation. I lived as if I was less than human. I won't go back there again. Now I'm going to go have a bath." She turned and stalked from the room.

After Hal had gone, Vincenz headed to their room to change and then met Julian back in the kitchen.

"That was a pretty stunning sight." Vincenz still couldn't quite get over the way Hannah had stood up for herself.

"Didn't notice it, I bet, but she had her hair back away from her face the whole time." Julian leaned in to kiss him and they slid into each other for a bit, coming home. "I missed you this week."

Vincenz licked over his bottom lip to savor Julian's taste just a little longer. "Missed you too. Masturbating just isn't the same as your hands on me. And we were traveling rough so the food I was eating couldn't come close to what I get here. Feed me and fuck me and I'm all yours."

Julian laughed, nipping Vincenz's chin. "I'm starving so why don't we take care of the feeding part first and the fucking part can come later."

They settled into their rhythm in the kitchen, Julian taking care of the cooking while Vincenz did the prep work.

Julian put a lid on something and turned back to Vincenz, who'd gone to pour some juice at the table. "The treatment is setting her on her ass. I don't like it."

"Hal said it would be much easier tomorrow. He said they'd be tapering to one day next week and then she'd be done." Vincenz shrugged. "I'm sure it's me being a man and all, but I liked seeing her pissed off. Not in that way she had before, all her rage at what they did to her. But normal-woman mad. You know what I mean."

Julian's smile tipped up. Just one corner of his mouth and a shiver went through Vincenz at the sight. "I do." He stretched like a big cat and a slice of his belly showed, muscles playing against the taut skin.

Vincenz drew closer and Julian's smile ticked up a little more until that dimple showed. "Not much more thrilling and terrifying as a beautiful woman. Never know what the fuck they'll do when you get 'em riled up."

Vincenz snorted. "Yes. Fierce in a way only a woman can be." He paused to light one of the nearby candles before looking back. "I'd love to take a bite of you right now." Vincenz walked past Julian and took a kiss instead. "She's getting better. She was shadows and reflections for a while. But this Hannah is no one's shadow."

"I was just thinking that earlier. She's gaining weight, looking better too." Julian patted his ass when he moved to take the soup from the cold box. "You know you can bite me any time you like."

"Mmm. I plan to. And to leave a mark."

They flirted a little more until dinner was ready and Julian had gone to tap on the bathroom door and tell her to come eat.

It was when Julian came back that Vincenz remembered. "We have to tell her about her parents. It's been two months now. She needs to be told."

"Can't we tell her tomorrow? Just let her have enough for one day?"

Vincenz felt similarly. But it had to be done. Pesch had been in support of not pushing the issue of her parents and she hadn't asked. In a way Vincenz had felt she knew but didn't want to admit it to herself so they left it alone.

She was strong enough now.

Still, the two of them seemed to have drawn ranks around Hannah to keep her safe. "You're protective of her."

Julian snorted. "Yes. She's just become mine. Like you're mine I guess. She needs me and I don't know, I like to make things better for her. You too, I've noticed."

Something there in those words.

"I saw her in that cell and from that moment on, she settled in. I like having her around and if I can protect her, gods know she needs someone to keep her safe after what's happened to her." He sighed and leaned his head against Julian's shoulder. "We'll tell her tomorrow. You're right, she needs respite right now."

That's when Hannah entered the room and then paused, blushing as her big brown eyes took them in. Not embarrassed. But perhaps hesitant to interrupt.

Vincenz held a hand out to her. "Come make us feel better by having a meal. Julian's been cooking, which is why it smells so good. And there's more cake." He'd decided to try not to push about how she was feeling. But he could see her hesitation and he didn't want it.

She took his hand and he guided her toward the table. Julian bent backward a little to kiss her as she passed and she blushed, smiling.

"You two are going to flirt me into heart palpitations."

Vincenz bowed after he pulled her chair out. "I like to hear you with a smile in your voice."

Julian put a bowl of soup before her. "First course. I just like it when she talks. Tea will be ready in a little while. I'm starving. Haven't eaten since this morning. From now on, you're included in our discussions about treatment."

Vincenz handed her a piece of buttered bread as he nodded.

"I'm sorry I yelled at you. I know you didn't mean it the way it felt."

And it was past.

They settled in at the table and began to talk. In the beginning, she'd talked a lot to herself but not always to them. Or when she did it was halting as she seemed to puzzle over how the words fit together.

Julian took it as a challenge, Vincenz knew. He'd never known anyone more talented at interrogation and intelligence gathering than Julian. People just told him things without meaning to. It was magical to watch in the field but with Hannah, it was tender and teasing. Sweet.

"So tell us about yourself." Julian poured a steaming mug of tea and placed it in front of Hannah.

She took a deep breath. "Cardamom. I haven't had cardamom in a very long time." She smiled at Julian and Vincenz's heart skipped a beat. "You know the story, Julian." She put her mug down and looked between them. "Tell me about my parents." Vincenz's gaze went to Julian. No matter how much they wanted to keep the news until the following day, they had to confront it now that she'd asked.

Vincenz took one of her hands and Julian the other. Her eyes widened and her skin paled.

"Tell me. What I'm imagining can't be worse than the truth."

"Your parents were killed. Seven months ago. It was recorded as a robbery gone wrong."

She pulled her hands back and shoved the chair back with a clatter. Shaking her head, she visibly tried to get herself together and he ached for her.

"Robbery? They lived in an enclave of university and research employees. This was *them*. *They* killed my parents. Were they buried properly? Where are their things? Can I go? See it?"

Vincenz hated this part the most. "The university interred them both. Their flat was emptied and assigned to another family. Officially we were told their possessions were sold or trashed. But that's not always the case so I sent someone out there. I have some boxes of their things. Not a lot, but it was what I could find. I'm sorry."

"I'd wake up and remember to ask about them. And then it would be time for treatment and then I'd forget. And when I remembered again I was too tired to ask. When they didn't come I knew something was wrong. But I was afraid to ask. Afraid they'd be hurt or worse. Afraid they'd rejected me because of what had happened. I find myself wishing they'd rejected me. At least they'd be alive." She headed to the other side of the room and they gave her the space. She looked out at her garden and he watched her reflection in the glass against the dark of night.

"You knew this for how long?"

"I was worried. You've had so much to deal with."

She'd been standing, looking out the back windows over the yard, but when she turned, she pressed her back to the wall where it made the corner.

"How long?" One of her eyebrows rose and the sight of the woman behind all the trauma snagged his attention the way it had earlier in the bathroom when she'd stripped down.

He shoved it away. "From the start."

She ran her palms up and down her arms and he and Julian looked to each other, unsure as to what to do as she trembled, so close but yet really far removed from them just at the moment.

"We did what we thought was best. They were dead anyway, Hannah. Telling you when you could barely make it through each day wasn't going to bring them back. We wanted to wait until you'd had some time. Time to find a way to deal with the news." Julian got up and went to her.

"What about my things? My parents were holding my possessions from my flat. When I moved to take the job with the foundation, we moved my stuff to their storage unit."

"I can look into that for you." Vincenz didn't hold much hope. But he could get started on tracking down people or agencies who might have taken her personal items and maybe track them down for her.

"What did they know? About me?"

"Your mother reported to the Federation contact for your foundation that you hadn't been in contact for two standard months. It's in their records. They assured her it was that you must have been so busy. Then the entire staff left suddenly. Literally one day they were there and the next the entire place was abandoned. We've got arrest warrants out for them." He wouldn't share how the local authorities had mucked it up so dreadfully they might be missing important information because their investigation was so flawed.

"They knew? Do you think that?" She pushed past Julian and paced. Eight steps, reverse, eight steps. He'd seen her do this in moments of stress before. But her hair was still away from her face. She wasn't hugging her body the way she would have just a month before.

"I don't know what they knew. We don't have enough answers at this point. Just some supposition."

"Bollocks!" She narrowed her eyes and the rage there hurt to see. "You're not just average passersby! This is what you both do. Oh don't be surprised that I figured it out. I'm crazy, not dumb. You have enough clout to hold off the entire Federation Military Corps from using the brain scans on me. You both leave for a few days at a time and never talk about specifics when you return. You have the ability to get me experimental treatment. Obviously the power you wield says you're both someone important. What do you *think*?"

Vincenz wisely held back a smile at her attitude. Upset or not, that she could have this heated discussion with them when even just a few weeks prior she could barely even speak to them meant she was improving.

"I think they knew. I think they had a part in your parents' murder and I think they left to escape to the Imperium. And those who didn't? They most likely ended up like your parents did."

"Will you find them?"

"Do you want us to? What then, beautiful Hannah?" Julian moved to her, encircling her from behind, and she relaxed back into his body just a little.

"I want you to figure out what they know and if they hurt my family and did this to me. I think you should kill them."

Vincenz cocked his head. "Is that really what you want? After all that, you'd have them killed?" Not that he judged that as a bad thing. He just wanted to be sure he got what she meant.

"Yes. I'd like them killed. A lot. If they hurt my parents, they've stolen everything from me. *Everything*. I want them to pay for that. They *should* pay for that!"

"Come back to the table and finish eating." Julian spoke to her quietly, his lips to her ear. "We'll take care of this for you. You know that. But you won't help anyone if you let yourself get even more run down than you are already."

She didn't even know what to feel. She'd been without them for a year, but had always imagined they'd be there when she escaped or was set free. She'd known on some level there was a problem, but she'd been too tired and too afraid to inquire for a long time. But now there was nothing at all. No pictures. Not her Mai's teapots. Not her father's medical texts with his neat and very precise notes in the margins. The quilts her mother had brought with her as a dowry from her family.

Nothing. Like it didn't happen.

"I need . . ." To be alone? It might be what she thought she needed, but she sure wasn't ready to face the reality of it.

"You need to let us help you." Vincenz spoke from his place at the table.

"Sleep in our bed tonight," Julian added. "Safer. Warmer and you can snuggle between us."

Hannah had been gazing at Vincenz as Julian had said that. Vincenz nodded. "We've got room."

"I don't want to interrupt anything."

Julian's laugh puffed her hair a little, tickling her ear. "You aren't."

She blushed then because of course she knew that. Had seen it and it still made her knees a little rubbery to remember it.

"It's all right to let yourself lean on us. Been a hard day for you."

That kindness was more than she could stand and the hated tears came back. "I won't even be able to look back on photographs if they got rid of everything."

Julian led her back to the table and Vincenz pulled her into his lap, wrapping his arms around her and rocking slowly. "They can't take your memories."

"Eat." She pointed at Julian, worrying about him.

She tried to get off Vincenz's lap, but he held her tight. "I can eat one-handed. Julian is already shoving food into his face. How about you eat too? Just a little more soup. The tea too?"

Chapter 7

*V*incenz eased from bed, pausing to look at Hannah all bundled in the blankets, Julian's arm over her. Her hair was over her face but she was beautiful anyway. The house was still very quiet. Even in the middle of a war it was quiet but for the soft hum of all the electronics in their communications hub.

He needed to check on an algorithm he started running before bed the night before. They'd brought back so much raw data on so many different things over the last four months. Each time one of the Phantom Corps teams went out they brought back more data. The picture began to fill in and it wasn't good. Not that they'd expected anything else.

He'd been deep in his head when her hand landed on his shoulder. "I apologize. I didn't mean to startle you."

The treatment may have been experimental, but it had been miraculous nonetheless. The shadows he suspected would always be in her eyes remained, but they were nothing like they had been. Her words were no longer halting, though she did get flustered at times and lost her train of thought, which frustrated her. That's when he and Julian would simply hug her, or grab her hands and look into her eyes to get her back on track.

While he could pretend it was only because she needed their help, he couldn't lie to himself. He liked to touch her. Liked the way she felt in between them in bed at night. Found himself eager to learn more about the Hannah beyond the injured woman he'd freed from the lab.

She was no longer the injured victim he first brought back. The Hannah beyond that had surfaced. The woman. The woman who held a lot more appeal than he ever could have imagined. The way he felt about her was changing, had been for some time. He wasn't sure of everything it meant just yet.

"Good morning." He smiled, taking her hand and kissing it. He'd opened his mouth to say more, but she was staring at his logbook. He moved to close it when she pointed at something he'd scribbled down.

"This is wrong."

"How so?" She didn't even know what it was. How could she know if it was right or not?

"You see here"—she pointed to the string of code just above—"it's correct. But here these three should be in a different order." She took a spare pencil and worked on a blank sheet of paper nearby. "Like this." She quickly revised the figures and he looked them over, intending to pacify her but realizing she'd been totally correct.

"You're a genius."

She laughed. "Many have this exact reaction when they meet me these days."

Beneath that mask she'd had on when he first brought her back to Mirage was a very dry sense of humor he really enjoyed.

"I've been working on this coding for a month. It took me a week just to get the section above this to work. I've been hung up for a week now and I guess I know why. I didn't know you did programming."

She pulled up a nearby chair. "This is a formula really. Chemistry and biosciences have always been something I connected with. It comes to me easier than say, creative writing or public speaking." She paused. "Numbers have always settled my thoughts. Further evidence of how crazy I am."

"You're not crazy. You've suffered trauma, but you're not crazy. Stop hurting yourself with that."

She paused and cocked her head. "You're very good to me." And then just as quickly she changed the subject. "Julian will be up soon to make me sweat." She grinned, referring to the workout regimen Julian had designed for her. "Would you like anything from the kitchen?"

He got up to follow her into the other room. "Let me get it."

"I'm not that horrid a cook. Julian's been giving me lessons with that too."

Big, tough Julian, who was incredibly patient with her, seemingly delighted by each thing she did. Though he didn't brook laziness, he clearly had a soft spot for Hannah. Which was all right with Vincenz as he had one as well.

"How are you . . . after the debrief?" He had no idea why he suddenly felt so shy around her. No, not shy. But . . . something had changed. Not in a bad way. At least he didn't think so.

They'd waited until after she finished her treatment before they did the brain scan debrief. He and Julian had been with her the whole time. It had been difficult for her and she'd been set back a week or two, but that had been a month before already. Ellis was on his way to them; he wanted to meet Hannah in person to talk with her about what they'd seen and learned. Julian had told him only the night before that he'd only allow it if she was ready.

Vincenz agreed.

"My brain . . . my thoughts aren't so jumbled. I can think about things I couldn't bear to before. I know you've all been waiting for the next step in debriefing me. You should just get it over with. Or try. All the time we waste is time you don't have. I know Ellis is on the way here."

"Julian and I won't let anything happen if you're uncomfortable with it. Wilhelm Ellis is a good man, but he's intense. You have nothing to fear from him though. I promise you."

She took his hands. "Thank you."

Julian sat in the sunshine, watching Hannah work in her garden. He'd gone through her workout that morning and as usual, she amazed him with how she never gave up. Even with sweat pouring from her and exhaustion in her muscles, she would finish her reps and turn to him, asking what was next. Her stamina could put many in the corps to shame.

He wanted to make her strong. As strong on the outside as she was within. Wanted to give her a measure of control, and in doing so, he supposed, he found some as well.

Being with her quieted all his rage. Soothed him. He wasn't sure why, but it was true anyway.

She was beautiful there on her knees, the big brim of the hat shading her face. Her constant chatter seemed to quiet out here in the open air. She hummed to herself and would occasionally speak to him, apologizing for interrupting and then he'd laugh and tell her he liked her interruptions and to stop telling him she was sorry. He didn't want to be something she apologized for and that in and of itself was curious.

He was debriefing her on his own schedule. They had a brief time before the rest of the world would come down around them, and he wanted to savor it. Wanted to unravel this for her and make her safer.

Things were heating up. Before long the war would consume him and Vincenz. They'd be sent off somewhere as a team. Somewhere away from her. Until then, they'd do their level best to keep her protected.

"You're distracted." She continued to work after she made the statement. Hannah had this way of seeing him right down to the bone and *understanding* him. And she did not recoil. Instead she accepted. Let him be.

"I'm debriefing you," he teased. "I have to pay attention."

"More than that. You don't have to talk about it. But if you want to . . ." She lifted her shoulders and they continued talking.

He'd learned that in the very beginning when they'd first brought her to the labs that they'd had her go over her notes multiple times. She didn't remember any specific emphasis on any one thing, but Julian figured the most obvious thing was that there was something she'd seen or touched on that they wanted to know more about. She just didn't see it at the time.

The brain scan was accurate of course. Took a print of sorts from her memories of her time in the labs. But because she'd been so mentally harmed, the impressions weren't as clear as they would have been otherwise. So it was his job to untangle it all and help her make a coherent history of what happened there.

"Were there any other people there from your offices at the foundation?"

She looked up from the earth she'd been digging in. "At first they had my research assistant, James. But then he went away. I don't know where." A shadow passed over her features and he knew she blamed herself.

"Was there a particular project you were working on with James?"

"He was my assistant. He worked on several projects with me."

"What was his specialty? Why did you choose him to work for you?"

"He had many of the same interests I did. Disease vectors. How different viruses spread. Speed of transmission. I chose him because I liked him best when I interviewed for the position. He's very personable. He's finishing up his degree and his advisor contacted me on his behalf. Not my favorite from my time at the institute, but he's well respected. A recommendation from someone that accomplished goes a long way." Hannah paused. "Am I saying too much? Not enough? I want to help."

"You're doing just fine, beautiful Hannah."

"Is this how you always do your interrogations?"

He frowned, thinking of the way he'd had to interrogate prisoners after Parron. "No."

She got up, brushing her knees off and tossing her gloves to the side before coming to him. It was when she went to her knees and put her head in his lap that he began to accept the way she brought so much comfort and solace.

"I'm sorry to have brought that memory to you."

He brushed a palm over the shiny black silk of her hair, so soft against his skin. "You didn't. My job isn't usually this pleasant. I'm not interrogating you at all. Just helping you get the story out. It's yours; I can only help you find a way to tell it. Interrogation is for people who don't want to help."

"Do you think that makes you bad?"

He snorted. "Not precisely."

"There are villains in the world, Julian. You are not one of them."

He leaned down and kissed her temple, pausing to take a deep breath, drawing her into his lungs and holding her there for long moments.

"I'm not a character in a children's story."

She laughed then, a real laugh, and he joined her there, on his knees in the dirt, getting face-to-face. "I love your laugh."

She paused and he hugged her. She seemed to melt into his embrace and that only made his . . . whatever it was with her . . . deeper.

Vincenz chose that moment to come outside. He paused and then smiled. Julian felt a twinge. Maybe guilt? No, he hadn't done anything wrong. But it wasn't that simple.

"Ellis is here."

Hannah froze in his arms and turned to Vincenz. "Do I have to leave?"

Julian stood and helped her to her feet, and Vincenz was with them in seconds. "No, baby. He's our boss. He wants to talk to you, but he's not going to take you anywhere."

Her eyes wide as saucers, she visibly pulled herself back together, taking a deep breath, brushing the soil from her clothes. "Will you be there?"

"Would you like that?" Vincenz asked.

She nodded, and Julian wanted to grab her and run the other way.

But Ellis wasn't a bad man. He was a good man and Julian knew, probably better than Vincenz did, that Ellis would instantly take to Hannah. He'd see her hurt and want to fix it. It was what made him such an effective leader.

That, and he had a soft spot for wounded birds. Hells, the entire Phantom Corps was made up of broken people Ellis had collected and given a purpose to.

"We'll both be there then."

"May I change my clothing and get cleaned up first?"

Her hands shook just a little and Julian took one, kissing it. "Go on. No rush. He's here and we'll need to have multiple meetings on all sorts of things."

She darted inside, avoiding the front room and headed toward her bedroom to change. Though most of the time she slept in their bed, she kept her room and retreated there when she needed to.

"How did it go?" Vincenz asked as they headed toward Ellis.

"She remembers more than she gives herself credit for. I'm beginning to think the reason they kept her so long was something to do with her work. Which is obvious and all, but I'll keep working with her."

Ellis was on a comm with someone when they entered the situation room. He signed off and gave them his full attention. "Operatives Haws and Cuomo." He looked around them. "Where's Ms. Black?"

"She's been in the garden. She went to clean up." Julian looked around the room and found a spot he thought she'd be most comfortable in. "She's asked to have me and Vin present when you debrief her."

"In case I attempt to ravish her like a rake?"

"She's fragile. People hurt her. She's wary." Vincenz sat at the table.

"I know. Julian, I think you should continue with your debrief. I'm sure it'll be better than mine anyway. It's your gift."

Julian had long since ceased to be surprised when Ellis said exactly the right thing. He just did and everyone in Phantom Corps accepted this fact.

"When we finish with Ms. Black, we have another series of meetings. Daniel is at Roman's and they'll comm in from there."

"And how is the babe then?" Abbie was Daniel's sister and the wife of Roman Lyons, the leader of the Federated Universes. She'd had a baby only two months before; in the midst of so much chaos, there had been joy. It was important to remember that.

"Mera is thriving. Not hard when every single person she sees dotes on her. As if Abbie would allow anything else." Wilhelm grinned as he shook his head.

"Sounds like her." Vincenz had a great deal of admiration for both Roman and his wife. They'd made a great deal of good in the Federated 'Verses, had brought them forward so much when it came to the extension of basic rights to their people. As a leader, Vincenz felt that Roman was peerless. He made hard choices and he did it well. He was courageous and intelligent and hard when he had to be.

"Ah, you must be Hannah." Wilhelm stood and Vincenz watched, amused, as Hannah's eyes widened when she took in nearly seven feet of Wilhelm Ellis, Comandante of the Military Corps. "I'm Wilhelm Ellis." He held his hand out, and she took a deep breath and returned his handshake. "Please, come in and join us." Wilhelm put her hand on his arm and led her to the chair Julian had put out for her.

"You're very large." She clapped her hand over her mouth. "I'm sorry. I didn't mean to be rude."

Instead of anger, Wilhelm laughed as he sat across from her. "Not rude at all, Hannah. I'm told my father was very tall as well. Must be where I got it." Ellis sobered. "My condolences and those of Roman Lyons and House Lyons for the loss of your family."

She blinked several times and nodded. "Thank you."

Ellis studied her intently but she held up under scrutiny. Vincenz had to clamp down on his instinct to rush in to protect her. He wanted to defend her against this, but he knew she needed to do this on her own. Knew it meant something to her and it definitely would with Ellis. Vincenz trusted Wilhelm Ellis more than anyone else he knew. He had to continue to do so.

Finally Ellis leaned forward. "I'm here . . . well, I suppose you must know one of the reasons I'm here. I wanted to thank you in person for submitting to the brain scan. I know it was . . . difficult for you, especially given your history with the Imperium."

"Julian told me the scan works better when—well, when the person's brain isn't murky and sort of broken. I understand you need more from me."

Ellis flicked his gaze to Julian and Vincenz knew understanding passed between them.

"Broken seems an inappropriate word for what your brain is, Ms. Black. To be blunt . . . as brains go, it's quite impressive. But yes, because of the mental trauma you endured, the scan was less than conclusive. So the real question is—they had you for some time and yet they didn't kill you. This is a good thing, obviously, as you're alive and we like that. But it's a puzzling thing. Do you know why?"

She sat straighter. "Why didn't they kill me? Why did they keep me alive on this side of the 'Verse line? You think I know something. Or that I've been implanted with something that poses a danger to the Federated Universes."

Ellis smiled and nodded approvingly. "You're very smart."

"I am if all the letters behind my name and the certificates I've earned aren't counterfeit. The treatment I underwent with Dr. Pesch mapped my brain. He tells me that while my brain has damaged spots, there's no evidence that I've been implanted or altered." She took a shaky breath and Vincenz handed her a mug of tea. After a few gulps she looked back up to them again.

"He made the same report to me. I was glad to hear it. But the puzzle remains, doesn't it? Killing you would have solved the problem if it was that you'd seen something you weren't supposed to. They killed nearly everyone else; why not you?"

Julian smoothly took over as Ellis settled into the background. "Indeed. Tell me what you think you know."

She sighed. "I've gone over it. The simplest answer is that it has something to do with my work. Communicable diseases. Some life threatening. But none of them were of a type I'd have recommended for biological warfare if that's what you think."

"That's good to know. I want you to add details like that if they occur to you. Did you get visitors from the Imperium?" Julian asked.

"Of course. It was a joint project between both the Federated Universes and the Imperium. About half of our funding came from them."

"Like who? People who worked with you? Other doctors and researchers? People who came from the Imperialist territories to oversee grant funding distribution? Who?"

She closed her eyes and Vincenz wanted to hold her hand, the one she had in a fist in her lap.

Fuck it. He reached out and took it, unfurling her fingers and placing it between his palms.

"We had six researchers. Four from our Edge 'Verses and two from theirs. A staff of ten more as lab techs, administrative help. I was one of three researchers with an assistant. Total staff excluding security was sixteen."

"With security?"

"Twenty-four."

Julian didn't look up, but Vincenz knew he found that number as interesting as Vincenz and Ellis did.

"That seems a lot. Is it a lot, Hannah?"

"I never worked in a similar situation so I can't say other than that I found it rather odd that they'd have so many guards. The building was well protected as it was. I had to show four pieces of identification just to get in each day. But it was politics." She shrugged and Ellis nodded. "The foundation had Imperium visitors at least several times each quarter year. Usually other researchers. Sometimes they had in-house training or lectures with guests from both sides of the 'Verses. Federation visitors on a regular basis as well."

Julian led her around through the story. He did it patiently and gently, backing off when Hannah got angry or upset and two hours later, it was Wilhelm who held a hand up.

"Young woman, you've said enough for now. You must be tired and in dire need of refreshment."

"We all are, I wager." Julian stood. "A meal and then, Hannah, you're fortunate enough to be free to skip all the other meetings we have to attend afterward."

Chapter 8

"We know they have one more portal-collapsing device."

Ellis said it without preamble once they'd come back to the table after lunch.

Daniel and Andrei also looked on via vid screen where they'd just joined the conference some moments before.

"What's the plan?" Vincenz sipped his kava.

Wil looked carefully at Vincenz and Julian. "You two need to go and destroy it, naturally."

This woman he'd met, Hannah, what a wild card she'd turned out to be. He didn't miss the way his operatives took care of her, protected her. Nor did he miss the intelligence of the woman herself.

They sat on a hinge point. He knew it in his gut. Things were building up and any one of those things could change the game in a big way.

"That was my belief when I'd concluded the interrogations as well." Julian sat back and sipped his kava. Wil had hated the necessity of using Julian in so many interrogations. Knew it took a toll on the man. But he hadn't been lying when he'd told Julian he had a gift. He did. And because of those interrogations with prisoners of war, they'd built up a wealth of intelligence.

Normally, both these men would have jumped at the opportunity to go in and destroy the device. But Wil didn't miss the quick check they both made toward where Hannah worked out in the garden.

"What do you think she knows?" He changed tack for the moment.

Julian took a deep breath. "I've gone over the logs and notes. They questioned her in a fairly narrow area. The timelines and the things they wanted to know from her seem to indicate she saw something. But their reaction in not killing her seems to indicate they needed it from her, that perhaps they didn't know it themselves. Or that they were missing a key element."

Wil nodded. He believed pretty much the same. "Pesch indicated several attempts to manipulate certain parts of her brain to stimulate recall." He smiled. "Which only seems to have made her will to resist them stronger."

"She's an asset." Julian leaned forward, his hands clasped in on the tabletop. "She understands Imperial culture in a way few do." Julian looked to Vincenz, who lifted his shoulders.

"When I first met you," he said to Vincenz, "I knew you had a path to walk. All these years you've proven yourself over and over to be one of our best people. You've got a head for formulas and for machines, which are fine skills. But now you are integral because Julian brings up an important point. You know the Imperialists. You know their motivations and the hows of what they do and why. It's why you need to be the one to head up this mission to destroy the last remaining device. If we control all the remaining Liberiam and they have nothing left to build a device with, they can't use them. This is the biggest weapon in their arsenal."

"Unless this thing Hannah knows has to do with another weapon." Daniel spoke from the vid screen.

"My father is no fool. He's arrogant, yes. Spoiled. But he's surrounded by smart and vicious men. They won't have only one weapon." Vincenz licked his lips. "There's another lab Hannah visited before they came to take her from the foundation."

"Do you think they might have the data we need there?" Wil asked.

"I don't know. But I think there's a good chance there may be some answers there. At the very least we'd be able to count things out." Vincenz pulled at his hair as he thought it over.

"You and Julian need to head the mission. We have some intel on the location of the labs where the portal-collapsing device is being built."

Julian huffed out a long breath and looked toward Hannah again.

Wil pretended he hadn't seen them both look to her so frequently. And he hoped these two were the last to go and get themselves tripped up by love. At least until the war was over. "We can send her to Ravena. She'll be safe there. You know Abbie and Carina will take her under their protection. Help her build a new life."

Vincenz pushed to stand and began to pace. "She . . . she's . . ."

"She needs to be with me and Vin." Julian put his mug down and leveled a look at Wilhelm.

About time. Wil looked them both over. "Is that so? And why do you say such a thing?"

"I think whatever she knows has something to do with her work. Just as *I* understand how things work in the Imperium, so does she. If she knows something, she's the best person to help us find it. I don't know a thing about medicine and science or how to even begin to figure out what to look for. I blow stuff up."

Wil smiled. Nicely done. He'd made the right choices with the people in his Phantom Corps. "She's not trained for this. And this op may have nothing to do with whatever she might know."

"We'll take care of the backup and defense. She's an asset here. One we can't afford to ignore."

"And?"

"Her entire world has been turned upside down. Her parents are dead. Her friends are dead. Her old job is gone. She has nothing here right now. Nothing but us, and we've made the commitment to her to be here."

It was the most impassioned he'd seen Julian since before Marame had been killed. Hannah Black was important. A bright point in the maze of all this insanity. She had a purpose and Wilhelm Ellis didn't like to ignore people's fate.

"All right."

Julian looked at him askance and he wanted to laugh. Instead he glowered.

"She's not classified as Phantom Corps like Piper. Just know that in advance. This is a onetime thing. I don't know why you all choose to lose your heads over a woman right at the worst possible time."

Vincenz opened his mouth to argue and then sat back. "That's not what this is."

"Pull the other one, boys. Stop lying to yourselves. As for the mission? You'll have to do both. Get that lab and the portal device. Make sure she's got some basic weapons training. I've got to meet with Brandt, who is stopping by on his way out of the Imperium. Coordinate with Daniel on this. Get it done, gentlemen."

* * *

"He seems to think we're romantically involved with Hannah." Julian sat at his data console pretending to read the screen, but in reality, he was thinking about Hannah.

"He's got a touch of prescience." Vincenz rustled around and found the card he needed.

"He knows. About you and me I mean."

Vincenz input a series of codes before looking up, amusement clear on his face. "Not much of a secret. Is it?"

Julian grinned. "Not if anyone has eyes."

"And after last night, ears."

They laughed, remembering the rather loud session they'd shared while Hannah had been in the bath.

"So why do you think he made that assumption then?" Julian asked again. "You know, about Hannah."

Vincenz put the data aside and met Julian's gaze. "Because he's got a touch of prescience, like I said. I see the way you look at her. I see the way you touch her, the way you hold her when she's in our bed."

Julian took a deep breath. "And does that bother you?"

"Yes, but not in the way you think."

"She gets to me. There's something about her. She moves past all my defenses and has curled up inside me."

Vincenz nodded. "I tried thinking it was fraternal. For a while. I thought she needed protection and I have a sister so she was like that to me. I can protect her and love her, but it's like Carina." He snorted. "Only that's a lie. It's nothing like Carina."

"No. Not even like Marame." The guilt rose. "It's hard, you know. Not to take my kisses deeper. I haven't though. You know that, right? Temptation doesn't mean anything. I wouldn't do that to you."

Vincenz laughed and reached across the table to squeeze Julian's hand. "I know you haven't. I think you and I are struggling in a similar way. She . . . *you* make me feel alive. Vibrant. There's no holding back with you and I have no desire to anyway. But she's there too. She's strong and fragile all at once. It makes me want to wrap her hair around my fist. Makes me want to lick up her neck." His faraway look sharpened as he focused on Julian again. "Makes me want her. *And* you. And I've felt like an asshole just thinking it. She's still recovering!"

"Me too. I've felt like I betrayed you." Julian breathed a little easier knowing he hadn't been alone in this.

"So we've agreed then? That we haven't? And then what?"

"And then who knows? Yes, she's recovering, but she's not the same as she was four months ago. She's clearheaded about herself and her goals and needs in a way she couldn't have contemplated before. When I'm debriefing her, I can track the strength of mind she has. The stability she's gained. She knows her mind." He snorted, thinking about how stubborn she could be at times.

He continued. "But for now we have a mission to plan. What we have is good. Let's just let this play out slowly and on her schedule. She may not be interested at all." Julian shrugged. He didn't believe it for a second. Granted, theirs was not the ideal situation, but he knew what was in her eyes.

Indeed they had work to do.

Hannah awoke and simply relaxed for long moments, breathing in Julian's skin as she lay on his biceps. His other arm was banded about her waist, holding her. Keeping her from floating away on bad dreams.

When she opened her eyes, it was to find Vincenz looking at her.

"Would you like to go on an adventure, Hannah Black?" he asked softly.

She thought carefully. Would she?

"What kind of adventure?"

He smiled and she wanted to simply curl into him with happiness.

"Sometimes it might be dangerous. It would involve travel."

He made it sound like a fairy story. "Would you be there?"

"I'd ask if that was something you wanted, but I think I know the answer. Yes, with me and Julian."

Julian's breathing changed and she didn't fail to note the hard cock resting against her ass. It was what happened in the morning for men, she told herself, even as her nipples hardened.

"Do you know me that well, then?"

"Sometimes." Vincenz's pupils swallowed nearly all the color of his eyes and her heart pounded as the moment stretched taut between them. She wanted . . . so much. In the months that she'd ended treatment, she'd entered into talk therapy with Dr. Pesch. The panic had long subsided and every day she gained a little more ground in her head. Enough to feel, so very fully, everything else she'd been stripped of in her time at the labs.

Foremost among those feelings was sexual desire.

And chief among the causes for that popping back into her life lay there in the bed with her. And she felt guilty about it. Yes, they'd made a place for her in their lives and in their bed. They showed each other affection in her presence in a way they never did in front of anyone else. On one hand it thrilled her to be so trusted with such a beautiful and intimate thing. They were so sexy together. And she never wanted to hurt that.

On the other, she wanted those hands on her. She wanted Vincenz to kiss her the way he kissed Julian. Well, not precisely. She found what they had together to be gorgeous. She didn't want to *replace* that. She wanted to have it too. In her own way. She wanted Julian's voice to change when he said her name. Not exactly how he did when he said Vincenz, but the change, the way it was clear he meant something to Julian simply by the way he uttered Vincenz's name. That's what she wanted.

Something beautiful and unique and not only with *one* of them.

So stupid to want such a thing. Stupid to think the way Julian touched her was more than just friendly, or to imagine the desire in Vincenz's gaze when she moved. They were together and she would never do anything to harm that.

"Where is this adventure then?" she murmured, swallowing hard and trying not to squirm against Julian, whose response to her attempt to get up just a breath earlier had been a tightening of his hold. Which . . . seemed to make her molten inside. It felt so good she wasn't sure how to respond.

"We're off to blow things up in the Imperium." Julian's lips brushed against her shoulder as he settled her back against his body, and yes, yes, he was still hard.

"You'd let me blow things up?"

Vincenz grinned at her. "Would you like to blow things up?"

"A year ago I'd have denied it. But I can't lie to either of you it seems. I would very much like to blow things up. But . . . you can't take me along. I'm not one of you."

Vincenz moved closer. So close the heat of him seemed to sear her skin through her nightdress. Probably because it tended to ride up when she slept and lodged at the top of her thighs.

"If you'd rather not, we can make arrangements for you to travel to Ravena. You'll be safe. Protected. Far, far away from anything that'll blow up. We'll be back after our mission is concluded."

"You'd send me away?"

Vincenz closed the last bit of space between them, pressing his body to her front as Julian cradled behind her. A full-body shiver of delight rolled through her along with a gasp.

"If you wanted to go, we'd make it happen."

Julian spoke in her ear. "But we wouldn't be happy."

Was she completely misunderstanding this situation? Was this no more than two friends surrounding her because that's what she needed? Was the cock at her ass really for Vincenz? Who had an answering hard-on at her belly. Each breath she took was filled with them. The warm, utterly male scent each of them carried on his skin.

She had no words. None that she could utter and not feel like a fool anyway.

Finally, she let herself take a leap. "Take me with you."

Vincenz brushed his lips across hers and she sighed into his mouth. Wanting so much. Needing and having no outlet.

She needed the bathing suite and some actual privacy. Because these men had created a problem and she had no choice but to fix it.

"I should go. To clean up." That she managed to remember all the words to put into the correct order was a testament to how far the treatments had taken her.

Vincenz kissed her again and she found herself clutching the front of his shirt, the softness of the material cool against her palms. She was dizzy with him, intoxicated by the moment.

"I like the way you taste, Hannah Black." He said this as he rolled over, bringing her atop him and then down to her feet on the floor next to the bed where she stood on shaky legs.

She blinked at them both so utterly male and satisfied in the bed. Staring at her.

Hannah had no idea what to say so she hurried from the room, closing the door behind her and leaning against it to catch her breath.

Flustered.

Her father had a word for being addled, *twitterpated*. Which seemed to be the perfect phrase for what she was.

Her reflection showed flushed skin, tousled hair, wide eyes and . . .

a grin. How long had it been since a man had rendered her so witless? What chance did she have against not just Vincenz but Julian too?

Needing something to do before she broke down into hysterical laughter, she pulled her nightdress off and stepped into the water closet before making her way to the shower enclosure and letting the water rush over her skin, letting it surround and warm her.

It had been a long time since she'd been touched.

Since leaving the labs the loss of the silence and the way people actually paid attention to her had been the most difficult things to deal with. Not that she craved silence, though she had come to remember what it felt like to need time alone in the bathing suite.

Julian had brought home three little cakes of soap. Each smelled like a different sort of flower. Today she chose the one that reminded her of the landsea on Sanctu. Salt and dry earth with a hint of sweet and wild.

Tough, broody Julian, who brought her gifts like little tributes. She loved his innate sweetness. Loved even more that he'd argue that he was sweet at all.

She closed her eyes and soaped up, the scent teasing her senses as the swirls of the washing cloth stimulated her skin.

Before she'd gone into the program and moved to work for the foundation, she'd had someone. A nice someone who asked her to marry him. It hadn't been hard to say no. Which still filled her with sadness.

Her work had been so important, far more important than marrying a man she enjoyed but didn't love. Sex was easy enough to find if that's what she needed.

And it was really what she needed right then.

She hadn't come. Not in over a year.

Her nipples ached, tightening as the soap slid over them, as her fingertips brushed against them and she imagined it was Julian's mouth. She loved his mouth. Loved the way his scruffy beard framed it.

The beard might tickle as she arched into him.

Or maybe she wouldn't be able to arch. Maybe Vincenz would hold her fast. Keep her where they wanted her to be. Bound by his arms or . . . it didn't matter. If it was him holding her, it would be all right. If it was him, or Julian, she'd struggle and like it, knowing it was a game.

But part of her, some deep, dark part that seemed to pulse with life whenever Julian cuffed her wrist with his hand, or when Vincenz held her still by the shoulders to look into her eyes, that part craved it.

Forehead against the cool of the tile, she imagined Vincenz pushing her thighs wide, holding her open as he licked through her pussy. One hand slid from her nipples down to her clit. She gasped at the first contact as a ripple of intense sensation moved through her.

A man like Vincenz . . . what would he be like as a lover? She'd wondered if he only liked men. Had seen enough to know he liked Julian a great deal. But from the way he'd kissed her a few minutes before, he seemed pretty interested. Maybe.

She shook her head, annoyed that she was second-guessing her stupid masturbatory fantasy into the ground. It was a *fantasy*. If he didn't like girls in real life, what did it matter one way or the other to her? Right then it was easy to imagine his mouth on her cunt. Kissing her like a lover while Julian kissed his way from one nipple to the other.

Her inner walls fluttered when she pressed two fingers inside, angling to brush her thumb across her now-aching clit.

Her rhythm was off, but she remembered well enough how things worked. Orgasm hung just out of reach as she tightened all her muscles, needing to come probably more than she ever had.

Vincenz would flip her over and she'd get to her knees as he slid into her that way. He'd order her to suck Julian's cock, which would be just fine with her. Each man would possess her in his own way. Thrust and pull away, a push and pull of three.

Tears mixed with the water, now turning tepid, streamed down her face as orgasm remained elusive.

Had they stolen this from her too? Was this broken?

The tug and roll of her nipples, even while imagining getting a hard fucking from Vincenz and a mouthful of Julian's cock, wasn't getting her that last little bit. Just a breath or two away from climax, she teetered on the edge, trying several heretofore guaranteed methods and none of them worked.

Frustrated, she stopped, turning to rinse off and wash her hair. Trying not to think. Trying not to worry.

It would be all right. She would go with them on their mission. Be with them instead of sent to Ravena or to a hospital.

It would be all right.

Chapter 9

Julian worked out as he thought about the way she'd felt against his body that morning. Each pull-up, the burn in his muscles, the stretch and strain of his upper arms and across his back meant he'd be strong enough not only to protect himself but to protect her as well.

He wasn't able to protect Marame, who'd always been so invincible to him.

But he wouldn't make the same mistake with Hannah. He and Vincenz would never give any opportunity for anyone to get a shot at her.

Vincenz had pushed her that morning, no doubt.

The moment she'd retreated into the bathing suite they'd been on each other, a mess of teeth and nails, cock to cock, writhing, sweating and in the end, he'd rolled to his back, breath heaving, fingers entangled still with Vincenz's and with the knowledge that things had changed for not only the two of them, but for the *three* of them.

There was suddenly something else, which complicated matters considerably. But without which he'd be lesser. He wasn't sure why or how it was that way, but she was part of his life, part of his life with Vincenz. Beautiful, skittish Hannah with her delightfully odd reactions to things they did. Any other woman, or man for that matter, would have run after a few days with them. But Hannah, though she didn't know it herself, was made of sterner stuff.

She ignored the way he and Vincenz bickered as they worked. Never so much as flinched if one of them turned to her mid-conversation to argue a point. She rolled her eyes and waved it away if Julian got grumpy or short.

The way she accepted him did something to him. Disarmed him. Charmed him. Made him feel understood and appreciated. So many people he knew and loved were afraid of his reaction after Marame. They were right to in some ways. He'd gone off the rails and if it hadn't been for work, and Vincenz, he may have fallen apart. The need to avenge her death had driven him hard, filling him with so much anger and darkness he stumbled his way through some days, barely hanging on. But Hannah wasn't afraid of his reactions. When she was around she filled his empty spots, made it all right to feel the desolation of loss. Without judgment.

He had no idea what that could feel like. Had no concept that such a seemingly simple thing would be a revelation. About himself but also about Hannah.

Humming to himself, he did the last set and hopped down to mop his face off.

Things had changed. But they'd be all right.

"Ah, Hannah, there you are." Vincenz looked up from his console to catch sight of her returning to the main room.

She'd been meeting with Dr. Pesch in the afternoons now. Each day she was stronger. She still had her moments, but he rarely found her in a corner anymore when he wasn't around.

"I don't want to bother you." Her smile was hesitant.

He went to her and pulled her into a hug. At first these hugs and kisses had been affectionate, to calm and soothe her. By that point though, he needed them too. Needed the sweet, calm assurance she filled him with when she hugged him back and smiled, blushing a little.

"No bother. In fact, Julian and I think you can be of some help to us as we plan our mission. Are you willing to be an honorary operative?"

Her eyes widened with pleasure and her smile widened. "Really?"

Julian came in and scooted his chair closer to hers, kissing her lips like he'd been doing it all along.

Vincenz shook his head, amused.

"Yes, really. Part of what we're going to do, lovely Hannah, is to check out the foundation's offices in Silesia."

"We figure you know a lot about not only how the Imperialists do things but also the subject matter. Julian and I don't know much about the science and medical stuff. We could upload their databases, and we will." Vincenz narrowed his gaze, remembering having to do that and discovering Hannah in one of the locked cells. "We need a technical expert."

Worry crossed her face, but she pushed it away, visibly sitting straighter in her seat. "What do you need from me?"

So brave. He wanted her to understand the danger but also that he and Julian would die before they'd let the Imperium take her again. "Julian and I will handle all the military aspects of the mission. This is non-negotiable. *We* will carry the weapons and *you* will be protected at all times."

She turned to him. "It is impossible to protect anyone at all times. This will slow you down and put you in danger."

Her delivery always loosened the knot he carried in his belly. Matter-of-fact. She had few filters, and he'd wondered if she was this way before her time in that cell.

"Vincenz is correct, Hannah. Consider us your personal guard." Julian's spine was ramrod straight and Hannah paused to study him.

"I should have a weapon too. Just in case."

Vincenz sighed. He should have known she'd negotiate instead of just letting them make the decisions. Still, it wasn't a bad idea, which is why Julian had already been so actively working on her physical training and strengthening.

"Don't think I can't see past your sneaky ways, Hannah," Julian teased with a wink. "You've been at me for weapons training all this time. I think it's a fine idea so we'll start with that today."

She hugged Julian, kissing his cheeks and returned her attention to Vincenz.

"How can I help now? What can I do? When do we leave? Will we take a big transport or a private one?"

They'd been at it for hours. Vincenz and Julian were used to such hours, but Vincenz worried about Hannah, who'd already proven herself integral to their mission several times. Her language skills were top-notch. She worked at his side interpreting documents. Julian worked at pulling together all the documentation they'd need. Maps, tickets, travel documents. He coordinated with some of the other special teams and back with command back on Ravena.

Vincenz rolled his head on his shoulders, working out the kinks. "You should go to bed. We'll be at this for another few hours, and you need your rest."

She sniffed delicately. "Do you think medical doctors are unfamiliar with long hours?" A smile played at the edge of her mouth.

"You're still recovering. Let your body do what it needs to." Julian spoke without looking up from his screen.

"I've gained fourteen pounds. I'm not having as many nightmares. I had a nap today anyway. I'm not feeble."

At that, Julian did look up. "No. Of all the words in all the 'Verses to describe you, *feeble* would never be one of them."

"Every one of those pounds looks good on you." And they did. She'd been thin and now she was softer, lusher. Her breasts, *seven hells*, they made his mouth water.

"Thank you, Vincenz. I'm spoiled now with all this delicious food. I'm not looking forward to the day when I have to worry over it again." She pointed to the display. "Coding should be reversed here."

He pushed the keyboard her way and watched as she clicked easily, her bottom lip caught between her teeth as she did the work, replacing his string of code quickly.

"I should have known that." It was logical after all, to have the code reflect how one culture or other communicated and broke down information.

"How long have you been here?" She got up and began to knead the muscles in his neck.

"Eleven standard years."

"Did you also do this sort of technical writing when you were next in line to run the Imperium?"

"I've always excelled at mathematics. But my training was not focused there."

"You learned it here?"

"One of the first jobs Ellis gave me was to comb through thousands of documents to look for information. Instead, I created an algorithm to find certain terms and phrases because it took up all my time the long way."

She laughed and it wasn't so rusty anymore. "He must have been delighted."

"Surprised I think. They suspected me as a plant for a very long time." He'd understood it, but it had hurt nonetheless.

A long pause as she looked him over. "It must have been very lonely for you. To be so misunderstood. To have done such an amazing, selfless thing and have people believe the worst of you."

He spun and pulled her into his lap, hugging her tight, burying his face in her hair.

She left him exposed because she saw right to the heart of him. And didn't flinch.

She held on tight. Her arms encircled his shoulders as her breathing slowed and she melted into his body. Those moments when it was as if she gave herself over to him raged through his memory, urging him on. Urging him to claim. To take and delight.

He dragged his eyelids up and met Julian's gaze. Julian licked his lips and stood, and it was as if time slowed with each step he took until he reached them both.

Vincenz stood and put her on her feet, swaying with her.

He looked into her eyes, so glossy and dazed. She was as affected as he was. Thank the gods above and below.

Moving to stand behind Vincenz, Julian took one of her hands and turned it palm up. When he pressed his lips there she gulped and made a sound. A low, needy moan dragged from her lips as if she was as surprised by it as he was.

Her taste. He needed more.

Cuffing her wrist, Julian didn't fail to notice the way her eyes widened and her pupils grew. Her lips parted, sweet and slick.

And he kissed that mouth.

He tried to take it slow, but there was no slow with her. Nothing halfway.

Surprised, she gasped and then breathed a sigh of pleasure into his mouth and he swallowed it, greedy for her.

Julian nipped her bottom lip the way he'd wanted to every day for weeks, maybe longer. Her fingers at his shoulder dug into the muscle there as she clung to him.

Moremoremoremore. Need was a drumbeat in his head, a throbbing bass in his gut, throttling through his veins like wildfire.

She tasted like spice and sweetness. Like something dark and forbidden and altogether precious and he needed her like he needed to breathe.

He kept Vincenz between them because he wanted to tear the clothes from her body to bare all that skin. He wanted to toss her on the table and bury his face in her cunt. She made him simultaneously want to dominate and cherish in a way that stripped all pretense away. Stripped him to his barest, basest urges.

He began to pull away from the kiss when she sucked his tongue and suddenly he couldn't think why it was a bad thing to claim this woman who'd come into their lives in the most unexpected kind of way and had turned everything on its ear.

Forehead to forehead they stood, leaning on Vincenz, who rested his weight against Julian as Hannah's hand remained clutched in the front of Vincenz's shirt.

"Why me?' she whispered.

"Because it's you."

Vincenz had said it as if he'd plucked it from Julian's brain.

"But . . . you two are already . . ."

Julian grinned. "Oh, yes. A great deal."

"But . . . I . . . how? I don't want to come between you."

Julian had to pause to gulp at the sight of Vincenz sliding a palm up her belly, between her breasts, up to collar her throat. Her eyes went half-mast and she blew out a gust of sound. A ragged sort of moan laced with entreaty.

"Looks like this time it's my turn to be in between you." Vin pulled her close enough to kiss. This time there was no soft or tentative brush of lips over hers. This was the kind of kiss that routinely turned Julian's knees to rubber.

When he broke the kiss she pursed her lips and then rolled them against her tongue.

"There's no *between us* in the sense you mean."

Julian knew she was fragile. He knew she'd been through a lot. But all that fell away when she slid the hand clutched at Vincenz's chest up around his neck and into his hair.

"Bed." Julian wanted the room to do all he wanted to them both.

Vincenz's dazed look sharpened as he turned his head to meet Julian's gaze.

So close to that mouth, Julian was helpless to do anything but kiss him. He tasted of Hannah, which only drove him madder for them both.

Julian nipped his bottom lip and then went back for hers. Surprising them both, she laughed, dispelling any last doubts he might have had that she wasn't on board with what was happening.

Vincenz flicked a few switches. "May as well let this do our work while we're busy."

Hannah had always believed herself a 'Verse-wide traveler. She was well read. Loved all sorts of new and exciting experiences. But this . . . well, this was something she'd never even really imagined. Aside from those moments in the shower earlier and a few fleeting wishes that they'd touch her the way they touched each other, she'd never thought it was actually something that she'd do.

They moved as a unit, these two men. That hadn't changed. She'd watched the way they moved from the very start. They knew each other so well they had a rhythm she found ridiculously masculine and sexy. But she'd had to sneak in those moments when she watched like a voyeur. And now she was more—a participant. She couldn't begin to fathom it.

She did know how grateful she was that she was able to appreciate it. That she was free and getting better and that neither of them considered her some sort of freak for what she'd endured.

Vincenz pulled his shirt off as they entered the bedchamber. She loved his body. Long and lean. Tight muscle lay over his body, bunching and flexing as he walked or moved.

Both men had slept in shirts and loose pants while she had been in the bed with them. But this . . .

Her gaze snagged on his belt where he paused to unbuckle and unzip his pants. Julian moved to stand behind her. "He's gorgeous, isn't he?"

She nodded, her breath catching as Vincenz pushed his trousers and shorts down and stepped from them. Totally, magnificently naked.

Without thinking she fanned her face and Vincenz caught the movement, swooping in and kissing her quickly. "That's a fine compliment."

Julian's hand, palm flat against her belly, held her in place against the swell of his cock at her ass.

She gulped. Totally out of her element but wanting this more than she'd wanted anything. Ever.

Vincenz reached for her, but Julian spun her and she tipped her chin up to see his features better. And then he ripped her shirt down the front, sending the little metal buttons pinging against the wall and floor.

"Oh!"

He shoved her shirt down to her wrists and twisted the material to hold her there.

Her clit swelled, hardening as her cunt slicked. The next sound she made was gut deep.

He kissed her collarbone, and when his hands were back to pop her bra open, spilling her breasts into his waiting palms, she knew somewhere in her head that Vincenz now held her hands captive.

She drowned in the sensation.

Julian dragged his thumbs back and forth over her nipples as she looked down her body to watch. As if it were happening to someone else. Someone very lucky.

"I saw those when you stripped the other day. You were so vexed at us that you gave no thought to me standing there in the bathroom. I'd dreamed of them, of the dark pink of your nipples when I'd catch their shadow through the material of your nightdress." Vincenz kissed her ear, sending her into overdrive.

"Tits like these make a man grateful each day woman was created." Julian underlined that with a pinch and tug of her nipples.

"I thought I was imagining it."

Julian paused and raised a brow. "Imagining how amazing your breasts are?"

She managed to find the humor in that statement. "No, silly. The way Vincenz looked at me. I thought I was projecting." And she'd given herself a talking-to about how she needed to realize they were kind to her like a sister, nothing else.

"At first it was . . . paternal perhaps? You were hurt and we wanted to protect you. And then it changed. Changed as you got stronger, as we got to know you, as Hannah the woman began to show herself. Then it became harder and harder to resist your beauty." Julian kissed her again, and she sighed wistfully when he pulled back.

She was glad they lost their willpower to resist. There was something incredibly empowering about their desire. Knowing they were so protective, it meant they judged her strong and healthy or they'd never have allowed themselves this with her.

"Why is she wearing pants?" Vincenz asked Julian, looking over her shoulder. Julian stretched and met Vincenz with a kiss. A kiss so very close to her face. If they hadn't been pressed against her, holding her wrists, keeping her in place she might have simply floated away at how ridiculously sexy it was to have them do this. She heard everything—the scratch of beard against beard, the sounds, oh, gods, the sound of lips meeting lips, of tongue sliding against mouth and tongue, the soft huff of a groan when the kiss broke.

"You've got her hands bound, Vin."

"Ah, well, then let me help with that." Again she was spun, this time with Julian holding her wrists as Vincenz dropped to his knees. Her heart stuttered as he pressed a kiss to her belly and then pulled her pants from her legs.

It wasn't as if she was a virgin. Or that she was a delicate flower when it came to sex. But two men seemed enough out of her normal range. Add to that the way Julian held her wrists, keeping her bound and making her like it, and she was sure she'd lost her mind.

She laughed at that. Vincenz looked up at her as he pulled her panties down, leaving her as naked as he.

"Laughing is an unexpected reaction to a man on his knees before you."

Hannah bit her lip. "It was a silly thought about my sanity, not about your very adept sex moves."

It was his turn to laugh at that. "Adept sex moves, eh?" He pressed a kiss to her mound, right above her labia and she saw stars as she gulped in a breath. He hadn't even touched the good parts yet and she was gasping and seeing stars. This when she couldn't even make herself come in the shower.

She worried then. What if she was horrible now? What if she could never come? Ever again?

"What's the furrow between your eyes, gorgeous?" The breath from Vincenz's words brushed against her pussy, testing her worries a little.

"Nothing."

His cock was so hard it stood and tapped his belly. She could see the smear of come at the head. That's what she should concentrate on, not a bunch of stupid what-ifs. Even if she couldn't come, she'd have this with them. Orgasms weren't the only point of sex.

"That's not a nothing face." Vincenz bent to brush a kiss over the inside of her knee, sending gooseflesh over her body.

"What?"

Julian's laugh in her ear made her lose her thoughts even more. "He does that to me when he's on his knees too. It's hard not to get befuddled with a man like Vincenz naked and focused on making you feel good. But that doesn't mean we don't want to know about what it is you're bothered by. Is it this? Too much?" He let go of the shirt and her wrists, and she made a sound of loss.

"I don't think that was it, Julian." Vincenz kissed her inner thigh.

Her thoughts burst apart like birds taking flight. "I don't want to talk about it. This is fine. I like this. A lot. I promise."

"You like it when you're bound?" He slid his palms down her arms and cuffed the wrists. His hands were huge and so very strong. She shivered, licking her lips.

And nodded. Why lie about it?

"I like it too."

"So what is it?" Vincenz gazed up at her, filling her with unbidden tenderness. She was off balance. Far too flustered to make up a reason, annoyed that her worry at making up a reason seemed to have sent that building pleasure back from the edge she'd been on, she huffed a frustrated breath.

"I said it was nothing. In case you've forgotten how women are, when we don't want to talk about it, we get frustrated when you push and push like the . . . pushy creatures you are."

Julian sent an amused look to Vincenz.

"Fair enough." He tightened his hold of her wrists and she sighed, losing the rigidity in her spine. Good.

She could keep on thinking they would let her get away with being upset without letting them help. But she'd come to learn that she was important to some pretty bossy men. Men who liked to fix things for people they cared about.

"I think you should spread her legs wider and eat that pussy," he murmured to Vincenz before he bent to kiss her shoulder.

Vincenz leaned in close and nuzzled her pussy with his lips, and she shivered in Julian's hold. It was an unbelievably sexy sight. The curves of Hannah's body against his. The perfection of her breasts, the flare of her hips, the darkness of her hair against the pale softness of her skin—magnificent.

She was everything he found beautiful about women. Including the way she responded to being restrained and bound. The way she yielded. He tightened his grip at her wrists and she went all pliant. Beautiful.

With his free hand, he tugged and rolled her nipple, all while he feasted on the sweetness of her neck and watched Vincenz with his face buried in her cunt, devastating her.

Devastating Julian too.

"Take her weight a little. Lean back." Vincenz spread her open wider, pulling her thigh up onto his shoulder and dove back in, leaving Julian to lick his lips.

"I can see his tongue on your clit at this angle. Open your eyes and look at him." Though his tone was gentle, it wasn't a request and she didn't take it as one. The blood in his cock thrummed as they both watched Vincenz. Took in the way he fluttered his tongue against her, the way his fingers dug into the muscles of her thighs and ass.

Her eyes, which had been sleepy and half lidded, widened and then she arched, pulling against his hold. He took note of her features. No fear. No panic. Pleasure glossed her eyes; her lips parted on a groan he felt as though it vibrated through every single cell and straight into his gut.

She came hard, so hard. It went on until Vincenz pushed her into another climax and she went utterly boneless.

Vincenz's smile was smug, Julian noted, as they helped her to the bed where Julian spread her out like a feast. She was soft then. Her features unmarred by the lines of concentration she often wore.

Until she started to cry and both of them moved to her quickly.

"What? Did we hurt you? Oh, gods." Julian hated himself then for rushing. He shouldn't have pushed. It was too soon for her. Obviously after what she'd endured. How could he have been so selfish?

She shook her head, covering her face with her hair and her hands. "No, you didn't hurt me."

"We rushed you. I'm sorry. We wanted you so much and it was stupid. I'm sorry."

She sat up then, taking each of their hands in her own. "No. It's not you. Not either of you. Not in the way you think. I . . . it's that I wasn't sure I could anymore. Come." She searched for more words but shook her head again.

Julian took his shirt off and got on the bed. Satisfied with the way her gaze lingered on him. "Why didn't you say?"

"Huh?"

It was Vincenz's turn to laugh. "You've captivated her with your body, Julian."

How they managed to make her feel included while still sharing their connection she wasn't sure, but she was glad for it nonetheless.

She lay and looked up, watching the two of them, so very dominant and yet totally different. It was exciting and sexy and though she'd come twice as it was, she wanted more of them.

"I like the way she looks in our bed." Vincenz spoke as he slid in beside her.

"I do too."

"You're not naked." Vincenz pushed Julian off and rolled on her himself. She smiled up at him as her thoughts slid away and she let herself feel.

So many times during her day she had to concentrate so hard, work so diligently to keep herself together. But with them, with *this* there was no need for that. She dove in and let herself experience. The roar of confusion eased into a hum in her belly. Warm.

"Hey!" But Julian's tone wasn't truly angry. He stood, quickly divesting himself of the rest of his clothing as Vincenz teased her with the head of his cock.

"I took care of the preliminaries earlier you see. Prepared as my teachers used to say."

Julian jumped back to the bed and, laughing, pulled Vincenz into a kiss that she watched, breathless.

"Villain. You've already been in that pretty pussy. I want my turn."

Vincenz rolled so that she was on top. Julian moved behind her. "Perhaps if she gets her mouth on your cock, I can make myself useful elsewhere."

At the same time?

"I don't know if I have the skill set for this." She turned her head to find Julian close.

"The skill set to let two men worship your body and make you feel pleasure? Do you think you could learn it? If, say, we practiced a great deal?"

Julian Marsters really was incorrigible. Irresistibly so.

"Perhaps."

He grinned and things tightened low in her belly and elsewhere.

"May I?" she asked Vincenz.

"Anything and everything. What is it you'd like me to give you permission for, beautiful Hannah?"

She wanted to learn him. To touch and kiss and explore.

"May I touch you?"

He took her hand and put it on his chest. "Please."

"On your knees," Julian said low, his breath stirring the hair at the base of her neck. "I'm going to put my cock in you like I've been dying to."

He helped her into just the position he wanted her in, which left her leaning on Vincenz. Close enough to kiss and touch just as she'd wanted.

She kissed across his chest, rubbing her face against him, loving the bristle of the pale hair on his belly.

Vincenz took her hands as she scooted down to kiss over his belly and along the trail of hair leading to his cock.

"Oh, no. Don't close your eyes, Hannah. When my cock is in your mouth, I want your gaze on me."

Oh. Julian had been the more verbally dominant until that moment, but she certainly had no complaints about this new development.

Gaze on his face, she grabbed his cock at the root and angled it. "I want to look at it. I can't look at it if I'm looking at your face."

Julian, who'd been kissing down her spine, paused to nip the flesh at her hip. "She's got a point."

"Look your fill."

Vincenz watched her as she held him, nuzzling the crown with her mouth, licking and pausing to study his reaction. He was pretty sure he'd expire before she got down to business, but also fairly convinced he'd go out a very happy man if that was the case.

And then her gaze locked with his as she took him into her mouth fully.

Julian had leaned out to watch, the voyeur he was.

"Gods above and below, I don't believe I've ever seen anything so sexy."

Vincenz agreed. Her mouth on him, her gaze on him, her body on display for both men. Unbelievable is what it was.

"From my angle I'd agree. The two of you above me reminds me of what a truly fortunate man I am."

She whimpered as Julian moved back, Vincenz assumed, to put his cock inside her inferno-hot cunt.

"So. Damned. Tight."

Her moans and whimpers around Vincenz's cock would have been sexy enough, but when Julian began to thrust, she moved forward on Vincenz, changing her angle. His balls crawled up into his body.

He'd had a threesome before. Twice. Never with a man he'd had as a lover. Never with a long-term female partner either. It had been exiting, tiring and messy, but he hadn't regretted it either time. But this was different. This was . . . he struggled to think as her mouth, hot and wet swallowed his cock over and over as Julian fucked her so hard her breasts swayed, her nipples burning against his thighs where she crouched above him.

This was more.

Julian had given up pretending this was a onetime event. Or that it was only a physical thing between the three of them.

Her cunt fit his cock like it was made for him. Slippery and so hot he tried not to lose his mind and come before he'd been in her a few minutes.

That she'd been afraid she'd never be able to come again had made him sad. Brought the urge to make her come at least once a day now, to remind her she wasn't in that cell anymore and that he and Vincenz had more in store for her. Something better and bigger and filled with more pleasure than she'd ever had before.

Julian couldn't tear his gaze from her mouth on Vincenz's cock, or of the look on Vincenz's face as he looked down at her. Her pale, dark-haired glory against Vincenz's sun-kissed skin and golden hair made Julian quite sure he was having the best time of his entire life right then.

"Yes, yes, that way. Deeper, you can take me deeper. I know you can."

Hannah's cunt squeezed him so hard Julian thought he might end up blind. "I think she liked that part, Vin."

She not only seemed all right with being dominated, she responded in ways Julian could trust far more than her verbal assurances. Her pussy told him she got off on it. Her pussy wasn't going to worry about hurting feelings.

At that last sign, he leaned to where his pants had landed, grabbing his belt quickly. The groan she made as he slipped the leather against her skin, wrapping the length of his belt around her upper arms shot straight to his cock. Her inner walls fluttered around him in response to the belt.

He tugged to pull her up and she lost her balance.

"Let him take your weight. Trust him," Vincenz crooned.

"Trust me to always take care of you," Julian said as he tightened the belt.

She let go then; Julian felt it in her muscles, trusting him and giving over totally.

Vincenz let out a snarled groan, his head whipping from side to side until he stiffened and came.

Julian then leaned his upper body back, tugging on the belt, which accentuated the curve of her back as he changed his angle, getting in even deeper.

"My hands are busy, Vin. Help Hannah out. I want to know what it feels like when she explodes around my cock."

Vincenz extricated himself carefully and moved down the bed. First kissing Julian and then as he settled on the mattress, he kissed Hannah long and slow until she was all soft and boneless again.

When Vincenz found her clit, he swept down to her gate to gather some of that juicy sweetness and back. Over and over, each time he moved back, he dragged his blunt nails down Julian's balls.

"She's close. Me too. Give us another, Hannah. Come again."

"Can't." She groaned.

"Oh, you can and you will because I want you to." Vincenz licked over the swell at the side of her breast. "Because Julian wants you to. Come around his cock, beautiful Hannah. Do it because I say."

She whimpered and then went stiff, her muscles locking and squeezing around him so hard he had no choice but to finally let go and come. So hard he saw stars against his closed eyes. So hard his head swam as he made his way to the bed, Hannah between them, lazy and satisfied.

As it should be.

Chapter 10

"Roman, do stop hovering." Abbie said it affectionately as she looked down at Mera, who blinked up with a sweet, toothless grin from her perch on their bed.

"She'll fall." He wasn't actually worried about that. His wife was as competent at mothering as she was everything else. But he liked this new interaction between them. This new journey they took as parents.

"I'm changing her nappy. She's here with one of my hands on her belly in the middle of our gigantic bed. I promise to do my best to not toss our daughter from the balcony or dip her in hot oil."

She bent and blew a raspberry on that sweet, soft belly and Mera pumped her little arms and legs, delighted. This precious baby girl with her father's eyes and the cant of his mouth. The rest was all Abbie though, which filled him with joy.

"I've done this before, you know." It amused him to rankle her, so he did. It was easier to think about that than the war.

"Go on and meet with Wil and Daniel. Mera and I are going down to the gardens to play with Corrin."

"Stop stealing this baby all for yourself." Daniel strolled into the room and headed straight for Mera, who he picked up ably, dropping kisses on her face. "Hello, my beauty." He even straightened the little dress Abbie had put her in.

"Stealing? I get to hold her less than you do. You have your own home and yet I keep finding you in mine." Roman sent a look to his brother-in-law.

"Abbie is atrociously ungenerous with her, I've noticed."

They started downstairs, Abbie ignoring their playful banter.

Wil came into the grand foyer and grinned. Roman deftly snatched Mera from Daniel and danced her past Wilhelm's grabbing hands. "And here is another male I find myself having to fend off. From my wife *and* my daughter."

"If only those people you all scare so routinely could see you felled by a wee baby." Abbie looked on, grinning. "Now, Mera, give your father a kiss. He has business and you and I have a date with your big brother. I wouldn't be surprised if we found *both* your brothers waiting."

Mera only knew she was loved. She only knew the safety of his arms, of his house, of a snuggle at her mother's breast and the constant attention from her family. He never wanted her to know the kind of fear so many of his citizens did at that point in their history. And he sure as seven hells wanted to assure a safe and healthy future for them as a result of the ugliness of the war.

She made a little gurgling coo, and he couldn't give her back to her mother just yet. "Will you be sure your mother keeps out of trouble, my darling girl? She's reckless."

He kissed the dark silk of Mera's hair, already thick like her mother's, and then handed her back to Abbie, pausing to kiss her as well. "Stay here today?"

She chafed at the situation, he knew. Wanted to get out and about, wanted to take Mera out to see her grandmother and aunt. Instead they all came to the house because it was safest. Safest in a world where the violence all around them could easily land anywhere, and he wanted his loved ones to be in the most well-defended place they could be.

"My mother is coming to visit when she finishes at work." She kissed him back and his heart sped. Only for her did he respond that way. Only Abigail got past all his filters and upbringing to have lodged her rabble-rousing self right in his heart. "I'll expect you for luncheon? Corrin and Deimos will be here as well. Mercy is making something suitably delicious."

Corrin and Deimos were his sons from his first marriage. Both adults and both utterly smitten not only with his wife but their new sister as well. If only everything else in the damned 'Verses was going so well.

"I'll be there unless something comes up. If Deimos is in the greenhouses, can you send him back to my office? He'll need to be in on this briefing."

She nodded and left, singing and laughing as their daughter snuggled into her hold.

"Now, let's get down to business, shall we?"

Once everyone had taken their seat, Roman turned on the display screens and nodded to Wil.

"As you can see, we've made major gains in the Imperial Edge 'Verses. We now control seventy percent of Silesia. Including the main portal station and those rogue portals we've located. We've got the upper hand on Fortuna, though the geography is more of a challenge than Silesia has been."

Wil let each person process what they saw on the screens and take notes. Roman had chosen well in the nearly seven-foot-tall Comandante. Wilhelm Ellis had a sense of justice and loyalty unlike any Roman had ever seen. He understood strategy but above all, he understood people and that made him more than just an asset, he was a weapon against an enemy who'd ceased caring about what people thought and why they did what they did. And that was one of the main reasons why the Federated Universes would take every single Imperialist 'Verse up to Caelinus.

There would be a bill for Ciro Fardelle to pay for killing so many Federation citizens. Roman Lyons would not only punish that violence on Fardelle's part, he'd take more territory than he needed to give the Federated 'Verses a wide buffer. Fardelle would not be in charge when this was said and done because it would not end until he was dead.

"Vincenz and Julian are working on a plan now to locate and destroy the last remaining portal-collapsing device. The woman they freed on Parron, Hannah Black, is in possession of information that could be integral to us, though we don't know what it is yet. Julian is continuing a long-term debrief and finds new information frequently as she gets better." Wil leaned back and looked them over.

"Why hasn't she been moved to the center?" Roman sipped his kava. These teams of operatives had their own rhythm and code; suddenly having an outside influence with other goals and needs not included in the parameters of the operation was a complication they didn't need.

"She has an uncanny ability to break down code. Vincenz says—and I'm quoting him—Hannah is a beast with code and numbers." Wil hid his expression behind his steepled fingers. "I've seen some of her work. It's impressive. She's developing some programs Vincenz will use when he arrives at the labs to extract, upload and destroy all data from the source."

"I've read the reports. She's not a military corpsman. She's not an operative. She's a woman who was mentally tortured for a year. She's unstable. I don't like the idea of her being on an op with my people." Roman trusted his people, but this woman was not someone he knew at all.

Wil had approved her to go on this caper and Roman respected his judgment. At the same time, he wanted to be convinced.

"I admit I had my concerns about this as well." Daniel sat forward. "But I've spoken in detail with Dr. Pesch and while he agrees her healing will take a long time, he does not harbor any fears of instability. In fact, he says her ability to pitch in and help has aided in her long-term recovery." He shrugged. "We need her and what she's doing."

Wil leaned forward. "Some of my operatives were born the way they are. Canny. Quick. Merciless when necessary. Three years ago I'm sure Hannah Black would have been entirely ill suited for such an assignment. This woman survived daily torture."

Wilhelm paused because he was still processing just what he thought of Hannah, but it was important for them to hear.

"I'm aware and I respect that. But it doesn't mean she's what these men are," Roman countered and Wil forged ahead.

"She isn't. She's something else entirely. What she's endured used to be called a trial by fire. She didn't choose what happened to her. But she didn't give up either. They caught her marking time in her cell and they'd go in and paint over where she had her tally marks. So she cut her scalp at the base of her skull so they couldn't see it. But *she* knew. That young woman never broke. The strength of fortitude that takes, the character of this person to agree to go on this mission is exactly the kind of strength I look for in all my operatives. She's not a permanent member of the team like Piper. I expect when this war is over she'll find a way to get back to work in her own field."

She had become part of Vincenz and Julian. He'd seen enough to know it was more than just brotherly concern. He didn't know how far it went and it wasn't any of his damned business. But he knew that since she'd been around Julian had been less angry and Vincenz more comfortable. Whatever part she played in that it was a good thing. Moreover, it would make the team stronger to have her there. And that was a point that couldn't be ignored.

"But will she slow them down? Who's to say she's not better off away from them? In a facility where she can get help? Or at least where she can see a doctor on a daily basis. Does this serve her? I have a responsibility to her as well."

Of course Roman cared about that. It was one of the myriad reasons Wilhelm trusted him without hesitation.

"Pesch states that putting her in any kind of facility would be disastrous to her recovery. And it is my sincere belief that if she is left behind, they'll be slowed down anyway because they'll be worried for her. Her place on the team makes them all stronger." He took a breath. "She's important." He didn't say he felt it, or that he guessed it. He knew it.

Since he'd been a young boy, sometimes Wil had just *understood* things in a different way. He'd known when someone was key, not always why or how, but that they were. It had served him throughout his life, especially as he got older and had lost the anger that'd propelled him through his tumultuous youth.

Roman looked at him and then nodded. "That's all I needed to hear."

They finished up and he sent everyone on their way, pausing to speak with Roman privately.

"I've got Andrei and Piper moving toward the Imperium. On the way they'll stop and look into all this talk of uprising."

Roman's jaw hardened, but Wil was totally convinced this path was necessary and it was his job to protect his government and his Federation.

"I thought we agreed to table this for now. They don't need the attention. They're not organized. It's that branch of the Walker Family who were disassociated. They have nothing but a grievance. To give them any attention only sends a message that they're worth worry. They aren't."

As if he were a novice on his first mission and would rush in with vid cameras and spotlights. He snorted and threw a sideways glare at Roman, who had the good sense to look a little guilty.

"And who makes sure that happens? I do, Roman. This is my job for a reason. You have enough to manage. As we suffer casualties and spend credits some Families are going to continue to call for us to withdraw and collapse the portals behind us to keep the Imperium out for good.

"This has the potential for a godsawful distraction and we can't afford it right now. We should know who they are and if necessary relieve them of this fantastic notion that they can take your seat and control of the Federated Universes."

"Abbie said the same thing to me yesterday."

"Your wife is a far more intelligent creature than you are. At least you have the wit to have captured her. Go be a husband and a father for now. There's a chill; you should take a shawl out to the gardens. The babe may be cool."

Roman raised a brow. "If I didn't know what a heartless cad you were, I'd suspect you've taken a shine to my ladies."

"I'm too crusty and set in my ways to be sweet on your ladies. I'm on my way out. I am to be in another meeting right at this very moment." Wil tipped his head in deference and with a wave and a quick turn on his heel was already headed out.

Coming to the house was an important reminder of everything

that was at stake. Deimos, Corrin and Mera were the next generation and they'd lead the Federated Universes. They and millions of young people all across the 'Verses deserved a future. A good future. And it was his job to help them achieve that.

Julian brought several boxes inside from where they'd been waiting. He put them near where she'd been sitting on the big rug.

She looked at them, and then up at him. "Would you stay?"

Vincenz had been gone the last day, out scouting. Julian had taken care of all the paper and documentation they'd need for their trip, but Vincenz had some important contacts left in the Imperium and they only spoke to him.

But out of the blue when she'd woken up that morning she'd informed him she was ready to go through the boxes of her parents' things Vincenz had managed to pull together.

He sat with her, leaning against the nearby couch. "Of course."

Gingerly, she opened the top and peeked inside and her breath caught as she drew out the first item. A misshapen green lump.

"I'm good with numbers, bad with clay." She met his gaze with a watery smile. "I made this in school and presented it to him quite proudly. He wasn't a man prone to a lot of emotional displays. He took it solemnly and looked it over. He thanked me with a kiss on my forehead. But it wasn't until years later that I caught sight of it on his desk. He'd had it there all along."

He watched her handle the death of her parents anew with each item she pulled from the two boxes. The odd photograph, a cuff link, her father's name badge. She took her time, examining each thing. Sometimes she'd offer him a story about it, others she firmed her mouth and moved to the next thing.

And then with a gasp, she pulled one last thing out.

"What is that?"

She put the two ends into her ears and placed the silver disc over his heart, smiling. Removing the buds from her ears, she placed them in his and put the disc over her own heart and he heard it.

"This is a stethoscope. An early diagnostic tool doctors used to listen to heart and lung sounds before the development of digicomps. He had this as long as I could remember. His father gave it to him, he said." She held it to her chest.

"Does it make you happy to have it?"

She closed the second box and then made her way into his lap, still holding the stethoscope. "Yes. It makes me . . . comforted to have this part of him. This part that connects us."

He held her tight, her head tucked in beneath his chin. "Good." He put this moment with her in that memory bank, the special one, where his most important life moments went. She and Vincenz shared so much of his heart and mind.

"He'd be wildly amused that I know how to use a blaster. My mother would have appreciated the economy of it. A useful skill, she'd have said. But he had a sense of humor, dry. His world was very academic; something like a weapon would have brought him no end of fascination."

He liked that.

"Thank you."

"For what?" He kissed her temple, his lips against her pulse beat.

"For being here while I went through the boxes. For listening to me. For respecting my need to do this." She took a deep breath and swiveled around, placing the stethoscope down and wrapping her legs around his waist. "People want to fix me. It's touching. But it's exhausting to deal with it. You don't do that. It means a lot to me that you don't constantly try to fix me. That you let me be."

He hugged her then, not knowing if he could manage to keep it together when she looked at him so honestly and openly.

"No one has ever given themselves to me without expecting something in return. Not the way you have. You're a gift, Hannah. One I am thankful for each and every day."

She sighed happily, melting into his embrace, and they remained there together for some time, just being.

Chapter 11

"Why do you call yourself Vincent Cuomo sometimes?" Hannah asked this as she sat on the floor, her body against his leg. She had been helping him untangle a string of encrypted data for the last few hours, curled up there like a cat.

They'd leave in a few hours to take the first leg of the trip toward the Imperium but as always, he was loath to move when she was near.

So he paused, sometimes still surprised by the suddenness of these types of questions. It seemed such a part of her by that point, the way she just blurted out whatever she happened to think.

But only with him and Julian. With others she was more reserved and tightly controlled. That trust and intimacy was a gift.

He hummed a pleased sigh, stroking a hand over the cool, smooth silk of her hair. "When I first arrived here after I . . . left, they asked me to use another name. Walking around with Fardelle as my last name given who my father is seemed a bad idea. Cuomo is a family name on my mother's side a few generations back. Vincent instead of Vincenz seemed to stick. Though I prefer Vincenz and only use Vincent when I'm on an op."

She turned to rest her chin on his knee and look up into his face. "I like Vincenz. It's very sexy."

He smiled, bending to kiss her. "Julian says that too. I'm glad it pleases you both. It was my great-grandsire's middle name."

"Was it odd then? To come here when you knew no one and have to change your name? Cutting ties but not being trusted all the way? I imagine you'd feel sort of . . . rootless."

She got him in a way that he supposed he'd be uncomfortable with in anyone but a very few.

"I was lonely for a long time. And then I began to make some friends in the corps." He shrugged, and she got up, dusting herself off. But he didn't want her to move away. He needed to touch her as much as she needed to be touched. He grabbed her hand and tugged her into his lap where she straddled him, sliding her arms around his shoulders and hugging him tight.

"Did you know Julian all this time? Was it slow for you, or did you know immediately?"

He laughed, leaning in to nip her bottom lip and trying to ignore the way she wriggled on his lap. "I've known Julian many years. We weren't especially close until the last months when he and Marame would come out here for work. I think I was as surprised by what developed between us as he was. After she had been killed, he . . ." Vincenz paused, not wanting to reveal more than Julian himself would feel comfortable with. But she was theirs now and she needed to know.

"He lost his way." Hannah looked at him with those wide eyes, understanding. "She was part of him. And she was gone and he had nothing to fill the spot she'd taken up in his heart. Nothing but anger."

"Yes. Yes I think that's true."

She put her palm over his heart. "Until you helped him fill it with something else."

He smiled. "I don't know if I'd say it like that, but I do hope I've given him some comfort in a bad time in his life. She was—Marame, I mean—the kind of person everyone liked. Smart, outgoing. Always laughing and joking. She was the light to his broody sort of dark. She died doing her job, which means something. To him and to me, to all of us."

Marame had balanced Julian. Her personality and the way they'd worked together had kept him from veering too far into the darkness. But then she was gone and Julian had no one left to stop that. No balance to keep him from tipping into all that rage and restless frustration.

And Hannah saw that. Knew it when most didn't get Julian's change at all.

"I'm sorry you both lost her."

He hugged her, content to simply be with her that way.

"But I'm not sorry you found me."

He tightened his hold, burying his face in her hair. "You're the best thing I've ever found."

"That was a very nice thing to hear. Thank you. For finding me and for making a place in your lives for me. I was afraid. Every day. For so long it was hard to remember there were other ways to feel. You and Julian reminded me of those other things."

The rage at what had been done to her coursed into his system again. Never far away.

"What they did to you will not go unavenged."

She pulled away to look at him. Her thoughts took her away somewhere for a while. And he waited as she worked it through. "I suppose sometimes I'm to say no. To say it's over and it's best to move on."

She tipped her head and her hair slid forward. He resisted the urge to brush it back. He hated that she ever found the need for those tic behaviors. But he respected that for her at times they were necessary.

"I want to hurt the people who did this to me. I want the people who make me tremble like a scared animal sometimes for no reason to be punished. I want to punish them for taking my parents. For stealing so much of my life." Her words blurred together as she sped her pace. Just to get it out, he figured.

There was still anger. But she *articulated* it now, as opposed to the rocking and shivering she'd done before. Pesch had said it was a good sign. But Vincenz still wanted to put a bullet into the head of every single person who'd harmed her.

"Beautiful Hannah, it doesn't make you a bad person to want to see the people who did this to you given their due."

Noise in the entry and a quick look toward the monitors told Vincenz Julian had returned.

"Is it time to go now?"

Vincenz stood and put her on her feet. "Soon."

Julian came into the room and grinned at them. He tossed a packet to Vincenz. "Documents all taken care of. Our berth is ready."

His expression softened when he turned his attention to Hannah. "Hello, my lovely." He pulled her into a hug and kissed her soundly.

"You taste of outside."

"Do I taste of how much I missed you and Vincenz today?"

She smiled, blushing. "Perhaps."

"I have a little something for you."

She barely refrained from clapping her hands and Vincenz leaned around her to kiss Julian. It was meant to be a quick, affectionate peck, but Julian stepped closer, pulling her between them, wedging Hannah between their bodies as Julian did what he did best.

Julian allowed himself to sink into the moment. Vincenz rushed through his senses. So sure in himself, Vincenz slid into a kiss the way he did everything else. With utter surety and total attention.

A nip of impatient teeth against kiss-swollen lips. A teasing taste and a promise of more.

"Yes, I think you taste exactly like you missed us today." Vincenz stole one more kiss before moving back.

Julian held them both to him. Getting used to something he shouldn't. It was absurd to think this could work given the crazy situation all around them. But there seemed to be nothing else he could do.

Hannah rested her head on Julian's chest. "Sometimes you two are so beautiful I wonder if I'm still in the lab. That maybe I've finally broken and this is all a lovely dream."

Julian swallowed around a knot of emotion lodged in his throat. He was a hard man. He'd seen a lot in his time. Very little had the ability to move him deeply. But the sum total of that stood right there against him. Hannah and her wild, brutal honesty, the well of strength she had no idea she possessed. So ridiculously intelligent even Vincenz had trouble keeping up at times.

He looked down into the face he'd give his very life for. Not just strong, not just intelligent, but beautiful. Lush. Her curves had filled in as she'd been with them. As each man had plied her appetite with treats as well as all the things she'd need to get better.

What could he say that could do justice to what she did to him? He bent his head to her mouth, brushing his lips to hers. She sighed into his kiss, giving herself to him.

"Don't you want your present?" he murmured against her mouth before pulling away.

"It's a terrible flaw. I'm avaricious."

She said it solemnly, but he saw the humor in her eyes.

He drew the long, slender silken pouch from his inside pocket and put it in her palm. Her eyes were wide with delight, a smile on her face; the flush on her cheeks was just exactly what he was going for. The way she reacted to his gifts did something to him. Eased some long deep knot in his chest.

He and Vincenz watched as she drew the deep blue lacquer hair sticks from their sheath. "Oh!" She looked up from the sticks and into his face. "They're beautiful. I think I'll wear them today." She tiptoed up to kiss him swiftly. "Thank you!"

He watched her disappear around the corner before turning back to Vincenz.

"I love it when you give her presents." Vincenz kissed him again. "Makes me happy to see your reaction as much as hers."

He shrugged and changed the subject. "We're booked on a standard transport to Asphodel where we'll pick up our private craft. I've gone over the cover with her; she's got a solid grasp on it. Certainly enough to get her out of most kinds of trouble."

"Do you think we're doing the right thing? Taking her with us?" Vincenz had worried, Julian knew. He did as well.

"What are our other choices, baby?" He cupped Vincenz's cheek. "Can you leave her? Even in Ravena where it's so much safer? Can you walk away and know she's back there without the people who understand her most? Who will hold her when she has the dreams? Who will know to leave her be when she lets her hair fall around her face? Hm?"

He'd developed a terrible selfishness when it came to her. But in all honesty he believed they were the best things for her.

And she them.

Vincenz nodded. "I know. I want her where I can touch her. And it's not a lie that she'll be helpful on his op."

"She needs to be useful. You know that. Hells, I feel it too. They took everything from her."

She came back, her hair held up with the pretty ornamental sticks. His heart stopped at her loveliness. And then wondered just what her life would have held for her without the horrible direction it had taken her in the year prior.

"They're very pretty. Thank you." She danced through the room to a song only she could hear. Vincenz put an arm around his waist and they watched her move.

"Are you ready to go?" Julian asked as she twirled to him and he caught her, laughing.

"If you're both still ready to have me."

"Where else in all the universes would you belong?" Vincenz asked and she paused, cocking her head at him.

"Nowhere." Her voice was serious.

"All right then. That's settled." Julian stole a kiss from each one of them before marshaling everyone to get them out the door and to the portal.

Chapter 12

The Portal city was loud. The air scented with the spice of the food carts, the acidic bite of the fuel used in the transports, the mélange of people from all over the Known Universes.

The hum of it lived in her belly, soothing her jangled nerves. Vincenz walked behind, Julian in front, the two of them keeping her from being jostled by the thick midday crowds.

Vincenz kept a hand at the small of her back. A lifeline.

They hadn't asked her over and over if she was okay. Which was nice or she may have screamed.

Vincenz kept an eye on her, Julian knew. But he wanted to kick himself for not getting them on a transport at a less busy time of day.

It wasn't that she had lost it. No, it was the way she so ruthlessly held herself together as they made their way through the lanes leading to the transports. The tension radiated from her body, but she continued to move, never betraying her anxiety to anyone but those who'd know her well.

"Almost there. It's a pretty day, isn't it?" Vincenz had moved from his place behind her to tuck her against his body. His gaze flicked to Julian, who nodded, readjusting his pace so that he came to her other side, his arm around her waist. They squeezed in a little more and the fine tremor in her muscles eased back a little.

She nodded, looking up at the sky.

"A picnic, I think," he said to cut the tension a little. "When we return, we need to take a blanket and a big feast up to the mountains. I know of a lake, crystal clear, surrounded by trees. Hot springs feed into little pools at the northernmost edge. You can swim there even at the height of the cold season."

The tension lines around her mouth eased. "Really? I do so love to swim. I've never gone in the cold season before. Aside from pools of course."

Vincenz pressed a kiss to her temple. "I had no idea you were a swimmer."

The joy on her features underlined how much Julian needed to make it happen. She certainly loved the bathing tub at home. He began to look forward to seeing her frolic through the water.

"It's a good way to keep in shape." She shrugged, but Julian knew it was far more than that to her.

"We need to go up the steps here. I'll keep in front." Julian moved to shield her.

The ticket taker looked him up and down with a smile. Hannah looked the ticket taker up and down right back. At least she didn't feel like throwing up from all the chaos around her. This woman had some cheek to flirt with Julian with Hannah right there.

She sniffed and Vincenz snorted a laugh in her ear. "He doesn't even notice the attention."

"I think he takes it as his due. He's quite delicious to look upon."

And who was she to feel jealous? He was Vincenz's before she came into the picture.

"I suppose. It's part of what makes him so alluring I think. He can render me totally witless sometimes."

"Do you feel that way about me?" she murmured as he pulled her against his body.

"Like I want to lick you all over?"

"Yes, that works." She smiled as Vincenz handed their documentation over to the ticket taker.

Julian took her hand, Vincenz keeping the other as they made their way into the big transport.

"This is a mass transit transport. I booked us into the VIP level. Should be less crowded."

She nodded, knowing her eyes were as wide as a girl's on her first time to the city. She wasn't a universe traveler, though she'd been on a portal transport a handful of times in her life. Of course, some of those were to kidnap her. But Vincenz and Julian were here. And she was with them of her own accord. No one had drugged her or coerced her.

She made her own choices now. Which seemed to help with the fear.

They took a lift up to the special levels and when they exited she saw how much quieter and less crowded it was. She squeezed Julian's hand in thanks.

Expertly, Vincenz led them to a seating area in a far off corner. The departure gongs sounded. A ten-minute warning. She wondered if she should have taken the offer of the medicine Hal had offered. A simple sedative. She would have been conscious the whole time. But the edge would have been dulled.

Thing was, she was done with that. She couldn't live her whole life with the edge dulled by medications. Couldn't avoid the public. She chose the fear over the numbness.

"I brought along something you might like." Vincenz rustled around in his coat pocket and procured a pretty pink box tied with a bow.

"Two in one day? It's not necessary for you two to spoil me so." She grabbed for the box even as she said it. Vincenz laughed.

"We like spoiling you. It's better than any vid to see the way you react to presents."

She hadn't received a lot of presents. Not that she grew up with privation and want. She came from a solidly middle unranked class family. Though her mother was from the Imperium. The community they lived in never seemed bothered by that. Her parents had been practical sorts. She always had enough to wear, enough to eat, a roof over her head and whenever she needed the credits for an extra class or something related to her schooling, her parents gave it to her gladly.

But she hadn't grown up with pink boxes filled with . . . "Oh! Chocolates. How did you know?" She remembered her manners in time and offered them each a piece before she looked down at the shiny dark brown shapes nestled in the tissue paper.

"Spoiling you is one of my greatest pleasures." Vincenz leaned forward and brushed a kiss over her lips.

Chocolate wasn't practical.

But, she thought as the sweetness of the caramel spread through her senses, it was beyond wonderful and she loved it.

"I never had chocolate until a few years ago."

The tug in her belly and the flickering of the lights signaled the transport had unmoored from the clamps and was sliding into place to enter the portal.

"Really?" Julian seemed surprised.

"Sweets aren't good for you. My mother was always worried

about my brain. She said sweets were a waste of calories and energy."
She shrugged. "When I went away to school I was a research assistant
for one of my professors. She made it a point to educate me on the
wonders of things like chocolate." And high heels. Hannah smiled at
the memory.

"Chocolate is totally impractical. Which is why it's so wondrous."
Julian grinned.

She popped another into her mouth, agreeing.

"What were they like?" Vincenz asked.

"My parents?" She swallowed past the lump in her throat. "As I
said, my mother was a practical woman. A daughter of traders, she
went out on trips with her father from quite a young age. I don't
think I can recall anything she wasn't good at. A confident woman,
but not . . ." She paused, thinking of the right words as they flittered
around in her head. "She was not fancy. But she loved books. That's
how she met my father. He was a student and she had a patch of grass
at the university where she sold her wares. He would come by every
day to moon over them. And then he noticed her. She says it took two
weeks for him to look away from the books and to her."

Vincenz laughed.

"She was what he needed. Where she was practical and accomplished, he was . . . he lived in his head. Brilliant, my father. But it was
hard for him sometimes to remember he had women to tend to. He
often stumbled from his offices, surprised to see us, as if he'd just
remembered he had a family. He was a good man. A good person. He
made a difference." She put the lid back on the little pink box and
methodically wound the ribbon back around, tying a bow. Trying very
hard not to let her bottom lip tremble.

Julian took her hand, kissing her fingers. Right at the same time
the transport slid into the portal and began to move. A free fall of
emotions skittered around in her belly.

"I'm sorry."

"It's not your fault. You didn't kill them." She did. Shoving that away, she looked to Vincenz. "In fact I know how many people you contacted to find my belongings. Thank you for that. Thank you both. For everything." Not all her things had been destroyed after all. Vincenz had recovered a large percentage of the things her parents had put into storage for her. She'd go through it all when . . . well, whenever she found the time she supposed. It seemed less important now that she was making a new life than it had been before.

It would be nice to have a day without this insanity messing up her every thought.

"The boxes should be at the house when we return. I was hoping they'd arrive before we left."

It had been hard enough looking through her parents' things. No, it was better to wait. Better not to have sifted through her old life right before she jumped into the wild beyond with these two men on some sort of secret mission.

That part was nearly as exciting as finding herself wedged between two of the most beautiful, sexy and thrilling men in all the 'Verses.

"What about your family?" she asked Julian.

"I don't know much. I grew up in an orphanage."

She cocked her head and looked at him. Sometimes he was so confident, ruthlessly so, in his abilities it was hard to imagine he had hurts of any sort. But it was clear by the brief appearance of the lines around his mouth that he had them.

"When did you . . . meet Wil?" Hanna wasn't sure how much she could say so she tried to keep it simple.

"I was nineteen standard. I'd done two years already in lockup." He looked at his hands and then back to her face. "He came in and interrogated me for over an hour. I don't know if I hated him or admired him. He really pissed me off that day. And then he left. He thanked me for my time and walked out. Two hours later he showed up again and sprung me."

What must that have been like? A man like Wilhelm Ellis through the eyes of a nineteen-year-old petty criminal?

Whatever it was about Ellis, she'd never seen anyone inspire so much loyalty.

"Were you shocked by the massive size of him?" She had to bite her lip to continue asking questions. She wanted to know them, but also understood the public nature of their situation just then.

Julian's gaze cleared and the smile came back into it. "I was just glad he wasn't a jailer there to beat me up. I was a young prick so it wasn't as if I was undeserving of such an event. But he came back and I went into the military."

And he'd met Marame. She rarely spoke of the other woman to him. Not because she was jealous or worried over a dead woman. But because she hated to see the pain in his gaze.

But the shadow didn't come so she left it alone. It seemed silly to feel accomplished just then, but she did. Because it felt normal. The sort of thing you do when you're with people you care about. It had seemed like another life when she'd been that person before. And she supposed it had been another life in a number of ways.

"Was it hard? Adjusting to that new life?"

"Before the military I don't think I'd ever been up so early in the morning. Every day. The only running I'd done regularly was from the polis so I was out of shape. Mentally and physically. There were some days when my legs felt like jelly and I wondered if they'd just fall off from all the running."

She actually giggled and Julian's smile widened. Probably to match the one Vincenz wore.

"Are you mocking me?" Julian teased.

She paused and then nodded her head, her hands over her mouth as she continued to laugh.

That moment seemed to have relaxed the three of them and Vincenz made sure she stayed distracted on the three-hour trip to Asphodel. So many people around made him heighten all his attention.

"When I . . . the last time I traveled things were different," she murmured as they finally reached the ground once they'd disembarked.

"What do you mean, beautiful Hannah?" Vincenz tried not to flinch when he noted the station just ahead. They'd all be scanned and while he and Julian carried no weapons at the moment, they'd all have to submit to a scan and physical pat down. He could use his security clearance to get them all past the scans, but that defeated the purpose of stealth. No, their cover was that of two ex-soldiers and Vincenz's fiancée, and they didn't go around security checkpoints. They went through them like everyone else.

"There are many more soldiers on the streets. They watch differently. Everyone is very tense."

"The war has changed things." Julian paused and tipped her chin up. "Do you remember when we talked about the enhanced security stations?"

Her eyes widened and Vincenz wished there was a way around it. She nodded and looked around until she caught sight of the station just up the lane.

"It will be quick. All right? Vin and I will be with you at all times. I won't ask if you can do this because I know you can. I promise to make you come extra hard when this is all over and we're settled into the private transport." Julian held her gaze as Vincenz caught the effort it took her to get herself together and nod.

"Can I help?" Vincenz brushed a kiss over her lips and watched her brighten a little.

"Pat me down or make me come?"

He laughed, hugging her. "Both. Later."

He knew the effort it took her to appear natural at the check-point. But she did. He knew her heart was pounding. Knew she trembled. Luckily there was no physical pat down so at least she didn't have to go through that part.

Vincenz put an arm around her and once they'd gotten away from the portal station he paused and pulled her into his embrace, but she pushed him back, shaking her head. "No. I can't right now. Just leave me be for a bit." Her voice wobbled just a little, and Vincenz had to stifle his need to comfort.

Instead, he nodded and took her hand, Julian the other, and they walked again until they caught sight of Liora Falk, another Phantom Corps operative, just up ahead.

Hannah took in the diminutive, pixie-faced operative and smiled hesitantly.

"You're Hannah." Liora pumped her hand up and down a few times. "I'm Liora. You two don't forget to check in before you pass through. I trust you know how to get out of the city and to the portal?"

She handed a package to Julian.

"Got it. Are you off in another direction?" Julian asked as he tossed their things into the back of the transport Liora had procured for them.

"Yes."

When she didn't elaborate, Julian simply nodded. "Be safe, Liora."

"And you. Hannah keep these two out of trouble."

She melted into the crowd on the walk across the way and Julian ushered them into the transport before getting them away.

Chapter 13

*O*nce they'd gotten everything loaded into the small private transport, Julian left them both in their small berth and went out to help pilot. The private portal was now under the control of the Federated Military Corps and would take them past the Waystation and directly into Imperial territory without any detection.

It was a slow trip because of the back-channel portals they had to use, but it was worth it to be sure no one saw them. Though the Waystation was now under Federation control after having arrested the Stationmaster and his nephew for treason, Wilhem didn't trust everyone there completely. So they'd sacrifice speed for stealth.

Hannah sighed heavily and burrowed under the blankets.

"Baby, tell me how I can make it better." He knelt at the side of the bed, laying his head near hers. He stroked a hand up and down her body, over the blankets, using the kind of pressure she preferred.

"I'll be all right," she muttered from the center of her nest.

"We're safe now. It's just you, me, Julian and a few other military people."

"I know. *I'll. Be. All. Right.*"

He smiled though he knew she couldn't see him. "Prickly."

She hmpfed.

"Shall I help you past your bad mood, pet? Hm?" He nuzzled her, pulling the blankets back to reveal her face. "I think I have a few ideas on how to take your mind off things."

She fought a smile and lost. "You're incorrigible."

"I am. But you're prickly because it's been a challenging day."

"Not for you." Her mouth set and he kissed it.

"I have my own challenges. Everyone has their own things to overcome. You think you're so special you get to not have something you have to recover from?" It was a teasing challenge, but one he knew she needed. Feeling sorry for her wasn't what she wanted, or what she needed.

Hannah narrowed her eyes at him. But he was implacable. The cad.

He pulled the blankets back and got in, resting his body atop hers, pulling her arms above her head and holding her wrists. She sucked in a breath, aroused to a full-body flush.

He was hard and heavy between her legs, the solid length of his cock against her pussy.

"Well, here you are, beautiful Hannah." He kissed her, gently at first and then he nipped her bottom lip and moved down, across her jaw and down her neck until he found the hollow of her throat and licked, bringing her skin to gooseflesh in the wake of his touch.

She writhed against him, knowing he'd let go if she truly wanted it. But she didn't.

He collared her throat and held her still to return to her mouth. A sound tore from her, from somewhere low and warm, a sound of need and longing. Giving a sound to what she felt every time she looked at one of them.

"What do you need? Tell me."

He wanted her to say.

She wanted to say.

"Ah, are you going to be stubborn?"

Yes. Oh, yes, she was. Because of what it brought from them.

He rolled off and she watched him through a narrowed gaze as he rustled through his bag. He turned and held out two long leather sheaths with buckles. Curious and titillated, she sat up to lean forward to get a closer look.

He held them out. "Do you know what these are?"

Already wet, nipples hard, she shook her head.

"They're gloves. For your hands and arms. But first, take your clothes off."

She stood on legs that were shaky and not from anxiety. Her hair had already been down, but she made equally quick work of her boots, pants, shirt and underthings. He liked to see all of her, so she gave it to him. The scars from the beatings had bothered her, still did to some extent, but the light in his eyes didn't dim when he saw them and so that was enough.

"Do you have any idea how beautiful you are?"

The transport's engines began to rumble and then hum and she closed her eyes just a moment.

"You're the beautiful one." She opened her eyes to stare at him. At that handsome face with his piercing eyes. Eyes that saw right through her.

He shook his head. "Turn around and kneel on the edge of the bed. Hands clasped at your lower back."

She did, not bothering to hide her eagerness.

The cool texture of the leather brushed against her hand. "I'm going to need this arm." She let him take her arm and he slid the leather up to nearly her shoulder. And the same on the other arm.

The sensation brought her breath out in hard pants. She had to close her eyes it felt so good, that squeezing leather over the whole of her arms. She was held, caressed, her skin totally surrounded.

And then it got better.

He leaned in and spoke to her, his lips against her ear. "I'm going to bind your arms together now."

She heard the clink of metal and then felt the tug at her upper arms as he must have fastened the metal clasp, joining her arms together.

She hung her head, unable to not give in to the languorous pleasure of being bound like that. The sensation of it washed through her, calming, soothing, pushing her distress so far away it wasn't even in her thoughts anymore.

Instead she floated in that warm, safe place as her muscles relaxed.

"Yes, I thought you'd like that."

He tipped her forward, keeping a grip on the gloves. Having learned the first time they'd all three been together, she let him take her weight, trusted him to hold her up.

"I'm going to fuck you, Hannah. So hard, so deep and so fast you won't have any time to worry about anything but my cock deep inside your cunt."

She tried to speak, but only managed to get a muffled groan of assent out. But it was enough because he was pushing in. "So wet. You have no idea what it does to me to know you're wet and ready for me at all times."

His cock continued that long push into her pussy until at long last he was buried to his balls.

He fucked into her as hard and deep as he'd claimed. And she loved it. Loved the way he held her up, loved the way he petted over her skin with his free hand, loved the soft croons and raw compliments. Loved that he trusted her enough to not always be so gentle with her.

He made her feel . . . ravished. And she craved more.

Craved that way he and Julian broke through her defenses and took what they wanted. Loved that they both seemed to need it as much as she did.

So she didn't think about whether or not it was normal, or right, only that it made her feel so good and cherished.

"When you go limp and pliant it brings the fine hairs on my arms up. Electric. You're electric, Hannah."

Her nipples brushed against the blankets beneath her body as she breathed in the scent of their sex on the air.

He reached around then, with his free hand, and found her clit, squeezing it between slippery fingers and bringing a rough burst of pleasure barreling through her system.

"I like it this way. When you come and your cunt hugs me so tight I see stars. Come all around my cock."

As if there was anything else she could do but come when his hands were on her. She still wasn't able to make herself come, but they had no such problems and she had no hesitation in letting them do it for her.

She writhed, pushing back against his thrusts as he brought her closer and closer. Her inner muscles flexed, fluttered around the invasion of his cock. Need crawled through her like fire until she burst with it. Arching her back, a long ragged groan of his name from her lips as he snarled and fucked into her body even harder.

Hannah loved that she could bring him to this. Loved that a complicated, strong man like Vincenz could need her this much.

As if he heard that inner dialog, he leaned down, bit the muscles of her left shoulder and pushed in so deep it snagged the long moan she'd been making.

He brought her to the bed then, surrounding her with his body as they both got their breath back. She remained bound, her arms at her back. It soothed nearly as much as his scent and the feel of the way he sheltered her, protected her. His body against hers did exactly what he'd claimed. All she could think about was him and what he'd done to her, with her.

She smiled.

$\mathcal{J}$ulian had come back to a cabin scented of sex and had promptly launched himself into the fray until everyone had ended up a sweaty, satisfied heap. He'd needed that reconnection with both of them. Had needed to touch Hannah, know she was safe, to touch Vincenz the way he'd grown used to in the time they'd had at home over the last months.

But he found himself awake in the late hours, always sleeping deeply after sex. Hannah wasn't in the room so he pulled on clothes to look for her, worried. Not about the other people on the transport. They were sneaking over along with a three-person special team who'd go their own way once they got over to the other side. But he didn't like her scared or lonely.

He found her curled up in a chair reading through the logs and making notes.

She looked up as he came in and smiled. The warmth of it swept over him, softening everything. But his cock, that was another story.

"Are you well?" She got up and moved into his arms where he received her gratefully.

"I woke up and you weren't there. Funny how fast I've grown used to you in my bed." He found so much solace in her. Depending on someone wasn't his strong point. He wasn't sure he should get used to either of them. Not that he had much of a choice; he couldn't seem to do without them. Was that weakness, as he'd been taught by his childhood? Each day he had them both, he disagreed more.

She blushed. "I woke up and couldn't get back to sleep so I figured I'd get work done. I didn't want to disturb either of you."

He sat and brought her with him, and she snuggled into his body with a contented sigh.

"I was proud of you today."

She startled. "Really? I'm sure I made things harder than if it had been just you and Vincenz."

He snorted. "You know what part of me you make harder. Otherwise, you made it easier. Thinking about you kept me focused on getting through without any problems. Would you like to watch a vid? There's a screen just across the room." He indicated the small set up for viewing.

"I used to love movies. So much I'd sneak away from work at midday to see whatever was playing at the cinema house on the edge of campus. When I went to the institute originally, the first thing I did was find the vid zones."

"Used to?"

"Oh, well, I'm sure I still do. I just . . ."

Tended to think in terms of how she was before and what she was now. He got that.

"Sometimes it felt like my thoughts had gone slippery and hard to hold. So I'd sort of re-watch the vids in my head. I had all my favorites memorized, but the last two I saw weren't very good. So I improved on them, re-wrote them as I went. Maybe I should have watched more of those soldier, assassin vids."

She very rarely spoke of her time in the lab, especially from this perspective. Each little bit she gave them only made him fall harder. She was so much more than she thought.

"That was pretty clever."

"It was the only way I could think of to hold on to myself sometimes."

He kissed the top of her head. "I'm glad you did."

"When do we arrive?" She changed the subject and for the time being, he let her.

"By midday tomorrow we should be making the first stop to drop Ash, Brandt and Sera off. And then we'll continue for another half day until we get to Silesia."

She nodded. "I've been to Silesia before. Only in the inner circle near the portal. Stayed at a hotel with my mother. My grandparents were still alive then and we visited them in Monteh and stopped in Silesia before we came home."

"What was it like? Having that foothold in two worlds?"

"I didn't know any differently really. My mother met my father and fell in love. I never thought of it as unusual, probably because in my father's life the academics and researchers also knew people from the Imperium who were colleagues. I had no real idea how hated we were until I was in my mid-teen years. By then it didn't matter as much because I had that connection and who were these strangers to me? It meant I got to eat fun foods no one heard of, or that my mother wore a different sort of clothing than others did. It wasn't anything to me but who I was and how I grew up. Until."

She and Vincenz were alike in many ways, Julian realized. They'd both had a world filled with juxtapositions. A foot in the past and one in the future. Dual loyalties and allegiances. It made them both stronger than either of them ever saw.

He'd carried her back to their bed some hours later after they'd watched a few vids. Vincenz had woken up long enough to encircle them both with his arms and he'd fallen asleep.

Chapter 14

*J*ulian snapped her shirt up over the body armor beneath. She wisely held back her complaints, but it was clear she wasn't comfortable or happy.

"You get used to it." He kept his tone gruff, training her still, even as he protected her.

One of her brows went up and he stifled a laugh. "Even if you don't, it'll keep you alive if you take a plas-blast or explosive projectile to the chest so you're wearing it."

Vincenz snorted in the background but continued to get all his gear in order.

She waited patiently, keeping out of the way until they needed her and Julian went into operative mode, checking his weapons and ammo, making sure all his tech was working and synched.

He'd checked in with Daniel before they'd slipped past the Waystation and they were a go to hit the processing plant. Andrei and Piper would meet them at a site near the plant, they'd handle the

munitions and takedown of the physical site while Vincenz and Hannah would hit all the comm stations to grab data. Julian would be
back up for them as they moved through the plant itself.

"We'll head east and hug that ridge." He pointed on the map he'd
spread out. "We've got to get moving and keep moving to stay in the
shadow as the sun moves."

Away from the Portal city, Silesia was a wild zone. Not always safe
with roving bands of workers who'd broken away form their nearly
indentured existence at the mines and processing plants ringing the
craters. Not that this was such a worry. They'd keep a good pace and
would be high enough that it was real work to get up there.

Hannah had been through the workout he'd custom designed for
her. Her upper body strength was above average. Over the months
she not only regained her stamina but built on it. Still, the hike would
be a challenge. He'd looked at other routes, but this one involved the
least risk. She'd flat out refused to go any other way once she'd heard
that.

Stubborn woman.

He pulled a hat from his bag. "Here. This will help with the heat.
I've got a camera you'll clip into the bill when we're ready. But for
now just use the hat."

She put it on, tucking the tail of her hair through the circle at the
back. Just then, her face devoid of cosmetics, glowing with natural
beauty, she looked incredibly young.

Vincenz pulled out sun shades and put them on her face. "Now
you're doubly protected. The light here isn't filtered as strongly as it
is in some other places."

Thanking him, she stood at the ready. Julian took a look at Vincenz and took point as they headed up the nearby hillside, up and up
until they'd reach the ridge above.

The trees were lush at first, protecting from the ridiculous heat, but thinned the higher they went. Vincenz made them stop here and there, mainly to hand her snacks and be sure she was hydrated.

"I'm not going to fall apart." Her brow furrowed, she fisted her hands and glared at them both as they approached the second-to-last incline. "I know how to ask for a break if I need one. I'm a doctor, I know how to keep fluids in me and rest when necessary. I don't want to slow you down. If I'm doing that, then why am I even here?"

"I need breaks too, you know. And neither of us thinks you'll fall apart. We wouldn't have brought you out here if we thought that. It wouldn't be good for us, or, more importantly, you. Let us take care of you, Hannah. It makes me happy to see you eat and I know you're getting enough water." Vincenz managed to make an order sound like a sweet request.

"That and I'm bossy, beautiful Hannah. I like knowing how the people I care about are feeling. So sit. We're going to take a dip in that pool over there in a few minutes. I want to do a little scouting first while Vincenz sets up some security on the perimeters. The sun is high and it's too hot to walk that ridge. We have to wait an hour or so."

"Swim?" Her features perked up.

Though she'd mentioned enjoying swimming, he had no idea she'd react so positively, but he loved it just the same. Loved bringing her happiness any way he could. Made him feel strong. A good provider for his woman.

He paused at the vista ahead, using the field glasses to spy on the valley below. No activity other than a few animals. There were people farther away but at their closest they still weren't near enough to pose a threat.

But there was a threat in any case. One he was far more vulnerable to and that was the fact he already considered Hannah his woman. He loved Marame with everything he was. Had considered her his, albeit not in the same way he saw Hannah. But the love was the same. The surety in your connection to that other person you trusted to know all of you.

But then his darkness had grown when Marame was lost. To his surprise it had been Vincenz who'd known that darkness and still loved. Surprising to have looked up one day and felt that zing.

His tip into that first kiss with Vincenz had been borne from a great deal of pent-up emotion. And he'd been feeling an attraction to Vincenz that seemed to deepen each time they'd been together.

A row over orders had been the spark. Vincenz had been pecking at him. Pushing him. Boxing him in until he had to look at it, look Vincenz right in the face and suddenly his mouth was on Vincenz's.

He hadn't even thought of having anyone else once they'd kissed that first time. Vincenz hadn't pushed a relationship. He'd let Julian set the pace. It had been all hot need. That heat still existed between them. Every time he looked at Vincenz he wanted him. But what they'd had deepened, roots digging in, uniting them emotionally as well as physically.

And then Hannah, who'd blown in like fluff and had put down roots. At first she was outwardly fragile. But each day she surfaced more. Each conversation they'd had brought him more of her.

She was by turns tenacious, beautiful, stubborn, sexy, vexing, funny. She was inherently provocative without meaning to be. There was something about her that caught the eye. Snagged the attention. The kind of person who listened more than she talked. She looked right at all his dark parts, all the secrets and blood, and she didn't care.

And by the time he figured out that because his defenses had been down with her, she'd gotten under his skin and into his heart, it was too late to do anything but admit his need for her. She lodged herself into all his jagged, empty spots as she gave herself to him and things had just clicked into place.

He sighed and tried to push away the worry. What would happen would happen, and there wasn't anything to do about it other than walk away. And he knew he wasn't strong enough, or foolish enough, to do that.

And what he had was more than that kid who didn't own a brand-new pair of shoes until he was old enough to lift one could have imagined. They had something special. Magical to be with two people who fit him so well.

He'd ride this crazy thing because there was nothing more in all the universes he wanted more. And he'd find a way to ignore his discomfort at feeling want. Because it was having them or not having them, and he knew which he preferred.

When he got back it was to find her sitting on a rock, her back against a nearby tree, her face tipped to the breeze, eyes closed. He didn't want to startle her, but he paused to just look for long moments before he made enough noise to get her attention.

"Vincenz has shown me how to set the security beacons." She grinned as she said it.

"Some women," he said as he dropped his pack and moved to her, "would get that look over a bauble. Not so this one." He bent to kiss her quickly.

She laughed. "So says the man who teased me for getting excited about his presents."

"I think it may be the case that Vincenz is just as pleased with you opening the presents as you are."

"Oh." Her brows flew up and she smirked. "So *Vincenz* is the one who likes that, hm?"

He kissed her again because he wanted to and because she tasted like sunshine. "Perhaps I may as well."

"You make me smile. I like to smile. It feels so new and wonderful."

He had no words for how that made him feel. No words for the depth of feeling she evoked.

Vincenz came back to their spot and sat to kick off his boots and socks. "Hot as hells out there. Beacons are set. Everything okay?" He indicated the spot where Julian had just been.

"Yes. We have about three quarters of an hour before we need to move again." He pulled his weapons off, placing them at the edge of the water.

"Swimming!" Her nude form dashed by them and into the water where she disappeared before resurfacing again a ways from shore. "It's cold, but not too much. Come in."

Julian stripped off completely and ran to join her, laughing as he did. Funny how a serious moment can still give way to laughter at times. He swam out to her. "Who knew you'd like swimming so much?" he teased.

"Oh, I do. It's one of my favorite things and I haven't done it since before they took me." A shadow flitted over her face and was gone. "And out in a lake for even longer. Did you ever visit the landsea back home?"

It was easy sometimes to forget they'd grown up in the same 'Verse.

"During the warm season, sometimes they'd take groups of us out of the city to the shore." It had been miraculous to him, the massive size, the roaring sound of the waves hitting the shore. He'd never seen anything like it before.

"We didn't vacation much and my mother frowned on frivolous activities as a waste of my potential. It's why I developed my love of vids. They were so taboo I'd sneak off to see them when I should have been in school." She blushed as she caught herself getting lost in a memory. "But it was so hot and the water was her weakness. So she'd take me all warm season long. My father would be working longer hours so we'd go. Spend the whole day in the sun just the two of us." She smiled but sadness edged it.

"When this is over, we'll go to Sanctu. For your family. And then we'll swim in the sea."

She brushed her fingertips over his lips. "I'd like that very much. You're good to me."

"No more than you and Vincenz are to me."

"What did he say to you? When Ellis came back to the lockup?"

Julian smiled, moving behind her as he swam, resting her on his chest as he did. Vincenz was doing laps. of course. Like a creature of the water, his man was.

Julian remembered exactly what Ellis had said. "You're an insufferable young prick who thinks he knows way more than he does. It's a dangerous quality. But it can be honed into a weapon. A weapon for something important. If you want to be important instead of yet another kid without a home who goes to lockup most of his life until he finally dies some silent, ignoble death, stay here. But if you can admit you're wrong and you want to learn"—he was quiet a long time— "if you want to be better than what you are now, grab your gear and let's go."

She didn't speak for a while as they lazily swam. She ducked under and came up close to him. Close enough to kiss him quickly. "And you went. He gave you a second chance and so I like him even more. He seems so frightening. But he's rather extraordinary at seeing people. He doesn't get caught up in appearances at all."

"Yes. He's got insight like I've never seen in anyone else."

"It must make you very proud that he chose you. Of all the people in all the 'Verses, he chose you because he knew you had potential."

He turned her, kissing her hard and fast. It hurt to be seen without any varnish. But it was a clean sort of necessary pain, being known by this woman.

Vincenz swam over slowly until he kissed Julian's shoulder and then his neck. "This was a good idea."

"It was." He leaned his head back against Vincenz for a time and they watched Hannah swim and dive.

"Who knew?" Vincenz spoke into his ear. "She's a fish."

"Clearly we need to make sure she has access to a pool at the very least."

"She seems relaxed. I should have guessed given how much time she spent in the bathtub." Vincenz snorted.

She surfaced, grinning. "I'm hungry."

*T*he muscles in her legs burned as they kept up their brutal pace along the ridge. She hummed to herself as she tore apart the code in her head. Reorganizing it. Taking it apart again.

It made the time move faster and helped her ignore the way the two of them seemed to not even be sweating in the heat and she, on the other hand, was a sweaty mess. Of course Vincenz looked like a vid star, still so handsome with his hat and sunshades. He filled his trousers out just perfectly as he jogged.

Jogged.

She withheld a sigh. She'd agreed to come on this operation and there was no way she'd complain. Outside of her head.

They'd notice anyway. They seemed so in tune with each other they picked up on her moods. And pushed. Which was a novelty. She'd never been involved with a pushy man before. And now she had two.

It confounded her. And since she was already generally confounded, she'd decided not to poke at it because it didn't matter why they were with her. She knew enough, felt enough to be secure in the knowledge that they truly cared about her. That was all she could handle just then.

She needed to buck up and handle it. So she dragged another breath into her lungs and kept moving.

They watched her, sometimes covertly, but usually openly. It made her smile, even as it frustrated her. Protecting. Shepherding. She knew they wanted to talk to her, wanted to call out to see how she was doing, but they'd been on radio silence, which had made her slightly nauseated at first. But it wasn't then, Hannah knew that. So she got past those memories.

They continued on for what seemed like an eternity. So long she wondered if her legs would turn into jelly after she stopped moving. But finally they began to slow and Vincenz held his fist up to stay them.

Julian moved to a crouch, took out his field glasses and took a long look out over the valley below and up ahead.

Vincenz came over to where she leaned against a big boulder, muscles jumping. "You all right?" he asked her in a low voice, his gaze roving over her body to verify the answer himself.

"Yes, of course," she lied valiantly.

He cracked a smile and leaned in to kiss her quickly. "Liar."

"My legs won't fall off." Even if she wanted them to just so she wouldn't have to feel them anymore.

"We'll be setting up a camp soon. Kip for several hours and then we'll hit the lab once the moon sets."

Julian joined them. "We're clear. There are a lot of what looks to be soldiers several klicks to the east. Shouldn't be an issue here though."

"I'm going to scout the plant. Let's move up ahead a little. Andrei and Piper should meet us soon." Vincenz put his hat into his back pocket.

Julian took her pack as though she'd asked him to, but she was too tired to argue. He put an arm around her waist and she leaned into his body, so warm and solid.

"I feel better now too," he murmured as he kissed the top of her head.

They walked some ways further and came up over a rise.

And there, in the middle of a hollowed-out niche in the valley on the other side, lay the plant. It looked a lot like the one back on Parron and her breath caught as fear clawed through her memory. She balked, her knees locking and Julian turned to face her.

"It's all right to be scared. But you need to understand that what happened to you on Parron won't happen again. Vin and I will protect you with our lives. We're better than they are, they can't win and we're not going to let them have you. Because you're ours."

He gripped her upper arms and she let herself find the comfort in that. Let herself wade through the fear and the pain and find a way to breathe again.

In her head, she chanted, *My name is Hannah Black. My parents are Shelby and Bertram Black. My name day is in midsummer as the grain is above my head.* Over and over until the haze of panic edged back enough to unlock her knees.

"There you are." Julian kissed her nose and took her hat off. "Sit down on that rock there." He pointed to a nearby rock overhang with a hollowed-out shelter. "I'm going to get a camp set up and you'll be able to rest a while."

"I can help." The fact that her teeth chattered a little didn't do much to bolster that claim.

He hugged her. "I know you can. But I've done this so many times it's easier for me to do it alone." He shrugged like he wasn't giving her a reason to get off her feet and she was just defeated enough to let him.

Vincenz had moved away from their little camp to do some scouting, but he came back some minutes later as Julian had handed her a wet cloth to clean up with.

He crouched to speak to Julian, putting a hand on Hannah's knee. "Intel was good. Looks like a full crew working security. We'll need to get into their system to shut down the automated weapons on the fences. I'll work with Andrei to get the charges mapped. Set a cascade that'll send their systems into crash and then we can take out the soldiers. Two dozen. None of them looked to be Skorpios."

Which was a relief given how terrifying Fardelle's shock troops were.

"Were you trained like them?"

Startled, Vincenz turned his attention to her. "Yes. My father felt it was necessary for me to have the military training they receive." He said it with his chin jutted out, as if he expected her to be repulsed.

As if she would be. "Good. It means you're well trained, right?"

He smiled and his spine relaxed. "So I'm told."

"Best of both worlds. I keep telling him that." Julian slid a hand through Vincenz's hair and grinned.

"You two are going to give me a swelled head." Vincenz shook his head, smiling.

"Gods, I hope so." Julian kissed Hannah's hand and moved back to where he'd been working nearby.

As they ate their meal, Hannah read the map over Vincenz's shoulder and thought about the security programming on the fences. Finally, she spoke. "I think I might know how to turn the weapons against them, instead of us."

Chapter 15

Vincenz was aware she worked on the comm, unraveling code as quickly as it appeared on her display. She appeared to intuit it. To look at it and see it as more than just characters and numbers, but as commands and actions *created* by that code.

He'd only known one or two other people over his life who saw it that way. He was fascinated by how her brain worked. He got the feeling she saw herself as odd and flawed, but she wasn't at all. She was unique. No one he knew thought in the way she did. It was beautiful and clever.

They clicked as they worked together. She would come in, batter a program and slide into a space she'd made to another, deeper level and he'd take the frayed edges she created and rewrite, unlocking levels in his wake and taking over.

All while Julian handled the munitions with Andrei and Piper, who'd arrived only minutes earlier.

She continued on, her face a mask of concentration, brow furrowed, that luscious bottom lip caught between her teeth. Every so often she'd make one of her frustrated snarls that perversely made his cock hard.

Finally, she gave a satisfied grunt and looked up. "Got it."

He followed her path, rewriting, tightening and yes, getting to the spot where she had indeed unlocked the automatic weapons at three layers of fencing around the plant.

He wanted to kiss her so bad he already tasted her on his tongue. "Genius. The way you've tweaked this here to create a command door for us on those guns is going to make things a lot easier."

She smiled at him, embarrassed, but her face flushed with pleasure.

"We're in." He looked back to Julian. "I've got the command now for the fences."

"Nice work."

"Are we ready then?" Piper winced when Andrei tightened her vest, but Vincenz noted she squeezed his hand in thanks.

"Let me get the cameras set in your caps." Julian moved quickly to do it as Vincenz followed her around the shelter.

"You took the vest off earlier. You need it."

She groaned but bent to retrieve it. He held it while she took her shirt off and managed not to get caught up in the glory of her tits.

"Wish I had more time to massage your sore muscles."

She rolled her eyes at him. "My breasts aren't sore."

"They wouldn't be after I massaged them with my cock, no?"

Her breath caught as he tightened the vest and then helped her back into her shirt. Julian came over with the cameras.

"What are you two up to? Looking flushed and guilty." Julian winked and then tested the video feed from his comm. Now that they were live, no more talk of coming on tits.

But it remained lodged in his gut and gave him a few ideas for later, where there'd be no cameras. Just the three of them. Naked.

"We're a go. You all right?" Julian took her hands and looked at her features carefully.

"As all right as I'm probably ever going to be." She nodded.

"Follow Julian. He's point and you remember what that means. If any of us gives you an order, obey it immediately. No matter what." Vincenz checked her weapon, which Julian had been giving her lessons with. "Weapons hot and live." Sort of like she was. "Kill them if you have to. Do you understand?"

This time her eyes were not wide, they had narrowed. When she nodded, it was from utter surety. And he liked that. In the us-versus-them arena, he was always okay with them instead of the us. Especially with what his father's people had done to all the people he cared about.

Sweat trickled down her spine as they paused. The stench of the smoke rising from the stacks at the nearby plant made her gorge rise. It wasn't helped by her general discomfort. She would overcome the fear, damn it.

Piper reached out and squeezed Hannah's hand. "You're here. That's your revenge."

Tears pricked the back of Hannah's eyes as she swallowed back the lump of emotion in her throat. She nodded her thanks before Piper and Andrei disappeared to their west to get about their own business.

If Piper could survive to get her revenge after these people had killed her brother on the last mission like this, Hannah could make it as well. Use her intelligence to help take Ciro Fardelle down once and for all.

She squared her shoulders and continued to inch along as quietly as she could, behind Julian.

Julian, who looked every inch the lethal weapon he was. Weapons strapped to his body, snug uniform pants, shirt stretched over his upper body like a caress. He moved so silently and gracefully it left her a little faint to watch.

As if he knew she'd been fantasizing about licking him, he turned and sent her a smile, tipping his head to indicate they head toward a small access door they'd identified as the best way to enter the plant.

She paused, riffling through their internal systems via her comm. "Wait." She remembered the hand sign and Vincenz clicked his mic to get Julian's attention without speaking.

"What's going on?" Vincenz asked her in very quiet tones. His gaze flitted around the area, always moving, always hyper-aware. His weapon had been drawn, at the ready. Her fear eased at how alert he was, even as she found herself fascinated by this side of him.

"There's a secondary camera back up in the system. There may be one near the door. Let me disable it first."

Julian led them to a more secluded spot, or as secluded as it got out there, while she made her way to the protocols buried in the maintenance programming.

She examined it as her finger hung above the button to execute the command. And shook her head.

"Get them back and away from the inner perimeter."

Julian didn't ask for more details, he just made that quick order in his headset and turned back to her.

"What is it?"

"There's a secondary system here for maintenance. Waste disposal, the incineration of medical waste, that sort of thing. And piggyback-ing that is this code here." She pointed at it and Vincenz hummed.

"Someone was smarter than I gave them credit for."

"Most likely it wasn't even meant to be used as a secret backup for security." But it would set off a full lockdown of the facility, which they didn't need.

"Can you disable it?" Julian asked.

Vincenz snorted and she grinned while she worked with him.

"Wait." She moved past Vincenz's coding and unraveled one last command. "We're all right now."

"Are you ready?" Vincenz asked, his lips to her ear.

It was too late to be anything else, so she nodded and straightened, ready to go.

On the other side of the complex, Julian knew Andrei and Piper had entered, so far catching no opposition.

It would come though. And so he let everything but the job go. The job that'd honed the boy who'd been quick with his fists and his anger into a highly trained weapon. As it did every time, he accepted it, accepted the low thrum of danger and the undeniable pleasure he found in that. More so that he was good at something so few could do. That sense of pride and fidelity to his people. The boy never could have imagined such a thing being important.

But the man knew honor was everything.

His focus shifted, deepened as he began to work through every possible outcome of every choice he made. Vincenz dealt with technology pathways, but Julian tossed himself into the percentages of human behavior.

He had a sense about people. About what choices they'd make. And he was almost always right. But he had to get a sense of who the people who ran this facility were and defeat them. The only way to do it was to go forward.

He took a deep breath, standing at the door a moment before opening it, sweeping his weapon and finding the inner hallway on the other side clear. He waved them into the building and closed the door. No interior security that he could detect. Sloppy.

"One level up." He indicated the stairwell with a tip of his chin.

The first level was storage, but according to the internal map Vincenz had uplinked to their comms, they needed to go to the far east corner to use another stairwell.

Julian approved of the construction choice. Exterior doors were always a problem. Traffic from the outside can breach your security on a regular basis. Directing traffic across the entire width of this second floor would give security enough time to determine if the trespasser was a threat or not.

Of course, he nearly sneered as he ran a scan of the area, that would have been a possibility only if any security at all was in place.

He held them up as they cleared the last long hallway. Three soldiers were at the stairwell they needed. Vincenz moved into position and Julian moved to Hannah, turned her around to face the hall where they'd come from and got back into place, checking his weapon and aiming.

His and Vincenz's breathing slowed as they targeted and without even looking at one another, they shot and then once more to get the last soldier before he could call for help.

Not that their internal comm system was working since Hannah had torn a hole in their security walls and Vincenz had planted the quit command.

He looked back to where she'd remained facing the hallway and took her hand. He'd expected upset, but what he saw was resolve. He squeezed her hand before moving again toward the bodies.

Vincenz had already dragged one of them into a nearby office. Hannah took watch, just as he'd shown her to, and he helped get the other two taken care of.

They moved up, quietly, carefully. He heard people speaking up ahead, just on the other side of the door to the next floor. And hardened his heart. Everyone there was working to make a machine that could, and had, caused death and destruction. They started this war and Julian was only too content to end it.

She clicked the mic and he turned. Four fingers.

Clever. She'd honed her senses while she'd been in that lab and if she heard four people, there were four people. Could be more though, who weren't talking, so they'd deal with that if it came up. The map of the floor had shown this as a processing area. They needed to gather some samples before blowing the place up and that was the next task.

But first.

He opened the door carefully and noted that yes, there were four workers standing near a large bin. He and Vincenz had taken out two of them before they'd noticed the intruders. Instinct took over as he moved, dodging some return fire as he took care of the last man standing.

She'd huddled behind a nearby table, smart woman. Even better, as he and Vincenz began to sweep through the area, she moved to a comm console and began to work, just as she and Vincenz had planned on the transport on the way.

Three more men came at him, slamming a door open and yelling.

Vincenz waded in, took care of one of them while Julian dealt with the other two. In his headset, he heard Andrei's report that the first level had been set for charges and they were moving upward and had taken out two more soldiers on the fourth floor.

Vincenz loaded the sample into his pack and headed to Hannah at the terminal.

"I've stripped the data." She spoke without looking up, her gaze intent on the screen. "The security is better than I thought it would be."

He moved to a terminal nearby. "I'll link in."

He was doing something real. Even as he stood there and aided Hannah in ripping through the Imperialist security wall, he was finally there casting a blow against his father. After all those years fighting on the other side of the line he was there doing what he was meant to.

No one was better to take Ciro Fardelle out but his son. He would avenge the deaths of all those people in the Federation, including those he knew and loved, like Marame.

In tandem, she moved through the data and he came in behind her, dismantling the security. And then once he was satisfied, he unleashed some code of his own and watched it spread out and take root. He'd issue the final command when they'd cleared the plant and knew there was no more data to find.

"Let's go. Three more floors."

And so they climbed again. Met some resistance, but continued to move. Continued to take data when they found it.

And then they got to the top floor.

She'd been so focused on making sure no one was trying to kill her in the hallway behind them that she didn't notice her surroundings fully at first.

It was the smell that snagged her attention. She halted in the doorway as if someone had jerked her backward. And then she looked around to see just exactly where she was.

A lab.

She took a deep breath. She'd been in labs of one sort or another since she could barely walk. This was no different. Or so she told herself as she put one foot in front of the other and continued into the room and headed toward the nearest comm station.

Vincenz looked her over carefully, but said nothing, letting her do her work. Trusting her not to fall apart, and it gave her the energy to continue moving. Continue with her hands on the keypad as she hit the first wall of security.

"Are you getting this?" Julian spoke into his mic, addressing, she assumed, the people watching wherever it was they were.

"This level of security is not present anywhere else we've been so far." Vincenz mumbled this as he continued working. "Too bad for them they had no idea Hannah would be here. Go on, Ms. Black. Rip it open for me."

Fear swamped her but she shoved it away. She would not fail them. She would help them and do her job.

Still, her hands shook a little as she hit wall after wall and then, finally, found a little, tiny flaw. Probably inconsequential to whoever did the coding given how tight it had been everywhere else. But it gave her a place to grasp so she could unravel the data.

Which she did with a growl of success.

It was only the camera in the bill of the hat that kept her from pulling it off and mopping her brow. And now that she'd finished her part of the job and Vincenz had taken over, she moved to get the data sticks in the other comm units to collect the contents as Julian prowled around the floor, keeping them safe.

Though he did look toward her from time to time, and she would be damned to all seven hells if she did anything that shook his faith in her, or undermined his job and the safety of the others.

At last Vincenz stepped back. "Done. This system is on a completely different network. Interesting, isn't it?"

She'd been thinking the same thing. What were they hiding up here that they weren't already hiding with the Liberiam and the production of the portal-collapsing device?

She shook it off. Stupid to make her situation more than an anomaly. There was no reason to imagine this had any link to the lab where she'd been.

Still, the fear made her belly leaden. Her skin cold and clammy even as she sweated.

One foot and then another, she kept moving, kept following them as they grabbed the data sticks and headed out.

"We need to head across this floor to the far southern stairwell. Andrei and Piper are waiting on the roof." Julian looked her over carefully but thankfully didn't ask if she was all right.

Because she wasn't and it was only sheer force of will that kept her upright and not hyperventilating.

Working quickly, everyone wanting to be done, she didn't notice the soldier until he was on her, knocking her to the ground.

The fight-or-flight impulse took over and the fear broke through as she clawed at his face and kneed him in the balls. He tried to hit her with his weapon but she dodged and sank her teeth into his wrist. The animal who had lived in her for so long surfaced, snarling, snapping, fighting for its life.

She heard them nearby, knew somewhere that they were also fighting with soldiers and that she was on her own.

On her own. The memories of the helplessness came back, threatening to suck her under. But she held on, fighting.

Then she heard Wilhelm Ellis in her ear.

"His weapon should be on your right side, Hannah. Make sure the safety is off and end this. You can do it."

Some part of her heard and registered, her fingers scrabbling through the blood to grab the weapon he'd dropped when she'd bitten him. It was him or her and it sure wasn't going to be her.

Vincenz managed to toss the soldier off and snap his neck, his every thought on Hannah. Julian could handle himself, but . . .

He found her then, on her back, covered in blood with a man nearly twice her size beating at her with a closed fist.

He wasn't even aware he had started growling until he'd propelled himself across the hallway and was nearly on them.

And then he heard weapon fire and time seemed to stop until she shoved the limp body of the soldier off, gasping and still kicking. Still caught in the nightmare.

He reached her then, on his knees, and pulled her to sit. "I'm here. It's over. It's over, beautiful Hannah."

She blinked quickly and he used his shirtsleeve to wipe the blood off her face. "Are you hurt?"

She swallowed and shook all over. "We have to go."

He helped her to her feet, keeping an arm around her waist until she took a shoring breath and straightened. "We have to go," she repeated.

Julian stalked over to them both, looking her over carefully. Long enough that she got vexed and Vincenz felt a little better to see it on her face.

"Most of it isn't my blood."

Julian tightened his jaw until Vincenz heard the click.

"Let's move."

She nodded once and straightened her shirt.

At the opposite end of the hall lay their exit. And as Vincenz also noted with a snarl, more labs.

He thought quite seriously about picking her up, tossing her over his shoulder and getting her out of there.

In fact he'd already begun to turn around to do it when she saw him and read his intent and shook her head. "*No*. Not like last time."

He was confused by her for long moments until Julian spoke. "Not like last time at all, Hannah. Look behind you on the floor. He tried to hurt you but you fought back. You're no one's victim."

The rage rolled from Julian in waves. Vincenz hadn't seen him this bad since the early days after Marame had died. His chest heaved with the effort to stay under control and idly Vincenz wondered what they thought of this back on Ravena as they watched.

She shook her head as if to clear it and with a great deal of effort, made herself walk through the doorway of the lab.

Vincenz wanted to save her, but Julian had the right of it. She was no one's victim, and if he carried her out, especially before he gave her the chance to do it herself, he'd be robbing her of the opportunity to rise above what happened to her.

Locked cells.

Julian stormed to each one and looked inside. "Nothing in here, baby. I promise."

She continued to walk, her gaze on the door to the stairwell.

And then she stopped and moved to the comm station, pulling out the data stick and getting to work with hands so shaky it took her three tries to get it in.

Tears streamed down her face but she kept working. Vincenz realized then that the burning in his chest wasn't just anger, but it was admiration and love.

Seven hells she undid him.

Her movements were jerky but she clamped her lips together and continued. Julian paced like a caged animal, keeping close to her.

Vincenz took up the station next to her, knowing she had to do this, hating that she did. Knowing his father made this happen.

And even so upset, her work was perfect. He followed her and did what he needed to, fighting the need to protect and comfort, knowing the quicker they finished, the quicker they could leave.

"There's a lot of encrypted data here," he murmured. So much he was sure they'd stumbled onto something important.

Her fingers weren't as confident on the keys as they had been before, but she finally stepped back, her job completed.

Julian glanced at Vincenz before approaching her slowly. She jerked her attention to him, eyes wide.

Julian paused, not moving any further but to take her hand, which she allowed.

"Nearly done." Vincenz ripped out the chip from inside the sheath of the comm unit. She'd already extracted the data from the system in there, but there was no harm in taking the chips, she'd argued back at their camp. He agreed.

The command now embedded in the system, he hit execute, and they headed to the stairs to get the seven hells out of there.

Andrei and Piper waited for them on the roof with an ultraquiet zipper. Vincenz had never been more relieved to see Andrei as they hustled inside and strapped in.

Hannah's gaze was glassy, her hands still trembling as Julian simply buckled her in and then himself. She didn't even shoot him an annoyed look.

Vincenz sat on her other side, pressing against her as they lifted off and moved away so very silently.

Andrei handed Hannah a little black square. "If you press that switch, the explosives will go off."

Her eyes cleared as she took him in, understanding he was letting her do the final work on destroying the plant and those labs.

"Now?" She swallowed hard.

Andrei nodded and squeezed her knee as he sat back.

With her gaze intent on the structure just out of shock wave range of the zipper, she flipped the switch.

At first nothing happened that they could see, but as Vincenz knew, it would be just a short time and then . . . ah, there it was, the first round of explosions and fire. The building shook and began to fall as more explosive packs went off.

"We can get you closer to the portal this time. That ridge was a bitch to climb," Piper said as she piloted away from the site once they were sure everything had been destroyed.

Chapter 16

Julian's head ached from having to control himself so tightly. They managed to get Hannah off the zipper. Andrei had indicated they'd meet again soon as Piper had hugged Hannah, speaking to her quietly.

Oh his sweet Hannah.

They were far closer to the portal and their transport, but would still have to spend another several minutes to get to it, skirting the Imperialist authorities, who'd been involved in clashes with Federated soldiers who'd landed just a few days before.

Vincenz had taken her pack, though she'd protested. He'd also paused to pull the shirt of Julian's she wore so often from it and hand it her way. Tears had brimmed in her eyes, the sight of it, and of the way she hugged his shirt around herself had torn through him.

Her hair was down, around her face, a face drawn with deep lines of concentration, and she'd most likely have a riot of bruises around her cheek and right eye from the beating she'd taken. But he knew she needed to get to the transport on her own steam. Needed to do it for herself. But he wanted to do it for her anyway.

He and Vincenz moved as quickly as they could, both needing to get her inside and safe.

The small clearing was empty and the security they'd set was still in place so they hadn't been discovered. In his earpiece he heard the chatter from the local authorities who'd discovered the processing plant had been burning and were on their way out to the site.

It was a good thing to have trouble in the opposite direction, keep their focus away from them until they were well and away from there.

Though, he thought as he prepared the transport while Vincenz fed data into the uplink, he wouldn't have turned his back on the opportunity to kill some Imperialist assholes.

It wasn't until sometime later, once he'd gotten the transport through the portal and on a set route, that he was able to step away and go to her.

Vincenz was still on the comm with Daniel so Julian passed, squeezed his shoulder and kept moving to her.

When he found her she had wrapped herself in a blanket and wedged her body between the bed and the wall. Her head rested on her knees, her hair obscuring her face.

Rage coursed through him. His hands fisted, wanting to punch someone, wanting to hear the crunch of bone. Wanted retribution for what they'd done to her. To Marame. To Vincenz, whose face so often bore guilty lines over what his father had done.

"Hey there, baby. Can I take a look at you? You took some hits in the hallway back there."

She looked up and as he'd suspected, bore the beginnings of quite a spectacular black eye. He pushed his anger back and opened up the first-aid kit.

"That your first black eye?"

"No. Before . . . just once. And then they didn't hit me in the face anymore."

He dragged a breath into his lungs and let it out slowly. "That doesn't count. You were abused. This time you got it brawling."

Her bottom lip trembled.

"Is it that you killed a man?" He tried to remain calm as he took a wet cloth to her face to clean off the remains of the blood spatter. He needed to be sure it wasn't her blood. And to focus on something other than wanting to go back to Silesia and take on the entirety of Fardelle's army.

She shook her head, allowing him to tip her chin and get the cut above her eyebrow cleaned and bandaged.

"I don't feel bad that I killed him." She winced as he unbuttoned her shirt and he found an abrasion on her neck. "Don't get mad that I took the vest off."

He paused, brushing the pad of his thumb over the curve of that trembling lip. "Can't be mad at you. It's impossible. As for not feeling bad? Guilt is wasted on doing what you have to do."

"Does it get easier?"

He helped her to her feet. "I need to take the shirt off." He'd learned early on to part her with his shirt and other things he'd given her with a careful approach. And her permission.

She held still while he looked her over, running his hands over her ribs to check for anything broken. He couldn't resist leaning down to kiss her shoulder, over the yellowy purple bloom of a bruise.

"To answer your question . . . it should never be easy to kill anyone. In that way, no, it doesn't. But over time I've become better at letting the parts that make sense matter to me more than the parts that don't."

She nodded, thinking over what he'd said.

Something he'd never said to anyone before.

"Sometimes we have to do things because they need doing and no one else is willing." He held up the small patch of pain medication. "I'm going to put this on. You're going to be very sore. Not just from the fight back at the plant, but the hike too. Just a standard pain blocker."

She held her arm out and he applied it.

"Thank you." She took his hand and kissed his knuckles, keeping hold. "My turn to check you over."

She dealt quickly and efficiently with the abrasions on his knuckles before she moved to the cuts on his face.

He allowed her to take his shirt off. "That's what you did on Ceres, isn't it? The hard thing no one else would do. The right thing." She cleaned the gash on the back of his right arm. "This needs some sealant." She reached past him to rustle through the kit until she found what she needed.

Yes, he supposed, it was exactly what he did in Ceres. Sometimes he'd felt so alone, but now he had Vincenz and Hannah. Hannah, who watched him with those big, startled eyes and understood everything. Vincenz who walked the path with him, knew the same demons and loved him anyway.

She cleaned his wounds quickly and efficiently as they both forgave themselves a little bit.

"Do you promise to always treat my gashes and bruises without a shirt on? It hurts far less when your breasts are part of the package."

She smiled a little, which had been his intent. "It might be simpler if you stopped getting injured."

"Wrong line of work for that. Still, might come in handy, having my own personal doctor."

"At some point I'm going to need a job again. I'll take a wild guess and say there would probably always be a need for one around you and Vincenz."

He bent to retrieve his shirt, drawing it around her body again to keep her warm. The deeper they went into the portal, the colder it would be, especially in such a small transport.

"Don't want you getting a chill. Come lay in the bed with me?" he asked, gently sliding his palm over her hair.

Her gaze met his and he wanted to growl at the shadows of anguish there. He wanted to ask if she'd like to sleep. If she needed a sedative. Anything at all that would soften what she was feeling. But he knew she wouldn't do it.

So he shook the blanket she'd been using out and pulled the bedding back so she could slide in. And he slid in after, pulling her close as he buried his face in her neck. She sighed, the sound catching slightly, as she snuggled back into his body.

Words he didn't know how to say lodged in his throat as the warm, solid feel of her body stirred him, even as he found a deep comfort there.

Let himself take the comfort from her, even as he gave her everything he had to give.

Moved, Julian closed his eyes and took a breath of her. He kissed her neck and she turned to him, tears in her eyes, her bottom lip trembling.

"Are you all right? Do you need a booster on the analgesic?"

"I'm sorry." She shook her head, wiping her eyes on his shirt, which made him smile even as he was annoyed by her apology.

"What in the Known Universes do you have to apologize for?"

"I fell apart."

"No, you didn't." He shook his head, keeping his arms around her, dipping his mouth to taste her briefly.

"I don't want to be like this."

His heart ached. "You're perfect the way you are."

She shook her head. "No."

"I wish you could see what I see."

She blinked up at him.

"Today you handled yourself as well as any other operative. Operatives who've had years of training. Operatives who grew up in rough, hard places. You're strong, Hannah Black. You're strong and smart and you forced yourself past some scary stuff because you knew there was a job to do. And you did it."

"You didn't have any trouble."

He laughed a little, but there wasn't much humor there. "Of course I did. I totally missed the soldiers in the hall." He raked his gaze over the bruises on her face, remembered the rage as he'd turned to see the man beating her with closed fists, but he was fighting his own battle, too far away to stop it.

"Ellis spoke to me. In my earpiece."

"He did? What did he say?"

"He told me where the man's weapon had fallen. Told me I could do it."

"And he was right. I'm sorry it was necessary."

Interesting that Ellis would break through and speak to her when he so very rarely ever commented while they were on an op. But Wilhelm had his own plans, and his own ways of making them happen, so Julian had ceased to question why he did what he did a long time ago.

She sighed, hiccupping a little, and burrowed into him. He tightened his embrace, noting the way the tension seemed to wisp away from her when he did. "Close your eyes and rest. I'll be right here. Vin and I will take care of you."

She shuddered and took a deep breath, her hand fisted in the front of his shirt.

Chapter 17

After having been out the entire day, Vincenz moved with purpose from the front entry to where he knew she'd be. In the doorway to their workroom, he paused. Simply watching her as she sat at the comm station—her comm station as it had come to be over the last months. Features intent, fingers flying over the keys, pausing only to grab a pen and take longhand notes.

In the days since they'd returned from Silesia, she'd dived into the data they'd mined from the plant. But he knew she still held herself responsible for nearly breaking down. He'd tried to disabuse her of that notion, as had Julian, but he saw the shadows there anyway.

It was time for a new approach.

She looked up and her concentration washed away with a smile. Love flooded his senses. "Hello there, Operative Cuomo. You look like sunshine today."

Oddly pleased, he got to his knees in front of her. "Why, hello there." He gripped the chair arms, caging her in, slow and steady, the tension between them building. "And why is that?" He leaned in and nipped her bottom lip. Breathed her in and fell into her mouth. Forcing himself to only take a taste.

"You've been in the sun. Your hair lightens when you've been in the sun."

"Ah." He took another taste, meandering through the wonder of kissing that mouth. She sighed, her fingers sliding through his hair. He pulled away but it didn't last long and he was back for more.

His tongue teased along the curve of her bottom lip before he sucked it into his mouth, grazing it with his teeth.

She shivered against him, moaning so very softly.

"You taste like late summer. Sweet, and ripe, delicious," he spoke into her mouth.

She smiled against the kiss. "I missed you today. It's hard to think without your sounds and the way you smell."

He rested his forehead to hers. "We have the entire house to ourselves. No visitors. I'm going to fuck you hard enough to make you scream."

Her pupils enlarged as she gasped. And gave herself over to him.

Greed sliced through him. "I don't remember a time when I didn't need you so much." He kissed the fluttering pulse in that sweet spot under her ear. She softened, exposing her throat to him.

"No one thinks worse of you that you had a rough time back on Silesia."

She stiffened and sighed, trying to straighten. But he kept his upper body against hers, his waist insinuated between her thighs.

She wavered between anger and searingly hot desire. She shouldn't get hot all over when he was this way with her. So aggressive and dominant. His way of holding her down was no less powerful than Julian's was.

Her reaction to and connection with it went to her bones. All the noise and chaos wisped away when he took over.

Her entire body had lit. Already wet. Each time he pressed himself against her, the seam of her panties tightened, pressing into her pussy, stroking against her clit. That wave of pleasure broke over her annoyance that he'd brought up Silesia. Sent all her thoughts of anything but his mouth on her neck, the slight sting when he bit and more pleasure when he licked over the bite, skittering away.

He pulled away quickly, leaving her gasping at his sudden absence, reaching for him. Covetous hands stroked over her arms, up her sides and over her breasts. He hummed his pleasure at the hollow of her throat, the vibrations sliding straight to her nipples, which now slid against his palms.

"Bare breasts. My favorite."

Before she got the chance to formulate a reply, he'd pulled the front of her shirt away from her body and then ripped it open, sending buttons everywhere. The shock of the cool air against her skin beaded her skin, but her nipples hardened because of the man kneeling between her thighs.

His gaze on her was a tangible thing and she suddenly felt a little bit like a mouse with hawks about. Only the fear was replaced with anticipation.

"It is not that you faltered when confronted with not only labs that looked a great deal like the one you were held in but a man who tried to kill you with his bare hands, having to kill that man and then had to walk through yet another set of labs, this one with cells."

She made a face, annoyed. Why did he keep bringing this up? She had no one to blame for her terrible performance but herself.

He stood. "I'll be right back. Don't move."

She frowned at his back. But didn't move.

When he returned it was with one of the little black bags he kept all manner of naughty toys in.

He bent, kissing her and before she knew it, her wrist was strapped to the arm of the chair. She pulled against the hold, sending white-hot shards of pleasure through her system.

At first she knew they *wanted* to be rougher with her than they were. But they remained ever so gentle as she healed. But it never felt totally real to her, their desire for her, their connection to her until the first time Vincenz had let his control go and gave her exactly what she wanted, how he wanted to.

And when he trusted her to know what she wanted, when he trusted himself to let himself want her, to give himself permission to *take* her, everything felt utterly right.

She kept her words, watching him as he bent to strap her other wrist to the chair.

"You and I have a problem, Hannah."

He knelt again, this time to strap her ankle to the chair. And then he paused to look into her face carefully, assessing, she knew, to be sure she was still all right with what he was doing.

"That's the difference, you know." Her face was solemn.

He rested his chin on her knee. "What do you mean?"

"Between what happened to me—what they did to me while they kept me prisoner—and what you do to me." She licked her lips just before he pinched her left nipple, tugging until she arched as well as she could against the leather pressing into the ultrasensitive skin at her wrists.

She stuttered a breath. "This is what I want. I choose this."

He paused, caressing her neck. So much emotion on his face. She was utterly helpless against what she felt for him. There was nothing she wanted more than to be here with him. To be his.

"I should cease to be surprised by you. I try to get you to see a truth and then you turn around and do the same to me." He swallowed hard. "I don't want to hurt you. I don't want to make you think about before."

"That was about *breaking* me. About stealing parts of me until there wasn't enough left to stay together. It was about humiliation and harm. What you do, what Julian does, it's different because it's about holding me together, not ripping me apart. For a time I felt as if I might fly away. I was so light, so empty, it felt as though I could lift up and float on the breeze until no one knew me anymore."

She needed him to understand, but she barely understood it herself.

"I can remember who I am when you touch me."

He bent to her nipple, licking over it. "It's because there is much about us that is the same. A foot in two worlds. Your story makes me think of my own though it's not entirely the same. You came to me, let me give you a place to call home and then you did the same for me."

"You're my heart." She sniffled.

"Then I want you to forgive yourself for being human."

She pulled against her restraints to get more contact as he pulled away.

"Ah, ah, ah." He bent to retrieve something. A blindfold. She looked at him and then down to the fabric he held.

She froze. And he moved closer. Her heart pounded.

He crowded her then and drew her in. The way he always did.

He drew the silk over her breasts and then let it rest against her shoulder. He held up a small silver clip and then he put it on her nipple. Slowly tightening it until right on the very knife-edge of pain before moving back and putting a similar clamp on the other nipple.

She drew in a shaky breath as the not quite pain bloomed into something warm and insanely pleasurable.

"Yes. Gods above and below, Hannah, you're beautiful." He kissed her again, leaving her panting, his taste painted all over her senses. He flicked a fingertip over one of her nipples and it sent a rush of wetness to her pussy.

Her words were all gone. Far, far away so she nodded. Hoping he knew that meant she wanted more. More of whatever he had to give.

Feeling exposed, drawn by this woman in ways he'd never have imagined before, Vincenz knew he'd have to push her harder to get her to admit the truth of the situation.

Her gaze had returned to that glossy state she'd had before he brought the issue of their trip to Silesia up.

"Do you trust me?" He kissed her neck and then down her chest down to the waist of her pants.

"With my life."

Her words were serious, as was the look on her face. He took the blindfold up and let it trail over her nipples, which he imagined had begun to throb in time with her heartbeat. And while she watched, he drew it into both hands and straightened.

He placed it over her eyes. She was stiff at first, but he kept caressing her, keeping his hands on her until she relaxed.

Moving to her ear, he whispered, "If it gets to be too much, you only have to say so."

But he knew her, knew that well of strength she possessed and he knew she'd never give in too soon. If she said it was too much, it would be.

She wouldn't be the only one excited with anticipation. He had to force himself to go slow, to make this something pleasurable, even as he broke through her defenses. The last thing he wanted was to remind her of the labs. But they were past that now, he believed. She let him put the blindfold on, and he could scent her desire. She was with him on this journey.

Rustling through the bag, he found what he needed. Heavy-duty scissors with curved tips to use on clothes.

Starting at her ankle, he took that delicate foot, bare, which made him smile, and held it still so he could cut the leg of her pants, all the way up her body to the waist.

She gasped, but there was no fear.

He paused to kiss the back of her knee, now exposed to his touch. She shivered, as he knew she would. As he did.

And then the other leg.

He pulled the tattered remains of her pants off, tossing them over his shoulder. She wore panties he knew Julian had given her. Bright pink against the cream of her skin. Startlingly pretty.

He kissed up her inner thigh, breathing hot air over her cunt, and then kissed his way down the other leg.

She pulled against the restraints, but not to get free.

To get more.

He hummed, his lips barely touching her through the material of her panties. She whimpered, arching into his touch.

"Contrary to what you might think, you're allowed to have moments where you have to pull yourself together sometimes."

She growled and he wanted to laugh. So fucking strong, even when she was being disobedient.

He opened his mouth over her and that growl dissolved into a whimper.

Smiling, he sat back on his heels. "You're not a trained soldier. And yet it was your work, your contribution to the mission that Julian and I, hells, Ellis and Daniel too, found to be the most useful."

"*Why?* Why now?"

He grinned at the stubborn line of her mouth.

"I've tried it the nice way. Julian's tried it the nice way. And now, well, I'm trying it the *really* nice way."

She smiled and shook her head.

"You're so beautiful." He leaned in and licked the underside of her breast, one and then the other. He kissed up the curve of her ribs. "And you're human."

"Don't want to talk about this."

He kissed over her lips, just a ghost of a touch, and then carefully touched the cool metal of the scissors to her hip, slitting the panties down one side and then the other.

"You're not in charge. I decide what to talk about now. Unless you want me to stop?" He said it, his lips just a breath away from her labia. Knowing she'd never use the words. Too stubborn, his beautiful Hannah. Too turned on. He slid his fingertip over her clit, juicy already.

Her head fell back and he stood. He kept close enough to make sure she heard each click of the zipper teeth as he pulled his trousers open and retrieved his cock.

Instinctively, she turned, her lips parting. There was nothing else to do but slide the head of his cock, glistening with pre-come, across her mouth, dipping inside just a moment, before stepping back.

It was good the blindfold was on so she couldn't see just how thin his control was right then.

His hands shook a little as he pushed the chair back against the table to keep it stable.

He teased her mouth with his cock until her lips were swollen and glossy and the need in his belly tore at him with sharp claws.

"Do you want my cock, Hannah?"

"Yes!"

"You didn't fail. You triumphed."

She groaned. "*You* didn't cry. Back at the plant."

Her pout only titillated him.

"So what? I don't do a lot of things you do. I pee standing up. Why do you hold on to your tears like it weakened you?"

"I don't want to talk about this anymore."

"I do. Anyway, you know what to say if you're done."

"I'm not done with the *sex* part. Just the talk about what happened on Silesia."

"Hm. Well, I think we established who was in charge already. Are you changing your mind about that?" He stroked his cock, thinking over the next steps. "I'm stroking my cock right now. I wish it was in you. In your mouth, in your cunt, between your tits. But it's in my hand instead."

Her features scrunched up and he had to bite his bottom lip to keep from laughing.

She struggled, trying to get closer.

"Please."

"Please stop punishing yourself first."

"Oh my gods! Vincenz, *why* are you torturing me?"

He bent to speak in her ear, pressing his body against her so she knew his cock was so very close. "Because I love you, Hannah Black. Because I think you're good. And intelligent. Stronger than anyone I know, and I hate seeing you punish yourself for being human. You had a slap in the face. A reminder of what they did to you and it got to you. But not enough to break you."

"They still have power over me!"

"Not in the way you mean. Or even in the way they meant it to. You didn't break. Not then, when they held you. And not when we were in that plant. You paused and then you did your job. You. Did. Not. Break. The rest is meaningless. They didn't win. *You did*. Every day when you wake up and keep doing this job you've taken on, every day when you open your eyes and greet the day and *live*, you win."

She sighed.

But the anger had left her posture.

He went to his knees again, kissing down her belly and straight to her pussy. He couldn't deny himself a taste of her.

Held open, strapped to the chair, blindfolded, he knew she felt every breath, every lick. He gorged himself of her. Licked and sucked, his fingers played against her gate and back to the tight star of her ass.

She shuddered and sighed his name.

He devoured that just as his mouth devoured her cunt. Tasted every part of her he could reach. Fucked her with his fingers. His cock was so hard it throbbed angrily, demanding to be where his fingers were.

Her muscles trembled and then tightened as orgasm approached.

And then he pulled back.

"I'm the one who gets to play at punishing you. The good way to be punished," he said, kissing the seam between leg and body.

He stood, undoing the hasps holding her body to the chair but leaving the blindfold.

"No!" She reached for him, found his shirt and held on.

"Oh, baby." He kissed her then. "I'm not leaving you. I'm not ever going to do that."

There were tears in her voice as he picked her up and walked her over to the main worktable and set her ass on the edge. "Don't move."

He brought the chair and situated himself between her thighs again and went back to work.

She came hard and fast, the sweetness of her on his tongue.

He leaned back into the chair and brought her down to his lap. Totally naked, her shirt having fallen off, all while he was still dressed. There was something ridiculously hot about that. About the utter decadence of her beautiful skin bared to his touch and gaze as she perched in his lap, her cunt just right above his cock.

"I'm going to fuck you awhile. To take the edge off. And then I may pull out and finish in your mouth."

She nodded, catching her lip between her teeth a moment.

And then he had her rise a little, enough to grab his cock and position it just so.

He held her there, the tip of his cock embedded in that wet heat. A pretty flush had built up her chest.

"Can I touch you?"

His breath gusted from his mouth and he let her weight take her down the length of his cock until he was buried in her to his balls. He took one of her hands to his mouth, kissing her palm. "Yes."

She caressed his shoulders as her pussy fluttered around his cock, driving him so close to the edge he had to work to keep himself from coming right then and there. Her fingers sifted through his hair until she got a better hold and pulled. "More. Please."

"You know how I love it when you beg."

She arched her back, taking him even deeper.

His hands at her waist held her still, pressed down against him, pubic bone to pubic bone. "You're dangerous. And human."

Remaining still, he had to concentrate on the way the blindfold was nearly indistinguishable from her hair it was so dark. Not as soft though.

Her mouth screwed into a displeased knot. He kissed it until she gasped, opening up and he took over, sliding in and owning. Taking. Making her his as she made soft sounds he swallowed up.

"You're going to stop this nonsense about how you shouldn't be allowed on further missions. First because you're important and we need you. Second because neither of us is leaving you behind. Lastly, because you're better at it than you'll let yourself admit and I'm not having any more. You gave yourself to me. To Julian, and we want you to stop being so hard on yourself."

"Soldiers don't cry."

He gave her four hard thrusts, sending her breasts bouncing and her head went to his shoulder as she held on.

When he stopped she made the sexiest little growl.

"You continued on with the job. That's what matters. Not that you faltered for the briefest of moments."

"I'm messed up. Broken and crazy. I can't even talk right anymore."

He snarled, ripping her blindfold off. "Give me your eyes."

She did, reluctantly.

"You are *not* crazy. You are *not* broken. And I'd challenge anyone to have come out of what you endured without being more messed up than you ever were." He kissed her hard, not closing his eyes, letting her see into his heart.

"As for how you talk? *I love the way you talk*. If I love it, and Julian loves it and you get the job done, who cares what anyone else thinks? Hm? Why do you allow any of that to matter?"

"I slow you down. Sera doesn't slow Ash and Brandt down. Piper doesn't slow Andrei down."

"You do no such thing." He rubbed himself across her upper body, making her writhe. "Sera and Piper have their own burdens to carry. But their men love them for all they are. Why do you think you're not prone to the very things that make me love you the most? Even with tears on your face you broke through those protocols and enabled me to load the virus."

"I hate that I can't be like I was before." Her bottom lip trembled and he nipped it.

"I hate that too. But you can't be. I can't be the same young man who arrived on this side of the Waystation all those years ago. Julian can't be the man he was before Marame was killed. *Everyone* is broken in some way, Hannah. You're special and beautiful, but you're not alone. Being a little messed up gives you perspective. Important perspective. I won't have you ripping yourself down about it. For being human and vulnerable."

He watched her finally understand. Saw the moment when she got it. And then moments later, accepted it. Maybe not all the way, maybe not forever. They'd always battle what happened to her in those labs. Sometimes it would come back and none of them would know why. But each day she could accept herself more. Let herself be who she was. If they could, she could.

"Ah. Yes?"

Tears running down her face, she hugged him tight and he let himself treasure her. Let himself be vulnerable too, to this woman who'd shown him so much without even intending to. She was his own sort of miracle and he never wanted her to forget that.

She nodded.

And he took off one of the nipple clamps.

Sensation rushed through her body, rocketing through her senses from nipple to cunt. She writhed on him, impaled, held by this gaze, by his cock and by his heart.

She touched his cheek. "Yes."

He grinned and stood, carrying her easily toward the bed chamber. Each step he took brought him deeper into her pussy as she held on tight, her legs wrapped around his waist.

But then he backed her against the doorway and she held on as he fucked into her body hard. Hard and fast. Her nails dug into his shoulder as his fingertips sank into the muscle and flesh of her ass, holding her just how he wanted.

His gaze never left her body. Roved over her hungrily, always returning to her face where she waited for that attention. Just like he expected. The warmth of that flushed through her, of knowing how much she affected him. Understanding he'd just stripped her to her very bones and let her see herself for what she wasn't as well as what she was.

"I want all of you, Hannah. I won't have any less than that."

She kissed him. "I've been yours since you walked into that cell and saved me."

Holding her up one handed, he removed the other clamp and she nearly knocked herself out when her head cracked the doorjamb. She couldn't control the yell, the rush of dark, sticky pleasure that claimed her, pulling her under.

"Make yourself come."

"I can't!"

"You can. I want it. You want to please me. Come around my cock."

She must have looked dubious because he continued speaking. "You're mine. They don't own you, they never did. Don't let them own your pleasure either. Finger your clit."

She took a deep breath but didn't let her gaze leave his face. He nodded, pleased.

He continued a hard, deep pace. Rendering her nearly mindless with pleasure.

Unashamed, she found her clit, reaching down to gather all that wetness he'd created to circle it up and around, over and over.

"You're already close," he murmured before he bit her ear, making her gasp. "Imagine Julian's mouth on you."

"As you fuck him."

He caught his breath and raised a brow at her. "Yes, yes, you do like it that way. So do I."

So she did. She remembered what it felt like to have Julian there, his broad shoulders holding her thighs wide open, Vincenz behind him on his knees, hand on Julian's cock. Each time Vincenz thrust into Julian, Julian's mouth slipped against her cunt in a different way.

Her nipples *throb-throb-throbbed*, each time a drumbeat in her clit answered as she touched herself. As Vincenz touched her. As he loved her.

And then it happened. The first rush of climax washed over her as she looked at him, surprised. He grinned. "Gods above and below thank you!" He went to his knees as she continued to come around him. Fucking her, pinning her, one of his hands rested at the back of her head to protect it from knocking against the door.

When he came, his mouth found hers in so much more than a kiss. He breathed her in, tasted her, reveled. And then bit her lip when he came, her name a low snarl on his lips as he stayed deep.

Chapter 18

Wilhelm looked across the table, finding Hannah's gaze. "Repeat that. Where do you get this information?"

She swallowed and took a moment, but then began to speak. "The data we retrieved from the second set of labs appears to refer to a bio-agent."

"Prove it to me."

Vincenz started to speak but Andrei kicked him in the shin. Wil didn't have to look to know this happened; he knew his people damned well. He appreciated Vincenz's protective nature, but Hannah was strong enough to make her case, or he'd chosen incorrectly when he'd let her come on the operation to start with.

She opened the file in front of where she sat. "I sent this to your comm earlier this morning once I'd made all the connections." She met his gaze. "And I did."

He resisted a grin. He had no doubts, but he still wanted her to prove it.

"As you know, my specialty is virology. The data here in this cluster refers to a virus. Two of them to be specific. One of them"—she paused to look at Vincenz briefly—"is what Petrus Fardelle is thought to have died from several standard years ago. The second is close to that one, but it's different in several small, but important ways."

"And those ways are?"

"The version Vincenz's brother died from was so virulent I'm quite frankly surprised more people didn't get sick before they put him into quarantine. If what I'm reading is correct, it did infect two other people, both of whom ended up dead as well." She paused to open a comm panel and sent an image to the screen at the head of the table and used the tip of her pen to point. "This is the adapted virus. You can see the differences here and here. It's been spliced with a few other viruses. I can't say with total certainty until I see the virus for myself, but if this data is reliable, what they've created is far heartier. And deadly.

"These notes say the incubation period is five to seven standard days and during that time the patient will not be contagious. Creating a false sense of calm. Apparently vomiting is a key side effect, which also sends contagion out in a fairly wide arc as well as serving to dehydrate an already deadly fever. Transmission is shockingly easy from person to person."

Wilhelm leaned back scrubbing his hands over his face. "So the second virus is longer lasting, not as fragile and created in such a way as to spread to even more people."

She nodded. "And to visit upon you a public health problem that would strain even the largest, healthiest government."

"The portal-collapsing devices were bad. This is . . . this is something far worse." Daniel spoke from his comm station back on Ravena.

"Daniel, work with our public health people there on some basic preventative measures and disaster plans. Liaise with Hannah. If this happens, we'll need to be ready on the ground." Wilhelm turned his attention back to the woman in question.

"You asked me . . . back on Mirage, what I think they wanted from my head. I believe this is what they think I saw." She kept his gaze.

He tended to agree with that. She had a brilliant mind and clearly they didn't want to waste it if they didn't have to. "*Have* you seen it?"

"Not this one. But I'm an expert, so I've seen and have studied most catastrophic viral illnesses. It's part of my specialty. There were some bouts with an illness from Earth called cholera, which is similar in some ways."

"The rumors of it breaking out in some of the frontier Imperialist 'Verses are true then?" Daniel asked.

"I was . . ." She licked her lips and visibly pulled herself back together. "I was still captive at that time, but from the reports I've studied and this data, yes. But this . . . well, the second version of this virus has markers quite similar to an ancient contagion called smallpox. The second version of this virus here has the blisters, though they don't show up until it's far too late to treat. Smallpox was one of the main foci for my research when I was getting my degree. It's why they brought me on at the Institute."

"How can all this have happened and we didn't know of it until now?" Daniel spoke again, his features hard, angry.

"We had some of the raw data. But we're impeded by the difficulty in getting any real information from the Imperium. Their closed nature kept this a secret." Wilhelm sighed and looked back to Hannah. "Am I correct?"

"Certainly the fact that the Imperialist 'Verses are closed and information is very closely guarded and censored would add to the levels of secrecy Fardelle's administration has put into play."

Wil knew there was more she wanted to say. Could see she held it back.

"Go on. Hard truths are truths nonetheless."

"In my experience, which is admittedly limited, the military has a focus and sometimes it makes them blind to other things." She paused and licked her lips. "What I mean is, there's this old saying about how when you're a carpenter every problem is solved with a hammer. Viruses aren't plas-rockets. They're imminently more dangerous. They're a strain on local and national government. They're difficult to treat once they hit the populace. They're like wildfire in the outback or in an inner city where people are on top of each other. For instance, there were several fast-moving viruses that hit the edge 'Verses in the Imperium fifteen standard years ago. Killed a third of the population in three weeks. My father helped create a vaccine for it. If I can get his academic papers, I might be able to find more. They wouldn't have destroyed them. Those papers would be in the University's archives somewhere. But he was only allowed in because of my mother and her citizenship. They refused help from others."

"So you think they knew this? That they kept you prisoner because of your father's vaccine?"

"I don't believe this is about my father. But I believe his work, and then my work, might have touched on some of this. At the Institute I refused to allow them to create a large amount of the virus I had been studying. The one related to version A, as it happens, though I had no idea at the time. I don't know why they felt they should keep me alive or break me."

He wished he knew. "Can Fardelle use this virus? The second version."

"I think he can. And I think he will. What I've found seems to indicate they haven't found the right way to release it."

"Why not just send some infected people into a transport?"

"It will burn out that way. To achieve a true, totally effective blanket of the virus they'd need to mount a large, complicated plan all at once. If it burns out, that gives the medical personnel time to treat and quarantine. Some people will have immunity; they'll make a vaccine. No, they have to find a way to launch it wide and at once. Cripple our systems with so many sick and not enough to treat them effectively. And they have to get it here, which isn't as easy as it sounds."

"How do you think we should deal with this then?"

"I thought you'd never ask." The corner of her mouth tipped into a smile and she tapped the keys to show new data on the comm screens.

Julian couldn't disguise his pride. She'd worked so hard on her presentation and totally nailed it. She had spent all her waking time on the research, calling some of her former professors and colleagues to get help on bits and pieces as she was allowed.

He'd been impressed by her tenacity. This was her arena. The thing she'd trained for for so much of her life. She'd been interested and helpful with their work. But with her work, her passion came through. She was sharp, focused, intent on answers. Her ease showed rather than the strain he knew she bore just making it through each day.

She'd come alive and he realized they were seeing part of the woman she was before. And felt the loss of her, even as he'd discussed with Vincenz that the woman she was now would be powerful in her own right.

But he thought about that loss a lot. Ached for her, even as he found himself irreparably changed by her presence in their lives.

Roman spoke via the screen from his office in Ravena. "Your data doesn't include any real locations for this research? A lab or facility?"

Vincenz smoothly took over. "Somewhere in the Imperium. Most likely in one of their Edge 'Verses. A 'Verse that is secure, so probably not Silesia as they get more traffic than most. As to exact details? There are still some parts of the data that are encrypted."

"The decryption program Vincenz already created will come in quite handy now." Julian said this as he followed along on screen.

Vincenz sent a look that was only for him. Julian smiled and then his gaze shifted to Hannah. She watched him through her lashes and smiled so very sweetly. Which was funny given that just beneath all that sweetness there was such a dirty, dirty girl. He shivered and tried to focus, but he couldn't get the mental picture from his head. The mental picture of the way she'd been just that morning, arms above her head, bound to the posts of the bed as he fucked her so hard all she could do was stutter out her moans of delight.

"How long?" Daniel interrupted.

Vincenz took a deep breath. "We're working on it on three shifts. Soon I hope. Within the day or two. This is far more complicated than the last data we had to decrypt."

"Is this about the data or about how easily we broke their encryption the last time?" Daniel asked.

Hannah snorted and then blushed furiously when everyone looked to her. "I apologize. It's just . . . easily seems an odd word to use. The program Vincenz wrote is pretty groundbreaking. Not an easy thing about it except probably when he hit the button to execute it."

Wilhelm struggled to hold a smile back. "You're correct, Ms. Black. We know how hard Operative Cuomo worked on the program. Why do you think I snatched him up the way I did? But the question was more referring to whether or not we were caught and they responded, or whether the data being protected was that much more integral that they locked it better."

"Fardelle isn't stupid. He's shortsighted, clearly, but he has goals."

Daniel tapped his pen. "Carina has given us a great deal of information as to how his inner circle works back on Caelinus. Added to the new developments and the way his security has tightened, I think it's safe to assume this is both very sensitive data *and* they know we cracked their program before."

"Well, of course they do."

"I want you to poke around a little with these revolutionaries. Figure out if it's cloud talk or if they have a real plan." Wilhelm sat back, clearly annoyed by the very idea.

Daniel appeared torn between amusement and agitation. Hannah simply looked at the screen, holding her eye contact with him. Julian didn't move, content to watch her come into her own again after jumping at shadows for much of the last several months. She found her courage when it was them. That was something he never ceased to be touched by.

"So what I propose is that we head back that way and get some intel the old-fashioned way as well," Daniel said at last.

Wilhelm sat back. "We're sending multiple teams in. Andrei, Piper, Julian, Vincenz and Hannah, you'll head to Asphodel. Use the private portals to head into the Imperium from there."

Nodding, Julian thought it would be a good team. Now that Daniel had been promoted, he spent more time in Ravena handling strategy. It was a natural progression of his career and Julian believed no one better for that job. But in the wake of Marame's death, it left two teams a few men down. Smart to put them together that way. Julian had worked with Piper before; the two of them would be able to collect intel as a team. Andrei would plan. Vincenz and Hannah could handle all the tech.

All in all, a smart choice. And he'd get to keep Hannah close by, which would make him and Vincenz feel better.

More talking. Roman was taking hits back home from those vocal opponents of the war with the Imperium. They wanted to collapse the portals in the Edge 'Verses to stop the ingress of any Imperialist traffic forever. But in doing that, it would also strand the farther-flung 'Verses because even at faster than light, a spacecraft would take years to get to any habitable 'Verses. It would be casting them adrift to sink or swim. Nearly two million Federation citizens suddenly abandoned.

Roman wouldn't allow it. Julian knew it. Understood it and respected it. There was no way he'd abandon the Edge. Ever. The Edge 'Verses would know that and follow Roman anywhere. It was actually smart as well as principled.

"Do you have the time to meet now? Set up the basic plan?" Julian turned to Andrei.

Ellis rapped the table with his knuckles. "I'll be part of this discussion if you don't mind. I have a few ideas."

Chapter 19

She'd never been to Asphodel except for a quick hop between public and rogue portals on the way to Silesia the last time. Now she had the time to take a closer look, and what a wonder it was.

Hannah couldn't help but stare out the window of the zipper Piper flew out toward her family's compound. "I'm glad you're out here with us," Piper murmured. Andrei sat in the nav seat at Piper's right feeding her information here and there. The two moved like a single unit. Hannah loved to watch them work together. The silent, brooding male and the vivacious, energetic and beautiful woman he so clearly adored.

"I've never been here." She pointed to a black gray swell in the sky off in the distance. "What's that?"

"Storm. Big one looks like. We'll set down and get inside. A storm like that isn't something to see firsthand." Julian had his leg resting against hers; she knew it was his way of touching her, calming her. She had no complaints about that. She wore his shirt beneath a sweater of her own. It felt good against her skin. Like him.

Piper spoke, interrupting them. "It's about ten minutes away. We're fine. You can tell when it has that reddish gray bloom at the bottom that it'll be large. Most likely started out in the deep desert."

Hannah had read about the storms, but it was a different thing entirely to see them firsthand. The descriptions she'd read had nothing on the reality. In the distance the sand swirled, large and alive.

"All right everyone, we're touching down in just a moment."

Effortlessly, Piper whipped the zipper around and set it in such a small spot on the ground if Hannah had been standing there, she wouldn't have believed a plane could have fit.

Several people came out immediately and helped them out before pushing the zipper into a small outbuilding.

"They'll tie it down. Cover all the places the sand can get in. It messes with the inner workings of everything," Piper explained.

"I like it that you tell me things. Can I help?"

Piper smiled and took her hand. "Yes. Come on. I'll show you what needs to be done."

Piper never treated her as if she were fragile. Though, Hannah thought as she locked the tie into place, Piper had seen Hannah at the very worst. Had seen her that day when Vincenz had come to free her. Then again, Piper had been drowning in her own grief at the time. Still, Hannah liked just how utterly matter-of-fact Piper was. Hannah never felt as if she had to hold herself together so tightly when she was with the other woman. It was a relief to build a slow friendship with someone who never seemed to want to fix her or think she was about to fall apart at any moment.

She only had that with Julian and Vincenz, though they both worried for her.

"Nice job," one of Piper's people said to her as he checked over Hannah's work. "Let's get inside. There's a feast waiting."

Julian approached, his hand out, and she took it, smiling. "Food."

"I know. You'll like it."

The air hummed against her skin as she turned her face up. There was so much chaos in the environment there. The shuss of sand and dirt sliding together off in the distance.

"Do you like how it feels here?" he asked as if she'd said it aloud instead of thinking it.

"It's raw." She licked her lips. There weren't a thousand barriers between Hannah's senses and the world around her. Not here. Here it was unvarnished. "What's the smell in the air?"

"Ozone. The spark of the big storms. It builds up and around, like a tunnel of wind and earth. Sometimes so fast it can tear the flesh from bone. Not here, but out in the wild areas. There's lightning in the center. Out in the wilderness there are patches of scorched earth turned to glass."

"Really?" How thrilling to see nature do something like that.

"Would you like to see it? After the storm breaks and it's all clear, of course."

She squeezed his hand. "Yes. Yes, please. I'd love to see that."

He pulled her toward the largest building. "Then that's what we'll do. Living quarters up here. Vin has taken our bags in already. Come on inside so they can lock down the rest of the house."

She followed him, breathing in the strangeness in the air.

"Stirred up."

He paused after he'd closed the door and latched it, setting a seal. "Me? Oh, yes, beautiful Hannah, you always stir me up."

She smiled, flattered. "Oh. That's nice. I meant the atmosphere here. It's twisty and turny. Nothing knows what it wants. So it does it all. Churning. The air, the elements all churn against one another. Beautiful chaos."

He leaned down and kissed her with so much gentleness it made her heart ache. "Your mind is so beautiful. That's exactly what it is here. That's why the storms are the way they are. The magnetic fields in the planet are unbalanced. Not in a catastrophic way. But not everyone could survive here."

She shook her head. "No." But she could. Maybe.

*I*nside the place was a happy sort of chaos. She knew Julian kept close, partly because he wanted to and partly because he was worried for her. But this sort of jostling, hugging, laughing reunion didn't stir up bad feelings or make her uncomfortable.

It was beautiful to watch the people in the room light up at the sight of Piper. She'd built something out there in the middle of nowhere. A family of sorts complete with children running around underfoot.

"You're Hannah." An elderly man took her hand in his own, gnarled with age and wasting disease.

Disarmed, she smiled. "I am. And who are you then?"

"My name's Arch Candless. Piper told me she was bringing you. Speaks highly of you."

That warmed her insides. "That's a lovely compliment. May I help?" She wrapped both her hands around his.

Surprised, he nodded. "With what, dear?"

She kneaded, gently, lightly, where she knew the muscles would be tightest, making his tendons brittle. "I can ease your pain. A little anyway."

He blinked and held his other hand out. Julian moved to the side.

"Why don't you sit?" She indicated the couch where she'd been about to plop down. He did and she joined him, Julian moved to her other side. "My landlady had Pendelton's Disease. Do you take medicine for it?"

"Hard to come by out here."

Not if she had anything to do with it. And she doubted Piper knew of this need, or he'd have his pills.

"The compound in the pills will help keep your tendons from becoming so brittle and painful." She took his hand in hers again and began to knead, massage, press warmth into the fingers she was sure had spent a lifetime of toil. "Do you use heat with them? To ease the discomfort?"

"Are you a med-tech too?"

"I'm a medical doctor."

He grinned at her and she responded, unable to do anything but return that sweet joy he'd just gifted to her. "Your Mai and Dai must be proud."

She blinked back tears and he understood. "I'm sorry. Did you lose them recently?"

"They were killed because of me."

Julian gripped her shoulder. "No, they weren't. They were killed because Ciro Fardelle is a heartless villain who figured it was easier to kill them than let out news that you were missing. And maybe to keep anyone from figuring out what he was up to. To hurt you. I don't know the whole of it, but I sure as seven hells know it wasn't because of you."

"Sounds to me like your man here has the right of it."

"Tell me, Mr. Candless, do you have a garden here?" She couldn't deal with what Julian had told her. Not just then.

"Ach, that's very nice." He moved his fingers a little as she worked on the heel of his hand. "We do. Kenner, that's Piper's older brother, he set up the greenhouses some years back. We can feed everyone through the rough times. 'Course, Andrei, he set up the cisterns so now we have enough water too."

"Until we can get some medicine to you, I can make a paste if you have the right botanicals. Put on a thick layer every night. Do you have gloves? Not heavy work gloves but something a little lighter. Wear them over the paste and let your body absorb. It'll give you some relief. If you wrap them in hot cloths that would be even better."

Piper approached. "There's a whole lot of food to be eaten." She bent to kiss Arch's forehead. "Hello there. I see you've met Hannah. Already holding hands? Julian, you and Vincenz had better watch out. In his day there wasn't a single man in Asphodel who could dance better than Arch."

"Me and my lovely Bettina. That's my wife. She passed three years ago." He sighed heavily and Hannah felt for him. "Hannah here is massaging my aching hands. Says if we have the right green bits in the greenhouses she can make some goo that'll help with the pain."

"If we don't, we'll get them." Piper's gaze met Hannah's. She'd talk with Piper about the medicine later. A man like Arch was likely not to want to have a fuss made, or to feel as if he was being given charity. So they'd make it happen quietly.

"I'll do your other hand and then get some food. You can tell me about your Bettina while Julian goes and gets himself a plate." She sent him a look and he narrowed his gaze. "I'm fine. I'll just be right here. Go on."

"It can wait. I'm fine here with you."

She looked at him. Loving each feature of his face. "You've been working all day. You haven't eaten in hours. Go on. I'll be in shortly. It's totally safe here, you know that."

His gaze darted to the dining room and then back to her. "I'll just be right there. Don't wait too long; you haven't eaten in hours either."

Arch watched him walk into the large dining/living space only to be greeted by hails of hellos and welcomes. He was a lively man, Julian. His smile was quick, but not always to the bone. But this place seemed to relax him a little and she was glad for it. She wasn't one for crowds really, but he was.

"He worries for you."

She continued to massage his hand and wrist. "He's a good man."

"More'n that. Most men in this house are good men. But that one has eyes for no one but you."

"He's afraid I'll lose my mind, I wager."

Arch leaned in close. "Looks all right to me. I doubt that's his worry. You got some pretty eyes, Hannah."

"You're a flirt, aren't you?"

"I know a pretty woman when I see one." He winked and she laughed. She laughed and it didn't feel like someone else was doing it. It didn't feel as if she had to laugh because if she didn't everyone would look at her funny.

"Tell me about her. Your Bettina."

"Vivacious. Oh, she could sing and dance. So pretty. She was no more than a kid when we met. I was a kid too, 'course. We courted awhile. Her Mai wasn't going to be having the likes of me sniffing around, getting her daughter pregnant and taking off. We married when she was seventeen standard. I was nineteen. Had our first babe two years later. The land here is hard on a woman's beauty. On her body and mind. But my Bettina was gorgeous until the day she left this world. Lovely. Had long pale hair she used to let me braid until my hands got too bad. We had six kids together. All of 'em here working this land with me. Some of 'em have kids of their own. Wives, husbands. Feels like I planted a crop with her and we still keep reaping the harvest."

She blinked back tears. "She sounds wonderful. I bet she loved you just as much as you loved her."

"We got on. She had a big job, you know. Me and six kids." He grinned again and her heart wanted to burst. "My grandsire used to say every lid had a pot. You know every person had their match. She was my lid."

Julian poked his head around the corner to catch sight of her kissing Arch's cheek.

"Do I need to keep an eye on you, Arch?"

"If you can't keep her, you don't deserve her."

Piper came in again. "Vin just finished up. He's asking after you. Come and eat."

Arch stood, holding his elbow out for her to take, which she did. "My hands sure do feel better. Thank you, very much."

"I can do the same tomorrow. Teach a few of the others, your grandchildren perhaps? To do the same. Then we'll work on that paste. Do you have a doctor here? A med-tech?"

He led her into the chaos of the dining room. Vincenz had come in from wherever he'd made his super-secret connection back to Ravena and only had eyes for her. Her heart tripped, slamming into her chest as he turned every single bit of his attention her way.

"We have a traveling med-tech. There's a clinic in town, but it's hard to make the trip very often."

She'd get the info about his medication and go from there. If she had to visit Asphodel twice a year to see to him, she would.

The doctor she was before they'd taken her stirred in her belly for the first time in longer than she cared to remember. The sharp relief of it brought her to halt a moment and take a deep breath before she could move again.

Chapter 20

Vincenz wanted her all to himself. They'd been surrounded by people every moment for the last few days except for the hours when they'd fallen, exhausted, into bed after hours of planning and preparation.

Julian had taken him aside when he'd completed his comm with Daniel and explained Hannah was with Arch, tending to his hands.

She was a medical doctor; it was her path. He knew this. But she'd been hesitant when he'd brought it up before, asked if she wanted to practice medicine again or work in a lab. It had been the first time he'd seen her tend to someone as a doctor. Not as triage, not because she had to, but because it was what she was.

It warmed him. Helped him believe they could get through all this, that she was getting better and that when all this was over and things slowed down, they had a future where all three of them did what made them happiest and came back together at the end of each day.

They'd shared a raucous meal with Piper's crew. She'd sat between him and Julian, content and relaxed. She'd clearly charmed Arch and because of that, pretty much everyone else.

But things finally got quiet. She and Piper headed out to the greenhouses, Andrei shadowing them along with Vincenz. Then she'd spent another hour making the paste for Arch, showing several of his grandchildren how as well.

This had been the first time he'd seen her in a social situation—apart from work, which was different. He liked watching her smile. Was gladdened that no one seemed to be the slightest bit bothered by the way she sometimes spoke or phrased things. He knew they were overprotective, but she was special, and theirs.

She came into their bedchamber smelling of sage and lavender. Pausing, she bent to kiss Julian's temple. "Thank you. The soap was perfect. Just what I needed."

Julian paused, his fingers on the keyboard halting before sliding up and into that river of dark hair. "Smells good."

Julian, the jokester. The man who pretended to never take anything seriously brought her gifts. Vincenz was sure Julian told himself it was for her, to make her happy. And it did, no doubt. But it did something for Julian too. Softened him, gave him that connection with her. Took him outside his normal reaction—pain, anger, defensiveness—and into something else. It wasn't reaction. It wasn't defense. It was just that he was happy pleasing her.

All that artifice slid away. With Hannah, even more than with Vincenz, Julian could be vulnerable.

She looked up to lock her gaze with his. "I feel like I haven't seen you in hours."

He was on his feet, pulling her into his arms before he'd even made the conscious choice to be there.

"I've been greedy for you. But instead of burning the place down to get you all to myself I had to be content enough to wait until the still of night when you were ours again." He brushed his lips against her mouth and she opened to him with a sigh.

Everything clicked into place.

Julian snorted from his place on the comm and Vincenz peered around her body. "Yes?" He helped himself to two handfuls of Hannah's ass as he did, snugging her to him tighter.

Julian growled but kept his fingers on the keys. "Not fair while I have to finish this."

Vincenz moved, his front to her back, spinning her to face Julian.

He unbuttoned her sweater, sliding his palms against her breasts through the material. She made a soft sound and rested her head against his shoulder.

"So many layers of clothing. Thwarting me," he murmured into her ear before he bit the lobe and her knees buckled just a little.

Julian continued to type but his gaze was locked onto Hannah, onto Vincenz's hands all over her.

He stood back enough to slide the sweater off and then came back to her, dealing with one of Julian's shirts she liked to wear. It was warm from her skin, scented of Julian and her both. Vincenz bent his head and kissed her shoulder as he bared it, sliding the shirt back.

All she had on beneath was a tank. He could see her nipples, pressing, begging for attention against the thin material.

"Mmmmm." He pulled the tank off and she was totally naked to the waist.

"Julian," Vincenz said as he thumbed her nipples, back and forth, back and forth. "You need to come over here and eat her pussy. I want you to bury your face between her thighs. Surround yourself with that sweet cunt. Make her come."

She shivered, writhing back against him, her ass sliding over his cock.

"You know she's wet. And she tastes so fucking good. If you don't, I will."

Julian stood and the chair clattered behind him. His pupils were so large they swallowed the color of his eyes. He moved to her like a starving man and fell to his knees with an anguished groan.

Vincenz slid one of his hands up, collaring her throat and she jumped a little as she moaned.

Julian pulled off the sleep pants she'd put on after her bath, leaving her in her pretty blue panties and nothing else. He slid his palms from her ankles up her legs. Pausing to bend and kiss the inside of her knee, the middle of her thigh, to breathe over her pussy but not touching.

"Take your cock out," Vincenz said quietly.

Julian's gaze locked with Vincenz as he unzipped his pants and pulled his cock from his shorts. He fisted it a few times until Hannah whimpered, reminding them she was in need.

"Eat her cunt and fuck your fist. But don't come yet."

Vincenz took two steps back to angle her body better as Julian pulled the panties from her legs, spread her open and took that first lick, his eyes still on Vincenz.

Hannah's fingers clutched the waist of Vincenz's trousers as her eyes fluttered closed.

Vincenz didn't know where to look. Julian on his knees with his mouth on Hannah's pussy made him so hard he thought he'd lose it. But Julian on his knees, his cock in his hand, pumping up and down slowly as he devoured Hannah was also ridiculously beautiful. Hot.

Tender.

He touched Hannah like she was something precious. Just watching it made Vincenz happy. This big, tough man filled with all the rage an army of angels could produce on his knees, his heart laid bare not only to Vincenz but to Hannah. She was that piece that had been missing.

She gasped in a breath and began to tremble. It wouldn't be long now, he knew. After her initial fears that she wouldn't be able to come, it happened that the two of them were quite good at making that happen. As good as she was at coming, though he realized he didn't know if she could make herself come when she was alone and needed to remember to ask. Maybe even to get a demonstration.

"Does she taste good, Julian?"

"Gods, yes," he managed against that slick, tender flesh.

She sobbed a moan as her nails dug into Vincenz's side. He continued to collar her throat. Her pulse beat steady against his open palm. Her nipple beaded hard against his fingers as he rolled and tugged.

She hitched a breath and arched, her upper body pushing back against him. Julian let go of his cock and hauled her close with both hands, his fingers digging into the flesh of her ass to hold her to his mouth as he brought her off.

"Shhh, remember we're surrounded by people sleeping." Vincenz smiled against her ear as she turned her face into him and whispered her cries until she went limp.

Julian stood, pulled her up and into his arms and laid her out on the bed. "I'll be right back." He kissed her hard before turning back to Vincenz. "You're in trouble now."

Julian's trousers were still open. His cock out, still hard, so hard it tapped his belly. His chest heaved as he nearly panted. The impact of all that arousal, of that utter supreme maleness hit Vincenz with so much force he grabbed Julian's forearm and suddenly it was all teeth and tongue as they met in a collision of a kiss that seared Vincenz right to his bones.

"You taste like our Hannah."

Julian's tongue slid along Vincenz's lips and then he nipped, hard enough to bring a gasp. "I do. And now you do too." Julian took his hand and led him back toward the bed. "You're going to suck my cock now, Vin."

Hannah hummed her pleasure. "Yes, please."

She lay there, tousled and mussed, a pinkish glow on her skin from the flush of climax. Totally comfortable as she watched her two men love each other. There was no shadow on her features. Just adoration.

"I'm trying to think of a way I can suck your cock and fuck that pretty pussy at the same time."

Both men got into bed as Hannah tried to roll from the way. Julian caught her and pulled her back, wedging her between them and she shivered and went into that soft place of submission and compliance.

"I like you right here. Your softness against me as I kiss Vincenz." Julian walked his fingers down the curve of her side and paused to crack her a sharp slap on her ass.

She sucked in a breath, her eyes wide. He traced his fingertips over the reddened skin and she broke over in gooseflesh. "Mmmm, do you like that too, beautiful Hannah?" Julian licked up her neck and met Vin's mouth as he kissed across her jaw. She liked being there between them, the pressure of their bodies against her. Loved watching them touch and kiss, loved the way the scent of their skin mixed and mingled into something deliriously sexy.

"You need to put his cock in your mouth, Vincenz. I need to see that too." Hannah ran her hands all over Vincenz's torso.

"I do. Roll over. Ass up, head down. I need in you first."

He moved back a little and she quickly obeyed. Julian got to his knees behind her and traced a fingertip down her spine. "So pretty." And then he scored his short, blunt nails down her back as she gasped and shuddered, making noises into the pillow instead of her normal vociferous cries.

"I love the way that looks." Vincenz kissed over the light red lines and then took himself in hand to tease around her gate. "The bed is low. If you stand next to us while I . . ." Vin's head tipped back for a moment as he pushed all the way into Hannah's cunt. "While I fuck Hannah, I can turn and suck your cock. Just how you like it." Vin's mouth tipped up into a knowing smile.

Julian scrambled from the bed, grabbed Vincenz by the hair and angled his mouth near enough to get his cock into it.

Hannah squeaked. "I can't see!"

"You don't need to see. You need to be fucked."

"Hmpf. Who says?"

Julian laughed at her cheek. "I say."

She pushed up to her elbows and Vincenz groaned, frustrated, around a mouthful of cock. "You do?"

"You're so in for it when . . . seven hells, Vin, yes, yes, fuck yes, swallow my cock, baby." Julian brushed his hand over Vin's hair as he watched his cock slide in and out of Vincenz's mouth, dark and wet.

Hannah moved, pulling forward and Vincenz growled.

"I want to see." She moved to her back and Julian couldn't argue with this view either.

"Fine. Make yourself come," Julian challenged and Vin hummed his agreement.

She blinked up at him, her mouth losing some of the sass she'd worn only moments before.

Vincenz pulled back. "Aw, baby. You come so beautifully. We know you're not shy. At least not with us. Are you worried you can't?"

"I can't. I mean, I can, obviously." She indicated her pussy and then Julian's mouth. "But not . . . I can't do it myself. I think I'm broken."

"The last thing you are is broken. I keep telling you that. Vin, get that mouth back on my cock or I'm going to get vexed."

Vincenz snorted but turned back to Julian's dick and got back to work. Julian kept his gaze on Hannah, on the rise and fall of her chest as she breathed. On her eyes, glossy with unshed tears of frustration.

Julian slid his fingers through Vin's hair and guided him, fucking into his mouth the way they both liked it. "Yes, yes, yes. Swallow all of me you can. Just like that."

Hannah lost the sadness around her mouth, but Julian wasn't about to let her retreat into a place where she felt broken either. For the moment though, he was content with Vin's mouth on him, with her legs entangled with Vincenz's on the bed.

"After I come down his throat, he's going to get back in you and fuck you so hard you can't think straight. And then I have other plans."

She gulped and nodded and he turned his attention back to Vincenz as she got to her knees to get at Vin's cock. It really was a wonder he lasted more than a minute and a half with these two in his bed.

"Are you fingering his ass?" she whispered into Vincenz's ear. Loud enough for Julian to hear and send him hurtling right to the edge. Then she took one of Vin's hands and sucked on his fingers, getting them wet. Julian watched in what felt like slow motion as Vin adjusted himself and reached between Julian's thighs to slide those wet, slick fingers over his asshole.

A belly-deep groan came from his lips as his cock surged, needing more. Tingles and heat spread outward from that spot Vin found so easily, stroking until Julian felt it in his back teeth. Orgasm built up, more and more until there was nothing but need. Until he exploded with a harsh snarled whisper of Vin's name.

Julian found his way back to the mattress but he wasn't sure how. Hannah petted him, kissing over his chest as Vincenz went to clean up quickly and was back.

"Vincenz is very hard, Hannah."

She nodded, reaching out to grab Vin's cock. "He is."

"He's going to fuck you."

Vincenz needed no more than that to roll over and settle between her thighs. She smiled up at him. "Hello."

He thrust and she arched to get more.

"Hold the head of the bed, Hannah. Don't let go until I say."

She nodded and obeyed as Vincenz thrust hard and deep. Each time he slammed home she made a sound.

"When you get close, pull out. Come on her cunt," he whispered to Vincenz, who sucked in a breath.

"Yes."

They both looked down at her and she narrowed her gaze. "I know that look."

"Good."

Vincenz wanted to take his time, but it was never possible. So much lay between the three of them that it was impossible not to be so ridiculously turned on that within minutes he was ready to come and come hard. This wasn't alleviated by the squeeze of her pussy, so wet and hot around him.

He thrust, pushing her thighs up and apart, changing the angle so he went even deeper. Holding her open to his gaze. To his touch.

And then Julian's fingers, wet again from her mouth, slid over his balls, already slick from her pussy, and then a tease against his asshole. A caress and then the burn of entry. Before long the heated pleasure as Julian pressed his every button. He cursed under his breath and Julian chuckled like the smug male he was. Doing to Vincenz just what Vincenz had done to him only minutes before.

Right on the very edge he pulled out and came in a hot rush, all over her beautiful, swollen, wet pussy.

"Oh!" Her eyes widened and she arched with a moan. "Gods . . ."

"I want you to use Vin's seed and make yourself come, Hannah. You can do this, baby. Do it for us."

She closed her eyes tight for so long Vincenz was convinced she wouldn't do it at all. And then she opened them and let go of the bed.

Julian joined him, both of them kneeling at her legs and watching, ensorcelled as she traced her fingertips over her nipples and down. Down some more, straight to her pussy.

She widened her thighs and began a slow circle of her clit, Vin's seed as her lube.

"I'm convinced I've never seen anything hotter than this in my whole life," Vincenz breathed out as they continued to watch.

"I *know* it."

She did this for some time and then huffed impatiently.

"Stop. You're talking yourself out of coming. Did you masturbate before? Before they took you?"

She nodded.

"And you came? No problem?"

She nodded again.

"You're just fine then. You're in our bed. My mouth has been on you. Vin has been inside you. I've been in his mouth. His come is all over your sweet, juicy cunt, and it's a crime, Hannah, a terrible crime to let them win. Come. You're here with us, covered in us, use that and don't let them win. Do as I tell you. You said you were mine, and I'm telling you to do it."

She didn't look totally convinced, but she went back to her pussy, her other hand playing over her nipples.

"Does it make you hot? To know we're both here looking at you finger yourself?" Vincenz slid a hand over her thigh. "So beautiful."

She shivered and slid two fingers into her pussy and angled her wrist to press her thumb over her clit.

They watched, breath held, as she continued and then she stiffened, arching, pressing the back of her free hand against her mouth as she came so hard it felt like he experienced it himself.

When she opened her eyes it was to send them both a smile. "Wow."

"See? I told you."

"Now I'm sticky in all the best ways."

Julian fell to bed next to her. "It's late enough that we can probably sneak in and I can wash down all your sticky parts."

"Deal."

Chapter 21

"Oh, for all the heavens' sake!" Hannah rounded on him, her hands on her hips. "I'm not incompetent. I'll live. Do you seriously expect to be at my side every moment of the next however many years? Do you fear I'll start fires or wander into a busy street like a wayward toddler?"

Julian appeared to have the good sense to appear chagrined. "Don't be glib."

"I'll be glib all I want. You don't get to control me that way. If we're naked, that's one thing. But we're not naked now." She took a deep breath and tried again. "I *know* you worry. And I appreciate it. But you have a job to do. We're at war. You're part of the plan to make sure we win. Go. Fight. Win. I'll be right here when you and Vincenz return."

He stalked to her and pulled her into his arms. "I hate leaving you."

Her anger washed away. "You'll have to. Unless you mean to dispose of me at some point, this is your job. There'll be other times, even after the war is over, when you have to leave me for a time."

"I like being around you. You fill all my empty spots."

Touched by that sweet admission, she reached up and slid her fingers through his hair. "I'm in them even when you're not with me. Let me fill those empty spaces and go do your job. You don't need to babysit me. I'm not going to fall apart, or go crazy and hurt someone."

Anger flashed over his features then as he shook his head. "Stop saying stuff like that. I don't think that. No one thinks that."

He'd never been angry like that with her before. Oh, sure, at other people and situations, but never at her. Instead of being upset, it filled her with joy. "You never get mad with me."

"You are *not* crazy." He took her face in his hands, tipping it to kiss her quickly. "I hate when you say that. Vin and I hate to leave you because we both love being with you. And because, yes, yes, we want to protect you against what happened to you before. I'm sorry I got mad at you."

She laughed. "No, it's a good thing. Don't you see? You and Vincenz snipe at each other back and forth all the time. You do the same with Daniel. But not with me. That you did, that you are now means you're comfortable enough to know I won't run away in the face of your anger. It means you want me to stay."

He looked adorably confused and she hugged him tight.

"Of course I want you to stay."

"I know. Now go."

"Don't go to town. Not until one of us can accompany you. Please."

She wanted to go to town to pick up some supplies so she could see to the medical needs of the people living out here on the compound. "I want to help. I need to go get those supplies. I'll go with several people. I won't be alone."

"Hannah, there's a war on. This place is already dangerous as it is.

The portal city is awash with ruffians and brigands on any given day, but these days it's particularly bad. Please. I'll go with you when I return. Or, since I'll be in the city this morning, if you give me a list, I can pick things up for you."

She sighed and nodded. She wanted to be independent but that didn't mean she had to be stupid about it.

"Thank you."

She dashed a quick list off and relayed it to his comm and he was off to do whatever he did. Vincenz had already headed off an hour before. Piper and Andrei had their own work as well so she got to task.

Julian sat across the table from one of his informants. He'd gone straight to the dispensary and ordered Hannah's supplies, paying extra to have the items delivered by someone Piper knew to be trust-worthy. That way she'd have her things to get to work.

And then he'd gone through the private portal to Ceres, ignoring why he was there last. Straight to the tavern he knew would be crawl-ing with mercs, thieves, brigands and all manner of assorted criminals. It was where he most often found out things he needed to know.

She looked him over carefully. "You've got a woman now."

At one time he would have elicited his information from this par-ticular informant horizontally while naked. But that seemed a life-time ago. Before Vin. Before Hannah. Funny how he tended to forget about that time. It seemed so long ago.

"I do. So tell me what you've been hearing lately."

He'd already passed credits her way. He trusted her enough to tell him without having to wheedle or con her out of the info before she was paid.

"War on. Good for business out here on the Edge. Still, hard to get around now that Lyons controls most of the private portals. Only so much you can secrete away in a transport when everyone's being scanned the way they are."

"Commerce finds a way."

She laughed. "Yes, and it drives up prices, which is also good for business. But you want to know about what sort of business someone from the other side might have here. Yes?"

He nodded.

"They're around. Here and there. Less, so I suppose Lyons was right to clamp down the way he has." She sipped her ale and looked at him over the rim of her mug. "Means something that he refuses to toss us away. You tell him that if you see him. Tell him that because he stands with the Edge, we stand with him." She paused again and gave him the names of several Imperium lackeys who'd been sniffing around asking questions and attempting to arrange transport of several things she found odd, but Julian understood immediately.

He gave her some extra credits. "Lay low for a while."

"Heard something interesting about Caelinus," she said as he stood to leave.

"That so?"

"Just heard from an associate who'd been traveling. Don't ask and I won't have to refuse to say where." She narrowed her gaze and he nodded. "Said when he passed through there had been a lot of troops just away from the main portal city. Said it seemed excessive, even for the Imperium."

He nodded. It was their capital 'Verse so it wouldn't be that surprising to have a massive troop buildup there. It was where Fardelle's home was as well. "Thank you. Be safe."

On the transport on his way back to Asphodel, he transmitted the info back to Ravena and thought.

* * *

$\mathcal{V}$incenz had been doing his own work, setting up some contacts with one of the people who'd helped smuggle him out of the Imperium all those years before.

He sat in the same place he had when he'd first seen his sister again after so many years. Vincenz had had no idea that the house they'd used all those months before had been owned by Beamus Scott.

"I suppose you're here about the war." Scott handed a mug of tea Vin's way and sat back to look out the wall of windows to the canyons beyond.

"I'm going to assume you know about the portal-collapsing devices."

Beamus nodded. "Sure. Been all over the vids on both sides of the line."

"And you know about Faelene?"

Beamus's gaze narrowed at the mention of the Imperialist 'Verse where the water had been contaminated, rendering large percentages of the population debilitated, killing the weakest among them, the elderly and children.

"Faelene has no elders anymore. And few children under five. Your father has destroyed a lot of people. He's going to have to pay for that. I take it that's why you're here and I'm happy to help you so let's get to the point."

Vincenz took a risk and told him a little about the virus.

"Each time I believe he's done his worst, he surprises me. I'm the criminal so what does it say that I have more morals than he does?" Beamus pushed up and began to pace in front of the windows.

"We believe he's been experimenting on our people for some time now. We don't know the full extent and even if we did, I wouldn't tell you. But I can tell you this virus has the power to kill millions."

"I'll look into it. Give me a day or two."

He didn't have to tell Beamus to be careful about what he revealed. The man was as canny as they came.

"I'll be back through and in contact. Thank you."

*W*hen Vincenz arrived back in Asphodel it was far after the suns had set, but still hot as seven hells. It didn't matter. He had a destination. Of course when he got to the compound Julian was still gone, Andrei was helping with repairs and Hannah wasn't in the main house.

"Where is she?" His pulse kicked higher at the idea of her being missing or harmed.

Shilo, one of the younger women living out there, looked him up and down. "She's down near the far northern cistern. Arch's son is with her. No one would let her get into trouble, you know."

"Thank you," he said over his shoulder, already moving in that direction.

Where he found her sitting on the ground, a small child across from her, looking up at her with big, curious eyes.

Hannah laughed and used a pen light to shine into the child's eyes. "I can see in your eyes with this. It shows me all is well. Nothing in there but lots of brains. It must be that you're very smart. Is that so?"

"Mai says so." The little boy nodded sagely.

"I gave her some tablets for you. You eat one every morning with your breakfast. She told me your favorite was griddle cakes. I love them too. Just chew the tablet and eat your breakfast and you'll keep on getting smarter and stronger. Can you do that for me? Your Dai has to take some too. You can be a good example for him."

The little boy, who'd appeared dubious about the pills, lost that suspicion and instead nodded eagerly at the idea of helping his father. She was good at this.

She stood and brushed off her delectable bottom.

"Thank you, Miss Hannah." He hugged her and was off.

She turned to see Vincenz and her smile grew. "Hello there. How long have you been back?"

He hugged her, breathing her in. "Not very long. I came straight to you once I'd tracked you down. Are you finished?"

"For now, yes. Oh!" She grinned and he did too because how could he not? "I think the program broke through. At least a few layers. I thought of something while I was out earlier and went back. I added some commands to the secondary encryption program; it might work."

"Let's go see then. Didn't you come out here with someone? I got scolded for assuming you'd be alone."

"They're quite nice to me here." He knew she blushed even without seeing it in the dark blue of evening. "Carel, that's one of Arch's sons, came out with me. He and his family live just there." She pointed. "Let me tell him I'm going back with an escort."

As they walked back to the main house he held her close, his arm around her shoulder, her medical bag slung over his free shoulder. "What all did you do today?"

"I'd planned to go to town to get supplies so I could see some of the people here. They lack basic health care and traveling to the portal city is hard on the elderly and the sick. But Julian did it for me and had things sent back here. Even that bag." She rested her head against his shoulder. "He's very thoughtful. I got Arch his medication. A several months' supply. I spoke with Carel so he knows the name of the pills and will go into town every few months to get it for him. And then I just went from building to building and talked with people."

"A medical doctor making house calls. I heard that was a myth of Earth," he teased.

"I never really envisioned myself as a family doctor, the door-to-door type especially. But I find I like it. It doesn't have to be forever. But it gives me a purpose while you are all out doing big, important deeds. It makes me happy to use my skills."

"There you are, Hannah! Come inside for the evening meal." Piper waved to them from the front steps.

"I'll be right in. I just want to check on something." Hannah squeezed Piper's hand as they passed, and Vincenz liked that she was making friends.

"Oh, well, hello there. I remember you."

Julian had stopped at a stall near the portal station. He wanted to bring some sweets back for Hannah. He turned to the woman standing on the steps of the partially reputable tavern just two doors down.

"Evening."

"Where's your friend?"

He looked at the package in his hand and thought of Hannah. And then realized two things. First, that he hadn't brought Hannah here so this woman wouldn't know her, and that the woman meant Marame.

"Dead." That simmering rage roiled through him at the thought that a woman half a world away from Ravena would remember Marame and that Marame wasn't alive anymore.

The woman sighed. "I'm sorry. Lots of that going around."

He began to walk toward where he'd left the conveyance he'd driven out from the compound.

*   *   *

*H*annah woke up from a very deep sleep. She reached out to find Julian's space empty. Vincenz had worked on the encryption for hours until he'd dropped into bed to get a few hours' kip. She'd given him a massage until he'd finally fallen asleep and then curled into him, safe and warm.

But it was so late and Julian was gone. Careful not to wake Vincenz, she rolled from bed and pulled a shirt and pants on and stepped into shoes.

There'd been three small storms earlier that day and the air still felt jittery. That it was jittery for a reason totally made sense to her in ways she couldn't understand.

The house was quiet as she made her way outside to stand and look up into the star-filled sky.

She was sure Julian was off doing his secret spy business, and she'd been the one to tell him to go and not worry about her. She hoped he was all right and sleeping, maybe even dreaming of her on some far-off 'Verse.

That's when she turned to go back inside and saw him off in the distance. She knew it was him without seeing his face or his features. Knew the way he held himself, the way he walked. And he walked with anger.

So she found herself moving to him, wanting to fix whatever it was that'd made him this way.

"Julian?"

He spun, hands fisted, mouth set in a grim line. "Oh, beautiful Hannah, are you a dream?"

Not worrying about those fists, she embraced him, hugging tight. "No, I'm real. And here. I missed you today."

He set himself away from her. "I'm not fit company right now. You should go back inside. You shouldn't be out here alone."

"I'm not alone. I'm with you. Tell me."

"No. Go inside and let me be, Hannah."

"Oh, I see. You can push me and poke around in my head and with my emotions to help me get over something, but I'm not allowed to do the same for you?"

Eyes narrowed, he huffed out a frustrated breath. "This isn't the same and I don't need to go over it."

"It's difficult, you know. To compete with the ghost of a woman you won't talk about."

"Don't."

"Don't what? You are in every part of me. Poking. Demanding. I give to you. But there's a part of you I can't get to because it belongs to Marame and you won't even discuss her with me."

"It wasn't that way. You know it. I can't believe you're jealous of a dead woman."

"I can't believe it either, but it exists just the same."

"I'm fucking another man and you don't care about that, but you're going to throw a fit over a dead woman I never touched romantically. That's beneath you."

She tried not to let him see how much that hurt. Knew he did it to keep her back.

"A fit? Is that what this is? I suppose I must have misunderstood the meaning of the word all these years. I can throw one if you like. Maybe that's what you need. As for you *fucking* another man, I know Vincenz. I see the love you two have. You let me share in. But Marame—"

He spun. "Stop saying her name!"

That hurt more than the slap he'd made just moments before. "Why?"

"Just leave me the fuck alone, okay? She and I had something special and I won't apologize for it. You don't need it to have other parts of me. When you back off and want to be left alone, I leave you alone."

She shook her head. "Balderdash. You poke and poke and poke. I'd never ask you to apologize for loving someone. Share with me, damn you."

"She's dead. There's nothing to share other than that. Now go back inside, Hannah; I'm not feeling romantic and I'm not the man to give you soft words. Not tonight."

"Did I ask you for soft words, Julian? Have I ever asked you for anything you didn't offer first? I'm asking you now. I'm asking you to share with me. You say I'm important to you and how you want me around in your life. Tell me about her."

"Go back to bed. I'll be in shortly."

She stood, watching him. Aching for the pain she knew he felt and for whatever reason didn't want to share.

"Go! I can't deal with fixing you right now." He turned his back on her.

She jerked back, tears coming so easily she didn't have much time to be amazed by it. That, after he'd told her just that morning that she didn't need to be fixed. After he'd scolded her for saying it of herself.

She turned and walked back toward the house. She knew he hadn't meant to hurt her. Knew he most likely hadn't meant it either. But he'd used one of her fears to hurt her and she didn't care to be around him for a while.

But she didn't want to get in bed either, she realized as she stood just outside the door to the bedchamber. Didn't want to smell him on the sheets. She looked down at the shirt she wore, his shirt.

$\mathcal{V}$incenz awoke and found her gone. The bed was cool in the Hannah-shaped space between them, so she'd been up awhile. Julian hadn't returned yet either, apparently. He needed kava and some food and to check in on the program to see what had unraveled in the few hours since he'd gone to bed. He noted the folded-up shirt on Julian's pillow. The one Hannah wore so often.

It was as he was pulling his trousers on that Julian came in. His gaze swept the room and the bed and then locked on the shirt.

"Fuck."

Alarmed, Vincenz grabbed a shirt of his own. "What?"

He picked up the shirt and buried his face in it. "Where is she?"

"What did you do, Julian?" His heart pounded.

"I said . . . I think I hurt her feelings."

Vincenz tipped his chin toward the shirt. "You think? Because that's more than a sulk. She's not prone to them anyway."

He opened the door and stalked out. The kitchen was full of people already, but none of them were Hannah.

"Have you seen Hannah?" Vincenz asked Piper, who handed him a mug of kava and he wanted to kiss her in thanks. But Andrei would frown on such liberties so he contented himself with a thank-you.

Piper smiled his way. "She was up when I came out. Working on the comm. She left you a note I think."

"Where is she?" Julian repeated.

Andrei raised a brow at Julian's tone. "Why?"

"Because we don't know where she is and we'd like to."

"You want to explain why you're giving me attitude, Julian?" Andrei leaned back against the counter as everyone else scattered.

"He's worried about her, silly." Piper patted his arm. "And perhaps he's done an incredibly male thing and made her upset and now that *he's* ready to make amends he's pissy she's not available for that."

"She talked to you." Julian nearly growled the words.

"Enough."

"What the fuck is going on?" Vincenz rounded on Julian.

"She came upon me when I was in a mood. Poked and pushed. I told her to leave me be."

Vincenz kept looking at him.

"I wasn't as gentle with her as I could have been."

"I'm going to assume you mean verbally."

Julian's features darkened. "Of course! Do you think I'd use my fists on a woman? Any woman, much less *our* woman?"

"No. I don't."

Piper sighed heavily. "She didn't give me any specifics other than you'd been short with her and said some things she was trying to not be bothered by. I assured her that men were sometimes dreadfully stupid and said things they didn't mean or even believe but that hurt anyway because they knew us so well. And then I told her if you were worthy, you'd get your groveling pants on and give her the begging she deserved."

Vincenz shook his head. "What. Did. You. Say?"

Andrei and Piper made to leave the room. "She went out with some of the others to the greenhouses. There's a rather large group so she's fine," Andrei said as they left.

"I don't want to talk about it." Julian sulked.

"Too fucking bad."

But he wanted to punch Julian in the face when the whole story came out.

"I'm stunned, Julian. I really am." He needed to find her. That she hadn't come back to bed, that she'd left the house to go elsewhere, that she'd given up that shirt made him anxious.

"I didn't mean it. I just needed some time alone. I don't have her to talk to anymore—Marame, I mean. I don't know how to . . ." Julian held up the shirt and shook his head.

"I need to find her. You don't. Let me deal with her alone. Then you can grovel. First I want to look at her note." He found it resting on the keyboard.

Looks like sectors A–F are now decrypted. I set the new program to piggyback on yours to double the data spread. Looks like references to cities and people you may be able to get a lock on the location from. I took the liberty of creating a data collector for the names and locations, at least those that appear to be. Not perfect, but a start. —Hannah

He looked down at the screen and saw the same three names over and over.

"Caelinus. The lab where my father is doing the research is on

Caelinus." He turned to Julian. "Get planning. I'm going out to find her and bring her back."

"Fuckall if you think I'm going to sit back here while you go find her."

"Didn't bother you for the however many hours in between when you told her you didn't have time to fix her until you came into the house."

Julian set his jaw. "I watched her to be sure she got back inside safely. Assumed it was to you. I won't let you make me feel bad for being human."

Vincenz sighed and pulled Julian to him, hugging him. "No, you shouldn't have to."

"I made a mess. You need to let me clean it up."

Vincenz kissed Julian's temple. "She's out there. Upset. Without you or me, and you want me to wait around while you go find her? When she may not even want you to find her?" He paused. "I'm sorry, that was shitty. It's just a stupid fight and it won't be the last, I'm sure. She's coming into herself now, finding a space between how she was before and what she'll be in the future. She's a strong woman, bedroom manner aside."

Julian put his forehead to Vincenz's. "I was wrong. I hurt her."

"You were and you did. You have to let go, you know. Marame is dead but that doesn't mean you can't ever talk about her, or share her with people. Of course Hannah was curious. She saw you hurting and wanted to make it better."

But before anything else could be said, Vincenz heard her laughter on the breeze.

"She's coming." Julian kissed the corner of Vincenz's mouth.

The back door opened and she came through with several other people. Her hair had been covered with a bright red scarf and she wore a sweater she'd brought with her. Nothing from either of them and the sight of it cut to his heart, though he had no reason to be so sad about it. She was still there, had worked, left him a note; there was nothing amiss.

One of Arch's grandsons—the boy was maybe twenty or twenty-one standard—gazed at her adoringly, and he wasn't the only one. Julian growled but Vincenz elbowed him in the side. "No."

He moved to her, drawn by the light she carried within. "I was just coming to find you," he said, entering the room where she'd already started washing up and cleaning the vegetables and fruit she'd brought back.

She looked up and smiled at him. Though it showed to her eyes, he saw the sadness there too.

"I've been in the greenhouses. When I meet Taryn I'm going to have to tell him how magnificent they were."

"Andrei helped too," Piper said as she came in from outside. "He rigged the cisterns so that we could water the plants. Without having to carry the water all the time and without having to ration it so tightly because we had a dedicated cistern for the greenhouses, our output grew."

"We preserve things, put them by for the leaner times." Her adoring fan said, never taking his gaze from her face, except to sneak peeks at her breasts. Vincenz didn't blame him, but the boy needed to remember his manners.

"Do you have the time to go over the results of the tests you were running?" Vincenz held his hand out.

She took it and the anxiety he'd been choking on for a while eased back. "I'd forgotten about that. Did you get my note?"

"I did and I think we've got some answers."

She turned back to the crew she'd come in with. "I've got to get back to work. Thank you for letting me tag along today."

He walked with her, slow and easy. Again realizing just how much he needed to touch her. Funny the things she'd brought to his life. Before her, before Julian even, he wasn't touched. Not every day. He'd had lovers, but no one like either of them. Now this woman would sit with him, her feet in his lap or her head on his shoulder. Touch seemed so integral when it was someone he loved doing it.

"I didn't want to wake you so after I set the new program up I decided I needed some time outside."

He put his arm around her waist. "I know about the fight with Julian."

She stiffened as she caught sight of him standing near the area she'd set up as her workspace. Vincenz noted that Julian had put out the sound dampeners the day before and that they were all functional. Which was good given the discussion they were about to have.

"Oh. Well. So the situation with the program. You said you found some answers?"

Oh, so she was like that when she was mad? Ouch. He made a mental note of it, not wanting to be on the receiving end. Not when she was normally so sweet and affectionate.

"Come walk with me, Hannah. Vin has to set up some travel plans." Julian wasn't going to let her push him back either. Good.

"I've done quite a bit of walking today, thank you. I don't need help. Or fixing."

Julian sighed. "I know. I'm sorry."

"Apology accepted. Now, is it Caelinus? I saw a name come up a few times and I tried to search for it but didn't find anything. I don't know why I felt it was. I just did."

Vincenz looked back and forth between them and decided to let Julian do his own groveling.

"It is." He pointed to the screen. "This term here? It's my father's tongue; I guess mine too."

"I thought Imperial was the standard all across the Imperialist Universes?"

"It is. Much like standard is what most of our citizens speak. But Caelinus had her own native tongue. I'm told it's a derivative of an old Earth language. Anyway, this is the valley the Imperialist palace sits in. No one has referred to it by that name for generations now."

Her eyes widened. "You mean to tell me his lab is there? In the palace?"

"It makes sense to a certain extent. He'd want it close so he could keep an eye on the progress. It's certainly the most well-fortified place he's got. It's big. The entire compound takes up several hectares."

"And it's surrounded by an entire column of Skorpios," Julian added.

She sniffed. "Oh, good. It'll be a snap to go and deal with that, then."

"Don't talk like you'll be there."

Hannah looked at him, her brows high. "Really? So all this talk about how integral I am was just bullshit?"

Vincenz sent a cautious look to Julian, who looked as surprised as Vincenz felt. She rarely used any sort of crude language. Outside their bed chamber anyway.

"Noo. Not that at all. You are integral. But Caelinus isn't Silesia."

"Oh. All right then. I had *no* idea. I'll just go back to . . . where would that be exactly? But I'll just go back there and wait for you to return like a good little woman." And with that, she spun and stormed out.

"I'm glad she's mad at you too."

He whacked the back of Julian's head. "We can't let her go on this op. This is beyond dangerous."

"It's all beyond dangerous, Vin. The shit back on Parron. Her facing those labs? Come on. Not to mention that without her we wouldn't have made it. She's the one who disabled all that security."

"I know a way into the palace."

"If we can only, you know, *get* to Caelinus."

"So you'd let her go to get back on her good side?"

"I heard that!" she called out from the other room.

"Fuck." Vincenz pulled at the ends of his hair, frustrated and freaked out.

"Not with me," she said loud enough for them to hear.

Vincenz winced. "This is your fault." He glared at Julian.

"You did just fine on your own. I already apologized." Julian put his hands up in defense.

Andrei cruised through the room and shook his head at both of them before waving them both outside.

"Really, both of you should be ashamed of yourselves."

"What? You think I should let her go to the single most danger-ous place in all the Known Universes? To get pussy?" Vincenz nearly sputtered it, he was so pissed off.

"Not going there. Yet. No, I mean the way you've both handled an angry female. I thought you both far smoother than this." Andrei pulled a pouch from his inner coat pocket and began to roll a smoke. "Julian, you have a reputation. Is it all fabricated? Have you never calmed a woman down after you've made her mad?"

"It would have been fine if Vincenz hadn't told her she couldn't go."

Andrei looked back to Vincenz and shook his head. "I know a few things about high-strung, intense women. You think Piper would take any of the nonsense you two spin to Hannah? And there's two of you, which means twice the opportunity to fuck up. And twice the opportunity to make up. Gods, boys, have you never experienced make-up sex?"

Vincenz wanted to laugh. He rarely saw this side of Andrei, who was normally incredibly reserved, a man of very few words.

"Oh." Julian pouted, but because he was Julian, it only made Vincenz want to bite him somewhere good and lick away the sting.

"Here's what I'm going to do. Piper tells me Hannah loves to swim. She's logged the coordinates for some heated pools out near the caldera. They're inside a series of large, open caves so be sure Hannah will be all right with that. It's a bitch to land, but Julian is totally capable. Don't break that zipper; it's Piper's favorite and unlike you two dolts, I like to keep my woman happy."

Vincenz quirked up a smile. "She probably would love that."

"Then Julian needs to grovel a lot more." Andrei glared at him. "I'm sorry? You said *I'm sorry* and thought that was enough?"

"I just wanted to be left alone and she wasn't going."

"You used something you knew would drive her away. I get it. But, Julian, you used something you knew would drive her away." Andrei repeated the last with emphasis. "That works with your friends and other assorted people, but some words can't be taken back. They come from you and into her and it begins to eat away at the foundations you've built. The trust she has in both of you."

"I'm fairly sure I've never heard you talk so much." Vincenz took the smoke Andrei handed him.

"I spent a few hours with Hannah earlier today. I'm not going to pretend and tell you what the three of you have will be easy. But she loves you both. To her bones. She is not helpless. She is not weak. She is not stupid. Don't treat her that way by manipulating her emotions because she's given herself to you both so freely. That's a gift."

"She told you about our sex life?" Julian didn't sound angry, just curious.

"Gods, no! I prefer not to know those details but thank you both for putting them in my head." He cleared his throat. "What I mean is, when you argue with someone you love, and who loves you, the dynamics change. Be mindful with the things you've been blessed with."

As it happened, it was damned good advice.

Vincenz heaved a sigh. "I know she's intelligent. One of the most intelligent people I've known. And courageous? Seven hells, yes. But she's not trained for an op like this. If I pretended I was all right with her going with us, I'd be lying."

Andrei looked him over carefully. "Do you think she'll endanger your goals? This is me speaking as your superior. Do you think she'll impede your mission?"

"She's not trained."

Andrei waved that away. "She's trained quite well for what she does. Remember we've got people trained in all sorts of ways."

"She has no weapons training."

"True." Andrei shrugged.

"But I do. And so does Vin. Each team has members with different strengths. That's the point. She has skills we need. She works with you seamlessly. She takes orders," Julian countered.

And he was right.

"What I can't face is the idea of losing her and being the cause."

Julian heard the anguish in his voice. *Understood*, because he felt it too.

Andrei nodded, still leaning against the fence around the tool shop he'd led them to. "There's that."

Oh, yes, Julian imagined Andrei got it. Piper was with him on

every op. Then again, Piper was a badass, bare-knuckled fighter. Totally unlike Hannah. And because Julian had lost Marame, who was
a better fighter than he was, Julian realized that things happened that
were out of your control and sometimes terrible outcomes happened
even when you didn't plan for them.

"I worry she'll get into the thick of it and someone who has been
trained to fight will get one up on her. And she'll be dead and it'll be
my fault and I'll have lost her nonetheless. And I don't think I can
deal with a world where she's not there, looking up as I walk into a
room and making me feel as if there was no one else in all the 'Verses
she wanted to see more."

Julian knew Vincenz would feel awkward if he moved to comfort
him just then. This conversation slid back and forth between work
and friendship between three men who generally kept their feelings
to themselves while on the job.

"Does she add to the operation? Will having her there make it
easier to do your job? Because, Vincenz, this is your father. Villain or
no, this won't be easy for a host of reasons. Will having her there give
you less reasons, or complicate things even more?" Andrei looked off
to the north, clearly still listening.

"If we go in to get rid of the thing we need to," Vincenz began,
mindful of what he said, "she's the one with the expertise."

Julian relaxed a little, realizing they were working the way through
to a solution they could both live with. Not that Hannah would appreciate them all coming out here to decide her fate, which was too
bad as he had no plans to stop protecting her.

"She knows the material in a way none of us do. This is why I
think she's integral to this op. I can shoot, you can shoot. We can handle that part. She can handle the other part."

"And what about you, Julian? Hm? I've watched you after we lost
Marame. Watched you fall apart, pull away from everyone who cared

about you. I've watched you drink too much, fuck too much and then you found a way to come back. Can you handle it if she's threatened? If she's hurt or . . ." Andrei wasn't just asking as his commander, but as his friend. But he didn't want to talk about it either way.

He scrubbed his hands over his face.

"You can't keep it locked up inside forever. It'll eat away at everything good. And you have so much that is good." Vincenz had so much emotion on his features it tore at Julian's reserve. "She begged you to share because she can see the pain written all over you. She's not one to let people she loves hurt. It's part of her makeup. You've seen her here. She's a doctor not only because she's got the training, but she's a nurturer. She's a caregiver and she knows you're in pain. She's not going to stop trying to make you better."

The fact that this was inescapable didn't make it any easier to hear. "How did the topic turn in this direction?"

"Because this is all twisted up, part of the overall issue. As your commanding officer I will tell you without reservation that I believe you need her on an op of this type. She's got the specialized knowledge we need. There will be a great deal of data here. And the possibilities of contagion are not to be ignored. She will think about things in ways you two can't because you're trained differently. That's how good teams get made. I wouldn't send her out on the overwhelming majority of the ops we do. But this one is tailor-made for her. And I can't say otherwise, though I respect and understand your hesitations. More than you know."

Men were so vexing sometimes.

She paced, not quite knowing what else to do.

First Julian with his sweet, befuddled half apology and then Vincenz with his overprotective chest beating about how she couldn't go on this operation because it was dangerous. Oh really? As if she didn't know that. She'd like to see them, either of them, figure out which virus was which. Seven hells, if they destroyed it incorrectly or it got airborne and they were exposed to it . . .

She growled and laughed when she sounded just like Julian.

She was going on this operation. Period. Julian would share this business about Marame. Period. If she was to be a full partner in this relationship, they had to stop trying to protect her, had to stop holding back. If they trusted her, they had to open up. If not . . . She huffed out a breath, not really wanting to confront what she'd do if it turned out she loved them and they only cared about her, or only cared about her enough to have sex and then they went off into their own world and left her behind.

Frowning, she sat down hard.

Piper tapped on the door before coming in and closing it behind her. "Are you all right?"

"I don't know."

Piper laughed. "I know how you feel."

"That's good because I'm not sure I do. I'm not sure about anything all the sudden. I'm jittery like the air."

"Do you want to talk about it?"

"I'm not very good at this relationships thing. I don't know how to relate to people. I don't know if I ever did."

"Really? Seems to me, Hannah, you do just fine. These people here are my family. I wouldn't let just anyone in. Wouldn't let just anyone treat their ailments and comfort them the way you have since you walked through the door and helped Arch. As for relationships of the romantic kind? You have your work cut out for you with those two. Julian with his wounded, broody alpha-male ways. Vincenz, who is that quietly intense protective alpha. He's got all this backstory and guilt over what his father has done. That's a lot of emotion just under the surface with them both. It's hard to manage that much testosterone. I feel for you. Andrei is a big enough job." She grinned and Hannah did too.

"It's just, I don't know. I thought I knew how they felt and then I just realized I don't know at all. I assumed, but that's not the same as knowing. They had this thing before I came along. They have their work to connect them. It's beautiful and I love them together. I guess I had just thought I fit too."

"And now you don't think so? Honey, Julian's little pouty stunt outside when he got defensive and pushed you away is what men do sometimes. They're so . . . ugh, they're pretty but sometimes they forget their manners and act like wounded animals. And these two are extra helpings of man. Seems to me you handle them just fine. Seems to me you fit with them just fine. If you didn't, you wouldn't be here. I see how they look at you. I hear how they talk to you, about you. It's more than just liking your bits."

"Vincenz doesn't want me to go to Caelinus to destroy the lab."

Piper nodded. "Sure. I imagine he doesn't. Dangerous. Highly protected. By Skorpios. Scary stuff. And his father is there. I wish you'd have met Carina already. She's his sister and gods help her, Daniel Haws's wife." Piper laughed. "Talk about broody and protective. Anyway, she'd have more insight on Vincenz. But he left years ago. Left without saying good-bye to his mother and sister. Left and came here and has been proving himself ever since."

"I know that. I know that he feels guilty for what his father has done." She knew too that he'd never found a sense of home, a man without a place for so long. He'd told her she gave that to him. She and Julian. "I can help on this operation. This virus is highly communicable and dangerous. I'm the perfect person to go. But I lost it. Back at the processing plant. You know that. Maybe they think I'll do it again. Maybe I'd slow them down."

Vincenz had convinced her otherwise just a week before. Had broken down all her walls and made her see she'd overcome, not failed. She didn't think it had been a lie. It had felt real. Each time he touched her it had felt real.

She stood and moved to look out the window. "I don't know what I'm doing."

"Welcome to the club. There are a few things. First, I agree that you're perfect for this operation. As does Andrei, though you have to pretend I didn't tell you that, and really, I believe Vincenz and Julian think so too, but they're scared. You're feeling out of sorts—not because of what you endured in the lab. You're feeling out of sorts because that's what love does to you. Turns you upside down and inside out and sets you down right on your ass. This is normal. All this." Piper waved her hand around. "This is boy meets . . . boy and then girl stuff. Fighting is normal. You'll have to manage them both. But they want that. Don't be confused about that part. Or about yourself. You're just fine."

Piper stood and went to the door.

"Thank you. For listening. And for helping me see the truth of it."

"That's what friends do, Hannah. Go make them see reason. Oh and grovel. Make-up sex is the best." Piper winked and was gone.

She'd made her first friend other than Vincenz and Julian, since before she'd been taken. She might never be normal, but having friends made her feel real. And real was better than normal any day.

Chapter 23

She was at the comm again when they came back inside. Vincenz's gaze swept the room until it landed on her. Her insides got jittery the way they did when he turned his attention her way.

"Would you like to go for a swim?" Julian came to a stop next to her chair. "So I can fully grovel. And because you love the water."

"Zipper is ready to go. Julian's going to fly us. The pools are in a large cave system but Piper thinks you'll be fine." Vincenz knelt on her other side.

"Just the three of us?"

Julian nodded.

"You *do* have some groveling left. And I suppose a swim could be lovely."

"We can talk a little about the op."

She held back the smile she totally felt. "All right. I don't have a bathing suit but I suppose I can borrow one. Or just use my panties."

Julian hauled her up. "Don't need one. It's just the three of us so you only need your skin. We've got drying cloths and some snacks already waiting."

She called out her good-bye to Piper, who gave both men a narrow-eyed look.

Hannah took the backseat, content to leave them both to their business. Vincenz was a very good navigator to Julian. She let her attention wander, looking out over the scenery as they flew along.

"Gonna be tight," Julian said finally, breaking into her attention.

"Hm?"

"The landing," Vincenz clarified. "He's got it. He always says this sort of thing and he never fails."

And he didn't, setting the zipper down quite easily on a tiny out-cropping.

The air out where they'd taken her was supercharged. The hair on her arms stood up and her teeth seemed to tingle.

"Just out there"—Julian pointed—"is the Caldera. The birthplace of a lot of the storms here. Not a lot of anything but dirt out this way."

No, he was wrong. There was a lot of electricity in the air. Energy just floating on the breeze. She breathed in deep. "I like it."

He smiled at her and held a hand out. "We've got directions. It's a ways down this path so watch your step."

The color of the canyon walls wasn't gray like it had been near Piper's compound. It was more blue. Blue with veins of bright, earthy red. As they headed down the path went into a tight little corner they had to go sideways to get through. On the other side they both watched her and she rolled her eyes.

"If I have a concern, I'll bring it up. This is fine. The sky above is open. I'm here of my own free will. It's not the same. I can tell the difference."

"Of course you can." Vincenz shoved the bag with the food and cloths in it into Julian's arms and took her hand. "My turn."

She favored him with a sniff and a raised brow but took his hand.

She wasn't sure what she'd expected from the description of the pools, but what she saw was far more magnificent than she could have envisioned. Light shafted over the walls inside from the small open spaces on the ceiling of the cave. The cave soared high up into the air. The room was open and just the right temperature.

It was magical. She'd pulled her clothes off and her hair free before the men had even put their things down.

Wandering past one large pool, she headed down a little to a smaller one just beyond. She dipped a toe in, groaning at the temperature. She wanted to jump in, but as she didn't know how deep it was or even if there were rocks she couldn't see, she waded in until she could push off and swim a lazy path from one end of the pool to the next.

The water was heavy in minerals, the texture silky, making her extra buoyant.

It wasn't long before she had company, but they left her alone for a while until she'd worked off her excess energy and most of her annoyance with them.

"This place is wonderful." She headed to a nearby rock outcropping. The stones were smooth from the water's caress. They made a nice seat and enabled her to keep her legs submerged as she watched the two of them swim toward her.

"I have reservations about your coming."

"I for one think you should shut up about that until we've fucked her into a much better mood." Julian turned every bit of his sexual attention her way and send a thrill right through her.

"Well, I can see the appeal of that plan." Vincenz swam up between her legs. "But I think she deserves this first. I'm sorry. It's not that I think you aren't smart enough or brave enough. You are. And we do need you. I just . . ." He swallowed hard and she gave in, allowing herself to touch him. "I don't want to risk you. If something happened to you, I don't know what I'd do."

"It's very difficult to be mad with you when you're so sweet. I know this virus, Vincenz. I know it. And you don't. And just let *me* say that if you touched it, or were exposed to it and got ill, chances are you'd die and then it would be because I wasn't there. How can *I* live with that? Don't you think it's awfully coincidental that you found me, brought me back to Mirage and opened your lives to me and I turn out to be the specialist in just exactly what you need? I'm a scientist. I believe in what I can see. In what I can prove. This is more than that. I'm meant to be here. I'm meant to go with you. Even if you don't want me, you know, romantically, after this all ends, I can help."

He pushed up, all the muscles on his chest and shoulders bunching as he exerted himself. He kissed her hard. "Have we failed then? In showing you what we feel? We must have if you don't know if we'd want you or not when this is over."

Vincenz pulled her into the water and Julian came up behind her, wedging her between them like she needed so much. She tried not to show it, tried to hold back the tears of doubt she'd been choking on since Julian had shoved her away.

They both hugged her tight. "Baby. Gods above and below." Julian kissed her neck and her ear. "I love you. I'm sorry, so very sorry I made you doubt that. I'm an asshole. But an asshole who loves you so much he's pretty scared by it."

Vincenz kissed her cheeks, taking in her tears. "Don't cry. Please. I can't stand seeing you like this because of us. Stay with me. Stay with Julian. Where you belong. I love you, beautiful Hannah."

She squirmed to turn halfway to throw an arm around each of them. "I thought I had read it wrong. Thought I had loved you both so much only to have you both move on and love each other while I had to rebuild, knowing you were somewhere but not with me."

Vincenz groaned, hugging her tight. "No. No. Never. Your place is with me and Julian. Beside us, between us."

"Below too. Oh and above." Julian hugged her other side as he moved them back to the shallows so they could stand.

"Let's lay out the blanket and have a snack. We can talk more." Vincenz got out and bent to find the blanket to spread while Hannah found the food and sat between them, her legs stretched, arms behind her, supporting her weight.

"I met Marame right after I got to basic training. I told you I grew up in an orphanage. So I never really had anyone I considered to be family until the corps." Julian lay flat, looking up at the ceiling and back into the past. She waited, so happy he would share, not wanting to spook him.

"I remember my parents. Or rather the last time I saw them. We were refugees from Catan. After the earthquakes there, the government sent in airlifts to take people out and move them to camps in other 'Verses. It was chaos. No food. Scant water. Not enough spots on the transport out. My mother shoved to the front of the line and tossed me into the crowd on the landing deck. I never saw her again. *Them* again. The records don't show them ever leaving."

Catan had been rendered virtually uninhabitable after a series of major earthquakes, which had started fires and all manner of other natural disasters. No one lived there now and it was only visited by researchers. Millions had died.

He hadn't saved them, she realized. Realized that even at three he'd seen it as his fault. He hadn't saved them and he'd grown up alone.

"Ellis saved my life and gave me a second chance. A third chance I suppose. But Marame became my family. The sister and mother I never had. She was my best friend. The person I trusted above all others. She always had my back. She never judged me. She made me laugh. Made every day better and that she's gone is such a fucking crime there are days I can barely get through because it *hurts* that I can't talk to her again. That I can never introduce you to her. She'd have loved you, by the way."

Hannah tried hard not to cry again, but his pain echoed through his skin where she'd laid her palm over his heart.

"And so last night I was buying you some sweets and a woman from the tavern recognized me. Asked about Marame. And she wasn't there. She was gone and I had no good reason for it and the stupidity of it sent me reeling. How can I say she's dead and have it just be words? There's no reason for it. *None*. It was pointless. And empty. And I can't take it back and make it not be true." And this strong man nearly sobbed as he said the last.

She lay beside him, curling into his body her hand clasped with Vincenz's, who bracketed Julian's other side.

"And sometimes I am so angry. I want to kill and maim, I want to rip people to shreds for taking my family away again. But never you. Do you understand me?"

She looked up at him and nodded. "Of course."

He seemed satisfied with that. "I didn't save her. I lived and she didn't and I feel guilty about it. And I look at you and then I don't. Which makes me feel guilty all over again."

"I'm sorry. I'm sorry I can't meet her. I'm sorry she was murdered. I'm sorry you have a hole inside where she used to be."

He laughed, rueful. "You and Vin fill my empty spaces. Even the jagged ones. I didn't mean it when I made the comment about fixing you. Gods, I'm sorry. You get to me and it makes me nervous because I can't defend against you. You lay me bare."

She attempted to keep her bottom lip from trembling but failed.

"I know you didn't. I mean, I wasn't totally sure and then I was worried I'd misread things and I'm not good with this, or with people and so I . . ."

He hauled her up, on top of him, his grip on her upper arms tight but not brutal and kissed every doubt out of her. He kissed her until she wasn't sure where her breath ended and his breath began. And it didn't matter.

His tongue slid into her mouth like a thief, sinuous, sensual, his taste making itself at home within her. He grabbed two handfuls of her ass and ground her against his cock. He nipped her lips, her chin, took a handful of her hair and pulled, angling her head to get at her neck.

He rolled her over, looming above her, eyes glittering in the low light, intent. He rained kisses across her face, over her closed eyes, the curve of her cheeks, back to her mouth where he took a long, leisurely tour.

"Hands and knees."

It was a good thing, as her knees were so rubbery she couldn't have stood.

He gave her ass three sharp smacks, at first because the sound appealed to him, but then for the pretty pink handprint.

"Get over here, Vin, and put your cock in that pretty mouth."

Vincenz got to his knees, caressing her hip as he leaned closer to Julian. "I need your mouth first."

Julian shivered and then gave over to the wonder of Vincenz's kiss. The sure, aggressive way his tongue slid over the seam of his lips and then inside. Vincenz tasted when he kissed. He sampled in little licks and then moved in to devour, as he did now.

Impatient for his cock, Hannah shifted and he slapped her ass another time, reveling in her squeal that ripened into a moan when he drew his fingertips over the spot, her skin hot to the touch.

It was his turn to moan as Vincenz sucked his tongue, fluttering his own against it. Julian's cock was so hard it could feel the pound, pound, pound of his pulse there.

Vin pulled back and then back in to kiss the base of his throat.

"That's better." He got back to Hannah, hunching to kiss her and swallow her cries as Julian wrapped her hair around his fist and pulled as he pressed his cock into her cunt.

Wet.

"Already wet."

She pushed back to meet him, sucking his cock in deep and bringing stars to his vision it felt so fucking good.

He yanked a little harder on her hair and her pussy rippled around him. That she responded the way she did made him feel like a king. Only he and Vin knew this part of her. This dirty, gorgeous woman who gave herself so freely.

"I wish I'd brought the clamps," Vincenz murmured as he broke the kiss.

"You used the clamps and I wasn't there?"

Vincenz grinned up at him. "They're in the drawer next to my side of the bed if you want to use them. Her nipples get so hard and puffy. And when I took them off . . ." He looked back down to her face tipped up from the grip Julian had in her hair. "When I took them off she came hard." He reached down and rubbed the head of his cock over her lips as Julian dug in and began to fuck her in deep, hard thrusts.

"Do you want this?"

"Yes." She licked her lips and Julian heard and saw Vincenz's breath hitch.

Provocative without even meaning to be. Seven hells, she was so powerful in her submission. It drove him to his metaphorical knees. The way he knew it did for Vincenz too.

"Don't neglect her clit." Vincenz gave in and began the slow press into her mouth.

"Wouldn't dream of it. I love her clit."

The two of them grinned, but then she tightened around his cock and he grunted. Vin's grunt echoed as Julian stretched forward to watch her suck Vin's cock, her tongue flat, pressing against the underside, just beneath the crown.

"He does like it right like that."

Vincenz couldn't tear his gaze from the sight of her mouth on his cock. Except that she gave him her eyes, just like he'd demanded. She gave him his pleasure and remembered his command. Which only made him hotter for her.

"I want to fuck your face." He sighed and she whimpered. Not in pain or distress.

Julian reached around her body and found her clit, swollen, hard and slick. He tickled it lightly until her sweet moans took on an edge of frustration.

"Do you want me to make you come?"

He was surprised he could get the words out around his clenched teeth. She felt so good the only thing holding him back from coming was his attention on her clit.

She squirmed, slamming back against him several times, pushing him hard and right to the very knife's edge. He squeezed gently, plumping her clit between his thumb and forefinger and she arched her back, making needy, demanding sounds around a mouthful of Vin's cock.

"Seven hells, your cunt is so hot and tight. Each time I squeeze your clit it's like a molten wave of flesh rippling around me. So. Fucking. Good."

But he didn't want to go without her so he added a little more pressure and that did the trick. She began to come, straining to push back and keep him deep as she spasmed around him so hard it pulled him right in and he came along with her as he fucked her deep, continuing to hold her hair, controlling her as he did.

Vincenz waited until Julian pulled out before he went back to work. "Now then, suck me the way I like it, beautiful Hannah."

He took her hair from Julian and yanked hard enough to elicit a startled cry from her. A cry that deepened into a moan as he let loose and thrust.

He'd wanted to fuck her face every time she got his cock in her mouth, but had held back, thinking she might not be ready.

But as usual, Hannah had her own mind and was far stronger and eager than he'd given her credit for.

"You hungry for it? Hmm?"

She hummed her assent as he thrust harder. She adjusted her breathing as he continued.

"Do you have any idea how beautiful you are this way? Hands and knees. Handprints on your sweet ass. All that gorgeous hair wrapped around my fist as I fuck that mouth of yours. And you love it. I don't know what I did to deserve this dream come true, but rest assured, Hannah, it's my plan to make you so satisfied for the rest of your days you'll never want for anything. But my cock."

She whimpered again. A needy sound that traveled up the stalk of him, up to the head, where she occasionally slid her tongue though the slit, and down to his balls.

He didn't have much time left. After her tears he was already laid to waste, and then Julian spoke about his childhood and losing Marame and that was more than he could bear. He needed to bury himself in them, in this thing they'd all created together.

Her tits swayed so prettily.

"I think we should get your nipples pierced. They'll look even prettier when I come all over them."

She closed her eyes just a moment before opening them again just as he began to come. "Take it, sweet Hannah. Swallow it all."

And she did.

Chapter 24

Wil rose from his chair and addressed the room. A gathering of the top Family members who had the sort of clearance they'd need to hear what he was about to say.

"We have destroyed the Imperium's ability to make the portal-collapsing devices. They will be unable to procure the key ingredient, Liberiam, which is found in only a few scattered 'Verses, all of them on our side of the line. We've installed detectors for air quality tests on each of them. If Liberiam is mined, we've found out it gives off a specific chemical signature. We can detect this signature with our tests."

No one took notes; they wouldn't have been allowed to leave the room with them anyway. So they nodded and if they had questions, Wil knew they'd ask.

"Up until recently this was the biggest threat Ciro Fardelle posed to us. We're a superior fighting force. We have more soldiers with better equipment and training. We've finally achieved the upper hand in Silesia. So much that we're able to declare it ours. The other edge 'Verses will go the same."

"What of casualties?" Vicktor Pela, the leader of House Pela asked. The man had been through the last battles at Varhana. Had lost an arm leading his column to victory there. He understood the costs of war better than most.

"Ours are minor. Theirs are not." They would of course continue to keep their aim locked on military targets to keep the counts as low as possible for civilians, but that was a fact of war and not one he liked to ignore. But they would continue and there was no way around it.

Pela nodded and indicated Wil should continue.

"As I said, up until recently we'd thought Fardelle's portal-collapsing device was our biggest worry. New data has come to light that this is not so. Fardelle has been testing a bio-weapon. A virus containing the most virulent and hearty elements of several of the most deadly viruses we've seen in the history of humanity. We don't know where he got the stock originally, but we know he's tested it on civilians, including his young son, who died after exposure."

The room roiled with angry outbursts and Ellis understood it. But they needed to get focused again so he rapped on the table with his knuckles. Roman smirked behind the hands he had steepled in front of his mouth, knowing Ellis could handle this but clearly amused by it.

"Hold your questions to the end, if you will, please. We've got our teams working on this at the highest priority. We've got specialists in virology consulting with us on not only identifying this virus but finding it and destroying it properly and removing any data there may be concerning this virus. This is not something we're taking public at this time. The panic would be devastating. We've got enough on our plates at this point that to add this would be foolish. And dangerous. There is *no* reason to believe this virus has made it into our territory.

But we do know there are links between a cross-border initiative, some of whose members were kidnapped and held against their will, subjected to mental and physical torture to obtain information. This information was not given by the Federated Universes' citizen who we freed. I've viewed her debrief, both a physical one on multiple occasions and just recently she submitted to a mental debrief. You should understand this woman was subjected to forms of torture designed to break her mind so submitting to our mental debrief process was a great sacrifice on her part."

He took a deep breath. Hannah Black was an unlikely savior, but saviors were rarely likely in his experience anyway.

"We are working with public health agencies on each Federated Universe under the guise of general preparedness. We have key personnel on our teams who can guide these agencies in having plans in place should a virus of this nature be released here in our territory, while keeping the specifics on a need-to-know basis."

They asked him questions for some time after he'd completed his presentation. He'd assured them the best he could, given the reality of the situation. He knew there was a team heading to Caelinus right as he spoke bent on destroying not only the lab and the virus stocks but Fardelle himself. They didn't need to know that information at this point and if things went as planned, no one ever needed to.

He hoped they went as planned.

He hurried out, late as usual for the next meeting. Such was his life since all this nonsense with the Imperium started.

His secretary gave him a narrow-eyed glance. "Have you eaten at all today?"

"I think so." Wil shuffled through the pile of papers he was sure were all important but found nothing so pressing the world would blow up if he didn't deal with right then.

"You could delegate some of this work to Daniel, you know."

A shiver went through him at the voice as he turned slowly to face Katrine Rooney. Today she wore one of those skirts, form hugging, tight at the knee so she'd walk just right. Along with a crisp white shirt. Her hair pulled back into a bun at the back of her head. Her eyes were so blue they reminded him of the sky back on Kwen Lun where he'd spent his first years. Before his parents had . . .

He shook his head to get rid of that memory.

"I'm sorry I'm late for our meeting. The last one went long."

She laughed and walked closer in those heels. *Click, click, click*. He wondered if underneath that skirt she wore garters. Something he frequently wondered about where Katrine was concerned. She'd taken over from her predecessor a standard year before and had done a far more competent job than he had. This had surprised Wilhelm because he was sure no one would take a woman who looked the way she did seriously.

But she was no ordinary woman. Bold. Sharp. Smart. She brooked nothing but the finest performance from everyone in her department. Since she'd come on, the relationship between the military corps and other branches of Federated governance had improved. Streamlined.

"Reuss contacted me to let me know. I always have other work and I know this is a busy time for you." She put a hand on her hip. "Come with me. I'm starving and you certainly need to eat as well." She winked at Reuss and he blushed. Wilhelm was fairly sure he'd never seen the man blush except when Abbie visited him. But she made everyone blush.

Just business, he told himself. He could have lunch with her and do his job. They had an appointment anyway.

Vincenz checked his kit bag one last time. Julian had gone into mission headspace and so Vincenz left him alone.

Hannah was doing an inventory of her bag across from him at the small, rough-hewn table. They'd made it to Monteh and had holed up in a safe house his connections had procured for them.

They'd head from here to a private portal, one of the last remaining in the Imperium, and straight to Caelinus. Full circle, he supposed. It felt odd, being back in the Imperium this far. Silesia was close enough to what the Edge felt like in Federated Territory. But Monteh was close to Caelinus; the culture was strikingly similar.

The carts at the edge of the town's main street had been selling seeded tea cakes. His grandmother, YaYa they'd called her, would serve cakes just like it when Vincenz and his sister Carina would spend their afternoons with her.

He'd spent a lot of time pretending not to miss this place that wasn't only his home, but all the 'Verses he'd been raised and trained to lead when he was old enough to take over from his father.

Before they'd left Mirage, Wilhelm had spoken with him privately. Asked him if he'd be willing to lead the Imperium after the war was over. He'd been taken aback, not even knowing how to answer.

It had always been his assumption that he'd do just that. Until his father had clamped down harder and harder on the people. Vincenz had opposed such brutality, had pushed his father to see reason. To open up their society and award his people the freedoms they deserved.

But from the start, his father—and more notably, his father's new advisors—had put into his mind that Vincenz was out to steal the leadership from Ciro. That Vincenz had been working on an assassination plot.

And then they'd created their own assassination plot to take Vincenz out. His grandmother had heard it and passed it to him and his mother. They'd wanted to hide it from Carina, keep her safe, but Vincenz had tried to find support to stay and deal with his father, but he'd been young and without the base he needed. He could have taken the Skorpios if he'd tried, but he hadn't been sure if they'd have held in the long run. Most of them were addicted to the drugs his father's people put in their food bars and were dependent on his father for their very survival. He couldn't promise them anything until he was in power enough to find a way to end their addiction.

In the end he'd had to get out with a great deal of information in his head and enough credits to get him to the Waystation.

And then of course they hadn't trusted him. Not for years. And he understood it on one level. His father wouldn't have been above sending his oldest son to infiltrate the enemy. And now he was a different person than he'd been when he first arrived. Stronger in most ways. Certainly buoyed by his connection to Julian and Hannah. He'd return a different man than he'd left.

That appealed to him in ways he couldn't quite put into words. He'd come back not having abandoned them, as had been whispered for years. But as the man who wanted to free them from the tyranny of the elder Fardelle.

He wanted to prove to his people that he hadn't forgotten.

But did that mean he wanted to stay? To run a government that would be in tatters by the time Roman Lyons was done?

He'd told Ellis that he had to think. That he wanted to do what was best for the people of the Imperium and for those in Federated Territories too.

Whatever he did in the end, his father had to be eradicated. He knew that. Knew certainly that Ellis felt the same. There could be no peace with the man who'd so ruthlessly attacked civilians—his own and those of the Federated Universes. For the man who considered using biological weapons agents on his enemy, who'd let his own son die from those same viruses.

He was a Fardelle. It was his job to deal with his father. And so he would.

"I know this is hard."

Hannah said this as she wrapped her things up, piece by piece, and put them into her pack. She didn't look up, probably knowing he couldn't handle her gaze just then.

"It is what it is."

"That's what people say when they don't know how to say the difficult stuff."

He snorted. Leave it to Hannah to just say it out loud. "Probably." He paused. "It's hard, yes."

"I like it here. I like the way people dress. It's like a bouquet of flowers."

He cocked his head and realized she was right. Greens, reds, yellows and blues dominated the clothing so close to the religious holiday season. "At home they'll also be dressed this way. I like that part. I've missed things. People."

She nodded. "I imagine so."

She didn't push. Didn't need to really. She understood Vincenz so well he often was humbled by it.

"I should very much like to see my mother again." That had been very hard. Esta Fardelle had been a fierce protector of her children. She'd risked her life over and over for both Carina and Vincenz. He wanted to hug her, hear her soft voice, see her eyes, which were so very like his sister's.

"I wager she'll be delighted." She swallowed, hard, and Vincenz knew she thought of her own mother, now dead, beyond one last hug.

"Whatever you need, you have." Julian stood, strapping a knife to his upper arm and pulling his sleeve to cover it. His gaze locked with Vincenz's.

He knew that too. Which is what made this part a little more bearable.

He stood. "Do you feel comfortable with the plans?" he asked Hannah.

She nodded. "I've got the map pretty well memorized. Yes, I'm wearing the dreadful vest." She sent Julian a glance and he laughed as he sent the clip into place in his weapon.

"Good. They will kill you, Hannah. They're trained to show no mercy."

"I remember."

He sighed, bending to kiss her quickly. "I know. It makes me feel better to remind you."

"I know."

"Let's get moving. The sun has set and we've got a very short window to get to the portal before moonrise."

He checked her pack and she let him without complaint. He checked Julian, who in turned checked them both and she held still for all their poking and prodding.

They headed out the back door of the house and into the field just beyond. It was growing season so the crops, a grain of some sort, were higher than their heads, giving the three of them great cover as they moved away from the town and toward the hinterlands where the private portal was.

Hannah liked it out in the middle of that field. Just the three of them; the sky burned overhead, heavy with stars. Vincenz had seemed to soften when they'd arrived. He'd taken in the stalls and Julian had stolen away to grab some of the tea cakes they knew he loved. She knew Julian would give them to Vincenz when he needed them most.

She remained quiet, humming in her head as she went over the plans over and over in her head. The last thing she wanted to do was to have pushed so hard to be allowed to come on this mission and then fail them in any way. So she kept her mouth shut and followed

Vincenz. Julian was right behind her; the two of them would die to keep her safe, which terrified and exhilarated her all at once.

They loved her.

They'd both told her back in that cave on Asphodel. She'd held the knowledge close to her heart as they'd planned and moved ever closer to Caelinus. When this was over, they'd have to regroup to figure out their future when there was no more war. But she knew they would and that was what counted so much.

After what seemed like an eternity, the moon had begun to rise, so large in the sky above. It sent silvery gold light everywhere. Vincenz had told her they didn't have night the same way she'd be used to, that the moon was so large and reflective it kept Monteh bathed in some kind of light most every part of the day. People had black-out curtains on their homes, he'd explained, so they could sleep. Businesses also used the same sort of curtains, she'd noted when she and Julian had gone to get a meal while Vincenz had met with his contacts the evening before.

They climbed into a small cleft in some rocks and up a rise only to climb down again and head toward a clearing off in the distance. Or so she thought; she couldn't see much with all the trees around. But she believed Vincenz and so she continued to walk, grateful to Julian who'd taken on her physical training when they'd retuned from Parron. Her legs would have fallen off with all the hiking, jogging and full-out running they'd done since they left Asphodel.

She felt the swell of energy and knew the portal was near. How something like a portal could remain undetected she didn't quite understand. The air and atmosphere as they approached the promised clearing was blatant, undisguised.

Vincenz held a fist up, indicating they hold in place and she stopped, Julian moving close enough to touch her back, reassuring.

"He'll go ahead. Wait." He whispered it into her ear and despite the seriousness of the moment, she shivered.

Vincenz came back into view some minutes later and she let out a breath she'd forgotten she'd been holding.

"Let's go. There's troop movement."

Her heart pounded and she forced herself not to be alarmed. They'd take care of it. She'd follow directions and everything would be fine. That was her mantra as they quickly got to the clearing and into the small transport that had been pushed from the trees just beyond.

It was very small.

She'd do it.

"It's a short trip," Julian said quietly as he took her pack and indicated she sit in a nearby jump seat. "Strap in."

She did, ignoring her shaking hands as Julian stowed their gear and went back up front with Vincenz. They'd handle it and she would hold on.

Closing her eyes as Julian keyed the engines over, she went over the plan again. Over the way she'd find the virus and get rid of it. They'd toyed with the idea of her bringing a sample back. But it wasn't totally safe. They didn't know enough to expose those in the Federated Territories to such a danger. The scientist in her wanted to bring it back so she could create a vaccine. Wanted to see what they'd done so she could figure out a way to combat it. But that same scientist knew risks weren't always worth it. The dangers here were manifold, the possible outcomes ghoulish.

So unless she could figure out how to do it and be as safe as possible, she'd destroy all the stocks of the virus and all the data she could find. After making copies for herself of course, to study when she got back.

Her stomach bottomed out as they entered the portal and began to travel. There wasn't a whole lot of insulation on these small transports they'd taken through the private portals. As a result it was colder and far louder than the other transports they'd have taken were they using the public portals. There was nothing luxurious about the ship she was in just then, but at least she was there with them.

Minutes later they both came back with her. "We'll arrive in less than two hours." Julian pulled his shirt off and handed it her way. "Put this on. It's lined and you'll hold heat in better."

"What about you?"

He rustled in his pack and pulled out another. "I have more than one." He frowned a moment. "I don't like it that you haven't worn any of my shirts since our argument."

"I've got one of your undershirts on. I wear it all the time." She blushed. "I thought you'd notice."

He laughed, the frown long gone. "By the time I get that close to your naked tits I'm not noticing if you're wearing my undershirt or not."

She unbuckled and stood to put the shirt on beneath her jacket.

Vincenz handed her a protein bar. "We've got some quiet down time right now. Eat when you can. Always think about your strength and make sure you can keep it up."

She unwrapped and took a bite. "Thank you." She tried not to curl her lip at the taste. Not horrible, but nothing she would seek out on her own if she wasn't on some dangerous, top secret mission to the very center of the Imperium.

"When this is over, I'll make you a dinner. All my childhood favorites." Vincenz sat across from her and took her feet up in his lap as he ate one of the bars himself. "Ellis offered me my father's job."

She'd been about to accept his offer of that dinner with gusto when he lobbed out the bit about Ellis. Not that she was surprised.

It made sense. Both that Ellis would ask and that Vincenz would want to chew it over before he said anything.

Julian raised a brow. "He did? And what do you think about that?" He realized he hadn't ever really taken that into consideration and how silly it had been not to have seen it from the start. Who better to lead the new Imperium after they removed Ciro Fardelle than his son?

"I don't know what I think. I've been working through it for a few days. I still don't know. There are bound to be people who are highly qualified to take over. I haven't been here for many years."

Vincenz was the kind of man more comfortable with praising others than shoving his own praiseworthy events to the fore. He'd be an impressive leader, he was born to it. But then he'd be elsewhere. They'd work it out, no matter what.

Hannah's gaze met his briefly before she turned back to Vin. "But you know your people. You were trained to lead. They're bound to feel better about you than someone your father was close to."

Vincenz shrugged. "He erased me from the public record. Disappeared me. All pictures and paintings with my likeness were destroyed. They may not remember."

Julian realized that was part of the problem. "And you think they'll have forgotten you existed."

Hannah shook her head, her mouth set. "From what I understand of being disappeared, people still keep secret shrines to those they've lost. How do you assume they'd remember their cousin or a neighbor, but not the son of their leader who suffered the same fate their own have?"

Julian leaned back and let Hannah do the digging around Vin's inner fortress. She had a way about her; it was impossible not to admire. Hells, he was wowed by it.

"But I didn't. Their loved ones were shot in the head and dumped into a ditch. Or they went into a dungeon and were never heard from again. I'm alive."

"Yes, you are. So why do you feel guilty about that? You're alive so you can liberate them at long last, Vincenz. People have long memories. People in repressive regimes especially. I'm not saying you should do it, especially if you don't want it or don't think you can do a good job with it. But I'd never forget you. You're real. Smart. Strong. Utterly capable and you've not only received training here, but in the Federation too. You are qualified to do your father's job, without any doubt."

Vincenz shifted uncomfortably but said nothing else for some time.

Chapter 25

*V*incenz stood at the hatch of the transport for a while before he got the courage to open it. Out there was the place of his birth. Was the land he'd learned how to ride, fight, lead on. The people out there were his people in a way he'd tried to forget over the last years. But he never had. They were in his blood.

Hannah leaned forward and kissed his shoulder. No words; she knew they weren't needed. Just that touch.

"Remember your training," he said quietly and opened the door to the dark beyond and stepped out, sweeping the area quickly before he gave the all clear. Hannah hopped down and Julian followed, setting the cloaking devices around the transport. They'd developed the device just a short time before. They masked the energy signature of the portal and the ship. Hopefully it was far enough away from the palace that there'd be no need, but being careful was better than getting caught.

They had a three-hour hike. He'd briefed Hannah; she knew they'd need to keep moving and stood at his side, ready.

On the way, as he kept them hugging the long, low ridge ringing the plains where the palace lay, he went over the plans again and again. Trying not to think about the discussion he'd had with Ellis.

Discussion wasn't really the word. Ellis had brought it up, let him know he believed Vincenz would do a good job, but had left the issue with him to decide.

The air there smelled like it did nowhere else in all the 'Verses. Clean, hot, dry earth. Sand, a little plains grass. Above the sky was brilliant with stars. The moon would rise soon enough and then a short while later the first of the two suns would rise and the day would become hotter and drier. Brighter. Until the zenith of the day when everyone but the heartiest of workers would head inside to break bread and have some ale and wait out the heat.

He wondered what they thought of the place. Wondered if he'd even want to know. Of course he did. They were two of the three most important people in his life. He knew his sister loved Caelinus as much as he did. Missed her terribly, made a promise to himself to speak with her when all this was over to get her opinion on whether or not he should take Roman Lyons up on his offer.

Nothing was simple. If he chose to stay, what would happen to Julian and Hannah? Certainly, Hannah could find plenty of people to help here. But Julian had a life back in the Federated Territories. A career with Phantom Corps. It wouldn't be fair to ask him to leave that to come here.

And did he want to really?

He knew he didn't want one of his father's cronies doing it. He knew he wanted this to be an opportunity for growth and good in the Imperium.

He shoved it from his head. He needed to be sharp for what was to come and dwelling on what ifs just then was stupid and dangerous.

And still he'd ruminated on it, at least in the back of his mind until they came to the spot they needed to stop.

He crouched and they followed. "This is where we head east. Up that hillside there. It's dusty so be careful not to kick up too much or we could be discovered."

Both of them nodded. Vincenz caught Julian eying her pack and wanted to laugh. She wasn't going to let him take it. He caught the same thought flash over Julian's features as they stood and headed upward.

He hoped the system of caves was still there and breathed a sigh of relief when it was. He led them deeper into the mouth of the cave before he allowed any light. The last thing they needed was to be discovered so close to their goal.

Counting his steps, he found the right depression in the wall and pressed in the appropriate places. Inside, he caught the click of the lock and the whoosh as the door opened inward. "Here we go."

Hannah took an audible breath. Julian took her hand in his and kissed it.

"I'm all right," she said, not sounding it.

Vincenz wanted to comfort her, enough that he was able to let go of his own anxiety to realize she needed to do this on her own. So he pushed his needs aside and settled for a quick kiss against her temple once he got them inside.

Once he'd got the door reset, they stood in the cool dark. Alone in the quiet. Each one with their own battle to fight. For some reason that made him feel better.

He clicked the torch on, taking a good look all around. Spiderwebs told him no one had been in this passage in years. Perhaps since he took that last trip out of the palace and into freedom.

"Everyone ready?"

She nodded, eyes wide. Julian gave a short tip of his chin and they began, following Vincenz down the long, long passage back to the palace where all this began.

"Is it all right to speak in here?" she asked Julian very quietly.

Of course Vincenz heard her because he was that attuned to her. "Yes. We're still a considerable distance from the palace. And we're surrounded by rock. Can't even be detected by someone standing right above us."

"Who made these passages?"

"And why doesn't my father know about them?" Vincenz kept walking, appreciating the distraction. "I only know bits and pieces from my YaYa, my paternal grandmother. Originally, the first Family who held Caelinus was aligned with the Federation. That was many, many generations ago. The family was the Cuomo Family and they held all the 'Verses from here to Silesia. There was a difference of opinion with House Lyons and they declared themselves independent. One of his daughters married a Fardelle and took over what had been a palace, which he constructed into a keep of sorts. He monitored the comings and goings of everyone, especially his family."

He kept going, on the look out for any other traffic or signs the passage had been discovered or used by anyone recently and found none.

"His wife had these tunnels made as a way to get away from her husband, who tended toward fits of rage. She wanted to be able to go where she wanted whenever she wanted. She passed this down to the next Fardelle wife and so on. My grandmother showed them to my mother, who showed them to Carina. Carina and I were very close and she showed them to me. In the end, it was me who used them to escape and leave the Imperium."

Hannah was silent for some time. Vincenz knew she was filtering through everything he'd said, most likely drawing conclusions and making predictions because that's what she did.

"Why didn't your mother escape?" It was Julian who asked.

"She was brought up to believe her place was at her husband's side, no matter the cost. They brought her here at a very young age. My grandmother raised her more than her own mother had. And my grandmother may have shown us the passages, but she stayed too." Bitterness washed through him.

"If she'd have left, who'd have taken care of you and your sister? She stayed to keep you safe. Even after you left."

He sucked in a quick breath at the truth of that.

"Which isn't your fault."

He smiled, though she couldn't have seen it. Smiled because she knew him so damned well.

"She did what she thought was right. What she was raised to believe. Helping you both get out was her job as a mother and she did it. That was her duty. That she didn't leave as well, where would she go?"

She could have come to him.

"I suppose you imagine she might have come to you. But would she know that? Would she have the contacts left to get out? And if so, how would she hide her absence from the palace? She's trapped. Not *because* of you two, but due to circumstances. So she did what she could to make things different. Better. And that is her gift. We can bring her back with us."

In just a few minutes Hannah had waltzed into his brain and beaten back every single doubt he'd had. Every resentment. And she'd provided a solution.

He took a deep breath and kept going.

* * *

They'd been steadily climbing for some time when they reached a junction in the passage. "We head left here. Each one of these has an outlet in the palace somewhere. As I don't know exactly how the keep may have changed since Carina escaped, I'm opting for the stables. They're likely to be unchanged. It's still early enough that it should be quiet with few people around. We'll change clothes when we get there."

And so that's how he found himself wearing the clothes he'd grown up in for the first time in eight years. Hannah was so lovely in the bright green dress he'd brought. Julian handsome in his simple trousers and shirt.

"Fancy enough that we could easily work inside the palace, but not so fancy we'd be looked at twice. Though of course Hannah is so beautiful people will look twice anyway."

She quickly braided her hair, leaving some wisps at the temples. She rarely wore it away from her face when they were outside the house, but he loved the way she looked right then. Her eyes wide with a little bit of fear, but more curiosity and excitement. Certainly a great deal of temerity. He grinned and kissed her hard enough to leave her lips pink and swollen. "Now you look even prettier."

Julian scratched over his scruffy beard, the bristles sounding loud in the quiet at the door. "I'd do you both right now if that wouldn't be wildly inappropriate. And we know I'm never inappropriate."

She took both their hands and squeezed. "We're here."

He opened the door carefully and they found themselves in the high hayloft. Alone in what would be the last hours before dawn.

They crawled out and stayed put until he got some readings.

He had some contacts left in Caelinus so they'd need to get to the marketplace, which would be setting up.

* * *

Hannah loved the large courtyard they headed out into once they'd left the stables. Dawn was beginning to imagine itself off in the distance and the first bustle of early morning had begun as the market stalls began to fill up with their wares.

The sky smelled different here inside the walls of the large keep. The electricity of the filters across the walls and ramparts around them hummed. Ozone, she remembered. Similar to Asphodel, but different. There was a repressed wildness, struggling all around her. Disconcerting while at the same time feral and comforting.

This place was where Vincenz was made. She could see it, could see his joy even though he tried to hide it.

She'd tell him later, when it was safe, just how much she liked it.

He straightened and raised a hand to hail a man setting up a dairy stall. "Hoy there, Ross."

The man's eyes lit at the sight of Vincenz. Curiosity ate at her belly. Wanting to know who these people were to him. How they knew him. What they meant to him. She hungered to understand Vincenz and these people had a part of him she'd never seen until now.

"Hoy! It's been some time." The man, stout and wide as a tree trunk, grinned.

They clasped forearms and Hannah noted Ross had given Vincenz a packet of some sort. Vincenz tucked it away in one deft movement. Sneaky and clever, her man.

"You must be hungry." Ross turned and rifled through a tub until he held up a small bundle wrapped in wax paper and tied with black string. "Get yourselves some bread at that stall there. Purri and nectarine season. Makes a fine breakfast."

"Thank you," Vincenz said, meaning more than the cheese.

"It's been far too long. I'm glad to see you well. Keep it that way." Ross turned back to his stall and Vincenz led them toward the bread stall.

That's when she saw the Skorpios strolling down the wide promenade, heading their way.

She shoved away the small furry animal fear that lurked in her gut. Or pretended to anyway. She cast her eyes downward because that's how it was when she'd dealt with them in the past.

Vincenz put an arm around her waist and held her to his side as they walked along. She found her breath as her heart beat loud in her ears. The comfort of his touch helped. Julian moved to her other side, staying close as well. That also helped.

The soldiers appeared to make everyone in their path nervous. Lots of heads going down. People busied themselves with anything but the men dressed all in black. She bet Vincenz had looked very handsome in one of those uniforms though.

It was that thought that helped her continue on even as she felt the regard of the soldiers on them. They were, after all, out of place. If they were watching this place as closely as she imagined, one of them might realize the three of them were not from around those parts.

Vincenz had used a pill to darken his usually pale hair. His beautiful eyes were brown to match. And yet he was still beautiful, still turned heads. Julian, well, of course he did too. Only he had a manner that made people approach him all the time. For such a well-guarded man when it came to his personal life, in public, when he was working, it was as if people were drawn to him so they could give him information. Remarkable.

They got to the bread stall and the woman there paused as she'd been placing crusty loaves into baskets. Her gaze quickly flicked over to the soldiers, but she continued her work.

"We'd like a loaf of that one there, with the seeds on top." Vincenz pointed and his hand went to the small counter and he tucked something into a small crack. He did it so quickly and stealthily she would have missed it had she not been watching him the way she was.

The woman picked out a loaf of the seeded bread and handed it to Hannah, who nodded her thanks in Imperial standard. The woman's mouth rose into a smile, transforming her face.

"Most welcome. My son made those fresh this morning."

Julian watched Hannah with the bread seller. Watched Hannah break down walls of distrust all by speaking to her in her own language. He knew she spoke Imperial. Her mother had been from here and she'd worked at the cross-border initiative. But hearing her here was different. She had a confidence, even as he knew she'd been frightened by the Skorpios prowling all around, that translated out to others.

He also noted the woman giving Vincenz something along with his change after he paid for the bread and the deft way Vin secreted it on his person.

"Do you have papers?" One of the Skorpios stopped, blocking their path to the fruit seller down the lane.

Vincenz handed over the packet of papers. He'd taken care to be sure the leather case they were in was worn and well used. A small detail, but important.

"Why are you here?" The Skorpios looked over the paperwork and then over to each one of them.

"Shipment of grain from Monteh. My wife is carrying our first babe; she wanted to come and see the palace." Vin pointed to the stamps on the paperwork that indicated they'd offloaded the grain at the portal a day before.

"Where are you lodging?"

"Last night at the Portal city. We planned to take our breakfast back to the public house at the second gate. My brother-in-law recommended we stay there."

"Second gate is a bit crowded these days. Black smoke from the plant might bother your wife. If you don't mind the walk, try the Dancing Bear. Rooms are cheap and clean. Nothing fancy as the Portal city hotels, but it's quiet and the air is cleaner." The soldier handed the packet back to Vincenz.

"Thank you." Vincenz inclined his head and they made their way past the soldier.

"Some fruit and I think we should try this Dancing Bear. Check in and perhaps rest for a while."

The tension radiated from Hannah, but Julian only knew this because he understood her so well. Outwardly, she looked like any other woman visiting the palace for the first time. But he saw the way her mouth flattened from time to time. Knew her heart pounded and her thoughts jumbled. He wanted to pull her close and smooth a hand over her hair. But he couldn't so he had to hope she knew he wanted to anyway.

After they'd procured the fruit and Julian imagined, the last bit of intel they needed, Vincenz led them up a small rise. "The public house is just over there."

The streets had filled in the hour or so they'd been there already. Men pushed water carts and Vincenz bought some. Women stood at stalls, calling out their specialty items as people passed by. The air was filled with noise, but none of it was communication. There was no real hum of conversation.

Like he noted every time he went to Nondal back in Federated Territory, or anywhere here, people kept a reserve in public. Especially where there were soldiers about. And they were out in abundance. Not just regular soldiers and polis, but Skorpios as well. It was clear there was a war on. Clear the keep itself was well defended. Thank the gods they had the passageways or this would have been a far more dangerous mission and he would have agreed with the need to keep Hannah back home.

Vincenz pushed the door open. They'd wanted to stay at the other place, near the second gate. Julian knew Vin felt it was safer. But once they'd been directed here by the soldier it would have been suspicious to have gone elsewhere. They'd manage it.

"Room for three please." Vincenz managed to make it sound as if they did it for economy and not that they were all going to sleep in the same bed. The clerk watched Julian from under her lashes and Hannah made a quick but sneaky step to her left to block her view. Julian held back a smile at that small jealousy. It made him feel better that she felt that way about him. The way he did every time a man paused to take a second or third look at Hannah.

Once they got upstairs and settled, Julian managed to do a surreptitious sweep of the room for eavesdropping devices and found a small bug that would transmit conversation. He left it in place but gave Vincenz a sign to let him know it was there. They'd give a show, talk about stupid mundane crap and then he'd jam it with a feedback loop of sound so they could have a little more freedom to speak. Though not much.

"Sit down, darling. Why don't you get us some bread and cheese while I get the water." Vin pulled the rickety chair out for her and she sat, busying herself with getting a meal together. Smart to distract her and to get some calories into her as well.

Julian sliced the fruit and fed her slices, leaning in to lick over her bottom lip to catch the sweetness of the nectarine.

She smiled back at him, handing a thick slice of bread and cheese his way. "Eat. Both of you." She did the same with Vincenz, who also dipped down to claim a kiss.

"I need to keep my strength up." He winked and she laughed.

Julian toyed with the end of her braid as he thought, running through all the options as they looked over the roughly drawn map to where the labs most likely were located.

Chapter 26

*V*incenz tried not to think about how stupidly dangerous it was to have Hannah there with them. He stood at the window of their room and ran through the map in his head. He knew there'd be more appropriate clothing for them in the hayloft. The labs were near his father's offices. In fact, they appeared to be two floors above it. Accessible only by an elevator located in his office.

That would be the tough part.

"We should see if we can find her." Hannah stood behind him, her arms around his waist, her lips very near his ear. He knew she meant his mother and the need to see her, the ache he had to simply put his arms around his mai one more time nearly took him to his knees.

He shouldn't be there. He was too close to the mission. He knew it. But he also knew no one else was better for it than he was. And so he would do it. He'd get them all three out of there alive and well and maybe, if he did it right, his mother too.

Esta Fardelle should live to hold her grandchildren. Live to breathe free. He wanted to give her everything for all she gave up for him and Carina.

He said nothing. Knowing Hannah would understand. Knowing she most likely followed the mental conversation he'd been having with himself.

Julian had put the jammer out just a few minutes before. The suns were at their zenith and people began to come inside to take refuge from the heat and take their midday meal and drink. He'd go down in a bit, see what he could see. But for now, he was there with them both.

"You did well today." He turned slowly and encircled her with his arms, swaying slowly.

"I love dancing with you. Everything else gets quiet and all I hear is our hearts."

He kissed the top of her head, loving her so fiercely it seemed to tear through him.

"We need to do it more often then. When we get home I promise to dance with you every day."

She tipped her head back to look up into his face. "That would be very fine indeed."

Julian came back into the room holding a basin. "Victorious." He placed it on the nearby table. The one they'd had had been cracked and wouldn't hold water. Hannah had protested, saying she was just fine to use a wet cloth to clean away the dust, but Julian had taken the old basin and disappeared, on a mission to get one she could use.

She twirled from Vincenz's arms and over to Julian, who she kissed soundly. "Thank you."

Vincenz and Julian lay back on the bed and watched as she removed the shirt, leaving the thin chemise beneath, and began to wash with the cloth. The water slid down her skin and she made happy sounds of pleasure as she washed away the grime of travel.

She loosened her hair and let it fall around her back and shoulders like a drape. It stole his breath to watch her like this. So beautiful. This private, simple and yet intimate moment. And when she turned, she paused, smiling in her way.

"You two make my heart pound in my chest. Make me short of breath."

Vincenz couldn't take his eyes off the front of her chemise. Wet from her impromptu bath, rendered transparent. The darkness of her nipples dried his mouth and brought his cock to attention.

"We don't have to be anywhere for a bit." Julian stood and began to disrobe. She moved to him quickly to help. "I'd rip that right off you if you had more than one." He slid a finger between the strap and her bare shoulder, pulling it down, baring her left breast.

Vincenz got up to help remove the skirt and the underskirt. Leaving her in her panties and stockings.

"Gods above and below." Julian raked his gaze over her.

"Indeed."

Vincenz disrobed quickly, wanting to be in her, on her, touching her in any way he could. Wanting his lips on Julian, those strong, bold hands on him.

"Do you know what?" Julian nearly purred it and Vincenz's heart skipped just a little at the promise in his tone.

"No, but I'm sure I'll like whatever you say next."

"On the bed on your back."

Vincenz obeyed quickly, anticipating whatever it was Julian had in store.

"Panties off and then I want you on his face."

Hannah blinked quickly, her hands shaking for just a moment. Vincenz's cock grew impossibly harder at the sight of it.

"Sit on his face, beautiful. I'll be busy with his cock."

Her eyes widened but she pulled her underpants off and got into position, and Vincenz wanted to sigh happily. Instead, he slid his palms up her thighs and held her in place. "Turn around."

She did and slid her fingers through his hair, yanking the way he thought she would. "Now. Take it from me."

She hummed and scooted forward just a little bit more, his hair still in her hand as she pulled him toward her sweet, juicy pussy. As if he needed the incentive.

That's when the mattress dipped as Julian got in the bed. When he spoke his lips were against Vincenz's cock. "I wish you could see her perched on your face this way. The pretty line of her back, the sweet curves of that ass."

She writhed with a small sound of delight and need. Vincenz closed his eyes and gave over to her, gave over to the insane pleasure as Julian's mouth surrounded his cock over and over.

One hand braced on the wall behind the bed, the other in his hair, pulling him closer, she turned her head on a gasp of pleasure to discover Julian watching her in the mirror just across the room.

The angle was perfect for such a thing and a warm flush raced through her as she couldn't tear her gaze from Julian, even as Vincenz did his damndest to devastate her and make her come right that instant.

The dark, heady power rushing through her as she continued her hold on his hair, all while she watched Julian suck Vincenz's cock and then . . . dear gods . . . began to slowly fuck his hand as he did, rendered her nearly mindless.

She managed to straighten a little, using her free hand to cup her breast, testing its weight. Julian narrowed his eyes a moment and then widened them again when she pinched the nipple hard enough to make herself catch her bottom lip between her teeth.

Julian couldn't tear his gaze from the sight of the three of them in the mirror. Hannah, all her glorious, thick, dark hair cascading down her back as she arched, pressing her cunt into Vin's face. Taking what she wanted without apology. Her nipples stood hard and dark. Breasts swaying slightly as she churned her hips.

Vin's face was nestled between her thighs, but the long, lean torso was burnished by the sun, the dusting of gold-blond hair on his chest, the trail leading from his belly button to his cock was visible.

He shifted his powerful thighs to wrap them around Julian's shoulders and that's when he had to shift to his side to get at his own cock. Needing relief.

And then her gaze had shifted until it snagged on his, moved to his hand on his cock and that beautiful woman of his began to tug and roll her nipple with a free hand.

He groaned around Vin's cock, sucking it back as deep into his throat as he could until Vincenz made a ragged sound. Hannah gasped as Julian knew it must have vibrated through her pussy. He watched in the mirror as Vincenz's fingers dug into the flesh of her ass and hauled her closer, holding her there.

It must have been stellar because Hannah's eyes went soft and faraway, glazed the way they did sometimes when he topped her. The hand that'd been on her nipple slapped the wall as she cried out.

A deep pink flush rose from her ass, up her back as she let her head fall forward when she came.

And then she got off and Vin pulled her in for a kiss and she swallowed Vin's groans as Julian took him deeper.

"Would you like some help?" She slid down to where Julian was, on the other side of Vincenz's body.

Vincenz snarled a curse, but Julian pulled off his cock to grin at her and capture that mouth in a kiss that tasted of her and now Vincenz. She squirmed to get closer as their kiss parted enough to admit Vincenz's cock with a flurry of lips and tongues.

Vincenz's hands gripped the bedding so tight his knuckles went white as he arched up to meet them both.

Julian broke the kiss. "When I'm done with him, I'm sticking my cock in you so deep you'll have trouble walking."

Before he could apologize for speaking without thinking, her lashes went half-mast and she purred, her mouth right above his, "Promise?"

At that, he and Vincenz both groaned.

"You're going to kill me."

Julian grinned at her and then went back to Vin's cock as she slid her palms over the both of them, over every part she could touch, all as she kissed, licked and nuzzled whatever part of Vincenz's cock that wasn't in his mouth, and his balls.

They hadn't done this yet, this unified cocksucking, and he hoped like seven hells she and Vincenz would try it on him someday. And then he wanted to laugh. Of course she would. Now that she'd seen how they both reacted, she'd do it because she loved to please them.

Vincenz writhed, restless, muscles tight as they continued. Every few strokes Hannah would return to his mouth and they'd kiss, a flutter of tongues against the head and crown of Vincenz's cock until he grabbed hold of both his and Hannah's hair, holding them in place, letting them know he was done being toyed with and wanted to come.

So Julian took him deep and steady, keeping him wet and the rhythm fast until Vin growled, thrust even deeper and came in a hot rush before falling boneless back to the bed.

Julian was on her in a heartbeat, rolling her to her belly and entering her from behind in one hard stroke.

He was in no mood to take it slow and easy. Need crawled over his skin, brought his balls up close to his body.

Vincenz watched them both with that satisfied smirk he often wore while they where all in bed together.

"You two are fucking hot." Vincenz took her hands and pulled, straightening her arms above her head as she arched her back to get more from Julian.

He slapped her ass. Hard. Three times until her whimpers went into breathy moans. "Can't take my eyes off that. So beautiful." Indeed she was, stretched out beneath him, her body receiving his, cunt a hot, wet vise around him, rippling and squeezing until he nearly lost his mind.

And when he finally came and fell to the side, Hannah wedged between them soft and warm, he let himself tumble into sleep. For just a little while. Because he knew he was safe.

Chapter 27

He'd gone over the plan with her several times. Enough that at the last attempt she narrowed her eyes and showed him her teeth.

"I know you get it. I just . . . it's dangerous."

They'd made their way to the passage up in the hayloft and had gone inside. It was the only place he'd felt safe discussing the logistics of the plan for the operation.

They needed to head to the heart of the palace, using the panel in his mother's suite of rooms. From the intel he'd received that morning, Carina's rooms had been given to someone else so they couldn't use those.

Ciro hadn't been sleeping in Esta's bed for some time, though he did still go to her for counsel from time to time. Which was good. It meant she still had some use for Ciro, which kept her alive.

Her suite of rooms was closest to her husband's offices, and hopefully they could get a better read on what was going in inside the palace from her once they were in.

"Don't take her job away."

"What do you mean?"

"I know you worry for her. About involving her. But she helped you and your sister both get out. She's already involved. You have to let her help. And you have to see her." Hannah sat, her back against the wall of the passage.

"It's not her job."

She waved it away lazily. "Of course it is. She's your mother. He's taken every single one of her children from her. I can't begin to imagine how angry that must make her. And perhaps getting you and Carina out safely was her way of telling your father that she would do her job no matter what. She couldn't save your younger brother. But I doubt she'd bypass the opportunity to not let his death be for naught."

Her delivery was patient. Quiet. She didn't try to talk him into seeing things her way. No. What made Hannah such a powerful force was that she herself was sure of what she said to him.

"It's too late anyway. We have no other options." He held his hand out and she took it, standing.

Julian came back around the corner. "I followed the passage all the way to her room. No one's been back here in a very long time." He marched right up to Vincenz and kissed him soundly. "You ready?"

"As I'll ever be."

And they walked. It didn't take very long.

"I'll go first." Hannah smoothed a hand down the front of her skirts.

"The fuck you will!"

She sighed like he was a moron. "I'm dressed like a personal attendant. If anyone sees me, they won't look twice. Hopefully. Anyway. You two . . ." She indicated them both with a flick of her wrist and a raised brow. "You two will catch attention in a woman's room, for goodness sake."

Oh.

"If you get yourself hurt, I will personally kick your pretty ass after I have to kill whoever hurt you." He took her upper arms and hauled her close. She smiled up at him.

"Do you think I'd argue with such a plan? I love you, Vincenz. I want to help, but I'm not stupid. I'll go through, be sure the area is clear, and you two can follow." She tiptoed up, kissed him softly and moved to Julian. "You too." She kissed the furrow between his brows. "I love you."

Julian hugged her tight. "Be careful."

And with that she squeezed through the low passage door and was gone.

She knew she'd come out in a large closet so that part wasn't a surprise. She held still and listened hard for any noise, but heard none. At the door she listened again, heard nothing and peeked. No one was around so she eased out into the pretty sitting room just beyond.

Her heart beat so hard it made her a little dizzy, but they needed her to do this. Vincenz needed her to do this for more reasons than one and so she did.

When she opened the door to the bedchamber it was to find Esta Fardelle sitting at her window seat, staring out at the dark night beyond. Startled, she stood and began to speak. Hannah put a finger to her lips and moved quickly to Vincenz's mother.

"Are you well?" She curtseyed and then straightened. "I'm new. My name is Yalta."

Esta's eyes widened and she nodded, looking all around. "Yalta, yes, I'm well. I didn't expect you. Is it just you then?"

Yalta had been Vincenz's first horse's name. Apparently this was a key phrase between him and his mother as they'd made to get him out of Caelinus. She clearly understood that there was something going on and let Hannah lead.

"I was mending one of your gowns in your closets. I hate to bother you about this, but would you take a look to be sure I'm doing it the way you'd like?"

Esta followed her to the closet and closed the door after them, locking it and pushing a low table to block access. Hannah went to the crawl space and opened it, standing to the side to allow Vincenz and Julian through.

When Esta saw Vincenz's face, she nearly crumpled, but he caught her. He caught her with a hushed cry and the two held each other for long moments. Hannah tried to hold her tears back but it was impossible as she watched them together. As she knew she'd never have this moment with her own mother again.

Vincenz and his mother both needed each other so much. It was moving simply to watch them fall apart and then help each other pull together again. Julian moved to Hannah to hold her to his side, his eyes glossy with unshed tears.

"We can speak in here." Esta tried to gather her wits as the embrace broke.

And then Vincenz told her what they were there for, what they needed and what Ciro had done to Petrus.

They switched to rapid-fire Imperial with the taste of Caelinus. It was difficult for even Hannah to follow and she'd grown up speaking Imperial as a second language.

"I hate him. I hate him and I want to destroy him the way he's destroyed everything and everyone I ever cared about."

"You're coming back with us when we finish this. Wait in the passageway so you won't be discovered."

"You'll need me here to run interference. You can't risk it."

"He'll be dead so don't fret about him." He said it in such a matter-of-fact way that even if she didn't know him, she would have believed his claim. He took his mother's hands. "I will not leave you here again."

Hannah realized Vincenz got his spine not from his father but from the woman who barely reached his chest currently staring him down.

"It's quiet now. Wait here and I'll go check on his office." Esta changed topics smoothly.

"Don't take any risks."

"Of course." She was gone in moments, leaving them all in her closet.

Hannah said nothing but took his hand, squeezing it. He took a deep, shuddering breath and pulled himself back together. "She's coming back with me even if I have to bundle her over my shoulder to do it."

"Of course she is."

Vincenz relaxed a little and turned to breathe her in. His Hannah. Home in so many ways. "Thank you, baby. I forgot to introduce her to you both."

Julian snorted a quiet laugh and stepped in to kiss Vin on the other side. "Let's just take this all one step at a time. She's had enough shocks for one day."

Vincenz waited what seemed like an eternity for his mother to come back. In fact he'd started to pace. Hannah and Julian had stood back to give him room. Julian tended to Hannah while he pretended not to and she pretended not to notice. He found their interplay charming and it eased some of his nervousness.

* * *

They'd kept the passage panel unlatched, at the ready should they need to jump back inside, but when there was noise out in the main room, he recognized the footfalls. Just one person. A small person. Had to be his mother and as they stood out of the direct sight of the opening door, she poked her head round and entered, closing it in her wake.

"There's no one in his office just now. There's a late-night feast down in the great hall so the guards are all there. You picked a good time to come, I suppose. I know where the elevator is. Let's go. It might be your only chance today."

Vin took a deep breath and nodded. His weapons were hot and ready to go. Hannah straightened and stood tall, ready. Julian led up the rear, getting their back. No more time to waste so he nodded at his mother. "I know where it is. You stay here. We can't take the risk of you being tied in with us if things go badly."

"He already suspects me. He rarely speaks to me anymore. I have nothing left to lose." With that she turned and headed to the door. "I've been taking chances with that monster my whole life. I want this over. He took every single one of my babies and I want him to pay."

Hannah sent him a look that told him he needed to let his mother do this, even if it was the last thing he wanted.

"Fine. But if I tell you to go, you have to go. Do you understand me?"

"Yes."

The hallways were the same as they'd been before. The same glossy black stone floors and walls. The same portraits in the long hall. Well, his was gone. Carina, being female had no such portrait to remove, but he was sure any and all mention of her had been expunged from the official records anyway.

She'd been right; the halls were empty in what would prove to be a disastrous breach of protocol for his father but a lucky one for them. Once they'd made ready to round the last turn to where his father's offices were, his mother held her hand up and waved them back. Vincenz stopped, holding them up as she continued to walk.

"Ma'am, can I help you with something?"

Must be a soldier.

"I'm looking for a guard. I heard a crash. Probably birds hitting the windows again, but one can never be too safe."

The sounds of their talking dimmed and shortly after, he peeked around the corner to find it empty, so the three of them moved to his father's office door. Hannah pushed herself to the front and began to hack into the system of locks and security on the door. She'd already disabled the surveillance system while they'd been in the closet earlier and they'd discovered his father's long hallway had no cameras at all. Gods only knew what he'd been up to that he'd make that stupid mistake.

She continued to work in that way of hers, all her focus on the task at hand until the door popped open and they slipped in, closing the door in their wake.

He indicated the next doors that led into what he and Carina had always joked was his father's throne room. Only now it had an actual throne on a dais. Seven hells.

Julian sent him a raised brow, but said nothing as Vincenz led them to the elevator just beyond. His mother wasn't the only one who knew where it was. He would have preferred to take the access stairs in the elevator shaft rather than the elevator, but it was inaccessible except for through what appeared to be a guard office on the other side of the thick walls. And they couldn't risk that.

Hannah got to work, and he came in behind her, propping the

system open as she ripped holes large enough for him to get in behind her. Soon enough the elevator arrived and they took the chance and got on.

No cameras in there either.

Hannah indicated they hold as she pulled on a respirator and some gloves. They had no idea what the lab would be like and she refused to let them take extra risks. He and Julian followed suit and pulled their weapons out, training them on the door as it slid open.

The lab beyond was impressive. Hannah had to admit it as she took a look around. The containment appeared to be solid, which made her relax a little, but also led her to believe there were some dangerous things there. They clearly had the right place.

She sent them a glare and mimed that she'd kill them both if they took the respirators off and not to touch anything but the comms they needed to get inside of.

And then she went to work.

From what she could tell as she went through each station's data, the lab was a veritable chamber of horrors of viral and biological agents. She wished she had a full containment suit, but as that wasn't an option she did her best as she downloaded the data and introduced the chlorine that would kill each one of the viruses in the containment units.

Any hope of bringing the material out to study back in the Federation was dashed. She couldn't take a risk with any of this. Better to destroy it all and study the data, which appeared to be quite extensive, than to expose anyone to agents that could kill millions.

She was about eighty-five percent done when the lights went off and flickered back again, this time blue.

Vincenz began to remove the respirator but she jogged to him, holding it in place. "No! You can't."

"They'll know there's been a breach. I need to move easier."

"You need to not be infected with one of the myriad ugly things in this room. You keep it on or I will kick you in the balls."

Julian snorted but kept his respirator on as he began to set up where they'd have to defend their position.

"Disable the elevator."

"I did." Vincenz glared at her. "You had no right to be in here if this was so dangerous."

"Be quiet and get your weapons ready." She turned and went back to her work.

He snarled, but she knew he did exactly that because that was what he needed to do. He'd lecture her later.

She found the virus at the very end, right as Julian and Vincenz began to talk about how the Skorpios had nearly gotten around their blocks. Pfft, they were amateurs and her blocks were very good. Together with Vincenz's work, they were nearly indestructible.

She had to trust it for at least another five minutes as she uploaded the data and replaced it with their data that would cascade through the system, not only destroying their entire system but any networked into it. That part, the communication to the other networked systems, had been working since she had finished the first station.

Hannah tried not to think about the data that scrolled up as she worked. All the people who'd been experimented on. So many had died horribly painful deaths all for the amusement and power greed of Ciro Fardelle and some of his ministers.

Finishing the last bit, she dropped the gas tab into the containment tubes and watched the gas turn colors as it ate at the contagion and destroyed it.

"Got it."

Vincenz looked at her one last time to be sure he heard right and then he sent out the command to initiate the internal destruction codes. Each comm screen flickered and then data began to flow in long strings as it all began to collapse.

"I think it's fair to assume they're going to be using the internal elevator shaft to override the hold we have on the elevator."

Julian nodded. "No way around it. We have to shoot our way out."

Vincenz looked back to Hannah. "Fuck."

"Just do your super-secret agent business. I know how to keep my head down and also how to use my weapon. Plus, remember you made me put on the vest. Let's go. The longer we're here, the more time they have to assemble a defense."

Vincenz wanted to scream. Instead, he opened the elevator and motioned her inside. "Stay the seven hells down. We'll do the shooting."

"If I may," she had the audacity to say and he narrowed his eyes, "if we keep the masks on they might think we have something with us from in here."

Julian nodded. "Good idea. It can't hurt."

"Hard to see around this respirator."

"Hard to see with a bullet in your head." Julian shrugged and Vincenz knew he was right.

He sighed. "Fine. But you still stay the fuck down."

She moved to the place he indicated as Julian opened the hatch in the ceiling of the elevator to check. "Movement below. Let's go. Now or never. Kill everyone you come across. We don't have the time and I sure don't have the inclination to spare anyone but your mother."

Hannah sucked in a breath, and he realized he didn't have the time to worry about the choices he'd made. They were made, and he'd need all of his attention to survive this.

She had her comm out so he waited until she'd finished, knowing she had a plan.

"I've disabled the light and sound announcements for when the elevator arrives on a floor."

"I'd kiss you for that, but you'll have to wait." Smart, their woman.

"All right, let's do this." He pushed the button and they began to descend.

They heard the Klaxons even before they'd arrived down in his father's office. It was clear their presence had been detected. He had a moment to worry over his mother before the doors slid open and he and Julian took as much cover as they could and began to shoot at whatever was waiting for them.

Hannah held up a hand grasping a silver cylinder.

"Back, you fools!" one of the Skorpios ordered.

Vincenz recognized that voice. Davis Dolce, the head of the Skorpios. The man who'd personally trained him.

The soldiers scrambled backward, weapons still aimed.

Vincenz had no use for any of them and so he and Julian took as many out as they could. Which turned out to be quite a few. One-handed, he grabbed Hannah, who'd attempted to stand on shaky legs, and hauled her out, keeping her behind him.

"What do you want?" Davis called out from his cover behind the throne.

Julian shot the throne with a pulse blaster and it cracked, falling apart.

"Where is he, Davis?"

"Vincenz?" Davis broke cover and stood alongside the rubble, making himself a target. "Is that you?"

He nodded and Davis threw his weapon down and went to one knee. "I pledge my fealty to you."

Well, that was unexpected.

Vincenz noted the remaining Skorpios had faltered at the sight of their commander on his knee. He lowered his weapon slightly and Hannah whacked his arm. "What are you doing!"

There was no way this was a trick. Most of the Skorpios corps might be addicted to his father's special bars loaded with stimulants and drugs, but they didn't surrender. Not even as a feint.

"It's all right." He nodded toward the doors. "Julian, secure the space."

"I'll take the weapons." Before he could argue with Hannah, she'd simply started to do it.

He growled. "Take care that they're dead before you go touching them." He turned his attention back to the soldier and ignored Hannah's grumble. "Stand up, Davis."

He did. "May I approach, sire?"

He was no one's sire. But suddenly he understood Ellis's offer better. If these men followed him, they could not only destroy his father's lab but his father's rule.

"Yes." He pulled the respirator off and Hannah threw her hands up in disgust.

"It is you." He clasped forearms with Vincenz. "Seven hells, it's good to see you. I thought you were dead."

"Not yet, but maybe soon. Who else is coming? What are we facing?" Vincenz simply took command as he'd been taught to do.

"I can handle my men. Rank and file are in the outer halls and in the streets though."

"Where is my father?"

"He was heading toward your mother's chambers." Davis's face paled and Vincenz felt sick. "One of your informants was picked up earlier and confessed. Not that it was you. But not many can stand up to torture."

Vincenz headed to the door and Hannah grabbed his arm, digging her heels in. "Not so fast. Make a plan first! You can't help her if you rush out there." She pulled her respirator and hat off, her hair all over the place as she shoved it back with her free hand.

"Hold for a moment." Davis spoke into his wrist mic, sending his men toward Esta's rooms with orders to let no one but him past. "Let's go."

They burst from the throne room and began an all-out run.

So well trained were Davis's men that not a one lifted a weapon, even when they saw Davis wasn't alone.

Vincenz kicked the doors open and went into a crouch as Julian swept the room on his left.

Hannah rushed past them both toward the place where Esta lay, crumpled and bleeding on the pale blue carpet.

"I need some first-aid supplies. Now!" she barked at one of the soldiers, who quickly dug through his pack and gave her one. "Vincenz . . ." She licked her lips. "She needs you now."

Hannah pulled her old gloves off and Julian helped her with the new ones before she threw herself into doctor mode.

Esta looked up at Vincenz as he fell to his knees on a broken cry. "Mai, I'm here. Hannah is a doctor. She's going to fix you. Where is he?"

"In my bedchamber." Even Vincenz heard the liquid in her voice.

Julian rushed past them, bursting through the doors only to come back some moments later. "He's dead."

Esta winced as Hannah tore open the front of her blouse. "I'm sorry. I need to get to your wound."

A wound it was. Close-fire blaster shot.

Hannah didn't even pause, didn't pale, just continued to work, cleaning, using a paste to deaden the nerves for pain relief. Her hands were gentle but her eyes held sorrow.

"He didn't expect me to kill him." His mother clasped his hand. "That's why he's dead now. I always expected him to kill me."

Hannah packed the wound. "Are you injured anywhere else?"

"Just there." She coughed, the blood bright red. Hannah handed him a clean cloth with one hand while she worked on his mother with the other. Vincenz wiped his mother's mouth and chin, relentlessly holding back the sob boiling up in his gut.

"He's dead. You won. We're going to get you better."

His mother shook her head. "No, you won't. I'm dead now, even if you won't admit it. Please know I did everything I could to keep you and Carina safe. I love you both so much. I'll be sorry not to hold your babies."

"She's married now. To the soldier who escorted her out of here." Julian crouched next to them. "You did a good job with your children, Mrs. Fardelle."

A sob broke from Vincenz as he watched his mother work to take each breath.

"Do something!" he yelled at Hannah, who flinched, but kept working.

Julian reached out and squeezed his forearm. "She is, Vin."

"A Fardelle has held this place for generations." Esta paused to take another breath, growing more pale with each moment. "Don't let that end. Be the man your father wasn't."

"Mai, please. Please don't let go."

"I can't hold any longer. I am grateful I was able to see you once more. I love you. Tell your sister I said the same of her." Her hold on his hand loosened as she slipped from this life.

It was as if all the things holding him up simply dissolved and he collapsed into a heap over her body, shoving Hannah's hands out of the way.

Hannah watched him fall apart. Watched all that careful reserve wisp away as he wept over his mother's body. Wept over the woman she couldn't save, even after Vincenz had saved Hannah.

Julian stood and addressed the man Vincenz had called Davis. "What is the status of your men?"

"We're under Vincenz's command. With Ciro dead, I don't foresee much resistance from our rank and file. But . . ."

"Speak freely."

The man looked Julian up and down and then over to Vincenz before he spoke again. "Ciro had ministers instrumental in whatever nightmares he had brewing in the lab. Once they find out Ciro is dead, they'll attempt to take over."

"Let's be ready to crush that then, shall we?" Julian looked down to Vincenz and squeezed his shoulder. "Cuomo, you need to be present for this."

Vincenz looked up. The front of his shirt and pants were covered in blood. He took a deep breath and stood.

"Does this mean you'll be leading us now, Vincenz?"

Hannah said nothing as she watched the man she loved so much pull himself together, wiping his hands on his pants, clearly thinking.

"Yes. Yes, unless there's someone else in the wings. I understand I have a brother."

"He's still in short pants. His mother is barely older than a child herself. Any real challengers have been disappeared. I believe the people would follow you. I believe the military would follow you."

Vincenz took a deep breath and before her eyes he took on the mantle of leadership. "Have my father's ministers arrested and brought before me. I need to contact some people on the other side. Get his body out of here. My mother needs to be prepared for interment. The military needs to stand down."

Hannah stood and handed the kit back to the soldier who'd given it to her. "Thank you." She noted his pupils and paused. "What is it you're a slave to?"

He started. "What do you mean?"

"What substance are you addicted to?" It couldn't be most things or he would be unable to be out in the field. She examined his skin, noting his pores and the hue of his fingertips. A stimulant, given the fingertips.

"It's the bars." Another one of the soldiers addressed her. He held up a protein cake of some sort.

"You are given these? On purpose?"

"Yes, ma'am. They give soldiers stamina in the field."

She sniffed, annoyed. "They create a physical addiction. You don't need this to be strong in the field. And you certainly don't need to be beholden to your commanders to receive your daily substance or go into withdrawal. I imagine it's quite painful."

"Hannah, we can deal with that later." Julian tried not to smile. It wasn't hard for her not to when all she wanted to do was cry.

She nodded and stepped back, not wanting to touch anything because she was covered in blood.

There'd be time to fall apart later. For now, she needed to contact Ravena to transmit the data she'd received. Julian and Vincenz got caught up in whatever they were doing so she asked one of the soldiers to lead her to a comm station, and she set up in a quiet office and began to work. He also brought her some clean clothes and a carafe of kava and some food.

Chapter 28

Vincenz looked up, bleary-eyed, numbed by grief and the sheer immensity of the task he'd agreed to undertake. "Where is Hannah?" He'd meant to reach out to touch her at least a dozen times and each time he'd been interrupted.

"The woman you came in with?" He'd been assigned an assistant already. Julian had been liaising with Ellis, who in turn was working with Roman to accept a peace agreement. They'd all meet sometime soon. His head spun at all the details.

"Yes."

"I'll find out." The man left and Vincenz went back to work.

The man came back some minutes later with a tray of food. "She's working in the library."

"Has she been fed? Shown to my rooms?" He stood. "Never mind, I'll see to her myself."

It was . . . odd to walk the halls of this place. The place he'd grown up. Only now he had no parents. He'd been away for years and had come back to sabotage his father only to take over in a bloodless coup.

He reeled, ached, filled with rage and frustrated impotence over his mother's death. He'd spoken with Carina some time ago and they'd cried together. Thank the gods Daniel had been there with her.

Speeding his steps, he moved to Hannah, needing to know she was all right. Realizing he hadn't connected with her since that scene in his mother's rooms. She was probably shaken up from the labs and all the chaos, and he hadn't been there for her.

And there she was. Still in the same clothing she'd worn earlier. Fatigue all over her features. Wrapped up tight in a blanket, her head on her knees as she looked off into space, seeing nothing.

"Beautiful Hannah, there you are."

Startled, she jumped and her gaze met his and . . . the absence of that warmth, that instant connection he felt every time she looked at him, slapped him.

She stood and papers went everywhere. "I'm sorry." She bent and began to pick them up and he joined her, taking her hands. So cold.

"Sorry?"

She pulled them back and resumed straightening the papers. "I've been trying to find someone who'll get me to town so I can get out but everyone's been busy."

He shook his head, confused and alarmed by her behavior. "What are you talking about? I know the day has been . . . long and horrible. Has someone done something?"

She shook her head and moved to stand, jerky and uncoordinated. He hadn't seen that in a long time.

"You're scaring me."

"Why? Why? Why don't you leave me alone? I'm trying to go. I couldn't . . ." She broke down, and he just didn't know what to do.

"Go? What are you talking about? Please talk to me. I'm all

fucked up and wrung out, I don't know what you need but I want to give it to you." He went to his knees but she backed up.

"I still have blood on my clothes."

He shouldn't have felt rejected, but he did anyway. "Come to our rooms. We'll get you a bath. You'll feel better after a bath and some sleep."

She dropped her head and her hair swept forward but not before he saw the tears in her eyes.

"You're scaring me, Hannah." He stood, being firm. "Come with me."

She gathered her papers and the blanket, holding them against her body and filling her hands so he couldn't take them.

"Have you seen Julian lately?" He tried to make small talk as he led her down the hall toward the rooms he'd taken over. Not his father's. Certainly not his mother's.

"A few hours ago."

He'd have to be sure she was taken care of better from then on.

"Have you eaten?" He hated this awkwardness between them. Made him feel out of sorts and cast adrift.

"I'm fine."

He opened the doors and as he did, someone else came down the hall, hailing him. He turned. "Not now. I'm going to be with my woman for a while. I'll find you when I'm ready. Can you find Julian please and send him in and have a meal for three brought up?" The man nodded and hurried off to carry out Vincenz's wishes.

When he turned back she remained, just inside the doors.

He took the stack of papers from her, placing them on a nearby table and closed the doors. "Bath first."

She followed him into the large bathing suite where he opened the taps to run a bath in the huge tub. Knowing she delighted in such things, he turned to her and found her standing, still clothed.

"I'll be out shortly."

"This has gone on long enough. What the seven hells is wrong? Is it me? You're disgusted by what my father has done and you think I'm capable of that?"

She gasped and took a step back, nearly falling. He reached out quick to grab her.

"No! I would never think that. You're good. Honorable and strong. You'll do right by these people."

Relief swept through him enough to loosen the tension in his muscles as he began to unbutton her shirt, though she tried to move away.

"If you don't tell me, how can I fix it? Hold still."

She slapped at his hands. "I can handle it myself. I don't need your pity."

"Now you're making me mad. Pity? Is that what you think this is? Are you so selfish you can't understand I had to take care of a million things today? After I watched my mother die? You can't give me some time to do something else but be with you?"

She went ramrod stiff and he regretted the words, but it was too late; they hung in the air between them, pushing them apart.

"Get out."

"Not until we talk."

"You've said enough. Now get out or I will."

"I'm sorry. I didn't mean it that way. I'm concerned about you."

"Get out!" She screamed it so loud it echoed from the marble and Julian burst into the room.

"What's wrong?"

"Get out. Get out. Get out!" She shoved at them both and slammed the door, locking it.

"What did you do?" Julian asked him, looking back to the door.

"I don't know. Well, that's not entirely true. I hurt her feelings. Fuck. Fuck. I am so tired I can't see straight."

He could hear her crying on the other side of the door. Even so, he was relieved when she got into the tub.

"This isn't over, baby. I'm going to get you some clean clothes and then we're all going to sit down and eat and talk this out."

"Fuck off!"

Julian sighed. "We're all tired and strung out today, baby." He pulled Vincenz close and hugged him. "We'll talk this over and work it through and all of us will sleep awhile. She's seen a lot today. I know you have too." He brushed a kiss over Vincenz's lips.

A knock at the door signaled the arrival of the food. An elderly woman he remembered from the kitchens long, long ago was with the man who brought the cart in. "Miss Hannah mentioned how much you loved these cakes. I remembered that from when you was a wee boy."

She had? He smiled at the sight of the cakes, and the idea Hannah had made mention of it. "Thank you. I do indeed have a weakness for them. I remember you. Vina, right?" He took both her hands and she blushed.

"Yes, that's right. So glad to have you home and, if you'll permit my boldness, to have a man like you in charge. Your mother will be mourned, but your arrival will be rejoiced. We raised the mourning flags earlier. Miss Hannah reminded one of the stewards about it and he got to it right away."

His agitation washed away, replaced by tenderness that even a world away from home, she took care of him.

"Thank you."

"There's tea. Drink it because I made it special for you. It'll quiet your nerves some. Make sure to get some protein into Miss Hannah. She ran herself ragged today."

"She did? What did she do, Vina?"

"Oh, well, she came into the kitchens to find cloths to clean up.

Poor bird was covered in blood." He needed to remember his people . . . gods, yes, *his* people . . . were far more matter-of-fact about death than many in the Federation were. "And when she got in there she set it all to rights. Made sure we sent you up food and snacks to keep you going all day. Made sure that one"—she motioned to Julian—"also kept his strength up with food and drink. She dealt with the mourning flags and the preparation of your mother's body and things. Took care of that secret hidey-hole of your father's too. Oh, and next time you walk down the hall of heroes, you should note your portrait is up again. Your mother had one secreted away; I told Miss Hannah where it was. She's a good girl. Loves you."

He sighed. No wonder she'd looked so fatigued. "Thank you for saying so. Did you see anything today that could have upset her somehow?"

Vina frowned. "No, sir. She made friends. Tended to a burn one of the cooks had. Was on her little comm for hours on end when she wasn't running around. Is she unwell? Can I help?"

Of course Hannah had already become someone the staff took to.

"No, thank you, Vina. I appreciate your coming up. It's good to see you here."

They set up the meal and left quietly.

Hannah couldn't avoid it a moment longer. She'd been in the tub so long she'd gone pruny and the water had gone cold. Even taking her time drying her hair could only go on so long. She had no clean clothes to change into and Vincenz was right outside.

Her anger at him had long since burned off and all that remained was her guilt. Her guilt and shame over her failure to save Esta. She'd never forget the entreaty in his eyes as he'd begged her to save his mother. And the desolation when she couldn't.

Her hands shook as she remembered the way he'd shoved her hands back when he'd slung himself over Esta's body as he shook with sobs.

After she'd transmitted the data back to Ravena, she'd gone up to the labs to be sure the decontamination process was being handled correctly. She'd been successful at destroying all the live virus, but she wanted to be sure the entire place was sterilized and everything that came and went was clean.

And then she'd tried to go. Had tried all day, but no one could be spared. She would have walked but the gates had been locked down. The portal had been closed to traffic once Vincenz had taken over.

So she'd gone to the kitchen to clean up most of the blood and Vina had taken to her immediately, plying her with some soup along with the clean blouse and the apron to go over her skirts.

That's when she'd decided to be sure the mourning flags went up, remembering how they'd done for her grandmother's death. It was while she was overseeing the removal of Esta's body that Esta's personal maid had come to Hannah to show her the cache well hidden in the passage behind Esta's rooms. The very same they'd arrived through. Just a few steps more and she'd found the portrait of Vincenz.

It had taken up time, kept her busy enough not to think. Julian had seen her for a few scant minutes in the late afternoon. He'd taken a walk with her over the west-facing ramparts. He'd been distracted, but she held his hand, loving the contact, loving that he'd come to her, seeking her out even for those stolen moments.

The lock turned over and Vincenz stood at the door. "My patience is exhausted." He handed her a pile of clothes. "Put these on. There's a meal waiting along with Julian and me."

She stood, still, until he sighed and left her alone to change.

Julian came in just as she finished. "Why you got your mad on, beautiful Hannah?" He took her hand and kissed her fingertips before wrapping it around his arm and steering her out of the room and toward Vincenz.

"I'm not mad. Not anymore. I deserved what was said."

Vincenz cocked his head, looking her over. "I don't like this Hannah. My Hannah would have told me to fuck off, like you did earlier."

Julian sat her down between them and Vincenz handed her a glass of mulled wine. It warmed her insides, gave her something to do with her hands. "Eat too. We saved you some meat and bread. And then you'll tell us both why you won't even look me in the eyes."

"How can I?" She put the wine down. "How can I when I know you must hate me and I don't think I could take it to see it in your eyes?"

He took her chin to tip it so he could see her face. "Do you see hate in my eyes? Hate of the most precious thing in the world to me? What are you thinking? How can you say that?"

"I didn't save her." The tears she thought she'd run out of came back with a fury. "You needed me and I failed you. I tried. I did. But it wasn't enough. I wasn't good enough when you needed the best, and she's dead and it's my fault."

He sat back, shock on his features. "I'm at a loss."

Julian smoothed a hand over her hair, moved closer so that his entire side brushed up against hers.

"The only person at fault for my mother's death was Ciro Fardelle. He's dead. She made him pay for it. Don't you think I know how hard you tried to save her? Do you think my love for you is so thin I'd blame you for something you couldn't control? Do you believe I'd send you away, that I'd want to send you away because you weren't able to save a woman who was already dead by the time we arrived?"

He brushed the pad of his thumb over her bottom lip.

"I'm sorry. I don't know anything. I . . ." It really only highlighted how messed up she was and she hated it.

"Stop. Stop it right now. I love you, Hannah. You fill all those empty spaces I had before you. You and Julian have become my home when I was sure I'd never have one again. What a pair we make, no? Me worried you'd both think less of me because of what Ciro had done. You worried I'd think less of you for not being superhuman. But in reality, we're a lot alike. Footholds in both worlds, both filled with positives and negatives. Thank the gods for Julian to balance us out, eh?"

Julian snorted, hugging them both. "Balance is indeed what we bring to the others. You soothe my anger, make me understand there is more to bring me joy in my future. I worry Vincenz will have no place for us now that he's here."

Hannah looked back and forth between them. "Me as well."

Vincenz groaned. "And me. I worry you two will reject this place and go back to your lives in the Federation. Live without me. It's one of the main reasons I hesitated to say yes. You can be a doctor here, Hannah. I mean, I understand that the Imperium has brought you pain and has taken the people you love. The people Julian loved. The people I loved too. I'll need men here I can trust in my inner circle, Julian. You're good with people on top of being an excellent soldier. I'd be risking Ellis's wrath for snatching you away from Phantom Corps, but I'd like you to be here. With me. Both of you."

Hannah's heart, which had been so heavy, lightened as she threw her arms around both of them. "Only if you're sure. Once I accept you're stuck with me. I'm not likely to ever be easy to live with. I may slam doors in your face and say very bad words when you annoy me."

She blushed. "I'm going to be irrational and demanding. We're going to get into spats and sometimes I will be wrong. I may actually admit it when I am but don't count on it."

Vincenz barked a laugh. "I've noticed these things. And yet, where would I be without you? Hm? The Hannah shaped spot in our lives would be empty and cold instead of warm and willing?"

Vincenz kissed her forehead and tipped her chin up. This time she met his gaze and saw what she'd been afraid she was only imagining before. Acceptance and love. Shadows, yes. Pain and loss, yes. But love.

Julian laughed, kissing them both. "I'll accept that very fine offer. Hannah, you and Vincenz are something wholly unexpected and I'd never let that go." He looked to Vincenz. "And you? The idea of serving with you, of helping you fill the role you were born to? To work with you at your side to build the Imperium into something better and stronger? That's something I want very much."

"Looks like we're stuck with you, Hannah." Vincenz grinned and she nodded, accepting it once and for all. "I'm your lid."

Julian paused and then dipped to kiss her bottom lip. "How's that?"

"Arch told me his wife was his lid. I'm your lid." She shrugged and Julian looked to Vincenz, who appeared as puzzled as he felt.

She sighed. "Silly. Every person has their fit with someone else. Every pot has a lid. I'm your lid. Both of you."

Which made Julian pretty damned happy. "Yes. Yes, that's it exactly."

Someone knocked on the outer door and Julian knew their moment of peace had passed. The real world had intruded again. They had a big job to do.

Chapter 29

*N*early a week later, Roman Lyons signed the last of the papers before him and then turned to Vincenz, who did the same.

"A peace has been declared between the Federated Universes and the Imperium. House Lyons and House Cuomo has now been witnessed and entered into the record."

Hannah watched Vincenz in his fancy uniform. The crest not of Fardelle but of Cuomo, the first to hold the Imperium. They'd decided it would be better that way. To embrace symbols of a better time and eschew those of repression and war. Julian stood to his left as Ellis stood to Roman Lyons's right.

They'd only arrived at the Waystation that morning. She'd been debriefed about the virus, with Piper at her side, holding her hand as Julian and Vincenz had gone into the final negotiations for the peace accord.

After a great deal of hand shaking, a beautiful blonde pushed her way through the crowd to approach. Carina Haws, Vincenz's sister.

"You're Hannah! I'm so pleased to meet you at last." Carina pulled her into a hug. "I hear you tended to my mother at the end. I wanted you to know that comforts me a great deal. That she passed from her life with Vincenz there, and you easing her pain . . . well, I'm thankful for it."

"I'm sorry I couldn't save her." That still weighed on her heart. Though she knew Vincenz did not blame her. Though she knew by the time they'd reached Esta it was far too late, it still hurt.

"I'm sorry you couldn't save her either, but it was our father who bears the responsibility. Thank you, by the way, for supporting my brother in his choice to lead the Imperium."

"Dear gods, what are you telling her about me?" Vincenz approached and put an arm around her shoulder. Julian joined on the other side, doing the same.

"Did you tell your sister we asked Hannah to marry us?" Multiple marriage was legal in the Imperium, though until then it had been used for multiple wives. Vincenz had been open about his relationship with both Hannah and Julian, which had surprised and pleased Julian deeply.

He had gone to Vincenz two evenings before after a long negotiation session and had said he wanted them all to be together officially. Vincenz had pulled out two rings, one that had belonged to his great grandfather and one that had belonged to his YaYa and had confessed he'd wanted the same.

Hannah went stiff and then she spun, looking up at both of them. "What?"

"Hannah, Vin and I have decided you should marry us. We have the papers. Funny how fast that happens when you're the big boss." Julian winked at Vincenz. "So what do you say? If we don't tie you to us really quickly, you're sure to get snatched up by one of your seeming millions of fans."

Carina laughed, clearly delighted. Hannah's eyes were wide, filled with excitement and a lot of happiness. Julian allowed that last bit of fear to fall away.

"All right then. But I still get to use the bath first before you two each day." She'd healed a great deal since they'd first brought her home, but occasionally she had panic attacks. The big bathtub was her place of refuge after a hectic day and he certainly had no complaints about his woman being naked and wet when he came home to her.

"That was suspiciously easy." Vincenz looked her over.

"I'll tell you a secret." Hannah leaned in toward them both. "I'm suspiciously easy where you're involved."

"Of course we'll have to go through all the Fardelle and Cuomo closets." Carina stepped in between them, linking her arm with Hannah. "My grandmother had something of a collection. It's probably down in the far north wing. I'm sure I won't know how to act walking around in the palace when I don't have to hide my every emotion. Daniel and I will be coming in a few days. We can look then."

Carina steered Hannah off toward some of the others, chattering a mile a minute. Andrei approached and shook Vincenz's hand. "Congratulations on the agreement. For what it's worth, you'll do a good job running things over there. Time for change."

"Time for lots of changes. We're taking it slow. But there will be a truth and reconciliation committee set up. Trials for those who don't wish to participate. We can't arrest everyone in the 'Verses for what they've done. But the men and women most responsible will have to stand up before the people and atone. We've got committees working on enhancing civil and human rights. It'll take years, but each step forward is a victory."

"By the time our sons are ready to lead, we'll have made a mark on the world for the better." Julian meant every word. He was proud of Vincenz, proud of his mind and his heart, of his limitless energy when it came to his people. Proud to call himself a member of the family and mean it.

He and Vin watched her as she floated around the room, shaking hands, leaning in to listen as people spoke. Her shy smile was a gift and he remembered back to the first time he'd realized there was a woman beneath all that pain. When he'd seen to the heart of her and had been captivated.

He wouldn't have had it any other way.

Author's Note

I mostly have this tracklist on shuffle as I work:

"Blackbird," The Beatles
"On Your Own," Blur
"Intimidated by Silence," Cars & Trains
"I'm Every Woman," Chaka Khan
"Beautiful," Christina Aguilera
"Police on My Back," The Clash
"The Game Has Changed," Daft Punk
"Heroes," David Bowie
"A Pain That I'm Used To," Depeche Mode
"Walking In My Shoes," Depeche Mode
"Cherry Cola," Eagles of Death Metal
"I Only Want You," Eagles of Death Metal
"I'd Rather Go Blind," Etta James
"Someone to Watch Over Me," Etta James
"Blinding," Florence + The Machine
"My Boy Builds Coffins," Florence + The Machine
"Crazy," Gnarls Barkley
"If," Janet Jackson
"Mouthwash," Kate Nash

"Frozen," Madonna

"Broken English," Marianne Faithfull

"The Beautiful People," Marilyn Manson

"The Speed of Pain," Marilyn Manson

"Complication," Nine Inch Nails

"Good-bye Blue Sky," Pink Floyd

"Is This Desire?" PJ Harvey

"Rub 'Til It Bleeds," PJ Harvey

"Paranoid Android," Radiohead

"Furious Angels," Rob Dougan

"Threshold," Sex Bob-Omb

"Moan," Trentemøller

"Maps," Yeah Yeah Yeahs